RUTHLESS HUNTER

The Institute

Book 1

A.K. ROSE

COSA NOSTRA
INSTITUTE

To all the bad boys out there doing good things.

And all the good girls watching them.

This one's for you.

Acknowledgments

This book wouldn't be as good without a wonderful friend of mine, Serena. Thank you so much for your guidance and your friendship. To my kickass Alpha readers, Jess and Shannon. You ladies just freaking rock. And finally, to my readers. Thank you for taking a chance on this, it means the world.

Please refer to my website for CW's

Prologue

ANNA

That was a hollow victory,

The kind that had dragged me under like a rope around my ankle until I'd left the light of my normal life behind. A life where I might've met a nice boring guy and had a nice boring future, one filled with promise. But that's not what I wound up with. My future wasn't up to me anymore, it was once, but now it's filled with danger. But it's all gone now, stolen by the burning need to escape. If only we hadn't tried to deceive them, we might've had a chance.

If only...

"Take it off, Anna."

His words had come from behind me as I lifted my trembling hands to missed buttons and torn lace. Still, I'd made do, wanting it. God, I'd wanted it. My lips throbbed from his kiss. My heart betrayed my own skin. It reacted to him...fluttering like a raven trapped in my chest.

"Make your decision, launderer," Finley Salvatore had murmured in my ear. "Be mine forever."

Forever. I knew what the word meant from someone like him. It meant there was no more fighting, no more finding a way out, no more trying to escape the unmerciful grip of the Salvatores. We'd be laundering their dirty money for as long as we lived.

Owned...by him, by Finley Salvatore...

"Anna...*no!*" my father screamed from the room next door. "Let her go, you *fucking bastard!*"

I closed my eyes to the feel of Finley, his warmth at my back as his hand closed around my throat. He had blood on his knuckles, blood he'd spilled for me.

But it wasn't his blood...

Not yet, at least.

He'd said he'd fight for me, said he'd inflict the kind of violence that'd make me scared of him. I knew what he'd done...I also knew he was capable of much worse. I knew that because he had everything now.

My loyalty and my lies.

Every dark, dirty secret I'd ever owned.

They were his demons to carry around now.

He'd said he'd wear them with pride.

If I'd had the chance to start over, would I have come here to this place...to Cosa Nostra Institute, a place controlled by the ruthless Mafia Commission? I wanted to say no.

I wanted to say the price was too great. You see, when you lay with lions, you weren't really protected. You just realize you weren't who you thought you were at all.

When you lay with lions...*you're just like them. A predator...*

I'd come here to find a way out of this world, but instead I'd been sucked deeper and deeper into it. So deep I can't find my way out of the darkness, so deep that all the laundering in the world won't make up for it. Maybe I don't want to anymore. Maybe here I could finally make a home...a home with him.

"Make your decision, Anna. Will you take my money?" he asked again. "Take it dirty and make it clean?"

We stared at each other. He knew I wanted more than that. He knew money wasn't something I craved. A billion dollars laundered? It meant nothing to me. But him, on other hand? Him I wanted so much, it burned.

My father roared his fury in the other room as I lifted my gaze to the mirror and the faint glow of the flames that flickered and danced on the thick wad of cash in his hand. *Launder their money*...the words consumed me. All their bloodstained, filthy money.

Did I want that? To belong to them? *To belong to him...*

The answer roared inside me, an answer I couldn't fight anymore.

Yes...

1

Anna

Code I
An invitation is only given freely
Anna

Two years before

"DON'T SPEAK UNLESS–"

"I know, Dad." I reached over and rested my hand on his arm. "Unless spoken to. I also know not to pick my nose in public, or ask outright if he's called *the Godfather.*"

Sweat glistened on his brow. He'd pulled the car over twice so far to breathe hard and heave until his skin was a pale shade of gray. Now he was driving like a granny.

"I don't know about this," he muttered. "I don't..."

"It's already too late," I answered, giving him the facts. "I'm eighteen, and I've been helping you launder their money for the last six months. I'm not stupid, Dad. I knew who those people were...and what they did."

He jerked a panicked gaze my way. "I should never have gotten you into this. I should've done forensic accounting or something boring."

"But you didn't." I slid my hand from his arm. "You did what most fathers wouldn't and couldn't do, and you did it for me."

He swallowed hard. "I was blindsided," he muttered, his focus back on the road.

"No," I answered and looked out the window as the Salvatore mansion came into view. "You were just damn good at your job."

We pulled up at the gates and the security detail stepped forward. It wasn't what I'd imagined. I don't know what I'd really imagined. But the guard dressed in a suit lowered his head and peered through dad's window directly at me.

"She's my daughter," dad said before the guard straightened.

No words were spoken, just a wave of his hand before the towering wrought iron gates started to move.

"We're going to have to get better security," dad muttered, his nerves fraying as he nosed the car along the long driveway and pulled up outside the slate-gray three-story mansion.

I was just secretly hoping for a newer car. "Shit, this is nice."

Dad cut me a somber look. "Looks can be deceiving." Still, he turned off the ignition. "Stay close to me, Button."

"Sure," I muttered and shoved opened the door to the old Chevrolet. The hinges howled, and the engine ticked and moaned with a near-death rattle. I pushed the door closed as the heaviness in my bladder turned to an ache. "I need to find a toilet."

"You should've gone before we left."

"I did," I answered. "But you drive slow and I'm nervous."

A look of concern flared and he already looked like he was going to pass out. I love my dad, but he was far too anxious for his own good.

He shoved his glasses back up the bridge of his nose and lifted his gaze as the front door opened. Two beefy-looking guys strode out wearing shoulder holsters over black turtlenecks. Okay, now *they* looked like Mafia.

"Max," dad greeted one of them.

A nod was all he was given before the guy gave me the once-over and turned, striding back through the open door. Okay, so not a talker.

I glanced at dad, who clambered up the stairs and hurried inside, forgetting for a second I was there. He'd met with *the Godfather* seven times now, and each time he came home a little more excited and a lot more anxious, working behind the closed door in his study until all hours of the night.

Stupid me, I wanted to know what for. So a month ago, I found one of his many passwords and I logged on. I saw the accounts...*hundreds of them.* I was hooked, following the patterns, tracing them back to one offshore account, then another, until the transactions started to blur. But I didn't realize six hours had passed as I processed what had been happening. Six hours gone in the blink of an eye.

Six hours was all it took for dad to bust me.

For three days, he didn't speak to me. Three days of silent torture, until one night at dinner, he stabbed a forkful of potatoes and sighed. "Okay, what do you want to know?"

The only problem was *I wanted to know everything.*

For the next hour, I grilled him.

What was he laundering and for who.

The what was shocking enough. But the who, that froze every thought I'd had up until that point. The Mafia weren't the kind of people we knew, or the kind of people we wanted to know. But the money...*the money was incredible.* The accounts I'd been tracing were all theirs. Ones that held millions of dollars in illegal money. Drugs, gambling, prostitution. It was all there, every filthy dollar they earned.

Dad was wearing himself out trying to keep up, working all night and most of the day, until the inevitable happened...*he became ill.* Sick enough to land him flat on his back, but the accounts still needed to be shuffled, layering and hiding their transactions. When he couldn't keep his eyes open, I shuffled them for him.

I was a fast learner. By the end of one week, I'd memorized their US accounts, by the end of the second, all their offshore ones, too. By the third week, I was picking up on details even dad had missed, and by the fourth week, I was coming to him with an idea. A crazy, out there idea...*cryptocurrency.*

We could anonymize funds to hide their source and break the paper trail. It was half-baked, and brilliant, and worked like nothing we'd ever seen before. So well, in fact, that my father's employer wanted a detailed explanation of what we were doing, and that's when my father's nervous word vomit came into play.

He used my name as the brains of the operation.

Mr. Salvatore was shrewd, but untrusting. He wanted to meet this 'brain' and right then she was walking through their front door.

"This way," Max, the bodyguard, called.

Dad followed, and I stared. Sleek black furnishings and expensive looking paintings that were strangely all of a woman with flaming red hair adorned dark sage walls. For a second, I forgot about my bladder as we strode along the hallway and stepped onto the biggest and most lavish study I'd ever seen.

"Holy shit," I mumbled under my breath.

"Dillon," the large man murmured, watching me with a piercing stare.

"Mr. Salvatore," dad nearly whispered as he stumbled forward and jerked a panicked gaze to me. "This is—"

"Anna," *The Godfather of all Godfathers'* low, rumbling tone tore through me. He rose from behind the gleaming red cedar desk and held out a massive hand. "It's nice to meet you. Your father's told me many things about you."

"You, too," I answered, grasping his hand with my own feeble grip.

He dwarfed me, but then again, Mr. Bloodmoney Salvatore would dwarf Santa Claus himself. "So," the giant almost hummed, looking me up and down. "This is the...*woman* who'll one day be the brains of your operation?"

One day?

How about now. Was now good for him? 'Cause I was pretty sure I could show him a thing or two about regulatory requirements. Only, dad didn't answer. He just stared, and Mr. Salvatore stared, while my bladder started to pang.

"One day...yes," Dad nodded, although he looked anything but happy.

"Sounds like she's running things just fine now. What say you, kitten?" The goliath rumbled and pinned me to the floor with his stare. "You going to come and work for me?"

Work for him? The way he said it made it sound like it wasn't an invitation...*but a command.*

"*Dad.*" I winced and shifted my weight from one foot to the other.

"Oh yes..." dad stuttered, turning to the man who'd invested millions of dollars illegally, and started talking.

Until the door suddenly opened behind us and the most beautiful woman I'd ever seen swept through like a summer breeze. *Her.* The sight hit me. *The woman from the paintings.*

"Dominic," she chuckled in the thickest Irish accent I'd ever heard.

All I saw was green eyes and thick, braided red hair. She radiated beauty, prestige, and somehow humility, all at the same time.

"Cian." The terrifying hulk of a man behind the desk beamed as he shifted his entire attention toward her.

She smiled at dad before turning that ray of happiness on me, stopped in the middle of the room, and plonked her hands on her hips. "Now, who do we have here?"

"Mrs. Salvatore, this is my daughter, Anna."

"And it's Cian, Dillon, *Cian.* How many times must I tell you to call me that?" She shook her head and came toward me.

But one nervous glance at Mr. Salvatore said dad would *never* call her that. It was all too familiar, all too smacking of the lack of respect.

"You are a pretty one, aren't you?" The woman grasped me and wrenched me against her, sliding strong arms around me. "You didn't tell me she was this pretty, Dillon. Beauty and brains, too?"

Heat rushed to my cheeks as she hugged me then pulled away. "We have to introduce her to Finley."

"He's busy," her husband growled, his happy smile hardening.

"Too busy to make a new friend?" She gave me a wink.

But my bladder was screaming now, spasming in painful clenches. "Your bathroom." I looked into her eyes. "Please."

"Dominic, this girl is almost bursting, what kind of a host are you?" she snapped, but there was nothing serious in her tone. She was all smiles, all winks. "A grumpy one, it seems."

One wave of his massive hand and Dominic Salvatore muttered, dismissing me without a glance. "Down the hall and to the left."

"Thank you." I tried to smile.

"Go," she directed, jerking her head toward the door as she swept around her husband's desk. "And when you come back, maybe we can find that son of mine, goodness knows what he's getting up to."

"My Irish Princess," Dominic murmured, swallowing her in an embrace.

Stars glinted in his eyes when he looked at her. It was the kind of love I hoped for one day, the kind I'd dreamed of. I was betting no one else made that underworld boss melt like a damn candy bar in the sun. But she did, and she laughed while she did it.

Dad just looked away, embarrassed, as she ran her fingers through Dominic's thinning hair and I hurried for the door.

Her throaty laugh carried along the hall as I stepped out of the doorway and almost ran into the bodyguard.

"Need to pee," I forced through clenched teeth and took off at a hurried walk.

Down the hall and to the left. Down the hall and to the left. Down the hall and to the left. I turned the corner and ran into a wall. A wall with a very nice painting, but that didn't help the cramping in my insides. I kept up the slow jog, turning, hurrying. Panic set in as I started to turn left and right in my attempt to find a bathroom in that maze. Why couldn't rich people have a damn map at the front door?

A dark walnut door waited at the end of a very long hallway. I all but sprinted for the thing, punched through the door, and stumbled into the tiled sanctuary, my hands already fumbling with the button of my jeans. One slam of the door, and I was yanking down my jeans, and plonking my ass on the seat. Relief swept through me with a shudder as I unleashed a torrent. I waited, closed my eyes and breathed, before wiping and flushing.

The mirror lights were harsh and unforgiving. I washed my hands, dried them, and strode from the bathroom and into the hall, trying to trace my way back. Numbers I was good at, remembering directions, not so much. I walked and turned, finding myself more lost than ever, until a familiar door waited and the low drone of voices beckoned.

"I'm sorry I took so long," I apologized as I bore down on the handle and strode through the doorway.

The *thud* of a fist on flesh was followed by a whimper. Blood was all I saw, that and the wide, terrified stare of a gagged man kneeling on the floor, his face a mess of blood.

"For fuck's sake," the guy standing in front of him took one look at me and roared. "Who the fuck is she?"

I lowered my gaze to his bloody knuckles.

"*Julius!*" the attacker roared, making me flinch.

They moved fast, faster than I could track. The heavy thudding of boots echoed in the space as I was dwarfed by the biggest, baddest looking men I'd ever seen. They surrounded me, glowering and snarling, all white teeth and savage stares. My bladder gave a tremble, thank god I'd just been or I would've peed on the spot.

The whisper of hinges came behind me and a soft commanding tone followed. "And who do we have here?" I spun and lifted my gaze, finding deep brown eyes and a chilling stare. One that was eerily familiar.

"Well?" he demanded softly, striding between the pillars of muscle.

They moved for him, taking a step backwards so he could come closer.

He was gorgeous, gorgeous *and* rich, by the looks of the rings on his fingers. He was near my age, maybe a little older, without the cockiness of the jocks I'd known in high school. His black t-shirt showed off a hard body honed by many hours at the gym. There was a surety about him, a quiet carefulness that spoke of power.

"Annalise" I mumbled.

"Annalise..."

"E-Eden," I stammered. "My dad works with your dad."

The smile was quick. "You mean he works *for* me?"

For me. I bit back a snarl of anger. I wanted to push the point. No, he worked *with* him. We could walk at any time, take our hard work and our brains and go any damn place we wanted.

"Finley," he held out his hand. "But my friends call me Fin."

"Finley," I repeated, making sure he knew we weren't going to be friends, as I shook his hand.

At first glance, he looked a lot like his father, but the sly, seductive smile was all his mother's. Thank god for that. A little too much of the patriarch in this family wasn't a good thing.

He shifted his gaze behind me to the man who whimpered and moaned. "I guess you're wondering what's going on here?"

Wondering? No. Trying to work out how I could scrub it from my memory...yes.

I gave a shrug. "It doesn't look like numbers to me," I said quietly. "Numbers are my business. They're all I care about, *nothing else.*"

I prayed he understood me, prayed this wasn't about to be the sudden violent end of my relatively boring life. But as a twinkle sparked in his eyes, he took one more step, lifted his finger to brush my cheek, and whispered, "Good answer."

2

Anna

Code II
Once in, there's no getting out
Anna

Six weeks before

MY PHONE ILLUMINATED WITH A BEEP.

Fin: You didn't come with your father tonight, what gives?

My pulse sped with the words. It was the first time he'd texted me after I gave him my number, to be used *in emergencies only*. Was this an emergency? I didn't think so.

What gives? Ah, how about last-minute meetings at midnight, asshole? My damn eye twitched and my thumbs slid across the screen as I opened up my messenger.

Why? Didn't think you'd notice my absence.

Like there was a lot to miss, mostly me sitting in his father's library while I studied dad's work. The front door thudded as the words on my screen started to blur. I stifled a yawn, rubbed my eyes, and checked the time. It *was* after midnight. Lucky I hadn't gone.

Fin: Looks like you were wrong. The numbers look shoddy. I think your dad is getting old.

I couldn't hide the smile. "Shoddy, my ass," I muttered under my breath. "What kind of self-respecting gangster uses the word *shoddy* anyway?"

I typed back: *You weren't even at the meeting, were you?*

I shifted my gaze to the bedroom door, waiting for it to crack open and my father's grumbled *"'night, Button"*, that'd eventually come.

Fin: Busted. Maybe next time we'll see each other?

"Yeah, right," I turned over in my bed. "I don't think so, you're way out of my league."

Three dots lit the screen. I waited for the message to come, watching as the dots pulsed, then went dark. *No message? Okay then...*

I swung my gaze to the door as I dropped the phone aside and crawled from my bed. Cold kissed my feet as they hit the tiled floor. But I didn't stop as I padded across my room and cracked open the door.

"Dad?"

There was no answer. That gnawing feeling in my stomach grew as I made my way downstairs and turned toward the back of the house. Lights were illuminated on the security panel at the front door. This place was wired with more security than the damn White House, a far cry from the hovel we'd lived in a few years ago.

There were guards outside, armed ones who patrolled the grounds inside the ten-foot fence topped with razor wire. There were floodlights on sensors and pressure triggers at the back door. Dad hadn't always so obsessive. Hadn't always so full of fear, but lately that'd been changing, and it had a lot to do with his employer...*a man called Dominic Salvatore.*

I rapped my knuckles against the door and waited.

"Dad, you in here?" I cracked open the door, to find the green glow of scrolling numbers.

The room was dark, darker than mine, making me blink until my eyes adjusted. Glass clinked as a shadow shifted.

"You should be asleep."

His tone was distant and hollow. *What, no, 'night, Button, I'm fine?*

"You okay?" I closed the door behind me. Four monitors sat across his desk. Numbers scrolled faster than the New York Stock Exchange in a frenzy. Still it wasn't fast enough. It was *never* fast enough. Our life revolved around transactions, around placement and hiding until there were just too many transactions to hide the illicit origin of funds. That was what we were...*launderers.*

"What's wrong?" I stepped closer, catching the silhouette of my father's slump.

"Nothing."

Nothing? That gnawing turned to a dull roar. "Doesn't sound like nothing." I moved closer to the desk and flicked on the lamp.

The bright light took me a second to adjust to, but as I lifted my gaze to dad's, I took in the haunted glaze of his eyes and the blood splatter on his shirt. "Are you hurt?"

His brow wrinkled, the question wasn't what he'd been expecting. "What?"

I took another step until I could reach out and touch his shoulder. "Dad, there's blood on your shirt. Are you hurt?"

"Hurt? No, I'm not hurt."

"Then whose blood is it?"

He was silent. The Salvatores. I glanced at my phone. "Did something happen?"

I waited for him to speak, for him to tell me everything was fine. That we were always going to be fine. Instead, the ice clinked in his glass as he shuddered. "I don't know how to stop this. I don't know how to stop a man like Dominic. He's a monster, Button... he's a fucking monster, and he's trying to pull me in."

Not just him...us.

An icy touch raced from my feet, finding my stomach instead.

"I can't get out of it." He lifted his gaze to mine and in that moment, I saw what fear looked like. "He's got me in so deep I can almost touch the bottom."

"We have his money tied up," I protested.

A slow nod. "And now he wants it back."

"That can't happen." My stomach rolled. "That'd take months, maybe even a year."

"The Salvatores are going to start a war, Anna. One we'll be dragged into."

"So how do we get out?"

What about the others? Brown eyes filled my mind and a sweet smile followed. *What about Finley?*

"There's someone who can help us."

The words drew me back. "What do you mean?"

Dad looked around the study, his gaze moving to the door before he grabbed my arm and pulled me closer. "Someone reached out to me, said they can get us out of this. I didn't think they were real at first, but they sent me this." He reached into the desk drawer and pulled out an image. It was dark...and blurry. I grabbed it and held it under the lamp, straining to see.

It was Dominic Salvatore and his bodyguards striding into some kind of room.

"That's the Commission he's going to, the *secret Commission*. Whoever this is, they're connected, well-connected, and they say they can get us out of this and far away from *them*."

Fear snaked along my spine.

All I saw was the blood splatter on dad's shirt and the panicked sound of his words. *Get away from them...them being the mafia...*

But I knew the men my father worked for. I knew what would happen if they even thought we were trying to get away. We weren't family. We weren't even friends. We were the people who washed and laundered their dirty money and we'd been doing it for a while.

"They won't let me leave. They even have me followed." Dad grabbed my hand. "So it has to be you, Button. It has to be you. I need you to meet with the contact. Then once you're out, come find me."

"Come find you?" My words sounded distant as reality set in.

I knew what he was saying now, knew what was at stake.

Maybe next time he wouldn't come home wearing someone else's blood on his shirt.

Maybe next time he wouldn't come home at all.

"I'm sorry it's all come down on your shoulders, Button." Dad's voice broke. "I'm just so fucking sorry."

"It's okay, Dad," I murmured, my words sounding strange.

My phone lit up with a soft *beep* and I lowered my gaze.

Fin: Are you asleep?

Asleep? The excitement of his words now lost their shine. I lifted my gaze to the blood splatter on dad's shirt. Finley Salvatore. The only guy who'd been remotely nice to me for two years, and the one guy I actually liked. Only now I wanted to get as far away from him as possible and keep us alive...

3

Finley

Code III
A family's blood must never be spilled at home
Finley

Six weeks before

"IT'S about time you showed up."

I stepped into the foyer, standing behind my dad. I said nothing, it was better that way.

"He's stalling." My father stared at the bright brake lights glowing in the dark as Anna's father left the compound. Dad's hands were fisted, bloodstained and trembling with rage as he finished. "And I want to know why."

"I don't think—" I started as he turned.

Heavy steps resounded in the foyer as he stepped away from the front door. A heavy smear of blood trailed from the entrance all the way to the dead body.

"Clean that up."

I fought a flinch at the savage tone and jerked my gaze to the pale splotches on the walls. They were bare now, bare as far as your eyes could see, because without her the house was fucking barren.

Max and Julius moved, each grasping a leg of the fat fuck, and dragged the body along the hallway, leaving a goddamn mess in their wake. I stared at that mess, stared until the red blurred against the marble white.

"I want my fucking money and I want it now."

My pulse stuttered. Hate welled in my gut.

We were going to war, the kind of war that wasn't just going to shake the Commission, but would break it. Those stark walls called to me, stark and bare and void of life. *Just like we were void of life.*

"Get me someone else," my father snapped. "Get me someone *to fucking kill!* Someone who knows something!"

His roar was deafening. But I didn't flinch at the tone. To flinch would show weakness, and that was one thing a Salvatore wouldn't allow.

Fin, honey...mom's voice lingered in my mind. If I lifted my gaze and found those blotches, would I see her face? I wanted to say yes...but I didn't think so. Now when I thought of her, half of her head was missing.

"I'll find them," I answered. "I'll find them all."

"You fucking better or you're no son of mine."

Hate seethed and writhed in my belly. I was his son...but I was also hers.

"The island," my father commanded as he stepped through the doorway of his study. "You're going."

I shook my head. "I don't think now is the time—"

My father whirled on me in an instant. *"You. Don't. Fucking. Think! You just DO!"*

I stood there while that savage shine in his eyes gleamed.

A savagery born from breaking the fucking Code we lived by.

A Code that was supposed to prevent something like this.

But the barren fucking walls and the poison in my gut whispered that that was long in the past. Someone had broken the Code...and brought death to our door. The death of someone beautiful, the death of someone kind. Someone not meant for the bloody hand this life offered. Someone who was now dead.

And now we were planning a war.

"They killed my fucking wife!" he screamed at me.

Still I didn't flinch.

All I could see was her body, lying right where that smear was now.

Shot in the head, assassin style.

Right in our fucking hallway...

They'd brought bad blood to our home.

My wife. Not *your mother.* That was the way it was with him, wasn't it? My wife. My money. My goddamn Commission. There was no room in his life for me, not unless it was his legacy. No position for anything other than an extension of him.

"You're going to that fucking island because the money bitch wants to go."

There was a twitch at the corner of my eye. *Bitch.* I bit back a snarl and held his stare. "What did you say?"

"That's right," my father sneered, coming alive with cruelty. "The launderer has made a fucking demand while he plays hostage with *my* money. He wants his daughter to go to the Institute, and I'm going to let her."

Go to the Institute? A chill came from somewhere. On an island in the middle of nowhere. An island made for connected assholes who liked to play Mafia boss.

"They want it open to women and fucking money." My father's lips curled as hate gleamed. "So that's what they'll get. But I don't trust him..." His gaze went to the doorway, searching for the glowing brake lights that were now long gone. "I don't trust him one fucking bit."

The launderer had said before that it'd take time, said it wasn't as simple as one transaction.

They'd laundered over a hundred million dollars of our money in their cryptocurrency schemes.

"So you're going," he ordered. "You're going to fucking watch her while I get every goddamn dollar I'm owed."

And if you don't? The question rose. *What happens then?*

"So you'll haunt that little bitch," my father commanded as he took a step into the study. "And you'll do what needs to be done."

Anna's face filled my mind. Anna who wasn't a goddamn daughter of a Boss and someone I had to like. That twitch came at the corner of my eye again, throbbing and grating. No, Anna I liked because she wasn't like the others. Not fucking stuck up and connected. She cared about numbers.

And fuck me...*I cared about her.*

4

Anna

The boat was swarmed by men dressed in black the moment we docked. I counted ten enforcers, maybe more in the frenzy. But at least double that waited for us on land, with guns drawn. Double the guards and double the attention.

I lifted my gaze to the mercenaries and met their brutal stares. I was supposed to meet a damn contact. One who'd promised they had found a way to get me and my father away from the most dangerous Mafia family of them all...*the Salvatores,* for good.

But as I watched the Mafia soldiers storm the boat, I knew I could kiss that hope goodbye, for tonight at least. No contact in their right mind would reach out to me, not until the chaos died down.

Shit.

"Building one." An older guy stabbed a bloodstained finger toward the top of the rise. "Get him to the infirmary."

"I don't need a fucking infirmary!" Baldeon screamed as the boat rocked and swayed, turning sideways against the dock. "Just find the bastard who shot me!"

Spent shells clinked and clattered around his feet, rolling with the boat's motion. Baldeon's white shirt was ruined, bloodsoaked and stuck to his skin. Bleeding was one thing, but it was the blowback to his reputation he cared about the most.

And in his world, reputation was worth dying for.

"I'm going to fucking murder him," he slurred, staring up at the beefy security guard who was holding him mostly upright. "Then I'm going to murder his *entire* fucking family."

Glass crunched under my boots as I huddled against the wall of the boat, far away from the others. I might be naive, but I wasn't dumb. We'd taken the hit thirty minutes after leaving the mainland, heading for a small island off the coast of Mauritius. Amongst the sea spray and the endless dark, I'd heard the terrifying *crack*.

A crack that ripped through the window beside me, shattered glass cascading to the deck in its wake. Baldeon had been chatting up a redhead, giving it his best effort, at least, when he jerked from the hit, spun, and went down.

When the shot rang out, I'd pressed my spine against the wall, and there I'd stayed, watching it all unfold like a goddamn coward. Guns were drawn in an instant. I'd never seen a storm erupt that fast...or that savagely. Bodyguards fired back, even Baldeon's guy did his best, driving himself to stand with a blood-curdling roar to empty his gun over the ocean.

Those were not your average guys.

They weren't even bad guys.

They were the worst of the worst. Connected in ways I didn't understand, and yet here I was, risking my damn life to find a way to get as far away from them as I could. I swallowed and watched the men moving throughout the boat. I mean how long would it take to make contact? If they were watching, maybe a few hours...a day at the most.

A day and I'd be out of here, huddled under some tarpaulin in the dead of night as we raced from the island in a speedboat. A day, then we'd find dad and leave. Then we'd never have to think about laundering dirty money ever again.

My world was numbers and algorithms, not guns, not...*Mafia*. Not a world where boats were shot up in the middle of the night, a world where men like Baldeon vowed the kind of revenge that made me shiver with fear. Not a world where imposing concrete buildings sat atop an island in the middle of nowhere.

Bloodcurdling screams came as they carried him from the boat. If gossip could be believed, he was the next in line for his family's Mafia throne. A throne that looked like it was about to be empty.

I lifted my gaze to the lights of the buildings. *Wait for the signal,* dad's words filled me. *They'll come get you, Button, and you won't have to hear the word Mafia ever again.*

Never hear about them again? After the last two years of watching dad work day and night to wash their blood money... that sounded like a second chance at life. One we were desperate for.

I swallowed a shudder and exhaled, dragging myself from the past. It took an entire minute before they started talking, like assassinations were an everyday thing. A whole minute before the brooding, armed Mafia Princes went back to staring down each other from across the room and the women dressed in Dior and Armani picked up where they'd left off mid-gossip.

Not all of them were Mafia, I'd figured that much on my own. Some were sons and daughters of the insanely wealthy, and I was guessing their world was as cut-throat as you could get, which made sense if they were going to a place like the Cosa Nostra Institute, run by someone or someones called the Commission.

I'd thought the Commission was a bunch of old men in wrinkled suits...*it looked like I was wrong*.

Only one of the rich didn't engage with the others. A millionaire redhead, going by the sparkling pink diamonds she wore. She stood separate from the others, with a glass of champagne, catching their careful stares and whispers.

I mentally counted the worth of her diamonds, figuring out what kind of stocks I'd buy instead. Stocks that could not only provide a stable income, but could be used to layer half a million a year in blockchain investments. The kind that traded dirty money for clean. She lifted her head and met my gaze, her smile quick, *hopeful*. I broke the stare and looked away, tucking away the calculations in my head.

Don't draw attention, just blend in.

Laundering money was the kind of information that'd get me in trouble. The kind of information that could get me killed. My phone beeped.

Dad: Button, answer me. Are you guys okay?

It was late. Ten-thirty by my phone.

The previous message from dad sat unanswered: *Are you okay?*

I still didn't know what to say. Was I okay? No, my mind was racing at a million miles an hour. Somewhere on the island was the person who had the kind of connections that could get us free...without getting us killed. For now, I had to pretend this was what I wanted. I had to pretend I was one of them.

Focus, Anna. I had to pretend I wanted to attend this...*Mafia institution,* or whatever it was. To make alliances. And, God forbid...*friends.*

Cosa Nostra Institute, where alliances and royalty are born.

That's what the damn brochure said, well...it would've *if* there'd been one. But to have a brochure about this place would mean it existed, and we all knew *that* was one of their damn Codes. *Never acknowledge anything illegal.* But even without the brochure, we all knew the reality of this place, or I did at least...it'd been drummed into me enough. I'd read about this place, researched more like it, what little there was out there to find. A secret island run by a secret organization, one protected under the rules of the Commission, the governing Mafia body that up until now had only allowed men on the island.

But now that had changed.

I lifted my gaze to the redhead as the engine of the boat died. But she was already moving, making her way toward the front of the boat. Three goddamn weeks...that's all this was. Three weeks of lies, deceit, and hiding my real name. If gunshot-guy was anything to go by, I doubted I'd survive the night.

"Okay," the gray-haired boat captain called as the boarding ramp slid into place. "Nice and easy, I don't need to explain to your parents how you rolled your fucking ankle on the first night."

Heels clattered, glasses of champagne were drained with a mutter. They strode through the trail of blood gunshot-guy had left behind as all twenty made their way off the boat and onto the dock.

I waited for them to leave, stepping out from my place against the wall, and swayed as the boat bobbed. Suitcases were hauled off by the island employees as they worked in the dark. I grabbed the steel railing and strode along the ramp. But the moment my boots hit the dock, the boat lurched sideways, throwing me forward. I stumbled, windmilling my arms, and hit the ground facefirst...*hard*.

Laughter cracked out like a shot as the metallic taste of blood bloomed in my mouth. *Fuck.* I lifted my head and shoved against the ground as one of the assholes from the boat laughed the loudest. My face burned.

"Fucking hell, nice spill," he roared, and the rest of the crowd sniggered.

"Shut-up, you asshole." The feminine growl drew my gaze.

The redhead shoved the guy aside and strode toward me. I wanted to die as a sudden hush washed over the crowd, then a deep, savage snarl took its place.

"Anna." My name thundered through the crowd.

I jerked my gaze high. *No...no...no...no.*

Terror washed through me as a tall figure cut through the crowd in long, sleek strides and I swallowed the flare of desire. "Fin? What the hell are you doing here?"

"Me?" He focussed a scowl on me. "I could ask you the same."

I bit my lip and winced. While my racing heart crawled into my throat, one stupid thought rose. *Please tell me he at least didn't see that swan-dive onto the goddamn dock.*

Heat moved into my cheeks as he lifted me. Finley Salvatore stood in front of me, all six-foot-two of bulging, yummy muscles, and utterly terrifying. "You okay?" He searched my face, his gaze stilling at my beginning-to-swell lip.

"Fine," I murmured, and winced at the sting.

The shrill laughter died instantly. But it didn't matter, not where Finley was concerned. He wrenched a savage gaze toward the chuckling idiot. "You think that's funny? What kind of piece of shit are you?"

The guy swallowed hard and lifted his hands, those laughing eyes not laughing anymore. "Finley...dude, I didn't know she was with you."

"I got her," the redhead murmured beside me.

"Didn't know she was with me," Finley repeated slowly, and turned toward the guy.

The movement itself was truly terrifying. I knew how the Salvatore name was whispered, knew better than most. Thugs. Killers. *Dangerous.* But it was more than that, I saw that now. Even amongst the heirs of the other families, they were feared.

"It's okay—" I started, until the redhead squeezed my arm.

She cut me a look, then slowly shook her head. *Let him do what he's made for.*

Made for...the words were trapped in my head, as though Fin was a recipe crafted to inflict pain and terror. Maybe he was. Maybe that's what someone like him was good at, breaking bones and ending reigns.

He took a step toward the asshole, cutting a glare across the others as he passed. A predatory wolf dressed in Valentino...one who was narrowed in on his kill.

He'd changed in the last eight months. For a while after the death of his mom, he'd tried, sending me messages in the middle of the night. Until the night dad had come home with blood on his shirt. After that, there was nothing. The ocean breeze turned cold. Now I saw what had kept him so goddamn busy...he'd been preoccupied with becoming his father.

This was about more than a fat lip and the lowlife scum who liked to bully and break. This was about loyalty...about not touching what was the Salvatores', and right now they were all looking at me like that...*like I belonged to him.*

"What's your fucking name?" Finley demanded.

The asshole's eyes widened, and those who stood next to him took three steps away in any direction they could.

"Your fucking *name.*"

"D-Dante..." the guy stuttered.

"Dante *who?*"

"C-Cavalaro."

"Cavalaro?" Finley let the name roll across his tongue, his gaze unmerciful. "I thought you guys were thrown out?" There was a shake of the guy's head, one that snapped sideways as Finley jerked him close with one hand. "Weren't you fucking thrown out of the fold, D-Dante C-Cavalaro?

"W-we were br-brought back in."

Splayed fingers clenched into a fist. The movement wasn't lost on Dante.

"You make fun of another woman again," Finley started, "especially *that* woman, and I'll make sure you're not only out...but you're so far fucking out they won't find you ever again. You got me?"

The guy nodded so hard I thought his head would snap off.

"Now get your shit and fuck off. Make sure I don't see your ugly goddamn face again, or I'll ram my fist through your teeth."

He let him go with a shove. This time it was the guy who hit the ground. Only no one was laughing, or staring. Not at Dante Cavalaro, anyway. They all stared at Finley...until he cut a glare through the rest of them and they quickly turned away.

Not one fucking word more was spoken...not until their Dolce and Gabbanas clattered as they scurried away. Then the low drone of their voices caught the wind, whispers and gossip I just knew would be about me.

Fin turned back toward me, glancing once at the stunning redhead at my side before striding my way. "You sure you're okay?" His thumb gently brushed my bloodied lip as he winced.

"A perfect way to make a first impression, right?" I muttered and glanced toward the rise as the others disappeared into the dark.

"Fuck what they think, I don't care," he answered, the crook of his finger capturing my chin.

No, no, don't do this, the words surfaced as a lick of heat moved through me. Movement came at my side, with awkward glances from the redhead. I'd forgotten she was still there.

With an awkward smile, I took a small step backwards. "Thank you."

His brows furrowed with a look of frustration before he cut the redhead a glance. I waited for the lightning strike to hit him, for that long, slow slide of his gaze down her wicked curves that would ultimately linger on the diamonds on her fingers.

Instead, he gave her a nod. "Finley Salvatore."

"Kat VanHalen," she answered.

VanHalen...as in THE VanHalens?

Jesus fucking Christ.

He was a goner for sure. I mean, why wouldn't he be? I mentally steeled myself for the crushing pain that would be inevitable as Finley fell head over heels in love with her. The ticking in my head resounded, until slowly I realized that wasn't happening at all. Instead, the Prince of bloodlust and mayhem just turned that brooding gaze to me. "Do you have your building yet?"

Do I have my building? I gave a nod and lifted my hand. The screen of my phone was shattered, long shards falling free as I moaned. "Shit."

"It's just a phone, Anna." Finley took the broken thing from my hand. "Use mine."

But it wasn't just a phone, was it? It was my portal to the world, passwords that I changed every ten days, all to keep information about us safe.

"It's got all my identification," I protested. *And all your messages...messages I'd saved.*

"You and your damn encryptions, Anna," he sighed.

"Finley," the low, familiar rumble came. Of course he was here. I glanced toward Max, who blended in with the surroundings in black, his shoulder holster packed with guns. "We have to go." One glance toward me, and the bodyguard nodded. "Anna."

He didn't like me, never had. I gave a nod. "Max."

"Give me a second." Fin's voice was etched with frustration as he pressed the button on my phone, illuminating the perfect smile of my Golden Retriever, Angel. "Anna, the code."

I shook my head and jerked my gaze to his. All I saw was the razor-sharp edges of the glass. "No...I..."

"Fin, man, we're already late," Max urged.

"*I said, give me a damn second!*" he snapped.

The bodyguard said nothing, just turned stony.

"Anna...the damn password," Finley urged, his tone softening.

For a second the old Finley was there, the sparkle in his eyes peeking out from the stony control of his father.

I shook my head, my damn face reddening.

"How else are you going to get your information? Just give me the damn password."

"Salvatoresucks," I whispered.

One brow instantly rose as I curled my shoulders, praying for the second time tonight the earth would swallow me whole.

The redhead jerked her gaze away as her hand rose to cover her mouth. But it did little to hide the smile, or stifle the snigger.

"Salvatore...sucks," he muttered, punching in the letters. "No special character?"

I wanted...to fucking die. "No, no special character."

Blood slipped along the cracks of my phone as the screen changed. *His blood.* I stared at the gash opening on his thumb as he murmured, "Building five...with a Miss VanHalen."

"Oh, that's me," the redhead said with not a hint of surprise.

The bodyguard shifted on his feet and dragged massive hands through his hair.

"I'll make sure she gets to her building, Mr. Salvatore."

The voice came from behind me, from one of the five men who'd unpacked the luxury cruiser tethered to the dock.

One nod from Finley, then he met my gaze. "Sleep, Anna. Classes start tomorrow. It's just an introduction, but you still need to be focused."

A shiver passed through me as he turned to the bodyguards at my back. "Make sure she's inside before you leave. Any problems, I want to be notified first. Do you understand?"

"Yes, Mr. Salvatore."

Finley just gave a nod and stilled for a second, before turning to me and leaning close to snarl, "And just for the record, Anna... the Salvatores not only *suck,* they lick and fuck, as well."

Oh my god.

5

Finley

I hated leaving her. Hated more that burning in the pit of my stomach over what I'd done to that asshole. But where duty lay... so did the need to protect, especially where Annalise Eden was concerned.

Not her...

She was a goddamn butterfly flapping around in a hornets' nest.

But to threaten not just violence...but death. *That was against the Code.*

The island wasn't a place for hotheads. It was a place where every son, and now every daughter, of those who made up the Commission attended. It was a place where no blood was dared to be spilled...because every attending family had something to lose.

An eye for an eye...or an heir for an heir.

Times were changing and for some at the head of the table, it couldn't change fast enough. This wasn't just a place for old, misogynistic values anymore. This was a place for women to be just as blood-thirsty and as brutal as the men. Women like Kat

VanHalen, whose daddy had made enough waves to get her here. Let's see how she liked the damn place in a day or two.

If you didn't have an heir, then you weren't in the fold. It was that simple. They wanted someone they could hold over you, someone that could be used as a target, because that's all we really were, weren't we? Targets. An end...*a fucking finality.*

This place wasn't a goddamn holiday. It was a place to train, to gain the kind of knowledge that made you powerful. Knowledge that would keep you safe. If your father couldn't be bothered to teach you, then he sent you here instead. Cosa Nostra Institute, where being bloodthirsty wasn't a crime...it was a fucking legacy.

Helicopters flew overhead, their blinding spotlights combing through the water, making sure the new arrivals were safe. Well, *safer,* at least.

Armed guards dressed in business suits stood sentry on the outskirts, more than normal. A perfect knee-jerk reaction from the Commission. It made sense, given the island housed the heirs to the most powerful Mafia families in the world. A place where bad blood was shelved while they were here and alliances were created. The kind of place where a beautiful Irish Mafia Princess could fall in love with a cold, heartless bastard like my father.

An Irish Mafia Princess was one thing, but the daughter of a launderer, even someone like The Ghost, was another alliance altogether. Shit, she shouldn't be here. She was too naive, too goddamn sweet. She was a genius with numbers, just like her father, and it was those numbers that had gotten her into trouble. With my father, at least.

My phone made a *beep,* drawing my focus from her. I yanked the cell out, staring at the message.

Pavlov: He's uncooperative.

Uncooperative, huh? Well, we'd see how long that lasts.

The roar of the ocean haunted my steps as I made my way to the lowest building in the rear. The place was a damn fortress. Towering buildings fitted with not just cameras, but every state-of-the-art tracking system known to man. Not even the damn treasury was this guarded...then again, the damn treasury didn't have us.

That fucking twitch in my eye came once more as Max pressed his thumb to the scanner and the locks disengaged. He shoved open the door and strode through the darkened foyer to the elevator. The light in the car illuminated, and I listened to the whirr as the elevator came from down below.

Fuck...he was already here.

The elevator doors opened as I worked the rings on my fingers. I followed Max inside as he pushed the button and the doors closed. We sank lower, past the first-level basement, to the one below. The one where shit like this happened away from view.

The doors opened and the salty scent of the ocean greeted me like a punch to the face. A low moan drifted out from the corner of the subbasement, the sound punctuated with the bubbled gasps of what sounded like a punctured lung. *What a goddamn shame.*

My fingers clenched into fists as I glanced at the discarded wetsuit jacket, then the guns, finding the sniper's rifle amongst the weapons. Rage seethed as I jerked my gaze to the hooded figure strapped to the chair, then to the icy stare of the man solely responsible for every-one on this damn island.

Clean-shaven, he was dressed in a black turtleneck under a steel-gray suit. A scar savaged one cheek. But it was his dark, hooded stare that made most people silent. He barely moved. If not for the faint rise and fall of his chest, I'd assume the male was dead standing up.

But it was the assassin I cared more about. Right now, I cared about one thing. Who was the real target and was it connected to my mom?

His arms were bound behind him, his wetsuit pants still on. One of my men, Pavlov, stood with three of the island's permanent staff enforcers. His sea-sprayed hair was still damp from the boat. His stony stare and bloodied knuckles told me he'd gotten to the bastard. But did he find out what we wanted without the Commander knowing? He lifted his gaze to mine, and without speaking, that savage stare gave me the damn answer. *No.*

One nod from the Commander and the hood was yanked free, leaving the hitman to blink and stare around the room.

I didn't know him...

"Do you know who I am?"

A chill raced through the room. Slowly, the asshole strapped to the chair lifted his head and leveled blue eyes at that unflinching stare. But I saw the flicker of recognition, that second where his breath stilled and his eyes widened. Yeah, he knew who the Commander was.

"If you do, then you know broke the Code." That chilling tone spilled through the basement. "So, I'm going to ask you once... and only once, and you are going to tell me what I want to know. Who sent you?"

"I didn't break any fucking Code," he grunted. "Wasn't on the island, so it's not your goddamn business, is it?"

The Commander took a step closer and bent down, staring into his eyes. "The second that *boat* left the mainland, you made it *my business.* You know the rules of the Commission. You know the fucking island is subject to this rule. No one spills blood under my watch. That rule is sworn to by every fucking member who has a damn seat. You fucking *know* that...and if you don't, that means you're not one of us...and there's no protecting you."

Silence.

Sometimes it spoke louder than words.

I was betting that right then, he was mentally calculating all the loved ones he'd leave behind.

"Don't bother trying to think of a way out of this." The Commander reached out, palm up.

One of the enforcers placed a gun, silencer attached, in his hand.

"Now I can make this painless...or you can die screaming. The choice is yours."

"Fuck you," the asshole snarled.

One nod was all it took. My gut clenched. *Not yet!* The words raged inside my head. "The target." I forced the words through clenched teeth. "Who was it?"

Anna's face rose from the darkness of my mind. If he said her name, I'd kill him here and now, Commander or not. I'd do what I'd been sent here for...find her goddamn contact and kill them. No matter who stood in my damn way.

"Baldeon," he finally answered, but his eyes sparkled with the lie.

My stomach tightened. "I don't believe you."

But the comment went unanswered.

"Who was your employer?" the Commander barked.

41

I flinched at the savagery.

"You know I can't give you that."

"The way I see it, you have two options," the Commander growled, aiming the gun at the bastard's groin. One of the enforcers paled and looked away. Jesus, the bastard's *balls*?

"You don't want to tell me? Fine, I'll make sure your mother knows what a spineless piece of shit you were before I blow her fucking brains out."

An icy touch snaked along my spine. He'd do it, too. I'd heard stories, ones that made me sick to my fucking stomach.

"You think they'd send someone who had any family left?" The bastard chuckled, then winced with a groan. "You have no idea who these people are. They're about to unleash a fucking shitstorm on your *precious* little island *and you with it.*"

He turned those bright blue eyes to me. Blue eyes that reminded me too much of a Rossi's. Was that who'd sent him? That burn reached a little higher. I wanted to smash and break, use water to pull the goddamn truth out of his mouth along with his teeth.

Teeth that glistened with blood as he roared with laughter. *"You have NO FUCKING IDEA!"*

I turned then, the thud of my boots ringing out in the dark as I strode past the sniper's rifle and headed for the elevator once more. But that hard fist in the middle of my gut hadn't eased. That twitch came again at the corner of my eye. This was basically over before it had barely begun and still I was left with *nothing.*

Thwack!

The shot was barely audible.

I wanted answers. I wanted blood. Did someone know the daughter of The Ghost was here?

How many would I have to kill?

As many as it took to keep her safe.

Salvatore sucks. Her whisper returned to my mind as the elevator doors opened. I lifted my thumb to my mouth, the gash opened by her shattered phone screen was deeper than I'd thought. Just like the memory of her face was deeper, reaching all the way into the depths of my hunger. Salvatore sucks alright. But we claimed what was ours to take.

6

Anna

Our footsteps rang out as we followed the guard pushing the luggage carrier a discrete five steps ahead. He was packing, that much I knew. I'd caught a glimpse of his gun two buildings back. I focused on that glint as Kat slowed beside me, and I matched her stride.

"So, Finley Salvatore," she said carefully.

I winced inwardly.

"You two...you know?"

I jerked my gaze to hers. "Fin? No...*definitely not.*"

She just gave a shrug and lifted her hands in surrender. "Look, I'm the last one to judge. But he seemed pretty into you back there."

Into me? No.

Maybe one time I'd thought we were friends.

But now...now after six months of not even a hello?

It was changed.

"No," I repeated, and swallowed hard. "We aren't a thing."

"Cool," she answered casually.

The way she said it made my body burn from the inside out. Him and someone like Kat? That made sense...a whole lot of sense. My breath caught with a sharp pang in the middle of my chest. *Ugh,* that's all I needed, indigestion from all the damn stress.

My steps slowed as I glanced toward her. "If you guys want to... you know, if you want to get together or anything, it won't be weird."

Her smile gave little away. The burn in my chest grew. Who was I trying to kid? I rubbed the damn ache and kept on walking.

"I'm not like that, just so you know," she answered finally. "The others, they'd take someone like Finley Salvatore in the blink of an eye and stab you in the back while they were doing it. But that shit...that's not me."

I exhaled hard, my heart not quite as battered and bruised. *Okay...that's good. Not that I was into him or anything.*

"Anyway," she continued and glanced my way. "I think we're gonna be busy being buddies."

"Buddies, huh?"

She gave me a killer smile. "Yep."

That nagging feeling rose once more. "Did you know we were going to be living together?"

"Me?" She feigned surprise, then narrowed her gaze on mine, letting the illusion fall away. "You could say that, yeah."

A VanHalen? Would someone like that be here to help me? I looked at her now, clicking her way in seven-inch heels.

"I checked the list, okay?" she said with a sigh. "Your name came up and you were someone I didn't know, so I took a chance, hoping you weren't like the others."

"You mean connected?"

"No," she denied, turning toward me. "A bitch."

I had to stifle a bark of laugher. Here I'd been thinking all someone like her cared about was money, power, and what she could get.

"Look at that," Kat murmured, changing the subject and jerking her gaze toward the brass sign. "Lucky number seven."

But I didn't move, scanning every inch of her face.

"You going to stand out here all night, or are you going to take a chance and trust me?" she murmured. "After all...don't you think I deserve at least that?"

I weighed her words. No one knew who I was. More importantly, no one knew who my dad was. No one other than Finley Salvatore, that was. I'd hidden behind my mother's maiden name, an untraceable name. My dad had made sure of that.

Make alliances, Anna. Dad's words filled my head. *Find the most powerful people you can and wait for my signal.*

A day, two at the most. I could play roommates and pretend like I wanted to be here. Until then, I needed powerful allies and right now, I was looking at one.

She'd made no move to out me on the boat. Instead, she'd come to my aid. I licked my swollen lip and winced. "Roomies, huh?" I murmured.

Her smile was big and bright, almost as bright as those two-hundred-thousand-dollar diamonds she wore. "Yep," she agreed. "Roomies."

I was grabbed, yanked forward, and slammed against her full breasts. "We're gonna have so much fun. I can't wait. Slumber parties, manicures and pedicures, and gossiping while drinking champagne. That's just going to be the first few nights. But don't worry." She gently pushed me backwards and stared into my eyes. "I got this. You're gonna love me."

"Or hate you."

The guard announced as we neared, "Classes start at eight sharp."

Her eyes widened. "Eight *AM?*"

"Eight AM, Miss VanHalen." He strode toward the elevator and hit the button.

We strode into the car and rode it all the way to the top floor.

"Wow." The word slipped from my lips as I stared, and kept on staring.

The tinted windows stretched across the entire side of the building. I took it all in, striding out of the elevator first and across the very lavish living room equipped with the biggest TV and fireplace I'd ever seen. The bedroom doors were open, our names engraved on special plaques.

"This will do," Kat said with a smile and spun. "What do you think, *roomie?*"

I thought I wanted off this nightmare of an island...but I could worry about that tomorrow.

Right now, this was heaven and as I slowly met her gaze, I answered, "I think it's perfect."

THIS WAS A DREAM...OR, more correctly, a damn nightmare. One I was praying to wake up from. But the moment I cracked open my eyes, I knew my damn torment and reality had collided. I was really here, trying to find the one person who could help us get away from the Salvatores.

And who just happened to turn up at the boat, when he'd been *very* vocal about not attending?

Finley goddamn Salvatore.

The son of the mobster we wanted to get away from.

A son who so far had been kind, unlike the other assholes here.

Now I not only had a billionaire heiress who'd adopted me as her new best friend, but I had to survive the place itself...a damn Mafia training camp. A place dad had told the Salvatores could help me learn how to serve them better.

Serve them.

The words stuck in the back of my throat, and sent a shiver coursing through me.

I rolled, and kept rolling, finally climbing out of the mammoth king-sized bed with its luxurious sage green bamboo sheets, and let my feet hit the plush fur rug before leaving it behind for the cold black marble.

Everything here was expensive. Marble, brushed steel, and dark tinted glass were everywhere...but not a damn door in sight. I stepped into the bathroom and stared at the doorway, glancing from one side to the other while the urge in my bladder grew teeth.

"What the hell?" I growled, running my fingers along the jamb. "No damn doors?"

I couldn't wait any longer, so I ground my teeth and glanced over my shoulder to the open bedroom door. Kat was probably still asleep, and wouldn't wake for at least another hour. If her reaction to eight AM classes was anything to go by, she wouldn't even hear me. I hurried to the toilet, yanked down the elastic waist of my PJ's, and spun, plonking my ass onto the cold seat.

Music started, spilling through the open doorway, something dark and sultry. I hurried to the shower, washed, rinsed, and stepped out, looking at myself in the mirror. Hazel green eyes, lackluster brown hair. I lowered the towel, taking in the smallness of my waist and the gentle flare of my hips before yanking the towel up once more.

Find the contact and leave. It was all pretend, right? Easy. Go to classes, smile and act like I wanted to be here, and wait. Dad didn't like the plan any more than I did. But the contact had been adamant it had to be here. So, while dad stalled with the Mafia's money, he made a simple demand, that I come here... where there was protection, and where I could learn how to follow in my father's footsteps *exclusively* for them.

But now that I was here, it felt weird.

Kat started singing in the room next door as I hurried to the walk-in closet. I wanted to hate this place. I wanted to hate everything here. But it wasn't hate that trembled inside me, even after the damn shooting.

Kat was nice, real damn nice, taking me by surprise. And this place was high end, as expensive as I'd ever seen before.

I slid on panties and a bra, then searched for my black denim jeans and the cream top with frills around my neck. Maybe it was too much? I winced. The mental ticking of a clock ultimately made the decision for me.

I sighed, slipped on flat black shoes, and dragged a brush through my still-wet hair. The blast of a hairdryer from Kat's room made me still. God, I couldn't go out looking like a drowned rat. I raced for the bathroom, searched the drawers, and found the dryer. Five minutes later I was looking a little better, even with flyaway strands and blotchy skin. I tugged at the frill around my neck. Still overdressed, but it'd have to do.

"Ready?"

I turned at her voice and stopped dead. "You're wearing *that* to class?"

"Like it?" She *radiated* in the silky green dress that hugged her boobs and was split to mid-thigh.

"You know we're going to class, right?" I couldn't stop staring.

She took a step closer. "Only class with some of the hottest, most dangerous Mafia guys in the world."

Her smile was devilish and I knew right then that she not only wanted to be *here*...she wanted to be around *them*, the corrupt, the merciless. That's what turned her on. "How are we going to be friends?" I questioned, and met her gaze. "We're total opposites."

"You know what they say about opposites." She came closer, perfect blood-red toenails peeking out of black, strappy pumps, and flicked my frilly, high-necked collar as she planted a kiss on my cheek. "Now, let's go knock 'em dead."

She spun, heart-stabbingly stunning, and strode away.

I followed her into the elevator and through the automatic doors in the foyer. The sun was already blinding as we stepped out and headed along the walk. I brought up my iPad, glancing her way as I punched in the unlock code. If she saw me watching her, she didn't say anything, instead she focused on chatting. "I mean, I do love Dior, but Chanel just has my heart...you get me, right?"

"Totally," I muttered, my eyes running over the numbers of the stock exchange. "A door has your heart."

She stopped suddenly, and I was so absorbed by the numbers, I didn't realize, not until it was too late. I slammed into her, the iPad crushed between my breasts and hers as she turned. "Are you even listening to me?"

"Sorry," I muttered. "It's just..."

"Not your thing, huh?"

My smile this time was genuine. "Yeah."

I was too much like my father. If you asked him, I was miles ahead of where he was at my age. Give me algorithms and identity verifications any day. That stuff I could live and breathe and talk about for days.

"Come on." Kat grabbed my hand and tugged me forward. "I bet I'm going to love that big, sexy brain of yours."

"Sexy," I barked. "Now that is definitely one thing I'm not."

Her phone buzzed and at first, I didn't know where she kept it, until her hand snuck into the side of her dress and pulled out her iPhone. "Come on, or we're going to be late. Christ, I hate these early mornings."

I didn't have the heart to tell her that eight AM was a normal time, most people were already hard at work by now and the stock exchange was already buzzing.

My iPad let out a *ding*. I lifted it and glanced at the message.

Psychology 101 - Weakness and Exploitation Techniques. Rooms 64 and 68, starting in five minutes.

Shit, if I didn't hurry, I was going to be late on my first day of classes.

Kat let my hand drop as the main buildings came into view. "Catch you after class?"

Fear punched through me. "Wait, you mean we're not together?"

"I have Kidnapping and Ransom Analysis, although," she said with a scowl, "I'd much rather attend *Running your Fortune 500 Company*. You?"

"Psychology."

"Bummer." She winced. "Maybe next time." She glanced at the map on her phone. "Looks like I'm over here. Catch you later, gorgeous."

"Later," I agreed, watching her leave.

My own map pointed straight ahead, through the massive glass doors and out of the sunlight. I stepped up to the doors, but this time they didn't open, leaving me to heave my weight against them and hurry inside.

The place was quiet, *too damn quiet*. A sweeping staircase was at my left, darkened hallways branched off to my right. *Sixty-four...sixty-four...sixty-four.* I hurried across the foyer, glancing at the signs at the entrances to the hallways, and sped down the second hallway marked *Rooms 60-72*.

Dangerous guys.

Mafia Princes.

*Finley Salvatore...*he was stuck in my head as I raced past closed doors. The further I went, the darker the damn hallway became. I peered at the numbers on the door and then slammed the handle and burst in. "Sorry I'm late," I apologized.

And was met with grunts and low, grinding moans.

My head snapped up and my gaze froze on the two people on the stainless steel table, a savagely stunning brunette and a tattooed hunk who was fucking her into next week. Her legs were splayed open, her ass squealing on the stainless table with every brutal thrust as the guy lowered his head and dug his fingers into her hips. "Fuck, you're so wet."

Red lips parted as her darkened eyes narrowed on me. "Oh, we have a visitor." She grunted and licked her lips. "Come and join...I like girls."

"I...*ahhh*..." I stepped backwards. "No thank you." Jesus, I sounded so polite.

There was a look of confusion before she muttered, "Suit yourself." Then she threw her head back and growled, "Harder, you goddamn pussy."

I all but lunged back out the doorway and slammed it closed behind me.

"Enjoying the classes so far?"

I whipped around, finding Finley right behind me. "Fin."

He shifted his gaze to the door behind me, where the guttural moans of heated sex filtered out. "The classes," he repeated as he moved closer, lifting his hand to brace against the wall, leaning over to peer through the glass at the couple inside before shifting that dangerous gaze on me once more. "Did you need help finding them?"

The sounds of flesh smacking flesh rang out, only this time there were no broken bones, only moans of desire, making heat race all the way up my cheeks. "No," I whispered.

"'Cause I can help you, Anna." He curled a finger under the point of my chin and lifted.

Lightning tore through me.

His warm breath blew against my lips as he lowered his head and whispered, "Fuck, you're sweet."

A shudder tore through me as I closed my eyes. The kiss was just a brush of his lips. But it was *fire*...

My pulse spiked, booming in my ears as the kiss deepened. He took without hesitation, devouring my mouth, making my damn body quiver and my pulse pound. Without thinking, I lifted my hand, my fingers skimming his arm before he broke the kiss.

"If you're sure then," he murmured against my lips.

Cool air engulfed me as he pulled away.

The classroom behind me was silent as he turned and strode away. For a moment, I couldn't move. My damn knees were shaking and my brain raced, a jumbled mess.

Sex.

Dark hallways.

And Finley Salvatore.

What else could possibly happen to me in the space of a few hours?

I was too terrified to guess. I hurried to the next classroom and double-checked the number on the door as a male voice grew louder, pushed down on the handle, and quietly stepped into the room.

Heads snapped up, gazes were filled with annoyance. I didn't look at them, just kept my eyes down.

"Sorry," I muttered, and glanced toward the instructor standing at the front of the class.

An instructor who was drop-dead gorgeous.

I took in his sleeves, rolled up on muscled forearms, and skintight jeans.

"No problem." He gave me a careful smile, scanned me from head to toe, then nodded toward the others. "Please take a seat... I was just explaining who I am. Jesse Silvestre, former head of forensics of the Federal Bureau of Investigation."

"Who finally woke up and now works for the dark side." Some guy called out from the back of the room.

I kept my head down and hurried to an empty seat at the side, away from the others. But they watched me with cold, hungry stares. I couldn't shake off the feeling and as the class wore on and Mr. Former FBI went through the various personality traits before moving on to the ways you can break down your opposition, that icy feeling at the back of my neck grew until it was unshakable.

In that moment I knew how it felt stepping into a snake pit... when you were the mouse.

7

Anna

I shifted in my seat and focused on my iPad, typing notes on specific Machiavellian and impulsive traits you could exploit. Everyone had triggers, Mr. Former FBI explained, and it was our job to find out what those triggers were. How that was going to help me was anyone's guess. I didn't want to be in the same damn zip code as most people, preferring monitors to faces and numbers to conversation. Except for Kat. Now she was someone I could chat with...in a normal sense at least.

"Okay guys, we've been going for about an hour. I think it's time for a small break." I jerked my head up from typing as he scanned the class, his gaze narrowing toward the back. "When we come back, I want to talk about loyalty, what that might mean to someone...and how it can be broken."

Chairs scraped and snarls and barks of insults and threats filled the air as the rest of the class headed for the door. I didn't dare risk a glance their way, didn't dare draw their attention. Christ, it was like the first day of high school all over again. The only difference was, these weren't the kind of people who wanted to belong...or to be liked. Fear and respect were the currency here and I was way out of my league.

Tattoos, designer brands, and lustful swaggers filled the space, heading for the door before Mr. FBI lifted his head and called out. "Finley, Harley, and Tate. Can I have a moment, guys? I have a little something extra I think you might be interested in."

Finley?

Christ, he was everywhere. My hand stopped sliding the iPad toward the end of my desk. I jerked my gaze upwards, then shifted it to the rest of the room. Everyone strode through the open door, except for one guy with the most platinum blond hair I'd ever seen and another tatted-up pretty-boy...and their shadows.

That icy feeling at the back of my neck only grew stronger, *then grew claws.*

Pulling my focus away from them.

His dark eyes bored into mine.

Controlled and composed.

Finley Salvatore was a loaded gun. One whose attention was pointed at me. He scowled and scanned me from head to toe, then pushed from his chair and strode toward the front of the room.

The two others followed him. I was betting everything came after Finley. He moved like he was the end result of everything. The finality. The goddamn answer to every fucking question that every existed.

Max and Pavlov moved with him, staring down the four other bodyguards in a pissing contest of epic proportions. Finley just waited, his tattooed hand ready to draw the gun tucked into the back of his waistband.

"Gentlemen, we're all friends here," Mr. FBI murmured, carefully crossing his arms over his chest, watching the displays of dominance. "And we abide by the Code."

But they weren't friends, that was easy to see...and still not a damn word was spoken. It was both terrifying...*and hot as hell.* Heat moved through me, licking and lingering in places it shouldn't as I watched the standoff of goons.

But it was Finley who gave a shrug, leaving his shadows to stare down the other four until a bark sounded.

"Just go," one of them muttered with a sigh. "Or I'll be here until I'm fucking eighty. Goddamn motherfucking Code."

They left then, tails tucked between their legs. A slight twitch of his lips, and Max chuckled. *Pissing contest won...I guess Max had the bigger dick after all.*

"Ahhemm." I jerked my gaze up at the sound, cheeks burning as Mr. FBI just stared at me. "Miss Eden?"

Shit. I jerked my gaze to Finley's bodyguard, who also stared at me.

I shoved to stand on trembling legs and scrambled like the damn mouse I was, clutched my iPad to my chest, and hurried for the open door.

Footsteps thudded behind me in commanding strides. I tore through the door and scanned the darkened hallway, my gaze instantly stopping on the closed door to the sex romp. *No way... not there...*

Panic thundered in the veins at the sides of my neck. I winced, and desperation drew me toward the low murmur of voices at the end of the hall. I made my way back to the foyer, glancing at the sweeping staircase and the massive water feature that I'd somehow missed hurrying to class. One panicked look over my shoulder and I found the hallway empty. *What the hell?*

"You should've seen how Finley Salvatore reacted toward her." The nasally blonde from the boat said loud enough that I could hear. I focused on the reason I was here and tried to ignore it. "Maybe he took pity on her. I mean, look at her, she looks like a nobody."

I turned, and took a seat near the fountain, nervously biting my lower lip. But in *my* world, looks could be deceiving. A nobody? I didn't think so. I had enough money invested in stocks that I could retire now at twenty and never have to work another day in my life. I didn't need to wear fifty thousand dollars on my body to get attention.

"Madi...stop staring." The guy leaned close. "Unless you want to...you know, *bang her*."

Gross.

My face burned as Finley's hungry stare came back to me.

"Jesus, there he is," she whispered at the steady thud of footsteps. "And there *they* are."

Speak of the Devil and he appears...I couldn't look away. He was thunder and lightning all at once, dark and brooding, his gaze sweeping through the crowd.

"She looks like a damn nun. Do we even know who she *is?*"

I inhaled as the words reached me, then slowly exhaled and busied myself with searching their faces, keeping my mind on the reason I was here, to find the damn contact.

Eden. My last name echoed in the space. I tugged at the high neckline of my top and cut my gaze toward them, watching as they turned their gazes away. This whole damn thing was a bad idea. How the hell had I ever thought I could fit in here? I should leave. I lowered my hand to the cold marble seat and went to stand.

But Finley still scanned the room, finding every woman before he moved on. That burn moved a little higher, reaching along my throat like a damn fist as that brooding gaze settled on me. *Control me.* That's what he wanted to do. It was written all over his damn face, carved into every furrow of his brow. Nothing more than a command on those lips.

My pulse quickened under his stare as I lowered mine to the floor.

I wanted to meet his ferocious stare with my own. I wanted to be ballsy, to be like *them,* and bark *back the fuck off...*

But I didn't...instead, I took a step sideways, the backs of my legs kissing the icy marble seat as I used those same assholes who'd made fun of me as a damn shield. Still, I caught the cant of his head as he narrowed in on the movement and turned his head to his bodyguard.

The blonde lifted her hand and waved at Finley when he turned back, but his gaze went right past her without a flicker of interest.

"What an asshole." I caught her nasally snark as she turned back to her companion.

"What did I tell you?" he muttered. "They aren't like us, Madelaide."

Madelaide? That was her damn name? And she made fun of *me?*

"Hey, Harley!" The bark filled the space.

Heads turned and I was just one of the crowd. I watched the dark-haired Harley stride toward a small group of guys who stood to the side. There were smirks, fist bumps, and slaps on the back. Finley watched the display with a careful gaze before searching the others for the blond.

Tate.

Tate *somebody*. Thick rings on his fingers, one trapped his thumb. Piercing blue eyes met Finley's gaze and didn't flinch. There was definitely no love lost there. It was like watching two trucks hurtling toward each other on the freeway in the same damn lane. Neither was going to look away...neither was going to swerve.

"Really? Fuck yeah, I want in. I'll put money on that..."

The words invaded in an instant, drawing me away from the staredown. A roll of money exchanged hands. A few thousand at least. Laughter slipped from Harley's lips before his fist clamped down around the wad and pocketed it.

An unseen touch crept up my spine at the exchange.

I glanced back at Tate as he turned away. Seemed like someone did flinch after all. He scrutinized every face, moving from one to the other, lingering on every female like they were prey *just like Finley had seconds ago.*

Money.

Sniggers.

And the three of them being called over by Mr. Former FBI.

Something was happening there. I swallowed hard as Tate-whoever zeroed in on me. Heat crept into my cheeks as I felt his gaze lingering. I looked down...looked anywhere else but at *him*. Something I didn't want to be part of.

"Ready, guys?"

They all turned at the voice and shuffled back toward him, muttering choice words as they dispersed...taking my cover with them. I stepped to the side, head down, taking careful steps as I avoided his gaze.

"Hey, do I know you?" Tate called out as I strode past.

"No, don't think so."

With every step, that sinking feeling grew. By the time I hit the classroom door, I was desperate to hide. I didn't look up as they strode in behind me and took their seats, hating every fucking second they made me feel weak.

"Okay, we're back to it." Mr. FBI clapped his hands. "Deception, pride, torture. What do those things have in common?"

The class was silent, waiting.

They were not the kids to raise their hands, nor were they the ones to ask for permission.

"Sounds like a regular fucking Saturday night to me," someone called out.

Others laughed, even Mr. FBI chuckled, nodding like it was all a joke, but in reality, we all knew it probably wasn't. He carefully deflected, moving into the various interrogation techniques used by law enforcement, terrorists, and organized crime, as if most times there was a fucking difference.

I settled back against my seat and forced myself to listen to Mr. Former FBI give us an in-depth rundown on suggestibility, but I couldn't stop my attention from drifting to the other side of the room. I lifted my hand, hiding the movement behind a brush of my hair, and looked.

Tate-what's-his-name stared at the nasally blonde, his focus so intense she shifted in her seat and cast sideways glances at the hawk features sitting next to her. He watched her, and Finley watched him, until finally Mr. Former FBI said, "Well, that's the rundown. I hope it helped, and more importantly, I hope you remember those practices so you can be better prepared."

"Better yet." A guy sporting a hundred-and-fifty-thousand-dollar Patek Philippe watch called out. "Call dad and watch the bastards run."

But Jesse just smiled, standing in front of the class. "Dad might not always be there when you call, Killian. One day *you're* going to be the one giving the orders. That's when those techniques come in handy."

"Got it," Killian muttered, his smile hardening to something cold and savage. "Thanks for the heads up."

I busied myself typing up the last few notes as they swarmed the doorway, leaving me behind. Tate followed Madelaide, shadowing her steps as she cast me a sideways glare and flicked her hair. I waited for them all to leave before I quietly slid from my seat.

"Miss Eden."

"I enjoyed your class, found it all very interesting."

"Did you?" He kept doing whatever it was he was doing, shuffling papers, not bothering to lift his head.

"Yes, and I'd really like to learn more about...*lying,* so I was hoping there might be some extra classes or something?"

"There're no extra classes."

I stilled. No classes? "But I thought..."

He didn't stop, just lifted his open book, not even giving me the goddamn respect I deserved.

"So what might they be interested in?" I clutched my iPad to my chest.

Now he looked up and his warm brown eyes met mine. "Excuse me?"

I glanced toward the doorway and tried to gather my nerves. "You asked them to stay behind." *Finley...you asked Finley to stay behind.* "I want to know what you told him—*them.* I want to know what *they* might be interested in."

He rounded the desk, leaned back, and crossed his arms, bringing my attention to the strained muscles under his shirt. He was gorgeous, careful, intense in a dangerous kind of way. I was thrown back to my eighth-grade science class where they discussed the boiling water analogy. But when I looked into his eyes, that's exactly how I felt...paddling...paddling, while the water grew warmer and warmer.

"Are you settling in?"

I frowned at the question. He was looking at me now, that careful stare trying to find a way inside my head. But he didn't know me. He didn't know there was *no* way inside my head. Others wore diamonds and expensive clothes and hid behind icy stares. I hid behind a firewall of pretense. A nobody, remember?

Careful, Anna. We keep up the facade, honey. Never let anyone rattle your cage.

My cage. I paced behind the bars and bit my lip before I murmured, "I don't think that answered—"

Mr. Former FBI was intrigued. "You don't look like them."

My frown deepened as inside my head I paced and paced and paced. *Interrogation techniques* 101 was printed on the paper beside him. *Defection techniques* were written underneath.

"You do that a lot, you know?"

I lifted my gaze to his. "What?"

He pushed off the desk and took a slow step toward me, his voice husky. "Bite your lip."

"You didn't answer my question before," I pushed. "What might they be interested in?"

A curt male snarl came over the speaker. *"All students required at the fingerprint and crime scene analysis in lecture hall 302. Class begins in five minutes."*

Mr. Former FBI was already moving, sliding his documents from the desk and striding toward the door. "Looks like you'll be late for your next class, Miss Eden. Enjoy your stay at the Institute."

8

Anna

I headed back along the hallway, that gnawing feeling welling in the pit of my stomach. I could do this. I could play their games and attend their damn classes. I could become the person I wasn't.

And not just because our damn existence depended on it. Because I was waiting for my chance to get out of here.

Only, to leave meant...

Finley's lips on mine were torture. And even though that burn lingered, so did that bite of annoyance.

Now he fucking kisses me?

Two goddamn years of working with his father, then radio silence for the last six months, and now a kiss?

He'd changed alright. Gone were the sweetness and the snark.

Here, he was someone else. Someone intense...someone dangerous.

I shoved that spark of desire away, pushing it all the way down under the need to survive. My steps were soft and quiet, barely making a sound as I came out of the hallway and into the empty foyer. Movement flickered through the glass at the end of the building, high up in the sky. A dark speck was growing larger in the distance and headed this way. I checked the map, finding the lecture halls one building over, and shoved through the doors.

Three more buildings stretched out on this side of the island, the one I needed was just in front. I lifted my hand to the glare of the afternoon sun and hurried as that dark blur grew above me. The faint *whop...whop...whop* of rotor blades grew louder as I raced down the hill and headed for the door.

Fingerprints.

Interrogation techniques.

I knew what the Institute was. It was more than a damn training camp. It was a test, one I needed to pass. Make alliances and keep my own identity secret...well, as much as I could. Kat knew who I really was, I don't know how...but she knew. Could I trust her? I wanted to. God, how I wanted to.

Cameras swiveled toward me as the building loomed. That damn chopper drew my gaze, flying low overhead like a hulking black beast before landing in the distance. Someone important had arrived. More important than the VanHalens and the Salvatores.

Tattooed and expensive

Just another way to say teeth and claws.

In my world at least.

I grabbed the handle, yanked open the door, and stepped into a fucking den...of vipers.

Heads turned my way, their reptilian stares chilling as they strode toward the open lecture hall door. I scanned twenty, thirty at most, and followed.

"Get *out* of my way." The snarl came a second before I was shoved to the side.

I stumbled and slammed into the doorjamb with a *thud*, pain tearing through my side as a gazelle dressed as a runway model strode past. Arctic blue eyes nailed me to the spot as she looked down from her seven-inch stilettos.

She lifted her gaze and kept on moving, her and her damn entourage. Black suits and muscled chests stalked her. I waited for her bodyguards to pass, then straightened my spine and lifted my gaze, meeting Kat's. She just watched me, not missing a damn thing. A smile was next, careful and full before she lifted her hand and waved me over.

She had guys all around her, one of them even attempting a conversation. But she barely noticed, instead she watched me as I turned sideways and stumbled my way between the rows of seats toward her.

"You're just an accident waiting to happen, aren't you?" she muttered, cutting the bitch who'd shoved me a hateful glare.

"I warned you." I slid into the seat next to her and glanced at the six-foot muscled guy who sat in front of her, attempting to have a conversation. She just smiled at him, fake but still a smile, and leaned forward enough to flash the tops of her breasts as she patted his arm. "Enough now. My friend is here."

He just stopped mid-sentence, then glanced my way in confusion.

But Kat was already moving on, her gaze following the bitch all the way across the lecture hall. I yanked the desk up and slid my iPad down, that eerie feeling of being watched heavy on the back of my head. I risked a glance over my shoulder. Finley sat three rows up and to the left, his icy attention on me, as was that of his two shadows.

My pulse sped, until flushed cheeks forced me to look away. "This place fucking terrifies me."

"Of course it does, sweetheart," Kat murmured, still staring daggers at the bitch. "You still have your baby teeth. But you'll grow out of them soon enough. Don't you worry 'bout a damn thing." She reached over and patted my thigh. "Kat's got your back."

My iPad gave a soft *ding* as an older man stepped up to the podium and his deep, gruff voice drifted through the speakers. I scanned the words scrawled on the whiteboard. *Crime Scene Analysis 101 - Leaving your mark.*

Why did those words conjure something heated inside me? Something I'd never normally think of? Something carnal and dark. A hand around a throat. Thrusting hard...the couple from the darkened classroom filled my mind—until slowly that image turned into a fantasy filled with Finley Salvatore...and me. It was his hand around my throat, his tattooed fingers clenched tight. Those intensely dark eyes boring into mine. His body...*God.* I shifted in my seat.

Jesus. Heat swept through me.

"Right. Settle down. I'm here to teach not hold your damn hands. Fingerprints. Don't leave your mark on anything you're not going to own."

Own...

I tried to shake off the fantasy of Finley's hands around my neck and punched in my password, finding a message from dad.

Dad: Everything okay?

I swallowed hard and tried to breathe. My fingers moved on the keypad. *Got here fine, the place is stunning.*

Dad: Didn't answer my question, Button.

The gruff voice at the front of the class echoed in stereo as I gave a slow exhale and typed. *I'm trying, Dad.*

I waited, and waited, shifting my gaze to the front of the class before the tiny *ding*.

Dad: I'm proud of you, Button. But I'm close if you need me.

A surge of adrenaline coursed through me with the message as the lecturer talked of arches, loops, and whirls. I swiped and typed. *Are you safe, Dad?*

We were safe because no one really knew him. To expose himself like that wasn't him...maybe not the data analyst, but it was the dad.

A message popped up.

Dad: Always.

"There's a party tonight," Kat murmured, leaning close. "And we're going."

I jerked my gaze to hers with a slow shake of my head. "I don't do—"

"You do *here*," she commanded. "Teeth, remember?"

Teeth, right.

I'm close if you need me...

Dad's message lingered as I tried to concentrate. But a murmur swept through the other side of the theatre as the lecturer spoke about gunshot residue like we were just a regular class. But we weren't...and we sure as hell weren't a class of would-be cops.

The gray-haired investigator paced behind the podium. "That's why gloves and coveralls are important."

"No blowback on this suit, it cost too damn much," some asshole muttered.

I winced as Kat rolled her eyes. "Showoff."

Before long, the instructor said, "Right, I think that's enough for the day. Bruno, Hunter, and Mr. Black. Can I see you guys down in front for a minute? I have a little something extra I think you might be interested in."

Really? Just like the class before. I frowned and glanced toward the movement.

"Anna...class is already over."

I jerked my gaze up. I was the only one still sitting. I shoved to my feet, finding the three guys slowly making their way to the front. Kat followed my focus. "What is it?"

"That's the exact same thing that happened in the class before."

"What?" she asked with a smirk, swinging her gaze back to me with a shrug. "Probably happens in every class."

"Kat, will I see you tonight?" the six-foot guy from before asked hopefully.

"Jake, you're a nice guy," she said sweetly. "But you're just not my type, *sorry.*"

"Not your type?" he muttered, and scowled.

The guy was Adonis in the flesh, muscled, tall...and *obviously* into her. But right now, all she cared about was me. I don't know which of us was more pathetic.

"He called them down and then..." I tried to find the words to explain.

But Kat just waited patiently, whipping a savage glare to anyone who dared snigger and look my way. "Come on." She grabbed my arm and gave me a gentle push. "We can discuss this at home."

Home. I tore my attention away from the front of the room and started walking, but my gaze gravitated over my shoulder as I smacked into a wall of muscle.

Midnight eyes bored into mine. "Anna," Finley murmured, lifting his hand and running his thumb across his lips, drawing my focus to his mouth.

The mouth that had claimed mine before.

My lips parted with a breath.

I swallowed hard.

With a wicked smirk, he was gone, cutting through the crowd, his two babysitters following close behind.

Everyone stopped for *him.*

Made room for *him.*

They worshipped him like some god.

A god who right now was setting my soul on fire.

I let Kat lead me away from the lecture hall, making our way around the next building, then the next, until we finally found our way to ours.

"Thank fuck that's over. You know, they actually made us do a personality test?" She shook her head and strode through the automatic doors into the foyer.

She put her hand on my shoulder, using me to keep herself steady, and slipped the pumps free. "God, that feels better."

"You need some flats like mine."

"Not even if my life depended on it," she answered with a wink.

The elevator doors opened and we were *home* before we knew it. Kat gravitated to the kitchen first, yanking open the black refrigerator doors and peering inside.

"This will do nicely." She plucked a bottle off the shelf, then turned before freezing. "Umm..."

"You don't know how to open a bottle, do you?" I stepped closer, shaking my head, and held my hand out. "Gimme."

"You're a wonder," she blew me a kiss. "'Cause I have to pee really fucking bad."

I worked off the wrapping and unwound the wire around the cork as the toilet flushed. *What is she even doing here*...the words repeated. *A nobody...just look at her.* I worked the cork free. But it was Finley's lips that claimed me. My pulse raced with the thought of him. I'd been kissed before...*but nothing like that.*

I wanted more. More of him, even if he was dangerous.

Pop!

The scent of the sweet champagne hit my nose.

"Kat?"

"Hmm..." she was there, sliding onto the leather seat on the other side of the island...

A tremble cut through me as I imagined myself with someone like him.

I lifted my gaze and met hers. "The party," I started. "You wouldn't happen to have anything I could borrow to wear?"

The squeal was piercing as she clapped her hands. She positively beamed. "Fuck, I never thought you'd ask. I have *the perfect dress* for you."

9

Finley

Christ, she was sweet, keeping her head down as she slid into the seat with barely a sound. I tracked her every move, staring as she curled a wisp of hair around her ear. Others watched me, like they always watched me. The goddamn outburst at the boat hadn't helped matters.

I tried to talk myself out of it, tried to get my damn head in the game, but the moment I'd seen her this morning, I couldn't stop myself. I *wanted* to kiss her, just like right now I wanted to again.

Find the money, track her every move. The thrill of this was a little too fucking addictive. I stiffened watching her, well aware how she triggered every fucking ravenous instinct inside me. I didn't like her here, in these classes and these halls. She needed to be back home, back within the walls I knew. She needed to be secret, she needed to be safe...

Every goddamn asshole who glanced her way I wanted to stab in the fucking eye. I drained my Scotch.

Don't look at her...

Don't fucking look at what's mine.

My phone gave a *beep*. I steeled myself and looked down.

Dad: My money better be fucking secure...

My money. Not *our* money. Just *mine...*

My money.

My reputation.

My fucking family.

Christ, this woman was going to spiral me out of control. I lifted my cell and my fingers moved across the screen.

I have it under control.

I hit send and waited. I didn't have to wait long.

Dad: You'd better.

I winced and cast the cell aside, letting it hit the sofa and fall. An ache spread through my jaw. I released the clench and rubbed the ache. *My money...*the words grated on me. I filled my glass once more. The silence of this place normally soothed me, but not tonight. I stood on the top floor and stared out. Darkness reflected behind me with barely a sparkle of light. All the sparkle was out there.

Streetlights shone, illuminating the paved paths around the Institute.

My gaze moved to the building in the distance. Darkness claimed each floor but the top one. That ache in my jaw moved deeper. I swallowed the Scotch, feeling the burn move through me. It was more than just my father that had me wound so fucking tight. It was the damn classes...more importantly, this fucking *initiation* handed out to a select few.

An initiation which was all about finding a damn target and exposing their secrets.

I knew the kinds of assholes who came here and what their intentions were.

Most would go for the weaker ones. The ones whose families were already hanging by a damn thread. But some...some weren't just interested in revenge or blood ties gone sour. *Some were here for the hunt.*

It was those bastards I had to watch out for, especially where Annalise was concerned.

My money.

I winced at the words and swallowed the heat, letting it move through me. The launderer was causing problems, making demands, demands like his daughter's safety. We'd pushed him too hard, expecting a man like him would buckle and do whatever we wanted.

We'd expected he wouldn't resist when we brought him into the fold.

To launder for the Salvatores alone.

The Ghost. His name whispered in certain circles piqued a lot of interest, too much interest. They'd heard about the five million washed in three months, washed by means that were known only by the man himself. So when he showed a backbone, it took us by surprise. He wanted to pull away from us, demanding to send his daughter to the island. To a place filled with the kind of people my father wanted her far away from. The kind of place *I* wanted to be far away from.

But I wasn't.

I was *here*.

Watching her.

As long as the fucking Rossis stayed away, I was happy. Those bastards I didn't have time for, not when I had Anna to watch.

My phone lit up, the brightness reflected in the dark, bullet-proof glass. I gave a sigh and strode forward, grabbing it from the plush leather seat.

Max: She's leaving now.

Leaving...to go to the damn party, striding in amongst all those hungry stares and carnal thoughts. I knew what she was walking into. I knew because if this had been anyone else, I'd be watching her, waiting to make my damn move. Her dad was a goddamn genius, layering out money into cryptocurrency in a way that made it virtually impossible to detect. It also took time to retrieve, time we'd had before we'd gotten word that someone wanted our launderer for themselves.

That someone was here, hiding on the island...waiting for a chance to take what was mine.

With a frustrated sigh, I unbuttoned my shirt and strode to the bedroom. It looked like I had a party to attend.

10

Anna

"This is stunning." I tugged the hemline of the dress.

"*You* are stunning in it," Kat murmured, and took a step back, surveying her masterpiece.

I swallowed hard and lifted my gaze to the mirror. But the woman I looked at wasn't me.

She was...*beautiful*. Her hair shimmered with the kind of deep chocolate shine I was envious of. But the dress. Black, sleek, the skirt flaring just a little, but still too short for my liking. But this wasn't just about what I liked, was it? It was about becoming someone I wasn't. Someone like all the other women here, and this dress was something they'd wear with pride.

The makeup was flawless, even my eyes were vibrant against my blood-red lips.

"You're a fucking knockout, Anna."

My pulse sped with the words. I swallowed hard, tearing my gaze from my bare thighs to the swell of my breasts. The push-up bra Kat let me borrow had done wonders. "Okay," I admitted, "I love it."

"Really?" Kat grinned.

I gave a slow nod, unable to tear my gaze away from the mirror. Now I knew how it felt to be one of those people who stared at their own reflection all the time. I smiled. "Really. I don't even know what to say. I feel incredible."

"Fuck, yes!" Kat nodded.

"Give me a minute to get ready." She rushed forward, planting a kiss on my cheek. She rushed from the room, leaving me to tear my gaze from the mirror and busy myself with a drink instead. I grabbed my jacket and slipped it on. The wind from the water could be icy.

"So, if you and Finley aren't...together, does that mean you're interested in anyone else?" Kat called out from her room.

I grabbed the bottle of champagne and poured. Interested in someone else? "You mean here?" I asked in surprise.

"Of course here, what do you think this place is for?" she replied. A flurry of fabric followed, then the slick sound of a zipper...a very *long* zipper.

Kat strode into the doorway looking drop-dead gorgeous, all shimmering silver and fiery red hair flaring around her face. She looked like royalty...if royalty was supermodel material.

"This place is more than classes and training, Anna." She strode forward. "How else do you make alliances other than in bed?"

Heat moved through me. Finley's face followed. I'd known it'd come down to that. I'd known it'd take more than a sworn blood oath. But was I ready for that? For...giving myself to someone dangerous? I met her gaze and saw the same hunger in Kat's eyes that welled in Finley's. "I don't know," I answered truthfully. "I guess I'm going to have to find out, aren't I?"

At twenty years old, it was time. I took a gulp of champagne as my body came alive, buzzing and warming with anticipation.

She eyed me up and down. "Now just make sure you take off the dress before the rough stuff, okay?"

"It's expensive, isn't it?"

"Very." She came close, her gaze narrowing. "How much are you worth anyway, Annalise Eden?"

My face grew hot.

Very hot.

"I...ummm..." I stuttered.

She burst out laughing. "I'm just joking," she chided. "Finish your drink, Anna, and let's get out of here."

Her phone beeped as we turned toward the door. I finished my champagne as she scowled at her screen.

"Everything okay?"

"Others are talking. Something about Stidda royalty?"

Stidda...I'd heard the name thrown around by my father. But it had always carried a sense of fear. Someone he didn't like... someone not to be trusted. Someone his ally, the Salvatores, hated with a vengeance. "He must be who came by helicopter today."

"Oh?" That drew her attention even as we got on the elevator. "Spill."

"I was hurrying and saw it land right before our class."

"That's who the helicopter was for? Interesting," she declared.

My mind slipped to my old life. A life behind a monitor. I wasn't made for parties. I was made for numbers and data. I was made for the glow of my screen and late nights tucked away in my bed, finding tumblers and mixers to split the clean money from the dirty amongst the many streams of data my dad had me check out.

I'd spent weeks researching, pages and pages of data, desperate to uncover what he needed me to find, all the while trying to find a way into his world. I'd been close...so damn close. But the moment I'd made any kind of headway, he'd dropped the bombshell of Cosa Nostra Institute, throwing me off my game, and I was still trying to claw my way back with the data.

"Helllooo..." Kat posed her face into my view. "Where were you just then?"

Careful.

"Nowhere," I lied, and forced a smile. "Thinking about the damn party you're dragging me to."

"You're going to *love it,*" she insisted, hooking her arm in mine.

And I had to think to myself for the hundredth time...*why?* Why her, why me? We strode toward one of the buildings, with music and laughter spilling from out from above. Glass doors were open, the balconies were filled with dancing and drinking. "Whose place is this, anyway?"

"Who cares," Kat laughed, and pulled me forward until we were running, and we all but careened into the foyer. Three guys waited at the elevators. They never even looked at me. All eyes were on Kat and she was more than fine with the attention, laughing and joking. But not once did she release my hand, not once did she push me away or make fun of me.

The elevator pinged as the doors opened. One of the guys motioned us forward, eyeing me up and down. "Ladies."

"Oh, look out, we have a gentleman in our midst," she winked, and strode inside, yanking me after her. I checked my jacket in the harsh glare of the elevator and smiled, lowering my gaze as the guys strode in and one pushed the button.

They were all tall, and gorgeous. One was wearing tight jeans and a black open-collared shirt. The one next to him had a black leather vest over a black-shirt and jeans. But the third guy had a tight t-shirt and a lot of tattoos. I couldn't stop staring. Wide, muscled shoulders bulged as he lifted his hand and rubbed the back of his neck.

I was starting to get the feeling this wasn't like any party I'd ever been to before.

Kat leaned close and murmured just loud enough for the guys to hear, "Close your mouth, Anna. You're drooling."

I jerked a glare toward her and swallowed hard as we glided to a stop. Music spilled through and laughter followed as the doors opened. We followed the guys, stepping out into the most lavish party I'd ever seen.

Kat commanded the room as she sashayed her way inside, heading straight for the kitchen, her hand firmly clasped around mine.

"*Hey!*" she replied as someone called her name. "Jacob." She winked at a guy chatting to a brunette at the end of the hallway, slowed long enough to lean in and kiss another strange guy on the cheek, then kept walking, dragging me with her.

"Isaac," she cried as she strode into the sleek stainless steel kitchen. The place was stunning, not quite as expensive looking as ours, but sleek and stylish.

"Kat, you showed." The guy turned, his tanned skin gorgeous under his open shirt. She released my hand as he handed her a glass with what I was betting was vodka. "And who's this?" He eyed me up and down.

Fear plunged deep and my breath caught.

"Family," she replied with a wink. "Who is damn thirsty for champagne."

Isaac turned and grabbed a glass as Kat gave me a careful wink. I exhaled, trying to dampen the panic inside me.

"Thanks." I grabbed the glass as he handed it over, and smiled.

His gaze lingered, scanning my face. "You don't look like family."

"No, we don't," Kat muttered, and scanned the crowd, not bothering to elaborate on the obvious lie.

I just sipped the drink. Awkward. The background chatter grew an octave as more people spilled into the apartment.

"How many share your apartment?" I asked, trying for polite conversation.

"Three on this floor, four on the others," he answered. "You?"

I just shrugged and glanced toward Kat. I hadn't seen anyone else in our building. There were no lights on the other floors, no *nothing*. "I think it's just the two of us."

"On your floor?"

"No," I sipped my drink. "In the entire building."

He didn't speak, just scowled and looked toward Kat, who'd been scanning the room, but now stopped on one face in particular.

"Well, help yourself to anything you want," Isaac offered, and strode away.

"Oh, we will," Kat murmured.

The slow, seductive beat of the music invaded. I looked around, finding some of the others somewhat familiar.

"You good for a minute?" Kat asked as she drained her glass and placed it on the counter.

"Sure," I answered, and gripped my glass a little tighter.

"I'll be right back."

She left me, striding across the floor. I thought I caught a glimpse of the bitch who'd shoved me into the door earlier, but then she was gone...and so was Kat, sliding amongst the sea of criminals like a damn daydream.

And all of a sudden, under the glare of the kitchen lights, I felt far too exposed.

I glanced along the counter, then grabbed the bottle of champagne and filled my glass until it lapped the edge. The buzz was starting to ease, and in its place was fear. That nagging voice came with it. *What the fuck are you doing, Anna? This isn't you...you don't belong here.*

I swallowed hard and took a sip before making my way out of the kitchen, edging into darkened shadows. Pale skin drew my gaze to a couple sitting in the corner. He pushed her dress aside, exposing her breast. One glance my way, and he went back to her, lowering his head to lick her nipple.

Heat moved through me in a rush. *Jesus.*

I glanced at a group of guys sitting around a table. Cash was piled high in the middle and each held a hand of cards. But this was no friendly wager. These guys protected their hands like a kilo of cocaine and they were playing for keeps. Silver glinted in the dimness as the nearest guy leaned forward to toss a card onto the table.

He was carrying, the gun tucked into the back waistband of his low riser jeans. I swallowed hard and looked away.

"Kneel for me." The command came from behind me.

I spun, champagne sloshing against the sides of my glass as I stared into a tattooed face of a guy I hadn't seen before. "I'm sorry?" I spluttered.

He met my gaze with a savage scowl, his gaze lowering to my neckline as he rubbed his chin. "In a dress like that, you want to be owned, pretty girl."

"No, she doesn't." Thunder dripped with the promise of pain behind me. I spun again, finding a malevolent stare from Finley Salvatore as he gave the male a hard look up and down. "Not by you, at least."

"Salvatore." The guy scowled, then looked back at me.

Finley was dressed to perfection, his black, open-collared shirt bared his muscled chest and tailored black trousers hugged every inch of his powerful frame. I couldn't stop staring.

One jerk of his head and the guy was gone. Then it was my turn to feel the weight of that stare, as if I hadn't felt it all damn day. "Fin, that guy—"

"Anna," he growled, his brow furrowed. "Stop."

But my name was different on his lips tonight, not groaned in frustration or sighed with disbelief. There was an edge about him. One I didn't understand and one I didn't like.

"You shouldn't be here." His gaze moved from my face and down my body. "Especially dressed like that."

Heat burned in my cheeks. God, I was stupid, so pathetically stupid. *I dressed for you,* the words were on my lips.

"I wanted to come," I forced, jutting my chin high. *For you...*

"Jesus Christ," came a bark from my right in a thick Irish accent.

Finley whipped that dangerous stare toward a gorgeous blond guy, one who gave zero fucks about Finley's glare. He narrowed in on me, scanning me from head to toe. "You are fucking stunning. What's your name, beautiful?"

"Anna—" I started, as Finely let out a savage sound. The hairs on my arms stood on end as my pulse leaped.

"Fuck off, Kilpatrick," Finley snarled.

But the cocky asshole didn't pay him any mind. Instead, he came closer...so close, I took a step backwards, leaving Finley behind.

"You are just delicious, aren't you?" Kilpatrick murmured. "You want to make some friends, delicious?"

I fought the need to find Finley's gaze. "I...*ah*..." I stuttered.

"Fuck me, you're sweet." He brushed his finger along my jaw, drawing my gaze to his. "I didn't think there were any of your kind left."

"I'm warning you, Bruno." Finley was savage at his back. "Leave walking, or in a fucking bodybag. The choice is yours."

Only then did my cocky blond suitor turn his head and meet Finley's stare. "You look positively enraged, Salvatore," he murmured with a grin. "Looks like someone needs to get laid."

The fist came from out of nowhere, landing on Kilpatrick's pointed chin with a *thud!* He stumbled, knocked off balance by the sheer, brutal force. My arm was grabbed in an instant and I was hauled toward the door.

"I'm going for a walk." I stepped away from him and turned. He looked too much like his father in that moment, seething with rage.

"No, you're not. You're leaving," Finley commanded. *"Now!"*

"The fuck I am." I bucked against his grasp, yanking my arm from his cruel hold, champagne spilling from my glass. "I have every goddamn right to be here. Finley...*stop!*"

He whirled on me in a blur, driving me back with the sheer savagery in his eyes. "This is not a place for someone like you!"

The room faded in that moment, and all I saw was his anger, all I felt was his rage. "What do you mean *someone like me?*"

He moved closer, his face inches from mine, his voice lowering as he raked his gaze over me. "You know damn well. A damn virgin."

I flinched at the word.

Voices hushed.

Just like they *always* hushed around him.

Heads turned toward me.

*No...nononono...*I was going to throw up.

"Now *that* makes this interesting," Kilpatrick murmured.

My face burned and that burn traveled down my body. There was a look of horror on Finley's face before he cut the room a bestial glare and strode away.

Champagne splashed on my hand as that fire inside me burned. I felt the weight of the stares of everyone in that room. A shudder coursed through me as Kat strode toward me. She glared toward the doorway as Finley left, then took one long look at me. "What happened?"

My throat thickened, strangling my words.

I looked away as tears threatened.

"Anna?" Kat's voice softened.

I shook my head. I couldn't tell her, my face was burning up with embarrassment.

"No." The word burst out as I wrenched my gaze toward the doorway where Finley Salvatore had disappeared seconds earlier. "No fucking way."

"Anna..." Kat warned.

But I was striding toward the doorway with the half empty glass of champagne in my hand, unable to quiet the roaring in my head a second longer.

Pathetic.

Unprotected.

Alone...

11

Anna

"*Hey!*" I barked as I charged through the doorway into the hall. Finley was striding toward the elevator, head down, shoulders hunched.

But he didn't stop at my yell, didn't even slow. He didn't acknowledge he'd heard me at all. Why would he? I was nothing, right, no *thing* and no *body*. Just a kid...just in his *fucking way*. Like I was in *everyone's* way.

"*You fucking asshole!*" I screamed and hurtled the glass at his head. "*How dare you speak to me like that!*"

It missed, shattering on the wall beside his head. Shards of glass flew through the air, hitting his face. But he did stop at that, freezing in the middle of the hallway. The two shadows at his sides were already turning and lifting their hands toward their guns. One careful wave from him and they were under control... like dogs on a tight leash.

Then he was moving, lunging toward me like a beast in full flight...terrifying...*and tormented*. He grabbed me around the throat with one hand. The sheer force of his body slammed me against the wall as we spun.

Agony tore through my head as I hit with a *boom*. Stunned, I stayed still, sparks colliding in my eyes.

"Anna," he growled, his mouth so fucking close. "You make me so fucking mad."

I couldn't hear the party anymore, couldn't hear the music or the laughter.

I couldn't hear anything *but him*.

Him, with his perfect lips and his dark eyes.

"Go on," I growled, my gaze boring into his.

His hand was on my throat, fingers curled like a fucking cage. My heart was hammering, the sound booming in my ears. Still, my fingers curled into fists at my sides.

"You. Belong. To. *Me*," he growled, leaning into me. "Don't you fucking *get* that by now?"

I couldn't speak, just stared into that bottomless soul of his. Hate and rage lurked in his eyes.

The cold rings on his fingers warmed against my skin as he searched my gaze. I couldn't think, couldn't fight, could only whisper, "What did you say?"

"You belong to me," he moaned, his tone daring me to say otherwise.

"No," I lied. "I don't. I'd thought maybe we could be friends, but now I see I was wrong."

"*Just friends?*" he sneered cruelly. "Because your dad works for me?"

I flinched at the words. My gaze shifted to the hallway, to his two shadows and the open door of the party. Kat moved onto the doorway, watching us.

"He doesn't work *for* you," I said quietly.

Careful.

"Yes...he *does.*" His gaze bored into mine. "And so do you. If you think I haven't thought about you every fucking day, then you're wrong. Two years, Anna. Two fucking years you've been there."

I've been there. Sure, while he had a steady stream of girlfriends. "Wow, how awful for you. I'm sure you buried your loneliness soon enough between the next woman's thighs."

"You mean the trophies?" The words were cutting and cruel. There wasn't a hint of warmth there, not one sparkle in his gaze...*not like there was with me.* "*You think I like them? I fucking hate it.* Nothing more than a Salvatore, nothing more than my fucking father's son."

Hate rolled through him with the venom and the pain. This was a side of him I'd never seen before, one he'd kept hidden, even from me.

"I fucking *own* you, Anna. So you better get real comfortable with that prospect real quick, because if you think you're going anywhere, you're not."

Going somewhere...does he know? I stared into his eyes, searching for the answer.

"Look out, boys. What the fuck do we have here? Pretty boy has a brand-new toy." The low murmur dripped with unspoken promises of violence.

Finley stiffened, and the twitch at the corner of his lip wasn't meant for me...*not this time.* He moved back slightly, unfurling his fingers from around my throat. But there was no ache he left behind, no pain, just barely restrained violence.

"But she still has her clothes on, Fin," the growl came once more. "And I don't see any wads of cash near her snatch."

Finley pushed off the wall, leaving me to turn.

Movement came toward us, slow, careful. I met the piercing eyes of the stranger, then glanced at the towering wall of muscle behind him. They were two of the biggest guys I'd ever seen, both wearing long coats, even on the goddamn island.

"Nope." The asshole eye-fucked me from head to toe and licked his lips. "No money and all her clothes still on. Don't tell me you're losing your touch."

"Fuck you, Lazarus."

Finley stepped in front of me, blocking my view. But still, I caught enough of the cruelty shining brightly in the asshole's gaze.

"Step aside, Finley," the bastard who obviously was the Stidda Prince commanded. "Let me see who's got this Ice Prince all worked up."

But Finley never budged, he just held his ground and I finally understood what he was doing. He wasn't standing in my view...*he was standing in his.*

"Come out from there, little one. Don't be shy, I won't hurt you." Lazarus took a step closer, his tone making a lie of his words. "Not unless you want me to. It's always the shy ones who want it fucking hard, isn't it, Fin? Always the pretty little unmarked ones who scream the loudest. Move aside, Fin...let me break her in for you."

Finley dropped his hand to his waist. His shadows moved instantly, drawing their weapons, and Lazarus's men did the same. In the space of a heartbeat, the hallway was filled with guns and the electricity of a tempest.

"Whoa..." Lazarus lifted his hand.

From around the wall of muscle in front of me, I caught the Stidda Prince's smile. Piercing blue eyes glittered as he held Finley's gaze. "This one's got you all riled up, hasn't she? Or is it just you, buddy? Just you with your moody fucking stare. What the hell are you doing here, anyway, Salvatore? Didn't think this was your style."

"Walk, Rossi," Finley warned with a snarl. "And keep on fucking walking."

My heart was hammering, driving against my ribs as Kat took a step out from the doorway, drawing Lazarus' gaze. He stilled, a scowl moving in for a second before it was swallowed by that cocky smirk. "And who might you be, sweetheart?"

"Too expensive for you," Kat answered flatly.

But the diversion was all I'd needed. I jerked my gaze to the side, finding my one hope of salvation...the stairwell door. I pushed away from the wall, took a couple of steps on trembling legs, and ran.

The bright hallway was a blur. I reached out, clawed the handle, and yanked. Dimness swallowed me the moment I stepped onto the landing, and the cold, fetid scent of concrete hit me like a blow.

"*Anna!*" Finley's roar was cut off by the *boom* of the door slamming behind me.

Then I was running, stumbling down flight after flight, with only the faint glow of the exit lights to guide my way.

Tears blurred my sight, sliding down my cheeks. Anger followed, making me jerk my hand up and slap the tears away as they slid down. I ran and kept on running, lunging down stair after stair until my ankles screamed with the pain of the impact.

"Anna, STOP!" Finley's voice kept coming and coming and coming.

"Stay the fuck away from me, Finley!" I screamed, the words resounding in the stairwell.

Green lights beckoned, making me stumble, and I shoved through a door. I blinked into the glare. The steady thump of music sounded high above me. My harsh breaths were frantic. I scanned the empty hallway and stumbled toward the elevator.

Hard grunts sounded from an open door. "Spread your legs, baby," a guy urged from inside a room. "Show me that perfect pussy."

My hand fluttered to my neck and the fingers grazed my flesh as I turned, frantically stabbing the button for the elevator. Jesus fucking Christ. This was not what I'd thought this place was going to be.

A woman's moan followed, carnal, almost bestial as the elevator shuddered and the doors opened wide. I yanked at the neckline of my dress and stumbled inside, punching the button for the door to close. I had to get out of there, away from Finley and this place.

No air...*no air.*

I couldn't breathe.

Couldn't get out of there fast enough.

Tears still slid down my cheeks as I squeezed my eyes shut, and the doors closed.

Just a goddamn virgin.

Humiliation burned my cheeks

Thunderous steps echoed from the hallway as the elevator sank. Cold night air drifted to me when it came to a stop and the doors opened. I opened my eyes and shoved forward, making for the glass doors.

My phone was in my hand before I knew it. My trembling fingers swiped, punching in the secure code to access my messages as I ran without thinking. I just wanted to get out of there as fast as I could.

"Anna," Dad's voice was filled with concern. "What's wrong?"

"I want out of here," I cried. "Dad, please."

The sound of bedsheets rustled. "What happened?"

My tears were warm against my cool cheeks. How the hell could I tell him? Tell him I was a failure...tell him I felt too fucking much here. "I'm sorry." I swallowed hard and swiped my tears again. "I can't find the cont—" I froze, the word still on my lips. "Dad, I—"

"Did...did anyone hurt you?"

I own you, Anna. The words mingled with the feel of his lips on mine. My pulse thundered and heat bloomed. "No."

"Hold tight, sweetheart." The hiss of his zipper sounded, the slur of sleep forgotten in his tone. "I'm on my way."

I pushed on and kept walking, feeling like a goddamn failure. Dad was coming, and Finley Salvatore would have his way—me as far away from this place as possible.

I fucking own you, Anna.

Finley's words filled my head.

I kept on walking, still swiping tears from my cheeks, wishing they'd dry up. "Fuck you."

"Anna!"

I swung my gaze over my shoulder. Desperation rose inside me, savage and hungry. I turned back and focused on where I was. It was another hallway...darkness sinking into nothing.

I wanted out of there and far away from *him*.

I swallowed hard and tried to think, tried to remember where the hell I was. The more I tried to find a way out of there, the worse my panic became.

"Stop running."

I flinched and clenched my jaw at the sound of his voice.

"Anna...*stop fucking running!*"

I ran from one door to the next, testing the handles. The *thud...thud...thud...* of his footsteps was deafening in the space. The sound of his boots mirrored the booming of my heart. Too close...too close...

Too fucking close.

12

Anna

"I said, *stop!*" he roared right behind me.

I lunged toward a dark doorway, smashed down the handle, and staggered inside. He was right after me, lunging like a predator to grab my arm and yank me around in the dark. "*Stop fucking running.*"

Motion-sensor-activated overhead lights blinked on, lighting up the space and the glint of steel all around me.

Guns...*everywhere.*

But he was unstoppable, driving me backwards with that grip on my arm. "I told you, don't run from me!"

He grabbed my wrists and wrenched me against him.

"Get the fuck *off me!*" I yanked one arm from his grasp and with instinct, I swung. The slap landed hard on his cheek, snapping his head to the side with a *crack!*

Sandy blond hair lashed his face. Harsh breaths claimed the air between us as he slowly turned that bottomless stare to mine. I swallowed hard as the skin of his cheek slowly turned red, the imprint of my hand clearly visible.

One shove and he pushed me backwards again with such force that I stumbled, then fell. My phone slipped from my hand, clattering to the floor with a *thud*. As I went down, I clawed for a hold, my nails raking the rolled-up sleeves of his black shirt, clinging onto him and taking him with me. He punched out, taking the brunt of the impact and softening the blow a second before my head hit.

But he refused to budge, his weight holding me against the floor.

"You..." he started.

"Yeah, I kn-know," I spat the words through clenched teeth. "Fucking pathetic, *right? Just a goddamn virgin.*"

I couldn't stop shaking, couldn't stop stuttering, couldn't believe this was happening. My stomach hardened into a stone. But he didn't move, all hard muscles and hot skin. He was shards of glass and bloody knuckles. He was hate and fucking angst all wrapped up in one perfect package like a fallen angel in disguise.

"You think I'm embarrassed about that?" He leaned closer. "Christ, thinking about that drives me wild. I waited for you to come to my house, watching as you slipped into my fucking life with your goddamn numbers and innocent smile. I fucking fisted my cock thinking about you. You make me so fucking insane."

My chest drove against his with a consuming breath. His big hands were on me, one pinning my wrist to the floor above my head as he stared at me with a gaze that both wanted to unburden his soul and devour me. "You...thought about me?"

The truth sparkled in his eyes. "Every fucking day."

Guns and weapons lay all around us. Honed knives, the blades built to plunge deep.

And yet he never noticed, unable to tear his gaze from mine.

"You want to *own me,* right?" Those dark eyes glittered at the words. I waited for him to say the words were an accident, that they weren't what he'd meant. But as I lay there with humiliation and hunger searing in my veins, I knew those words weren't coming. Because he'd meant what he said.

"I shouldn't have said that in front of the others," he said carefully.

I jerked my gaze back to his, that fire like a goddamn inferno inside me. *"No, you shouldn't have.* It was private."

"Private," he repeated, and lowered his head as he licked his lips. "So fucking private."

Then in one blinding blur, his lips crashed against mine.

He was consuming and commanding.

And all over me.

My wrist was pushed higher, stretching me out under him. I was helpless to fight...helpless to do anything but comply.

He'd kissed me without warning.

Without permission.

Without boundaries, driving his mouth so hard against mine that I burned.

His hard moan plunged down my throat. Hips ground against mine until that fire reached between my thighs. That burning rage inside me was an inferno, blistering and raging...leaving nothing behind but ash and scars. He kissed me until I forgot about leaving, forgot the darkness of this place. He kissed me until I forgot...*everything.*

His thighs thrust between mine. His hand stroked my cheek, then traveled down to cup my breast. I closed my eyes with a shudder. I wore his touch like a brand, like it was meant *for me.*

"If you'd just let me." His hand went to my thigh, pushing my dress higher. I was on fire as my eyes jerked open with the brush of his fingers between us, sliding between my thighs. "I could make it so no one looked at you again...not unless they wanted to lose their goddamn eyes."

He was a fucking force, inside me and out. My hips rocked against his touch. *Yes.* The word was in my mouth, sliding along my tongue, aching for my lips.

His hand left a trail of molten lava in its wake as it trailed across the elastic of my panties. I met his gaze, unable to watch his hand.

"Fuck me, you're perfect," he murmured, sliding his finger under the barrier.

My mind was racing, part screaming *WAIT!* while the rest moaned...*yes...please god, yes.*

My hand trembled as I lashed out and grasped his wrist, stopping him cold. "Finley."

"Do you trust me, Anna?" Stars glittered in his eyes.

There was the galaxy once more, the one trapped inside the darkness, the one that shone for me.

"I'm not going to do anything you don't want me to," he reassured.

My grip eased, fingers sliding from their hold, leaving him to travel lower...and lower. The contact of his fingers against the top of my crease had me trembling.

He knew exactly where to go, sliding in just enough to circle that part of me that made me whimper and bite my lip. He watched me, enjoying every tremble, his lips parting when I moaned.

"Just like this." His finger danced over my clit, skimming and teasing, making my hips rise with every stroke. "If you'd just let me..."

He moved lower, stealing his gaze from mine as he moved down my body. I watched him as his focus became my black lace panties instead. "Just a fucking taste," he murmured, dropping his hand to the back of my knee.

I was helpless to fight him, helpless to do anything but do whatever he wanted. My knees rose, thighs pushed wide as he lowered his head. His dark hair glistened under the armory lights. I shuddered, heat moving like an inferno through me as he tugged the edge of my panties aside...and licked me.

His tongue pushed deeper. A guttural growl vibrated against my tender flesh. My hand went to the back of his head, my fingers speared through those dark strands. God, his mouth...his mouth had me trembling.

I closed my eyes, my hand stroking his head as he dipped lower, taking me higher than I'd ever been before. I was losing myself, falling under his spell, sliding deep.

"Finley..." his name was a moan on my lips.

"Let go, Anna," he urged. "Let me give you this."

The heat was building, lashing against the edges as he licked and sucked, dragging my swollen nub into his mouth. *Fuck me.*

My hips bucked as that fire moved through me, making me twitch and writhe against his mouth. His fingers slid along me, the tips of two slid inside. "Fuck me, you're perfect."

"Fin," came a low growl from outside the door.

But there was no stopping this. I opened wider as his fingers slid deeper. "Turn your fucking head, Max," he commanded with chilling savagery. "Or I'll put a bullet in it."

The heat was rising once more, making me groan and quiver around his fingers.

"I want to be here," he growled, slipping them in deeper. "Right here."

"Fin, there's a problem," his bodyguard insisted from outside.

But I was already jerking my hips into the air as I arched my spine, already seeing stars as they ignited. A tremor rippled through me, coursing up the center of me as he slipped his fingers along my crease and slowly pulled away.

"I told you before, Anna. You belong to me," he whispered and adjusted my panties. Harsh breaths consumed me as he rose from the floor in one swift move. "Now it's time to prove it."

In the space of a breath, he was gone, turning toward the door and leaving me behind. I waited for a second, listening to his footsteps before I rose.

Shell-shocked and numb, I rose to stand on trembling legs. My body didn't move right, warm and fluid as I made my way out of the armory and along the hall.

"Anna!" Kat called my name as I came out of the building, following the path. "What the hell happened?"

I couldn't speak, couldn't find the words. My body and mind were at war. Hating him and wanting him, at the same time. But in the crisp night air, clarity found me.

Dad...Dad was coming for me. The words were a cold shock to my system. Had that really just happened?

"It's okay, Kat. I'm leaving."

"Leaving?" She stopped walking beside me and fell behind. "What the fuck do you mean, leaving?"

I was too tired to explain and too numb to think anymore. Instead, I just kept on walking, desperate to find my way back to my room and get to the dock.

"You can't leave."

"Can and will," I answered. "I'm not meant for this place."

"The *fuck* you're not." She caught up and matched me with long, angry strides. "If you're not, then who the hell is?"

I shook my head. "You don't know me, Kat."

"No, I don't. But I was starting to, at least." She threw her arms wide. "What are you so fucking afraid of?"

"Afraid? Don't you even know?"

We're afraid of all of you...of the Salvatores and the Rossis and the goddamn war that's just waiting to happen.

Blood money.

That's what we dealt in.

Money to be layered and hidden until the government can't tell which is legit...and which is dirty.

Tell her...tell her who you really are.

"I can't do this..." I forced through clenched teeth. "I can't keep lying and hiding. I can't keep being afraid."

"Then don't." She took a step closer, her hand so fucking gentle on my arm. I shivered from the contact as she assured me in a murmur, "You can trust me, Anna."

Trust.

I didn't have friends, not ones I trusted with the truth.

Leave.

Stay.

Stop.

Run.

The tug-of-war ripped me apart. I stopped, my shoulders hunching as the sobs came.

"Oh, honey." Kat was there. Her arms felt so good...so damn good as they wrapped around me, holding me as I cried.

I held onto her until the shudders slowed and the tears finished trailing down my cheeks. Out of the tears and heartache...came his face, his tortured, beautiful face. Those dark brown eyes stayed with me as I lifted my gaze to hers. I knew what I'd seen when he'd kissed me. I knew there was an entire uncharted galaxy just waiting for someone brave enough.

"Kat," I started.

"Yes, honey?" she responded, and stepped back.

I swallowed hard, my heart hammering, and whispered, "I need your help."

13

Finley

The speedboat's engine spluttered and surged, slamming the hull against the dock with the choppy swell of the waves. Still, with all the battering and the obviously incompetent helmsman, the damn thing didn't die. I was impressed.

Dillon Shaw was frantic, his hands flailing in the air inches in front of the Commander's face, as he demanded his daughter off the island...and far away from me.

I didn't blame him.

I wouldn't want her here either.

Not with the way I wanted her.

Yet...here she was.

"I want her in my goddamn boat *now!*" Dillon screamed. "Right this fucking minute."

"The rules, Mr. Eden." The Commander's tone was unshakeable, hiding the Ghost's real name. The guy was dressed in his usual immaculate steel gray suit. He adjusted the jacket.

"Cannot be broken. Not for you, not for anyone. It was made perfectly clear in our conversation."

"Fuck your rules!" Anna's father spat.

Still, the man looked ridiculous. Dressed in sodden brown trousers and bare feet, he'd left in a hurry, that's for sure. It was both obvious and interesting as hell.

Two years, I'd known him. Two years, I'd watched as he turned frantic in front of my father, explaining how *his* millions of dollars were laundered in cryptocurrency, hidden in layers upon layers of accounts. An idea forged by his daughter. An idea my father had benefited from. Two years, I'd watched him haunt my family home, but I'd never seen the man this panicked.

His daughter had arrived on the island's cruiser along with all the other sons and daughters of those who made up the Commission. The thought of her here made me feel fucking enraged. I didn't want her here, or anywhere near *them*. Vipers, every single one of them. One whiff of someone like Annalise and they'd tear each other apart to sink their fangs in deep.

But my father had allowed it, sending her at the request of her father. Now, here I was, following her every goddamn move, watching and aching, desperate to corner her in one of these classrooms once more to find out the real reason someone as smart and as sweet as Annalise Shaw was here.

I'd told my father it was a bad idea she was here, said it was even a worse idea to send me to guard her. I didn't want to protect the woman. I didn't want to be that fucking nice.

The Commission spared no expense on the transfer, sending four armed bodyguards to collect the descendants of the Mafia bloodlines. After all...the island was sacred—*it was one of the goddamn rules*. So, if Dillon Shaw's daughter was protected on the island...*why wasn't he back home getting my father his fucking money?*

I shifted my focus to Anna, and my damn pulse sped.

"Your father should know about this," Max growled at my side.

The bodyguard missed nothing.

"Not yet," I responded. "Not until I know more."

Kat VanHalen was at Anna's side. The heiress was a damn rock, rubbing her arm, murmuring words I assumed were of comfort. Still, I couldn't stop watching my little launderer, riveted by the way she wrung her hands and smoothed her dress. The same dress I'd pushed high a couple of hours before. I licked my lips. The same damn dress I wanted to take from her fucking body and show her just what she did to me.

Stop fucking running!

The roar resounded in my head.

If you'd just let me, I could make it so no one looked at you again...not unless they wanted to lose their goddamn eyes.

I'd kissed her and touched her. Christ, what a goddamn stupid fucking move. I dragged my fingers through my hair, hating how the feel of her returned in an instant. I could still feel her around my fingers, still taste her on my tongue. Perfect and sweet, like my sweet, dark secret.

"Anna," Dillon called. His shoulders were hunched in defeat as the idea of his daughter being my private little conquest tore through me like a drug. One I fucking liked.

I turned then, finding hazel eyes. "Follow him."

Pavlov gave a nod, his gaze shifting to the fool who, for a goddamn genius at financial rules and regulations, was surprisingly shit at reading the island's fine print. I turned, took a step, and stopped. "First, I want you to do something."

"Whatever you need," the bodyguard assented.

"I want you in her room...*unseen.*" I gave him the command, watching as his gaze narrowed before he finally nodded.

He left, sinking into the darkness, as I focussed on Dillon Shaw once more. The guy took a panicked lunge toward his daughter and was blocked by the Commander in one swift move. He was outmaneuvered and way out of his fucking league.

He'd leave, either of his own accord or by force.

Either way, Anna wasn't getting off this island, not anytime soon.

Max's phone chirped. One glance from the bodyguard, and he turned my way. "Baldeon's awake."

Still alive? The asshole was stronger than I'd thought. "Good."

I left Dillon Shaw then, hating how I left her, as well. But there were too many damn questions lingering in the air tonight and not anywhere near enough answers. Max followed as I made my way up the rise and across the grounds, keeping to the shadows.

The infirmary was at the back of Building One. Secure offices and electronic vaults. But it was the state-of-the-art medical facility that received the most attention, with a small and sophisticated emergency ward, that for a fucking island, was unusually busy.

But I didn't head straight there. Instead, I made for the building further back. The one pushed against the steep, sheer cliffs of the island and the one hidden in the dark. The one permanently reserved for the Salvatores.

Finley...her moan resounded in my head as I cut through the gardens and stepped up to the scanner.

The green light was piercing in my eye for a split second before the electric doors opened and I strode in.

Let go, Anna. Let me give you this.

I clenched my jaw as the memory deepened. Max stabbed the button for the elevator and stepped away, his hands clasped in front, near the guns. But it wasn't the fucking guard I cared about right now.

"Give me a minute," I muttered as the elevator doors opened.

I lowered my head, stepped into the harsh lights, and waited for the doors to close. She was too fucking real for me in that moment. Too raw. Too fucking...*blinding*. The elevator rose, coming to a stop at the penthouse before the doors opened.

Steel clinked softly as a dark beast rose from the corner of the room.

"Leale, down."

He sank once more, his watchful eyes following me as I strode to the bedroom. It was dark in here. My world, nothing more than shadows and sin...*right where I belonged*.

Finley...

Her voice plunged deep as I rubbed my thumb across my fingers. Fuck me, her pussy was perfect, warm and soft. I licked my lips, finding the salt of the sea, chasing a remnant of her. Just a fucking taste, one goddamn feel. My cock hardened, aching with need as I strode to the window.

The island was in darkness. But she was out there, frightened and panicked. Her mind racing at a million miles an hour, just like mine.

I lowered my hand to the button of my pants and lowered the zipper. I couldn't fucking concentrate...too hungry for her. Heat moved through me. I imagined her tight and warm, stretching around my fingers. *Do you trust me, Anna?* I fisted my length, and bit back a growl. *I'm not going to do anything you don't want to.*

I could say the goddamn words all day long. But the truth was, I wanted what I wanted. Two fucking years, I'd thought about her. I squeezed my cock, sliding all the way to the hilt. Two years of fucking texting. Two years of being...*friends.*

I braced my hand against the cold glass and closed my eyes. Slick and eager. My fingers sank into her with ease. She'd wanted me. I knew that now. Wanted me as much as I'd wanted her. Fuck me, she'd been wet. Her eyes closed with need. Those fucking lips parted as I slipped my fingers inside her.

I wanted to be inside her now.

A low, savage sound rumbled in the back of my throat as I fisted tighter, pumping harder, the slick bead snatched away under the roughness of my fist.

"Anna." Her name was nothing more than a grunt.

But the impact was brutal. My cock twitched at the sound of her name. The frenzy drove my breaths deeper and my fist harder. I was too close to the end, too fucking desperate. That thick vein pulsed as warmth spread between my fingers. I opened my eyes to the streetlights in the distance, the ones near her building. The ones I knew intimately.

"You belong to me."

The growl staked a claim. One I planned on enforcing every fucking chance I got. No matter how much she wanted to deny it. My sweet, goddamn secret wanted me too.

I zipped and buttoned my pants and made my way into the bathroom to wash my hands.. I couldn't afford to be distracted, and right now, that's all I was. I strode from the bathroom into the kitchen, snatched the opened bottle of Macallan from the marble counter, and made for the elevator once more.

I rode it all the way down, getting off at the foyer where Max waited.

He fell in step as I left the building and made for the back door of Building One. I pressed my thumb to the sensor and waited for the automatic door to unlock. There were certain perks with being a founding member, and one was access to the majority of the island...including the building where Anna lived.

Soft lights illuminated the way as I strode along the hallway, driving deeper into the building. A light was on in the distance, the glow cutting through the glass walls, coming from the part of the building my code didn't reach, a part exclusive for the Commander alone. Movement cut through the shine. He was there...working.

I turned once more and pushed open the door to the infirmary.

"Did you fucking hear what I said?" Baldeon's irritating voice sounded from one room. "Get me my fucking gun!"

I stepped into the hospital room under the solemn stare of the poor bastard who stood at the end of the bed. The doctor, I was guessing, who'd just spent the last twenty-four hours saving and putting up with this demanding asshole. He jerked his gaze toward me as I stepped around the curtain.

"Doc," I muttered and gave a nod.

His brows furrowed and panic flared for a second as he took in Max behind me.

"It's okay," I reassured him as I swept the curtain aside, to find the sallow fucking bastard barking demands on the bed. "Wow, you're alive. That's shit."

"Fuck you, Salvatore," Baldeon snarled, his gaze dropping to the bottle in my hand.

"I don't think you should—" the doctor started as I lifted the Scotch.

"If a bullet didn't kill me, a drink won't," Baldeon growled, reaching for the bottle in an instant, his tongue already skimming his lips in anticipation. "Just do your damn job."

I stared at the doctor, until his eyes widened and his breaths deepened. He gave a mutter, something I was guessing along the lines of, *"it's your funeral"* before he turned and left.

"Looks like it hurts." I surveyed the thick white bandage wrapped under his arm and over his shoulder.

"Like a fucking bitch," Baldeon bit out, and took a long draw from the bottle.

I strode to the front of the room, to where the tinted glass walls gave him a view of the island.

"Did you find out who sent him?"

In the reflection of the glass, I saw his face. Hopeful. Savage...*and utterly terrified.*

"No."

"Did the bastard at least scream before they ended him?"

I turned then, finding that cruel part of his nature rising in his eyes. That glint we all had, every single one of us. "Yeah, he screamed."

"Good." Baldeon nodded slowly. "Good." And he lifted the bottle once more.

"You have no idea who it was?" I pushed.

Baldeon jerked his gaze high, his pupils dancing as his mind raced. He licked his lips. "It's all I've been thinking about since I...you know, I woke up. But there's nothin'. Nothin' I can think of."

"Has your father...called?"

"Yeah," he took another swallow. "Twice now, the old man's spitting it, screaming for blood. He's going through everyone who has a problem with the Baldeons. But there's no one that'd have a beef like this. No one would want me..."

Dead. He still couldn't say it. They wanted him dead.

I swallowed hard, my gaze shifting to the bottle in his hand. He flinched and his gaze focused on mine as he lifted the bottle to me.

I just shook my head. "Keep it," and turned for the door.

"Finley." He stopped me two steps from leaving. But his voice had that tone now, that softer fucking tone. The one filled with all the shit I didn't need to hear. "About your mom."

One nod was all he got. One simple fucking nod as my throat flared with a savage ache. I left Baldeon, striding along the quiet hallways with my damn shadow at my back.

About your mom...

That ache traveled down through my throat to clench like a fist in my chest.

Screams filled my world. Only they weren't the screams of an assassin.

They were mine.

14

Anna

"Anna," Kat called me. "Come on, honey, let's go."

I tore my gaze from the point where I'd lost sight of Dad's boat and tried to still the chattering of my teeth.

Her fingers brushed my arm. "Look at you, you're freezing."

*Anna...*Dad's desperate plea surfaced in my mind. The look on his face followed, his features twisted, his frantic eyes whipping from that man who'd greeted him at the dock to me. The man who was all hard edges and chiseled features, the man who scared Dad. I could see it in his eyes. I swallowed that awful ache in my chest and let her pull me away.

"Let's get back home and get you something warm to wear. Then we can talk, okay?"

Talk.

The one thing I couldn't do.

Talking meant more than an unburdening—a tremor coursed from my belly—no matter how heavy that weighed on my soul.

No, talking meant something far more tangible to me in that moment. A bullet to the brain.

Still, I let her pull me with her, let her slip her arm in mine. Let her guide me as we made our way back along the path to our building. Warmth wrapped around me the moment we strode through the automatic doors to the foyer and stopped at the elevator.

Kat cast me a careful look and urged me inside as the doors opened. She thought this was all because I wanted off the island. She thought it was because of what had happened at the party. Her brows were furrowed and she was silent...careful, which was so not her. But it wasn't just about this place, or the party.

It was what had happened after.

I told you before, Anna. You belong to me.

The elevator doors closed and we rose in silence. My breaths deepened and my pulse sped. If I licked my lips, I'd find them aching and swollen. But I didn't need to do that. Every step made my thighs rub, igniting the memory of his fingers...and his goddamn tongue. My body hummed just thinking about it.

"Come on," Kat urged as the doors opened.

I headed for my room, head down, the pressure inside building, and stopped at the doorway.

"What is it?"

She watched me, filled with concern. A tear slipped from the corner of my eye. "I...I need..."

She was beside me in an instant, sliding her hand along my arm. Her voice turned small and careful. "You can trust me, Anna, with whatever you're going through."

I met her gaze. Could I? Because right now, the walls were closing in and I wanted to run. I glanced around at the perfect apartment, knowing that in a place like this, someone listening was a given. My mind turned to that cold, stoic male at the jetty, the one who'd manhandled my father like he was nothing more than a two-year-old. Someone like him would listen to anything I said...*and act on it.*

My teeth gnashed as Kat moved, taking a soundless step, her eyes wide as she whispered. "Not here?"

I swallowed hard as my pulse thundered. I shook my head.

There was a flare of concern. "Grab your jacket. I know of a place."

A nod of her head urged me forward. I hurried in, tossed my phone onto the bed, and headed for the closet. I wanted out of that dress and away from those memories. But all that could wait. The words were lodged in my throat, stuck like a bone. One I could nether swallow nor dislodge. I grabbed the warmest jacket I'd brought as Kat stepped into the room.

"Ready?"

My mind was racing, filled with my father's panicked stare and Finley's words. She was dwarfed by the thick black parka with a fur-lined hood, but she tugged it over her head as I shrugged into mine. My jacket wasn't as thick as hers, but it was warm and a little of home and right now, I was sick with need. I followed her back down and out of the building, hurrying after her when she led me from the path and headed toward the crash of the waves once more.

"I saw this place from my bedroom window this morning," she explained, grabbing my arm and tugging me forward. "Heels," she gasped, out of breath. "Don't want to sprain your ankle."

I lifted my foot, sliding off one heel, then the other. My feet throbbed with relief, sinking into the cold grass before I stepped forward, down the incline until we hit the soft, gritty sand. My sigh was snatched by the wind, but the sensation was pure bliss, easing that tightness in my chest.

My hair lashed my cheek, forcing me to turn my face to the wind. For a second, I didn't understand why here, until Kat pulled me down to the sand beside her.

"They can't hear here. So you're safe."

They couldn't, not with the gusts of wind and the crash of the waves in the background. Out here I was free to say anything I wanted. The only problem was...how much could I say?

"Okay, so let me tell you what I've figured out so far on my own. Which, let me tell you right at the start, I'm *not* one of those fucking busybodies out to gossip. So, whatever you say to me stays right here...with me."

Jesus, my heart thundered.

"You and Finley. There's something going on there, isn't there?" She studied my every flinch. When I swallowed hard and looked away, she growled. *"I knew it!* A goddamn Salvatore? Holy shit girl, you're in for a world of hurt."

As if I didn't know that already.

"Go on," I murmured quietly, finding her piercing gaze once more. Maybe she was here as a contact, maybe she wasn't. Either way, I needed to know what she'd figured out on her own.

"He wasn't supposed to be here, was he?" I shook my head, watching as her eyes widened, like a hound hooked on the scent. "And *neither were you.*"

"No. *He* wasn't, but I wanted to come."

"Wanted to come, huh? Honey." She placed her hand on my arm. "You stick out like a middle-aged hooker at a high-end whore's club."

"Jesus, Kat."

She just smiled and gave me a wink, but slowly that grin faded for a more solemn look. "Anna, are you in some kind of trouble?"

A chill crept along my spine. "Trouble?"

"Yeah, you're not...you know, running from him, by any chance?"

I coughed and spluttered, sucking in the salt air. "Finley?"

His father's savage gaze rose in my mind.

"Yeah, Finley," she repeated carefully.

"No," I answered, feeling the heat rising in my cheeks. If it wasn't for the cold ocean air, it would've been a dead giveaway. "I'm not running from Finley."

His father, on the other hand...

"Okay," Kat leaned back with a sigh. "Okay, that's good. 'Cause if you were...you know my family could help you. We're connected. Maybe not *that* connected. But still, I'd help any way I could."

Not *that* connected. The words slammed into me. Still, she kept talking.

"I dated a son of one of the Commission once. It was fucking *awful*...a daddy's boy, through and through. The guy couldn't even take a piss without checking he wasn't violating 'one of the rules', pfft. Still, they aren't the kind of guys girls like you tangle with...not without getting hurt."

Her phone let out a *beep*. She tore her gaze from mine for a second, reached down and pressed the button, staring at the screen. She froze at the message, her eyes grew dull, fear moving deep.

"What's wrong?"

"Nothing," she answered, still staring at the screen, then she forced a smile and put her phone away. "Everything's fine."

Getting hurt. I swallowed hard as panic rose. Would Finley hurt me? Would he use and discard me? Jesus, I could still feel his hands on my body. *I want to be here.* Heat bloomed between my thighs at the memory of his fingers sliding inside me. *Right here.*

"Oh, honey." Kat pulled me closer as I shuddered. "It's going to be okay. You got yourself tangled up, then you got yourself away. I'm glad you came here to the island. I'm glad we're friends. 'Cause it's all going to be okay. I told you before, I got your back." Her voice went quiet. If she hadn't pulled me against her, I'd never have heard her. "We all have demons, Anna. Every single fucking one of us. The secret is to look him in the eyes, *then kick him right in the balls.*"

When I thought about the demon we were running away from, it wasn't Finley I saw.

It was his father.

His cruel, controlling father, and the millions of his dollars we had hidden away.

She held me like that, pressed against her. There was a tremble in her hand as she clutched me tight. In that moment I didn't know who needed the comfort more—me or her.

The crash of the waves lulled us, until the silence settled that ache inside me to stone. There was a haunted look in Kat's eyes when I pulled away, one I hadn't seen before, until she forced a smile. "Feel better?"

"Yeah," I answered as she slowly climbed to her feet.

I lifted my gaze to the waves, knowing Dad was out there. He'd risked his life coming to get me, and for what? To find out this island not only protects...it imprisons as well. There was no getting away from the Institute, not until this was done. Maybe that's what the contact was banking on? Maybe that was why we were so safe. Unless you were part of the Commission...the *Cosa Nostra*.

Maybe they lived outside *'the code'*, maybe for them there was no damn code at all?

"Come on," Kat said with a jerk of her head. "It's getting late and we've got classes tomorrow."

I followed her back to our building, hating how part of me was a little relieved I was stuck here. The elevator lights were unforgiving, casting shadows under Kat's eyes as we rode in silence to the penthouse. A penthouse Kat's father had spared no expense getting for his daughter, *and in turn, for me.*

Still, I wanted to ask about her demons. The ones who seemed to haunt her as she lowered her head and made for her room.

"Kat."

She lifted her head and met my gaze. "Yeah?"

"Are you okay?"

Her smile was quick and small. "Just tired, Anna. I'll see you in the morning, roomie."

"Okay." I watched her disappear into her room. "'Night."

I yanked off the parka and made my way to the bathroom. A warm shower and a good sleep were what I needed. Tomorrow would be different. Tomorrow, I'd pull myself together. I lifted my gaze to the mirror as I undressed and stared into my eyes. Tomorrow, I'd find the damn contact and get away from here, far away from Finley and the torture of his lips. The hiss of the shower came from the room next door. The only problem was, I was starting to like this place...*a lot.*

I showered, dried, and got ready for bed. But when I slipped between the soft sheets of the king-sized bed, that chill inside didn't leave. Instead, when I closed my eyes, I thought of him... the one person I wanted to never think of again.

Only then did my body warm.

To the memory of his lips on mine and his tongue in places no one had touched me before.

That warmth spread between my thighs as the memory of his fingers filled me, and the way his eyes had raged warmed me even deeper than his touch could. *Jesus...*

I shifted in the bed, tossing and turning, and after an hour of the goddamn torture, my will became weak, leaving me to slide my fingers between my thighs. *I fucking fisted my cock thinking about you.* I squeezed my eyes closed, rubbing and sliding, replacing his touch with mine, hating how even now I wanted him...*demon and all.*

A DAMN TRUCK had hit me during the night, I was sure of it. Then it backed up and had another attempt or two at doing me in. My feet ached and my mind was foggy. I blinked, stretched, and inhaled the perfect bitter tang of freshly brewed coffee. It was the only thing that wrenched me awake in an instant.

I shoved my hand out, fingers curled, searching for my phone. But there was nothing. I scowled, lifted my head, and forced my eyes to focus. Memories slipped in. The beach, talking to Kat, but before that...I lifted my gaze to the discarded parka on the floor, then to the bed where I was sure I...

A white box sat on the nightstand next to me. I pushed upwards as the blur in my eyes cleared. "What the hell?"

I grabbed the thing, finding a note stuck to the top.

You need a new damn password.
Fin.

Cold plunged through to the center of me. My heart thundered as I drew the box close. *"No fucking way,"* I growled as I opened it.

"Anna?" Kat called and the soft sound of bare feet against the marble came before she appeared in the doorway, carrying two steaming mugs. "Everything okay?"

I just stared at the note...and the brand new iPhone.

"Rose gold? Ooo, that's pretty," she said, her voice strained.

I met her gaze, and saw the dark circles haunting her eyes. "What's wrong?"

The smile was instant before it was hidden by a sip of coffee. "Nothing," she answered, and jerked her head toward my hand. "Except for that."

That was the new phone...a phone that had been placed beside my bed, *while I was sleeping*. A chill worked its way down my spine. But it wasn't just about the damn phone. It was more about the fact that someone had been inside the apartment...and in my room.

It had weirdo, stalker vibes all over it.

My hands shook as I yanked off the sticky note and opened the phone. My old phone was nowhere to be seen. The cords were perfectly wrapped, but the tape was gone. The moment I tossed the pretty rose gold phone onto the bed and pressed the button, the screen came alive.

The damn thing was charged...*and all my apps were loaded.* "Motherfucker..."

Kat let out a small bark of laughter. "That mouth," she chuckled, and came closer, sat on the end of the bed, and handed me a cup.

"Thanks." I grabbed the cup and took a sip.

But the moment I tried to log into my password, it prompted me to log in for the first time. So, he hadn't gotten my details, just copied my old apps over?

"Fin, huh?" Kat murmured, taking another sip of her coffee, and nodded toward the discarded note as she rose from the bed with a smirk. "Not entangled, my ass..."

She left me with the coffee and the awful feeling of falling. I swiped my thumb across the screen, finding a new message waiting...

Fin: I'm sorry for last night.

My stomach clenched as I typed: *Because you broke into my damn room?*

The reply was instant.

Fin: No. I'm talking about what I said at the party.

Anger welled in my belly. He was everywhere, in my classes, at the party, here in my room while I slept. My pulse raced at the image of that, him standing beside my bed, watching me in the dark. *I thought of him last night, my hands between my thighs.* My cheeks burned with the memory.

"Of course, you wouldn't be sorry for breaking in, would you?" I growled and typed: *Fuck you, Finley.*

I tossed the phone onto the bed and stared out the window. The sun was shining, the sky perfect and blue. I took another swallow of coffee as my new phone let out a *beep.*

I stared at the pretty pink phone, hating how he knew I'd wanted one.

Hating more how he'd bought it for me.

Until curiosity made me grab it and turn it over.

Fin: Fuck me? I think you might like that, Anna...I think you might like that very much.

"You goddamn cocky asshole," I muttered, my mind returning to the feel of his hands on my body.

The danger was, he was right.

15

Finley

Fuck you, Finley.

Not Fin.

Not asshole.

Just...*Finley.*

I smiled. She was trying to put distance between us, trying to force me away from someone familiar and instead shove me square into the fucking friend zone. The friend zone, where she didn't have to think about how wet I made her and how, for a second last night, she'd wanted me as much as I wanted her.

The goddamn friend zone...like I was just some goddamn schmuck. "Let's see how long that lasts, Anna."

Leale gave a whine and shifted his weight on the sofa, turning to lick my face. I reached and rubbed his ears, making the beautiful beast shake his head. His thick jowls swayed with the motion as those black eyes fixed on me, glinting with intelligence.

The Rottweiler had been my one fucking demand here on the island, a gift from my mom and my one constant. *Leale*...the word meant loyal in Italian and he was, faithful and smart...and mine in a world where everything belonged to my damn father.

The huge dog gave a whine, tearing me from the aches of my life and dragging me back to the present with a sloppy lick of my cheek.

"I love you, too," I murmured rubbing his ears, then pushed upwards. "But I've got things to do, buddy. Can't just lie around with you all day."

Bright rays of the sun poured through the tinted windows. For a second, I just stood there, basking in the glare, and slowly closed my eyes. I wanted to feel the heat of the rays, wanted to feel anything other than the thrumming in my veins and that *hunger* when I thought of her.

But there was no heat from the glare. Not even a flicker of warmth. Nothing...until the image of her under me came roaring back to the surface of my mind. *Then I burned.* Fevered and sick, my hands shook against my thighs. I wanted her. Fuck me, I wanted her. I strode into the bathroom, shoved my boxers low, and fisted my cock.

The woman was making me jerk off like a goddamn teenager. *Jesus fucking Christ.*

I hit the shower faucet, slamming icy needles of the cold spray against the tiles, and stepped inside. The impact was instant and brutal. Still, I pumped as the shock of the water stole the rock hard ache. I lowered my head, letting the cold hit my shoulders, then adjusted the water temperature, shifting my grip and letting it slide all the way to the tip before I squeezed.

No matter how desperately I wanted my mind to wander, she was there, with her sweet fucking smile and innocent eyes. The one spark of pure light in my brutal, blood-stained world. I thrust my hips, turning against the wall until my breaths deepened and the release came all too fast. I lowered my hand and splayed my fingers, letting my come wash away. The end was always too fast when it came to her. Still, it barely took the edge off.

I washed my hair and my body and ended the spray, grabbing a towel to wrap around my hips. I'd been sent here to do more than just jerk off. Anna was on the island for a damn good reason, while her father worked at undoing everything he'd created in the last two years. I needed to not just find out what that reason was, I was here to expose every thought, every...*secret* she ever had. The only problem was...did I want to do all that for my father, or for me?

I dressed, yanking on a slate gray t-shirt, black fitted jeans, and heavy boots, before I slipped on my leather jacket. Leale just watched me from the sofa as I strode out, cocking his head and waiting patiently for attention. "Okay," I murmured, "I see you."

I gave him a rub between the ears, grabbed my phone, and headed for the elevator. She hadn't responded to my last message...I smiled and slipped it into my pocket.

Classes...what a crock of shit. More like a diversion from the real game. *The initiation.* It was a dangerous game, filled with lies and deceit, but what other game did you give a bunch of rich and *bored* motherfuckers to do?

The elevator doors opened and I lifted my gaze to Max and Pavlov. A nod was all that was needed before they fell in step and I strode toward the door.

I wasn't fucking naive. They'd play their petty game any fucking way they could and try for their pound of Salvatore flesh. First, they'd try to dig up dirt on my name however they could, and when they found nothing, they'd come after me.

My thoughts shifted to Ross. That vile piece of shit would be fucking ruthless. He'd already seen Anna at the party and that bastard was like a bloodhound hooked on her scent. I needed to make sure he stayed away, like the other side of the island away.

Fuck, Anna...why the hell did you have to come here? I rubbed the back of my neck. The answer to that would explain a lot to me.

My phone gave a *beep*. I snatched it from my pocket and glanced at the message:

Class 105: The Code and its creation - Part 1, Room 214. This class is compulsory.

"More fucking bullshit." I shoved the phone back into my pocket. "How many fucking parts of the goddamn code do we need?

I wanted to turn up on Rossi's doorstep and unnerve the fucker, see what rattled his goddamn cage, not get caught up listening to a hundred-year-old recount of the first blood laws of the Mafia. The roar of the ocean pushed in, forcing me to turn my head toward the shimmering blue before I sighed and turned back. "Plans have changed, looks like I'm heading to class."

"You want me to follow him?" Pavlov stopped and waited.

He would, too, the former Special Forces ex-sniper was menacing, brutal, and the stealthiest motherfucker I knew. I shook my head. "No. We have time. Let him come to us."

Max was quiet as he fell in step, adjusting his jacket, his one goddamn tell.

"Speak, Max," I muttered, and headed to building two's lecture hall.

"I don't like this," he answered. "I don't like you being here, and I sure as *hell* don't like her being here."

He knew how to cut it down the middle. "Neither do I." I strode out, pulling away from my shadows. "Neither do I."

The phone was a perfect example. I had bugged her new one. Her old one was still in my apartment, and every file had been checked, what ones we could access, anyway. She was smart, setting up an almost-impossible-to-hack file, the password changing every ten days when she changed it. I'd thought she was neurotic at first. Little anxious Anna. But it seemed like she'd gotten a few things past me, and that didn't sit well at all.

The last call on her open phone log glared at me. She'd called her father as she ran from me. Like I was some goddamn stalker to her. Like *I* was the one she wanted to avoid.

What do you mean, someone like me? Her words rang in my head as I lengthened my stride. But it was my own response that really hit home. *You know damn well. A goddamn virgin.*

I shouldn't have said what I did...It was that fucking simple.

I'd betrayed her and exposed my hand in front of every fucking family there.

I rubbed my damn neck as Building Two rose in front of me. I'd fucking spill my own blood just to take the words back.

"*Salvatore!*" the thick Irish accent cut through the air.

"Not now, Bruno," I responded.

But the asshole didn't listen. He never did, just took a drag of his cigarette before flicking it against the wall, and broke into a jog alongside me.

"The game," he started. "Do you have a target?"

The game...the goddamn *game*. It was just fucking fun for them. "No."

"'Cause I was thinking...if you were willing, we could team up and join forces."

I cut him a chilling glare and punched my fist against the damn door before striding through. "I don't think so."

"You haven't heard the target." He followed me in, threw his hands wide, and lowered his voice to a whisper. "My good old pal...*Kilpatrick.*"

I stopped walking, just stood in the foyer, staring at him as voices rebounded from the classroom above. At least the Irish asshole had kept it down. I met his gaze, catching the mischievous glint in his eyes. He combed his fingers through his long blond hair and grinned. "You interested?"

"What makes you think that?" I didn't fall for that shit, not anymore.

"Something's not right with him, you know...not since his brother." He lifted his hand, pointing a pretend gun at his temple.

The Bernardis didn't like the Kilpatricks, that was easy to see. But to go after the bastard when his brother was still in a psych ward...that was a low blow, even for him. I held his gaze and saw that hunger, like a beast prowling just under the surface. They all wanted a piece of each other here, they all wanted to bring each other down...

Down into the mud and filth.

Where we all belonged.

The smug bastard just gave a shrug. "You're interested. I can tell. We can talk about it over cards tonight?" He chuckled, then lifted a hand, and his thumb and pinkie became a phone. "Call me."

"Fuck you, Bruno." I gave a hint of a smirk and turned away.

Christ, now I was getting into bed with the Welsh? What more could go wrong? I left the grinning idiot behind and climbed the stairs two at a time as the other students crowded through the door. Shit, this was the second time I'd been to the Institute and it was two times too many.

The first time had been fun, until even the violence became boring. And this time? I glanced over my shoulder as Bernardi watched me leave. The Kilpatricks were first cousins to the Byrnes...my mother's Irish kin. Like I needed a goddamn reminder she was gone.

Bruno lifted his head, catching my gaze. Those blue eyes glinted. But there was no smug smirk now. Just a connection, one I didn't need or want. I turned away to scan every face. They all looked the same, cold eyes glinting. Anna was the only one who stood out. But she wasn't here...not yet.

I lowered my gaze, shoved my hands into the pockets of my leather jacket, and made for the back of the classroom, sliding into an empty seat. But the moment I sat, I caught sight of the one goddamn person I most *didn't* want to see.

He smiled. He *always* fucking smiled. I wanted to wipe it off his face...*with my goddamn fist.*

"Salvatore," Lazarus Rossi said, and slid into the seat two over from me.

I ignored him. Instead, I focused on those at the front of the room as the last few students slipped through the open door.

"Looking for anyone in particular?"

I clenched my jaw, my gaze cutting to Max and Pavlov standing just inside the door, along with all the other shadows.

"Oh, that's right. Your little girlfriend from the party."

"She's *not* my girlfriend," I ground out the words, not bothering to even look toward him. "I barely know her."

"Hmm," the bastard clucked his tongue. "Didn't look like that to me."

"Who gives a shit what it looked like to you?"

Two more came through the door as the instructor, some fat old fuck, cleared his throat and called out, "Let's get started."

"Oh no," Lazarus gasped in mock horror. "Looks like little girl-friend isn't here. Don't tell me she's avoiding you?"

I clenched my fist so fucking hard my knuckles popped. A glance at Max and the stony bastard just held my stare. *Don't do it*...those brown eyes warned. Don't...fucking...do...it.

"The origins of the code date back to the nineteen-twenties..." the lecturer started, his voice booming.

He thought he sounded important, thought he gave the speech *with confidence*. Instead, he was just loud and out-*fucking*-dated, reminding me of my father. I shifted in my seat, then unfurled my fist, leaving crescent marks in the palm of my hand as I grabbed the edge of the desk.

"Damn," Rossi muttered. "That one's got you all riled up, hasn't she?"

I reacted in an instant, fear and desperation punching through, driving me from my seat until I had the bastard's shirtfront clenched in my fist.

Movement came from the doorway as Max drove a path through the others to get to me.

"One more fucking comment, Rossi," I snarled as I dragged him from his seat. "*One...more...motherfucking...comment.*"

But he wasn't one to shove around anymore. Gone was the bony, awkward kid I'd pushed around and clocked a few times under the guise of a wrestling match. The asshole had been working out. He was built now...*and savage.*

But he didn't react, never even lifted his hands as the entire classroom turned quiet. Instead, those piercing blue eyes just carved through me like a blade, then lowered to my fists.

"You're unraveling, Salvatore," the bastard said coldly, sliding that menacing gaze to mine once more, and for the first time in my life a shudder of fear coursed through me. "You're splitting at the edges, coming apart at the seams."

"Fin," Max urged behind me.

Hard breaths were consuming me. Still, Lazarus just held my stare, that smothered flicker of amusement shining through. I just shoved the bastard, but he didn't stumble as much as I wanted, barely even moved. Max's hand settled on my shoulder. I jerked my arm, shrugging off the connection.

*Coming apart at the seams...*the words stayed with me. Even Bernardi was watching me as I strode from the room and made my way down the stairs to the empty, echoing foyer. "Where the fuck are you, Anna?" I whispered under my breath.

Shadows shifted behind me as Max and Pavlov followed. But I just couldn't handle their protection...not right now. I waved them behind, the command desperate. Space, I needed goddamn space. I needed to think and to breathe and to find out...*why the fuck she's really here.*

I left the building, making my way out. Maybe I just needed to go to the gym? Pump some weights, work the bag, get some of this tension out of me. I shoved my fists into my pockets and left, making my way back toward my building as a soft bark of laughter was snatched by the wind.

Laughter that sounded all too familiar.

Laughter that came from Anna.

I jerked my gaze toward the sound as she ran around the corner with her new best friend and disappeared. They were playing hooky...on their second day here. A sting of pissed-off frustration lashed like a whip inside me. This place cost hundreds of thousands of dollars for a few fucking classes and countless opportunities, and they're *just skipping?*

"Just like that, huh?" I ground my teeth, left my damn shadows behind...and followed.

16

Anna

"Kat," I stumbled as we tore around the building, running headlong to I didn't know where. "What the hell are we doing?"

She whipped her gaze over her shoulder to meet mine. Her eyes sparkled and her red hair lashed her face. "Helping you find your demon, silly...so you can kick him where it hurts."

She laughed as we ran, and for a second, those shadows that'd haunted her gaze all morning disappeared. I'd tried to ask her what was bothering her, tried to pry out the truth. But the woman avoided my questions like a hedge fund avoiding the SEC.

"Class has already started," I groaned, but still letting her pull me forward as we raced along the pathway and toward a low building.

"You're *supposed* to be rebellious, Anna," she laughed. "It's what the rich are, right? Rebellious, with zero fucks given."

Being rebellious was one thing, but I was here for a reason and it wasn't to skip classes. Especially classes that might have a contact waiting for me to appear. "Kat..."

"I *love* it when you say my name like that," she moaned.

We cut through a garden filled with lush green ferns and past the glass wall of a building. I scanned the rooms as we passed, catching the blur of what looked like a hospital bed. Someone lay in the bed. He lifted his head, catching our movement and in that second, our gazes connected.

Baldeon.

His brows furrowed and his lips parted. But then I was gone, tearing past with the wave of my hand. He winced, then lifted his hand in return. And for a second, I thought I knew him, like I knew this life and these people...*like I really belonged.*

"Come on,'" Kat called, charging forward, head down, as we rounded the end of Building One, until the far side of the island opened up.

Only one building stood separate from the others and instantly, I knew...it was *his*.

I lifted my gaze to the tinted glass windows and the cold concrete walls. This building was smaller than the others, a mere three stories high. It was a statement, one that said: exclusive.

This was a guest that never shared and *always* stood separate from everyone else.

Untouchable, even. The thought of that made my heart race. I'd seen Finley with women before, watched as he strolled through those hallways dressed to perfection, his hand discreetly placed on the small of their backs.

Yes, I'd watched him from the shadows and each time that ache in my chest grew stronger...a savage pain.

My steps slowed and my hand slid from Kat's as she raced ahead. I sucked in harsh breaths as I returned to that pain now, that realization that Finley existed outside my sphere. That by his own last name, he lived in an entirely different world.

If you'd just let me, I could make it so no one looked at you again...not unless they wanted to lose their goddamn eyes.

Those words returned to me as I lifted my gaze to the top floor of the building. A shadow moved in the corner of the room, low, hulking. My pulse sped...*Leale.*

My lips parted. *He'd brought Leale.*

I loved that dog...loved him like he was my own.

I lifted my hand, stupidly, I know. "Leale! Over here, boy!"

The dark shadow moved, pressing his big body against the glass.

"Anna, *come on,*" Kat called, at the scanner to his building. She pressed her access card against the pad, but there was no green light...and no release of the locks. A tightness filled my chest as I searched for Leale once more. Even if Finley had somehow become a stranger to me...I knew his dog.

I'd been there the day his mother had brought him home, and I fell head over heels in love as the eight-week-old puppy stumbled and bounced along the hall of their home.

"He's perfect, right?" Mrs. Salvatore had asked, smiling.

"He's perfect," I'd answered. "Finley is going to love him."

And even in the weeks and months of horror that followed, Finley clung to that dog harder than anyone. Part of me wished somehow he'd clung to me the same way. Instead, he'd become distant, the infrequent text messages my only form of communication.

He was hurting. I *knew* he was hurting. How could he not be... when he was the one who'd found his mom?

"Fuck you, *Finley!*" Kat called out, reckless. "Let us in! You creeped on us, right? It's only fair we get to creep on you!"

She laughed and turned to me. I chuckled at how vibrant she was in that moment. But no matter how much I laughed, the sadness still lingered. I was furious and desperate for him, all at the same time. My fists curled. I'd clock him in the jaw right here and now if I saw him. Hit and yell and *kiss*.

I swallowed hard as the memory of that came raging to the surface. *I waited for you to come to my house, watching as you slipped into my fucking life with your goddamn numbers and innocent smile.*

He'd broken in to our apartment and brought me a damn phone. Did that sound like a sane man? Did that sound like someone normal?

"Finley!" Kat stabbed the intercom and barked into the speaker. "Stay the fuck away from her. She doesn't want you...she doesn't want anything to do with you."

A nerve at my temple pulsed, driving a spear of agony through my head with the words. A lie. That's what the agony said. My hands shook with the thought. I lifted my gaze to Leale standing faithfully at the window, staring at me. I could almost see the happiness in his eyes, almost hear that pleading whine. Almost see his little tail wagging.

"We can't get in," Kat complained. "Maybe we can trash his garden instead? Would that work?"

Leale suddenly turned away from me, moving further along the wall...his focus somewhere else.

"Anna?" Kat turned back and kicked a fern. "You want me to send him a message, 'cause I will, if you want me to?"

I spun on my heel, finding movement in the distance, almost hidden by the jutting wall of Building One. Finley. Standing there....

My heart punched at the sight. He looked *pissed*, his dark eyes almost black, his hands fisted in his jacket pockets. He looked like he was ready to explode...*at me.*

"No," I answered carefully, took a step backwards, and turned. "Let's get out of here."

Kat didn't see him, half hidden by the towering green ferns that surrounded the front of the building. All she saw was me as I hurried forward, grabbed her hand, and tugged her after me. "I want to go."

"Okay." Confusion flared in her eyes for a second.

But then we were running, tearing around the other side of Finley's building, leaving that surly, thunderous gaze behind. The faster I ran, the harder my heart thundered. I risked a glance over my shoulder to the corner of the building in the distance.

The corner I knew hid the one man I wanted...and right now feared.

"What do you want to do, then?" Kat threw her hands into the air.

What I wanted to do, she wouldn't like. I wanted to find the contact...or I wanted to be where the contact would find me. I scanned the buildings and perfect landscape of the island, my mind racing.

"Where can we go?"

The answer was, anywhere Finley wasn't...so where would that be? Around other people. "Who else do you know here on the island?" I glanced at Kat, hopeful.

"Me?" She cut me a look and shook her head. "Most of the assholes I know here aren't worth knowing, believe me. Entitled pricks, the lot of them." She pursed her lips, the furrow of her brow deepening. "But there's one I know and another I've been meaning to introduce myself to. Give me a second."

She whipped out her phone and started typing. Seconds later, there was a reply. "Sneaky, sneaky, sneaky," Kat muttered, and tucked her phone away. "You ready to meet someone who's gonna rock your world?"

"More than ready."

She gave me a wink. "Then let's go."

I followed her, leaving the top side of the island behind. But that eerie feeling came on the back of my neck as we walked. I glanced over my shoulder, watching for movement, knowing all too well who'd have the balls and the motive to follow.

Well, he could pout and rage all he wanted. I wanted far away from Finley Salvatore and his possessiveness. We walked until we came to the third building, set further back from ours, which stood in the distance. Kat's heels echoed on the pavement as she left the bright sunlight behind and sank into the shadows. She stopped at the intercom, pressed the button, and leaned down. "It's me."

The door buzzed, the locks released, and we were inside, striding toward the elevator.

"So, all the buildings are the same, huh?" I murmured, trying for conversation as we rose floor after floor.

"You're nervous, aren't you?" Kat glanced my way with a shrug. "Don't be."

I was walking into a stranger's building with only my apprehension as a weapon, damn right I was nervous. For all I knew, they

A.K. ROSE

could be drug dealers, thugs, like Finley's family...or worse, *murderers*. But the moment the elevator doors opened, the throaty, seductive sound of a woman's voice floated through the air.

"Fuck that, X. I want money, *real* money, not that playing shit you have."

"Real money, huh?" A throat growl thick with what sounded like a Welsh accent filled the air. "For someone I just met you think you know me?"

"Here in the island, we're all the same. Greedy, rich muther-fuckers...I just want to be richer."

"True that, bitch. True that."

Kat flashed a smile at me over her shoulder, flicked her hair back, and sauntered through the apartment. "I'm here, bitches, and there better be alcohol."

Movement came from the living room as two women glanced toward us. The blonde was drop-dead-fucking stunning, sitting crossed-legged on a high-backed chair as she turned her head toward us.

"Guys, meet Anna. Anna, this is Xael and Evan," Kat said casually before plonking herself down next to a brunette who hid the most banging body I'd ever seen under baggy pants and an open baseball jersey.

"What are we talking about?" Kat asked as she glanced from one to the other.

But both Evan and Xael were watching me cautiously.

"Evan." The blonde moved first, rising from her seat, her hand stretched out.

I grabbed her hand in mine. "Nice to meet you."

"Anna, huh?" the brunette muttered with a thick accent, giving me a once-over. "Got a last name, *Anna?*"

"Eden," I answered, and swallowed.

"Eden," Evan repeated slowly, and sat once more. "Not sure I know that name."

"Jesus, guys, really?" Kat rolled her eyes and leaned across Xael for the glass of champagne just out of reach. "She's with me, isn't she?"

"No offense, Kat," Xael muttered as Kat straightened with the brunette's liquor in hand. "But you're too goddamn trusting."

"Only when it *doesn't* come to family, am I right?" Kat stared at the champagne, then drank.

"It's okay," I said, moving to the vacant sofa, and sat. "I'd be just as cautious, fire away."

"Family?" Evan asked. "Or money?"

"God, no," I answered, practicing the lie in my head. "Neither. I mean, we do some work for the Salvatores, mostly trading stocks. Nothing too big, so more like...*contacts.*"

"Trading stocks, huh?" Xael reached for the platter on the coffee table in front of them and grabbed a massive strawberry. "You any good?"

I just gave a shrug. "It's my dad mostly, I just watch."

"Look at that," Xael murmured, and carefully took a bite of the strawberry. "We've got ourselves a voyeur."

Heat raced to my cheeks.

"And a blushing one, too," she added.

"Your daddy isn't The Ghost, by chance, is he?" Evan asked with a slow chuckle.

But the humor was a lie. Under the pretense was the kind of stare that could pierce armor. I just smiled and shook my head. "I wish. I could use a new wardrobe."

"It's true," Kat nodded my way as she helped herself to the strawberries. "She could."

"Maybe you can help me with my dilemma?" Evan crossed her legs once more.

"I can try."

"I've got about five hundred sitting in an offshore account." She licked her lips, that killing edge gleaming in her eyes. "I'm needing a way to...transfer said funds."

"You mean clean it, right?" I answered carefully.

She just gave a shrug. "Or not."

But there was something more...*dangerous* in her eyes. Something hungry, something that made my breath catch in my chest. Evan made me nervous, more nervous than Dominic Salvatore, and that was saying something. This was a test, one I needed to pass to gain even a flicker of trust from them. My thoughts raced with scenarios, trying to stay away from my own home game. "Well, I've heard some chatter about auctions."

Evan uncrossed her legs and recrossed them the other way. "Hmmm, interesting. Go on."

"You could, by chance, purchase an item to be auctioned online but, of course, the purchasing would need to be careful, with proxy servers and anonymizing software to hide ISPs."

"Of course," she murmured carefully. But those brown eyes glinted with excitement.

I gave a shrug. "Just what I heard, anyway. Could be an uncomplicated away to move five hundred thousand."

Her lips curled. "I said five hundred, didn't say anything about five hundred *thousand.*"

"Bitch, *please,*" Kat groaned. "You're drinking Dom at nine AM in the goddamn morning on a fucking island in Mauritius, surrounded by some of the most influential women of our goddamn age."

"True." Xael nodded, giving Kat a high five.

The *slap* echoed through the air. Still Evan watched me carefully. I stayed right away from my real talent, instead giving her the kind of information any two-bit hedge-fund idiot would use to impress...*and she damn well knew it.*

"Okay," Evan said cautiously, with a slow nod of her head.

"What the fuck are you two skipping, anyway?" Xael took another bite of her strawberry and sucked.

"The Origins of the Code." Kat eased back into her seat and lifted her feet into Xael's lap.

Christ, the woman looked like a younger version of Angelina Jolie, all lips and attitude. She shifted her gaze to mine, nailing me to the seat with dark, bedroom eyes that screamed sex. "It's all fucking bullshit anyway."

"What is?" Kat answered.

Xael rubbed Kat's bare leg, running her hand along her shin toward her knee. My breath deepened with the possessive touch, my gaze riveted as she grasped Kat's knee and pushed her skirt higher. "The crap they're spewing in the class, like some of us don't know the real story of what happened."

Kat pushed upright, dislodging Xael's hand. "Wait a minute. I don't know the real story."

"Then you're in for a doozy," Evan muttered, grabbing the glass of what looked like Scotch beside her. "We were just discussing this, were we not?"

"That and everything else about the damn seats." Xael shook her head and then glanced my way.

But we were captivated, watching Xael as she just smiled, drained her champagne and sighed.

"*This* is the one not even the Commission will tell you," Xael started, and held out her hand to Evan.

With a sigh and a few choice words, the blonde handed over her glass.

Xael drained the glass and handed it back. "So, originally there were six families, right?"

Six?

"You mean five," Kat muttered. "I know that much."

"No," Xael smirked. "There were *six*. Six families that controlled everything up and down the east and west coasts. Six families that fucking hated each other, but they hated another family even more. A family who was bigger, stronger, and more fucking ruthless. A family whose name is *never* uttered, not in any kind of conversation. The story is, they disappeared...like every fucking son, every goddamn daughter, and every man who'd ever worked for them. *Poof!* Just like that. You *think* the goddamn Commission was built to stop the pissing matches over who controls what. But, no. It was a blood pact, pure and simple. A fucking blood pact they hate. Why else do you think there's so much bad fucking blood between them? That's what the goddamn code is built on. Not loyalty...*fucking mistrust*."

"Jesus Christ," Kat muttered, her eyes wide.

"How do you know all that?" I asked.

"I'm a goddamn Davies, that's how."

A *Davies*...one of the so-called Families.

"You know who was the founding member, right? The one family with more to lose than any of them?"

Cold plunged deep inside me. I didn't want to hear it...didn't want to know.

Because deep down, I'd always known there was something very wrong with them.

Still, Xael smiled and plunged that unseen blade home. "The fucking Salvatores."

17

Finley

She went into that damn building and she didn't come out...not for fucking hours. Twenty goddamn messages from Max and a deliberately missed call from my father later and still, I couldn't take my eyes off the place.

I waited for her.

Sweating like a bastard. The muscles clenched at the back of my neck.

What the fuck was going on up there?

I knew who stayed in that apartment, and knew well enough to stay the hell away. From the both of them. Evan Valachi and Xael Davies were two women I had *no* intention of tangling with. Not only were they goddamn Commission daughters, they weren't my type.

Self-opinionated, loud, and fucking reckless. Man-eaters, the both of them. It made sense someone like Kat VanHalen was friends with them, but I didn't like Anna there. Not with their damn questions...*not with anything.*

But finally, the front doors opened and they walked out, all four of them, laughing and smiling. Best fucking friends now. That goddamn twitch came at the corner of my eye, jerking and dancing, making me lick my lips and clench my teeth.

I hung back, watching Xael and Evan break off with a wave and a bark of laughter. I lowered my head, stepped around the thick foliage of the ferns, and followed with my damn heart booming in my chest. A second later Anna glanced over her shoulder, scanned the grounds, and stepped off the path, heading for Building Two, and left Kat behind.

I lifted my phone and pulled up her class schedule. *Weapons class 301: Introduction to Unarmed Combat for Beginners.*

And she was a beginner, that's for sure.

I left the safety of Building One behind and stepped out into view, haunting her steps like a goddamn stalker, reminding myself this was why I was here. This was *family business.*

Head down, hands shoved in pockets, I pushed through the door of Building Three. That ache inside was like a damn fist pressed against my chest.

"Hey, Fin, *buddy!*" some guy called, and ran toward me.

But I didn't lift my head, didn't meet his gaze. She was all there was, crammed so fucking tight inside my mind I couldn't avoid her even if I wanted to...and I didn't fucking want to.

"We're having drinks for Bal later." He slowed and smiled. "They're letting him out of the infirmary today. Hoping I might see you there?"

I stopped then, turned, and looked at him. Clean cut, fucking boy-next-door, with his damn eyes sparkling. I licked my lips, "Zakharov, right?"

He gave a nod and took a step closer. The movement made me twitch.

There was hope in his gaze. I knew damn well what he was thinking, that somehow the rumors weren't true and I wasn't as cold as they said. He hoped we'd be best friends, hoped that maybe he'd dance with the danger of my world...for a little while at least. *It's what they all thought...at first.*

I took a step, ran my fingers through my hair, and steeled that savage part of my nature. "You don't know me. So, let me take this opportunity to rectify that." That spark of hope in his eyes dulled. "We're not friends, Zakharov, and we're *never* going to be friends. You think because your family has money that that is how it is here? It's not. There's always going to be *you*, and then there's *me*. So, *buddy,* have your goddamn parties and your little group of friends, snort your fucking coke, and fuck your girls. But count me out. I don't involve myself with your kind, not now...*not fucking ever.*"

I turned and shoved my hands back into my pockets, hate and resignation like fucking tar coating the inside of my gut. That was just how it was.

"You're a real fucking prick, you know that?" Zakharov called out as I strode away.

"Yeah, I know," I muttered, lifting my gaze and finding Rossi standing there, his arms crossed, that permanent fucking smirk on his face.

"Jeez, you just make friends everywhere you go, don't you, Salvatore?" Lazarus chuckled.

I just slammed my shoulder against his and kept on walking, taking the ramp down to the lower floor.

Them and me. That's how it was in this world. *That's how it was when you were a Salvatore son.*

As I passed through familiar hallways and darkened rooms, I hunched my shoulders, hating how my goddamn blood made me. *Alone. Distant. Fucking ruined after finding my mom dead in our goddamn house.*

Hearing the sound of voices in the distance, I shoved the thought aside. I followed the hallway, turning, and turning again. This fucking place was a maze. But the voices grew louder, laughter spilled out before one dominating voice told them to settle down. "Okay guys, team up and let's get started."

Team up? I lengthened my stride, my pulse hammering.

I shoved open the door and stepped into the training room, with its mats on the floor and benches against the walls filled with weapons. The instructor glanced my way and stilled, his focus on my eyes before they shifted to my hands fisted in my pockets. "Can I help you?"

But the others in the class didn't notice, they were too busy *teaming up*. Murmurs spilled out. I narrowed in on one voice in particular, and scanned the room.

She stood with her back to me. She should *never* do that. Not to me...not to any of them. The asshole who faced her just grinned and lunged. He grabbed her, hands everywhere, trying his best to pull her against him.

She started to fight, clawing his hold. Her panic...*was all mine.*

I was moving before I knew it, cleaving through the others spread out across the mats.

"Hey!" the instructor called.

But I was already grabbing the guy who had her, already yanking him close and snarling, "Get your fucking hands *off her.*"

"Finley!" Anna barked my name.

But that fire inside was burning, blistering my veins and roaring in my ears. The guy's eyes widened, fear instant as he realized who I was. They all knew me...*and if they didn't, they would soon enough.* I shoved him backwards so hard he tripped and fell.

He was a punk. Just a fucking punk with a bankroll. So I left him behind. There was anger in her eyes when I turned.

"You like to be handled, Anna?" I growled, then bent and wrapped my arms around her thighs before throwing her over my shoulder and heading for the doorway. "I'll give you what you goddamn need."

"Finley, *put me down, now!*" she demanded.

Movement came toward me as one of the students stepped in my way. His gaze moved from Anna to me. A fucking hero...*there was always one.*

My lips curled in response. "Make one fucking move, and I'll pistol-whip you so fucking bad you'll lose a goddamn eye."

I kept walking, past the chump with the brand new conscience, and strode past the instructor. "Don't worry, I'm not going to hurt her."

But the asshole was already stepping backwards and reaching for his cell. The Commander would be called soon enough. But curtesy spoke volumes around here...and so did not touching what *belonged to me.*

I yanked open the door and strode from the room as she thrashed and punched me, the heavy *thud* of her fists on my back strangely comforting. I wanted her to hit me. I wanted her to fight, 'cause, Christ, I wasn't in my right mind right now.

I took a wrong turn. But then again, every goddamn turn was wrong when it came to her. Darkened rooms waited behind each door as I strode past.

"Finley!" She tried to throw herself backwards.

I reached up and flattened my hand against her spine. "Stop it, you'll hurt yourself."

But she didn't listen, just kept kicking and clawing. I swallowed a groan with the sting of her nails, then scanned the hallway, finding a familiar room. I slapped the handle and strode inside. I held her against me, feeling the slide of her body against mine before her feet found the floor.

She stumbled backwards, her wide eyes fixed on me. *"You stay the fuck away from me."*

I opened my hands and didn't move. "I'm right here, Anna. I'm not going to hurt you."

"You..." she started, her chest heaving with hard breaths.

She glanced at the open door behind me. *Try it, and see what happens.*

It was a test. I licked my lips. A fucking test. If she ran, would I let her?

Christ, who was the one being tested here?

Me.

Or.

Her?

But she didn't run. Instead, she dragged those fierce eyes to mine. They all thought she was small, thought she was harmless, thought because she was weaker that she was prey. But we both knew different. I knew who she was...*and I'd seen her violence.*

I knew her, seen her with her sleeves rolled high. I'd seen her work tirelessly, her honey-brown eyes unflinching. She wasn't a mouse. She was a damn lioness in waiting, ready to pounce.

"You shouldn't let them touch you like that," I said carefully. "You don't know what they're like."

She tilted her head, jutting her chin high. "Oh, I think I have a good idea."

"What the fuck are you doing here, Anna?"

Her chest stilled mid-breath, before it started again. Jesus, the woman was so fucking easy to read...all you had to do was to know her trigger, and fuck me, I did...the memory of her body returned. I knew every fucking button, knew every point. I took a step toward her, slow and careful. I knew I turned her on.

She'd accepted my phone.

Accepted my texts.

Allowed my hands on her body.

My cock grew hard.

"Stay back," she commanded, taking a step backwards. "One more fucking step, Finley."

"And what, Anna? You gonna call daddy?"

There was a flicker of panic in her eyes.

"You can't leave, can you?" I tried to keep the hunger from my tone. "You can't escape. There's only one thing left." I took another step, pushing her against the end of the bench.

A bench that looked all too familiar.

A Glock sat dismantled. The slide, the pin...and the magazine side by side. It was the same fucking weapons room from last night. Jesus, my cock hardened even more in response. "Just tell me the truth, Anna. Tell me why you're here." She was riveted on me as I reached out, bracing my hands on either side of her. "You can trust me."

"Trust you?" she repeated as I moved against her.

Warmth pressed against me. I couldn't fight her, not the feel of her body, or the sweet scent of her shampoo. I lowered my head and moved one last time, finding peace.

"You know you can," I murmured against her ear. "You've always known."

She didn't push me away, just stood there, her hands at her sides.

"You know what this room is, right?" I ground my cock against her. "I could do it all different. Take my time. I could give you the kind of pleasure you couldn't walk away from."

Her bark of laughter was thick and seductive. "You're so fucking full of yourself."

"Oh yeah?" I pushed against her. "You think so?"

She lifted her head and met my gaze. "Yes, I do."

Defiance blazed, but fuck me, so did desire.

The sight tore through me like a punch to the chest.

She didn't have to sample any more of the product.

She was already hooked.

"You broke into my room." She licked her lips, that throaty hunger so goddamn raw. "And stole my phone. *Now you want me to trust you?* Fuck you, Finley."

They were the same words she'd told me before. The same words that'd had me riled.

I lowered my head and inhaled the scent of her. "I told you before, you might like that." Her body quivered with the words. I swore there was heat. Gone was that hardness. There was only desperation within her. "Anna...I..."

"You what, Finley? You what?"

"I want you to..." *give in.* "Talk to me. Like you used to. I want you back. Fuck me, Anna, I want you back."

Silence lingered between us, until the low creak of the door interrupted.

"Everything okay here?" The cold, hard fucking tone broke through.

I lifted my gaze and stared at the wall, but didn't move. "Yes."

"No," Anna growled.

"Mr. Salvatore." The sonofabitch chose now to be formal?

I sucked in a hard breath and moved my gaze to hers. "This isn't over, Anna...*not by a long shot.*"

She shoved me then, drove her force against my wrist to break the cage of my body around her. I fell forward, catching myself as she slipped away and hurried toward the door.

"Miss Eden," the Commander acknowledged as she marched into the hallway.

The *click* of the lock sounded before his careful words. "Second time, Finley. This is the second time with her. You're unraveling."

"Unraveling?" I growled and turned, finding him leaning against the closed door, his hands behind him.

"Yes," that stony stare was all for me this time. "*Unraveling.*"

I'd watched the bastard order a hit just last night. There was blood on his hands, blood all over his fucking touch, and yet *I* was the one unraveling? He turned his head toward the door. "Why her?"

"Stay the fuck out of my family business, Mateo," I warned.

"Family business, huh?" he repeated. "Looked awfully personal to me. You sure you're not clouded?"

I took a step closer and clenched my fist. "No, I'm not fucking *clouded*."

The nod was careful as he turned that steely gaze to mine. "I'm glad to hear it. I wouldn't want anything to get back to your father."

I bared my teeth. "Who the fuck do you think sent me?"

18

Anna

Don't run...don't run...don't...run.

My fingers shook as I grabbed my phone. The hallways blurred. All I could feel was his body and hear the pain in his words. *Fuck me, Anna, I want you back.* My steps stuttered. The corner up ahead was my salvation.

Those words plunged right through me and spilled through my mind.

He wanted me back....

But I knew the truth now.

A truth that had rocked my world.

You know who was the founding member, right? The one family with more to lose than any of them?

It all made sense now. All the terror in my dad's voice, the desperation to get me here, far away from Dominic Salvatore...

With Xael's words ringing in my ears, I ran, my head down, swiping my thumb across the screen and punching in the code to unlock the phone as I rounded the corner and slammed into a wall.

"Fuck!" The roar was brutal.

My phone went flying and I hit the wall again, bouncing before rough hands grabbed me.

Papers scattered as a savage gaze burned right through me. "What the fuck were you running from, a goddamn bear?"

I couldn't speak, couldn't think. My throat thickened, my breaths too shallow as I knelt and began to gather the fallen papers from the floor. "No...I'm s-sorry...*I*..."

He knelt, too, his big hands grabbing two of his books before he stilled. "Miss Eden?"

I jerked my gaze to his. He knew my name...he *knew my name.*

I tried to force my mind to work, tried to push back the panic, tried to scan my memory. "Do I know you?"

"Fifty First Dates, is it?" The lecturer gave a wink. "Yesterday you wanted extra tutoring and today I'm barely remembered. What a lasting impression."

Former FBI guy. The realization hit me. "Psychology."

The smile was fast. "Glad you finally remember." A nod toward my head. "And there's no concussion."

I tried to smile, but feared it came across more as a grimace as I shoved the papers in my hand toward him and rose. "I'm sorry, totally my fault."

Concern filled his brown eyes. Eyes that seemed to bore into mine before slipping behind me. Shit, he was gorgeous. "Are you okay?" he asked. "You seemed to be running from something."

"Fine," I answered a little too fast as he grabbed my phone from the floor and held it out to me.

The pretty brand new phone with its rose gold cover, the phone bought by Finley. A tortured moan tore free with the pang in my chest.

Confusion in Mr. FBI's gaze turned to concern. "Are you hurt? Can I call someone?"

Am I hurt? Yeah...you could say that. I licked my lips, that ache in my chest pounding. Ripped in two, does that count? Running from a goddamn monster, the same people who murdered an entire family and everyone who worked for them. That kind of evil never goes away.

"No. No, I'm fine, honest." I grabbed my phone from his hand and took a step backwards before turning. "I'm sorry for slamming into you like that."

He looked like a nice guy, a really nice guy. Still, I left him behind and ran. I shoved my way out the doors and ran, my shoes slapping on the concrete path until I hit the door to our building.

Murky gloom consumed me as I strode through the automatic doors. I sucked in savage breaths and hit the button for the elevator. The Salvatores were dangerous...I'd known that.

But I hadn't known *how* dangerous...

Now I knew.

All those deaths...all that terror. The Salvatores wiped out an entire family? We had their goddamn money and there're just the two of us. Two of us with no one to care if we simply disappeared.

"Jesus." I wrapped my arms around my middle and I stepped inside the elevator car, stabbing the button before I closed my eyes.

Bad blood like that doesn't just go away. It turns into someone like Dominic Salvatore. A man who was planning retribution, a man determined to go to war. A man who was born to spill blood. "Stupid," my voice was thick as I shook my head. "So *fucking* stupid."

My stomach clenched and acid burned in the back of my throat. I was afraid I was going to be sick.

The elevator doors opened and I stumbled out.

"Anna?" Kat called.

I jerked my gaze up at the sound, panic fluttering in my chest. I licked my lips, scanned the apartment, and found her curled up in the corner of the sofa. "It's me," I managed as I forced a smile.

She didn't move for a moment, turning her head toward the window. Her hands fluttered against her cheeks as I turned to the kitchen. I clenched my fists and released them, trying to still the trembling. "Want something from the kitchen?"

"I'm good." She lifted a half-filled glass and drained the contents.

She was drinking...*a lot*. Her haunted gaze and the shine on her cheeks told me she'd been crying. "You okay?"

"Family shit, you know?"

I cracked open a bottle of water and drank, making my way toward her. One minute, Kat was up, like *really* up, then she spiraled. I wasn't used to seeing someone hit rock bottom that fast. "Are you in some kind of trouble?"

She let out a bark of laughter and reached over, filling her glass once more. "Anna, *I'm always in trouble.*" She smiled a sad, empty smile, and drank. "But enough of my shit. I don't even want to think about it. I thought you wanted to go to class?"

"So did I," I answered, leaning against the arm of the sofa.

But Finley...always Finley. He was everywhere I turned. I couldn't breathe without thinking about him. Hating him and wanting him at the same time. He frightened me, but not like his father.

No, his father was terrifying.

And Finley was...*Finley was...hurting.*

"Fuck this shit," Kat groaned and unfurled from the sofa to pad bare-footed toward me. "Let's get drunk."

I laughed and lifted my water. Kat just rolled her eyes and shook her head. "Drinks at Evan's in an hour?"

"Maybe I'll just stay in this time," I muttered, remembering last night.

Kat shoved her hand on her hip. "You're here to meet other people, right?"

"You're right," I nodded, and she just smiled. I was here to meet the contact and I couldn't do that sitting here alone. "But I'm not dressing up tonight. It's casual for me."

She just gave a shrug, but her smile was beaming as she grabbed me in a massive hug. "We're going to have a kickass night. You wait and see. Finley Salvatore won't dare show his face at Evan's."

For a second, I was swept away in her fever, smiling and laughing once more as she pulled away and skipped to her room. The happy Kat was back and for a second, everything was okay.

Music spilled out of her room, something lively and fun. They were always lively and fun. There was always singing, always the bright, blinding sun...

Until there wasn't.

My smile died as I glanced at the half empty bottle in front of the sofa. Kat had demons, alright. A shiver coursed through me as I moved my focus to the open door of her bedroom. She didn't want to talk about it, that was for sure. That storm I felt bearing down wasn't just confined to my world. Now it spilled out, dark and seething, searching for a crack into this world.

My phone let out a *beep*.

I clenched my jaw.

"You just can't leave me alone, can you, Finley?" I muttered, and yanked my phone up.

Unknown number: You need to be careful, Miss Shaw.

Shaw.

Shaw...

My heart hammered as I stared at the message. I jerked my gaze to the windows, then around the room. It was the contact...*it had to be.* I swallowed hard.

"Are you getting ready or are you going in today's clothes?" Kat called out. "At least change your shirt. You don't know how picky those bitches can be. You'll be judged even if they love you."

I just gave a slow nod as a tingling raced through my body. The walls were closing in, narrowing and pushing, brick by brick I was being confined. Still, I moved automatically, making my way to my room and stripped in the closet.

I didn't know what I pulled out, a top, jeans, nice boots. I strode into the bathroom and took my time showering and drying.

You need to be careful, Miss Shaw.

They were watching. Were they watching me now? My hands froze, hovering over my breasts, fear making me shiver under the warm spray. I hit the faucets and stepped out, hurried to the towel, and wrapped it tightly around my body.

First Finley spied on me, and now this...I felt naked, *exposed*. That tingling found me, growing cold and cruel. I hurried from the bathroom, tugging on my panties under the towel and stepped into the walk-in closet, shrugging into my bra before I slid on the jeans and my top.

I brushed my hair then slid on lip gloss and a light brush of shadow as Kat poked her head around my doorway. "For someone who doesn't try, you sure look like a knockout."

I smiled and stepped backwards, pushing that chill aside. A knockout. That was one word I'd never associated with my looks, but standing there, my gaze sliding down the black top that hugged my curves and the dark blue jeans, I felt...*different*. Powerful.

You need to be careful, Miss Shaw.

"I do, don't I?" I agreed.

Whoever the contact was...they were watching. I gave a small smile and turned, striding from the bathroom and through my bedroom, sliding the key card for the building into my back pocket. I'd come to the island to make contact...and I had.

One box ticked and one step closer to getting out of here and far away from this world.

"You and I are going to have so much fun tonight." Kat hooked her arm into mine.

But to leave this world meant I'd be leaving Kat behind.

That ache moved deeper, tainting my happiness. The truth was, she was pulling me into her world. Her claws went deep, even as she purred. I met her gaze as we strode into the elevator. She was laughing, chatting about Evan and her power trips. She was happy, and in that moment, I didn't care what she said. All that mattered in that moment was that I was there. "I'm going to really miss you." The words out there before I knew it.

Kat just froze, her mouth open, her words forgotten as her gaze narrowed in on me. "Anna, you missed a very important lesson on Kat somewhere, a mandatory lesson. One that would've told you that when I love, I love hard and fast. And honey, I love you. You're not going to miss me at all. I'm in your life now...for good."

She pulled away a little, just enough to keep her comfortable. Her finger swiped against the corner of her mouth as she looked at her reflection on the elevator wall and murmured, "Okay?"

"Okay," I answered. "Friends for life." As if I knew what that meant.

"Friends for life. Fuck knows we need them," she answered with a wink as the doors opened.

We made our way back to Evan's before classes were even finished for the day. This was going to be one long fucking party.

They were already drinking when we arrived, dressed in something a little more glamorous. Evan had on a barely there, shimmering gold dress that just floored me. She smiled as we walked in, her honey brown eyes twinkling as she rose and made her way toward us. "Margaritas on the counter, we're partying like we're in Ibiza apparently."

"Fucking A." Xael shoved her half empty glass into the air.

I smiled and helped myself as the elevator doors opened and more people spilled out. Guys and women, most I didn't even know. But I was introduced to each and every one of them. I nodded, shook hands...and became tongue-tied as Evan pointed to the most beautiful man I'd ever seen.

"This is Damon." Evan smiled, watching my reaction as heat found my cheeks.

"Zakharov." He offered his hand. "Nice to meet you."

My mouth dropped open as his amber eyes glinted. He was tall, and built, with wide shoulders and a tight ass and the kind of hair you wanted to run your fingers through. "Has anyone ever told you that you look exactly like Shawn Mendes?"

He just smiled...*and there were dimples.* "Yeah, I get that a lot."

"Not only is he hot, he's fucking loaded," Kat called out behind me. "He's perfect for you, Anna. A good way to get Salvatore off your case."

My cheeks burned hotter.

"Finley Salvatore?" Damon narrowed his focus on me.

"He has a hard-on for our friend, Anna here," Kat muttered.

"That guy's a real asshole." He shook his head and turned toward her. "You know, I even invited him for drinks later, and the sonofabitch had the balls to look down at me like I was fucking *nothing*."

"Tell me about it." Evan sipped her drink. "You know, my parents even considered forcing me to marry the prick? I told them if they *ever* wanted grandkids that there was no way I'd be forced to marry a cold fucking bastard like Finley Salvatore."

"You'd be better off being married to a fucking fish." Damon moved off and left me behind.

But I didn't smile when they did, and I didn't laugh at Finley's expense. Cold. Detached. *Cruel.* I turned as they filled their glasses. Kat watched me with a careful stare, her eyes twinkling as she realized I'd said nothing.

Because the truth was, he was anything but cold around me.

To me...he was bruised lips and burning passion, leaving behind nothing but desolation in his wake.

"You okay?" Kat murmured, stepping closer.

Still they laughed and joked. I turned away and smiled. "Sure."

"You know, if you like him it's totally okay."

I widened my eyes. "You mean Damon?"

"No, I don't mean Damon," she answered carefully, her voice low under the roar. "You look different when we talk about *him*, like he's under your skin somehow and deep in your veins. We've all had our fantasies about Finley Salvatore, so it's okay to entertain the thought. Just know that's *all* it is, okay? Finley is...just a thought. I don't want you to get your heart broken."

"I won't," I smiled, and drank my margarita that tasted far too sweet.

But the thought of him marrying someone like Evan sent a flare of agony through me. She was perfect, harder in a boyish way, and meant for his world. She looked like she could hold her own. She looked like she *belonged.*

Just like all the other girls he'd brought home. But that wasn't me.

Their laughter sounded hollow. I turned, filled my glass again, and drank. No, I wasn't supposed to be in their world. I was a nobody with a particular set of skills...that's all. I was stupid and naive. I was destined to be the girl to be heartbroken. A fucking statistic if there ever was one.

Collateral damage, isn't that what Dad had said we'd be?

But the truth was, I was already collateral damage for Finley.

I drank until that ache inside me eased, and made my way to the sofa. I even laughed when they changed the conversation to some stupid story about how Damon's father had been caught banging his third mistress by not only his wife, but mistresses one and two, and now he was living at the Hilton.

The way he said it made it all seem so funny, and for a second I was swept away oblivious to the sky darkening outside, until Damon rose from his seat and everyone followed.

"You coming?" Xael asked, draining her glass of Scotch.

I narrowed my gaze. "Where?"

"Baldeon's getting out," Kat replied. "So we're having a few drinks at Damon's."

"They're letting him out already?" I was surprised the guy had even survived. "Sure." I pushed up from the sofa, and felt the room sway.

"Easy." Kat grabbed my arm, steadying me. "You okay?"

The buzz was perfect. "Yeah," I muttered, with a wave of my hand. "Lead the way."

"Come on, Kat!" Evan called from the elevator.

We followed and crowded into the car. Someone grabbed my ass and in that moment, I didn't really care.

Finley was destined to marry someone else and I was just waiting to get away from here. I glanced at Kat and smiled.

Maybe I could send her encrypted emails via a VPN. Maybe I didn't have to leave *everyone* behind.

We stumbled out into the cool air, finding the faint, bruised sky of a fading sunset.

"Lead the way, Shawn!" Kat called, laughing.

"Not funny, Kat," Damon grumbled. "It's bad enough I get compared to my brother, now I have to be compared to a goddamn singer, too."

"I dunno." Kat veered closer and slipped her hand under Damon's elbow. "I always thought Shawn Mendes was hot as fuck."

Damon looked down at her and grinned. "Really? How hot are we talking about, Katerina?"

She just giggled, but there was that electricity about them, that *hunger* that sizzled in the air.

"Looks like Valachi's gettin' lucky tonight," Xael murmured, watching them with a ravenous gleam in her eyes.

I followed them, letting the cool, salty air fill my lungs as we made our way to Damon's building that was one over from where we were last night. I left the memories of that behind. I was sure I'd been the topic of conversation last night. The virgin who threw a glass at Finley's head.

If I had been, none of them had let on. I pretended none of that had happened as we stepped into the building and waited. Damon and Kat were cozy as hell, cuddling and staring into each other's eyes as they stepped into the elevator.

"We'll catch the next one," Evan declared, giving me a gentle shove.

"You go ahead," I muttered.

Kat just smiled, letting Evan press the button, and they disappeared.

"I'm not high enough for this." Xael dragged her fingers through her hair. "E, you have something?"

Evan slipped her hand into the top of her dress and plucked out a small bag of white powder. "Always."

I stepped into the car when the doors opened and tried not to stare as Xael sniffed Evan's hand and moaned in ecstasy. The apartment was already packed when we arrived. Music with a heavy beat spilled out. I knew NF when I heard him singing about love and pain.

As I went inside, a champagne glass was pushed into my hand with a wink by a cute guy.. I scanned the room, searching for Kat, and found her with her back to the wall and Damon all over her.

"Don't expect to see her the rest of the night," Evan warned, nodding toward the two soon-to-be lovers as the cute guy handed her some champagne.

"Looks like it. That your scene?" I questioned, meeting her gaze as I sipped my drink.

"A hook-up? Hell, no. I still have my v-card."

"Evan's turned on by power, isn't that right, E?" Xael speared her fingers through Evan's wild blonde mane and pulled her close.

So close, I thought they were going to kiss.

"Damn right," Evan whispered, staring into Xael's eyes, until finally Evan broke away, lust raging in her eyes.

"Let's drink and wait for that asshole to get here," Xael muttered, shoving her empty champagne glass at the cute guy. "What the fuck is this shit, anyway?"

The way she spoke in her thick accent made me chuckle. The guy just laughed, reached over and snagged the bottle of vodka from the counter, and pushed it toward Xael.

"Now, we're talkin'," she cheered, and took a swig.

We made our way over to the sofa. Evan introduced me to people along the way. Xael just stared daggers at another woman dressed in Dior until she left with a mutter. Then we settled in, drinking and laughing. Evan and Xael took me under their wing, pointing out who was who as the party raged.

Until the elevator opened and in walked Lazarus Rossi.

"That guy right there," Xael muttered without shifting her hard gaze. "You wanna stay right away from him, okay, Anna? That asshole is where nice girls like you go to die."

He didn't even give us a glance, striding through the apartment like a lion on the hunt, looking for someone, until his gaze stopped on me. He shifted that gaze to Evan, then to Xael as she flipped him the bird. With a laugh, he looked away.

I wasn't gonna lie. The guy scared me. He had an *unhinged* look about him. Rings glinted on his fingers as he shoved them into the pockets of his ripped black jeans. That guy didn't give a shit about designer labels. His currency was malice. He slipped away into the hallway that led to the bedrooms.

"Looks like someone's in trouble," Evan said, and grabbed Xael's bottle.

The music raged and the voices were deafening, still Lazarus didn't return, not for ages. When he did, his jaw was clenched, and his gaze was cold...like he'd seen something he didn't like, something he was planning on correcting.

"Where the fuck is this guy, anyway?" Xael grumbled, and checked her phone.

It was after nine already.

We'd been partying and drinking here for well over four hours, and still no sign of Baldeon.

Kat and Damon stumbled back in a few minutes later. Kat adjusted her dress. Damon's hair was ruffled and his shirt was unbuttoned.

So that's what'd pissed Lazarus off? Had he watched them?

The thought of that was explosive.

The elevators doors opened again and a collective cheer swept through the room as all heads turned. But it wasn't Baldeon who strode into apartment. It was the one they called the Commander. The same guy who'd met my father at the dock and told him to leave, without me.

But this time he wasn't alone.

He was flanked by security. Men dressed in suits who scanned every face in the apartment. Fear plunged deep...*they knew*...the thought hit me. *They were after me.* The cheer turned into mutters of concern.

"Quiet, everyone," the Commander lifted his hand, quieting the wave of fear. "I'm sorry, but the party is over. I need everyone...*and I mean everyone,* to go back to their apartments. You'll be escorted by security. I want to assure you, this is for your protection."

"Why?" a guy called out from behind me. "Where's Bal, and what the hell is going on?"

There was nothing comforting in his eyes.

Nothing comforting at all.

Concern exploded into panic, that swept through the room like a storm.

"Okay...*okay*," the Commander called for quiet. "There's been a development and the truth is, we don't know where Baldeon is. He was released this afternoon from the infirmary and hasn't been seen since. So, if anyone has any information, I urge you to come forward. The rest of you need to go home." He turned to the guards behind him and swept his hand through the air. "You'll be guarded until we know more."

I expected terror. I expected screams.

But this wasn't a normal crowd and my mind was cast back to the first time I'd meet Finley when I'd stumbled into that room I shouldn't have seen, back when I was stupid and naive, one that'd seen its fair share of blood and pain. But I wasn't naive now. I knew all too well what was happening.

Evan and Xael just rose. Xael took the bottle as she slipped her hand into Evan's and glanced toward me. "Straight home, Anna, or you can come and stay with us?"

"No." I forced a smile and rose. "I'll be okay."

Kat huddled against Damon, her face pale. One look my way, and I knew tonight I'd be on my own. I gave Kat a nod. "Stay, I'm fine."

"You sure?" she mouthed.

No. "Yes," I answered with a smile.

"Okay, let's go people. I want to be the one notified the first instant you hear from Baldeon," the Commander spoke as they headed to the elevator in pairs and small groups. Smiles had been replaced with hard gazes.

"Mr. Rossi," the Commander spoke, looking at Lazarus. "Can I expect you in my office?"

But Lazarus didn't shift his gaze from Kat, who turned and clung to Damon. "Sure, you can expect me," he muttered, and severed his stare. "But you're not going to fucking like it."

The Commander and Lazarus left.

Evan and Xael were gone.

I followed the others, crowding into the elevator along with the guards. There were more men in suits waiting downstairs. Each one broke away as we stepped out of the elevator and walked through the foyer in somber silence.

Baldeon was missing...

And suddenly the night stretched before me...cold and very much alone.

19

Finley

Blood.

It was everywhere.

Pooling under his body lying face down on the concrete floor.

The white gauze bandage over his shoulder showed stark crimson in the bright neon lights.

"He died screaming," the doctor sighed beside me.

I turned away from the sight, the image of Baldeon's head burned into my mind. "Yeah, he died screaming."

Footsteps echoed in the distance. Max and Pavlov were focused, their guns in their hands, muzzles trained on the resounding thuds.

"Easy, it's us," the Commander called from the darkness before he stepped into the light.

Rossi was behind him, his hands curled into fists. His gaze, already savage, had been pushed to the edge before he even got here. His blue eyes met mine and there they stayed.

There was no love lost between us, that was for sure. Our families had been at war for a fucking century. Still, in that moment there was no hate, no rage...just a knowing...*this could've been either of us.*

His guards spread out, moving around the basement of Baldeon's own apartment building as the Commander's voice echoed. "What the fuck happened?"

The doctor took that opportunity to bend beside the body and turn it over. "Lacerations in a crisscross pattern across his chest." He probed gloved fingers into a couple of the wounds. "Just from here, I'm counting five, six stab wounds deep enough to cause death. But I'm guessing the cut across his throat was the final straw."

The body...not Baldeon anymore.

Like I hadn't spent the last twenty-two years of my life knowing him.

Like he meant nothing at all.

Like the hemorrhaging in his eyes and the smashed front teeth in his open mouth meant nothing at all.

Nothing. Nothing at all. Because this wasn't real...this couldn't touch me.

Steel walls slammed down in my mind as my gaze lowered again to the sickening sight.

"Jesus," the Commander muttered, those unflinching eyes missing nothing as he moved to closely eye the knife embedded hilt deep in the calf muscle of Baldeon's leg.

This had been no assassination...

It was well past that now.

This was a fucking message.

Plain and simple.

I turned away. There was nothing for me to do now. Nothing but to call my father...and give him the news.

One more son down.

Lucky for the Baldeons, they had a backup. Kinda sucks for the Salvatores.

I saw the same knowledge in Lazarus's eyes as he lifted his gaze to mine. There were no words exchanged here, not of war or of comfort. There was nothing but the hollowness of the pit we played in. A pit that'd one day become our grave.

Max and Pavlov fell in behind me as I made my way out of the basement, taking the elevator to the foyer once more. Fucking hours old. That's all this was, just hours since the moment he was released to his guards. The same two guards who'd been found with double-tapped shots to the back of the head in his apartment upstairs.

Whoever had come here was good...*and goddamn quiet.* I rose in silence, Max on one side and Pavlov on the other.

"That's not going to be you," Max murmured as we approached the outer doors. "Let's get that out of your head right now."

He could say the words all he wanted. But it didn't change the fact this had happened right under our noses.

My mind drifting to Anna, I grabbed my phone, slid my thumb across the screen, and pulled up my messages as I strode out of the building, my shadows on either side.

Anna...

Her name at the top of my short list.

My gaze drifted to Baldeon's message under hers.

Baldeon: See you soon, brother. The message sent mere hours ago.

"Yeah." I hit the button, killing the screen. "I'll be seeing you real soon."

I made my way back to my building. Movement came from the side as more guards swept the grounds. I could hear Leale's booming bark as I stepped through the electric doors and hit the button for the elevator.

"It's all clear up there," one of the Commander's men reported as he left.

Three more guards still moved through my apartment. But Max and Pavlov were still through the doors first, moving with military precision, guns drawn, sweeping through the space as the three guards headed for the door. "That's one big fucking beast you have there," one muttered with a shake of his head.

Thunder echoed inside the walls. "Leale, down," I commanded, and the sound stopped.

Every room was searched before Max holstered his weapon and rubbed Leale's ears. My bodyguard turned his head and those dark eyes met mine before the mountain of a man straightened. "You want me to stay?"

"No."

"We'll be right downstairs then." Max motioned to Pavlov. "One of us will be awake all night in case you need us."

I swallowed hard and gave a nod, my breaths trapped in my chest until the moment they left and the elevator doors closed. Then there was nothing but the rush...

Nothing but the loneliness. Nothing but the call I didn't want to make.

I needed a fucking drink first.

I stared at the counter and scowled.

There'd been a bottle of Macallan...I flinched as though slapped, remembering Baldeon.

That's right.

I strode toward the stocked bar, grabbed a fresh bottle, and tore off the cap, spilling a little as my fucking hands shook. Still, enough hit the bottom of the tumbler before I drank. Fire lashed the back of my throat I needed that burn, chasing it like a damn drug as I poured again and swallowed.

And when the boom of my pulse quieted in my ears, I made my way over to the sofa. "Get this fucking over with," I breathed.

I placed the bottle and the glass on the coffee table as I fished my phone free and hit the button. It rang...and rang, picked up on the third ring. "Yes?"

I winced at the cold tone.

Silence stretched before us, just like it always had.

"Baldeon's second son is gone."

"A hit?"

I swallowed hard. "Yeah, a hit. It was a message."

"A message."

Yes, a fucking message!

"And the launderer?"

I closed my eyes as Anna's face filled my mind. I tried to force it away...but there wasn't enough alcohol in my body to do that...*yet.* "There's nothing to report."

"I'm quickly losing my patience, Finley. Get me something or you'll be back home. There's still time for me to take matters into my own hands."

My stomach rolled at the thought. "I'll have something for you soon...and Dad—" I started, but the line was already dead, just like the connection between us, dead as the night my mother had died. "I'm okay, *if you ever fucking wondered. I'm just fine.*"

I lowered the phone, sliding it onto the coffee table, and filled my glass once more.

It lit up with a *beep*.

I barked a fucking laugh and picked it up. "You've *got* to be kidding me."

Anna: Are you safe?

I stared at the message, blinked, shook my head, then looked again. "Am I safe?"

I grabbed the phone and took it with me as I went to the bedroom. Darkness smothered me, that message bright and glaring. *Am I safe...*I took a drink and sank to sit on the bed. *Am I fucking safe?*

I dragged my teeth across my lower lip as my thumbs moved across the screen.

Finley: Why?

A cruel smile curled my lips. Let's see if she responds now. She won't. I'd scared her today. Fucking terrified her—

Anna: Because I want you safe.

"You want me safe? You want me fucking safe?" It was the alcohol talking, and it almost smothered her message.

Finley: And if I said no, what then, Anna?

Anna: Then I'd say lock your doors, grab a gun, and don't sleep tonight.

Finley: Careful there. You almost sound like you care.

I waited.

Waited.

The smirk on my lips trembled.

Fear punched through.

Anna: I do care, Finley.

The words hit me harder than the Macallan ever could. Still, I drank, my thumbs flying across the screen.

Finley: We found him, did they tell you that?

Nothing. There was nothing for so long, I thought it was done, that whatever we had was *done*. Gone and buried, snuffed out before it ever began.

Until the phone rang.

I stared at the screen as it sounded with a different tone. I punched off the video and answered the call. "What do you want, Anna?"

"Talk to me," she murmured quietly into the phone.

I closed my eyes at the sound of her voice. Pain quaked through me, making my voice husky. "I can't do this."

The sound of sheets rustling came through the phone as she moved.

I opened my eyes in an instant, my senses firing, my breath growing harsh. "Where are you?"

I winced at the tone. Still, she answered. "I'm in my apartment. Turn your video on."

"Alone?" I scowled, fear driving ice through my veins.

"Yes, alone, Finley. Don't worry, Kat's not here, no one can hear us."

She's alone, all alone...the image of Baldeon punched to the surface of my mind. "You think I give a shit about that? What do you mean, Kat's not there?"

Fear bled into her tone. The sheets whispered again. "She's at Damon's."

"And she left you there on your own?" I forced the words through clenched teeth. I was already moving, shoving up from the bed, that savage part of me burning with need. "Stay right where you are. I'm on my way."

"No. Finley, *stop*," she commanded, stopping me cold before her voice softened. "There're two guards downstairs. I'm perfectly safe here."

But that was a lie.

I knew it.

And so did she.

"Safe, huh?" I licked my lips as a hurricane moved through my chest. Safe...how could she be safe *when she wasn't with me?*

"Talk to me," she urged, her voice low and seductive, taking the edge off my anger.

And when she said those words, it didn't feel cruel like others' usually did. It didn't feel like she was just after the forty details of my world. It felt like...*home*. I eased back down onto the bed and lowered my head, the truth spilling from my lips. "It was bad, Anna...it was so fucking bad."

"Turn the video on, Finley," she urged. "Let me see you."

The Scotch burned in my belly. "You want to see me?"

My hand trembled as I punched on the video and stared at the screen. Shadows and sorrow stared back at me. But then the image in the middle flickered and she was there, those brown eyes big and haunting. I stared at her mouth...and fuck me, I wanted to feel it. I wanted to feel her. I wanted to taste her more than I wanted anything in that moment.

The camera shifted as she moved, bringing her close. I hit the button and expanded the angle, and she was there, filling the screen. I wanted her perfect face projected on the wall, as big as I could. I wanted it burned into my memory, but deep down, I knew it was already too late for that.

She was burned and scarred and tattooed onto the quiet parts of me. The parts that still stayed small, that were still intact...the parts where the good parts of me were locked away.

"Are you alone?" Her voice was so small, so damn quiet I almost missed it.

"Yeah," I answered. "I'm alone."

"I want to see you," she urged, and licked her lips.

"Is your video not working?" I pressed the button, bringing my screen-in-screen video into view.

"Yes," she answered. "But I want more."

"More?" I lifted the camera. "You want more?"

All of a sudden, pain ripped through me. She wanted more, they all wanted more. What about what *I* wanted? I acted without thinking, grasped the corner of my t-shirt and yanked it over my head. Faint lights from the apartment chased shadows from my shoulder away. "Is this what you want?"

Her eyes were mesmerized, making my pulse jackhammer as she stared at the screen. I was exposed here, raw and vulnerable. Sheets shifted as she moved. The silky pajama top she had on slipped from view, leaving her shoulder bare.

Fuck me...

The hollow of her collarbones was like an inky pool. My fingers curled, itching to sweep through its depths. She barely gave me anything, but it was the most erotic thing I'd ever seen. So perfect...so pure. Fragility burned in her eyes.

"More," she whispered.

My cock grew hard. I wanted her. I wanted her so much it burned. I wanted to touch her, to taste her. I wanted to be her first...because I was never first, was I? I'd never had anything that was just for me. But Anna...

Anna, with her perfect, innocent eyes. Anna, who was tucked away in secret. I lowered the camera, letting it slide down my chest. Goosebumps raced as I watched her take in every inch of me. "Is this what you want?"

"Yes."

The silence wasn't empty between us this time. It was filled with desire.

"Lower," she commanded.

In that moment, I wasn't the one calling the shots. I wasn't the one giving the commands. In that moment, I wasn't the one taking...*instead, I gave to her.* Only her. Always her.

"You said something to me," she murmured. "You told me you... touched yourself when you thought of me."

I stiffened, my cock twitching, the head throbbing. "Is that what you want?" My voice was deep and aching.

She licked her lips, her breaths rushing through the speaker as she drew the phone close. The phone I'd bought her, the phone I given her. "Yes," she answered. "That's what I want. It's only fair, right? After you saw me when you took my phone."

I held the phone and lowered my other hand. Completely vulnerable. My zipper sounded so loud through the phone...and she was captivated as I pushed my jeans low, completely exposed now.

"Lie back on the bed," she directed.

The camera moved as she shifted in her bed. I licked my lips. Jesus, this was the hottest thing I'd ever done. "What did you just do?"

The camera view left her face and for a second, I almost barked in frustration until the camera's view danced across her milky skin. I caught sight of the small swell of her breast, her nipple so tight and puckered. My lips parted at the sight before the view was gone. The ridges of her ribs came into view, then they fell away, becoming the dip of her belly. Then she was there, the dark thatch of her hair on the screen.

"Just to make sure you know you're not the only one vulnerable here," she reassured.

I knew in an instant what she was doing. She was making sure I knew I was safe here. That she had as much to lose in this as I did, that I wasn't the only one exposed. Desire burned inside me. She did this for me...after all I'd done to her, she was prepared to put my feelings first.

"So show me what I want, Finley. Show me how bad you want this. Show me how much you care."

Her words blistered and blazed, making me stand and jerk off my boots. I shoved my jeans low, letting my erection spring free, and lowered the camera.

Fuck me, I filled her screen, long and veined, darkness closing around the length with my fist. "Touch yourself," I growled. "I want to see you touch yourself."

Her thighs parted, and the camera was shaky as her hand dipped low. The slick sounds of her fingers were followed by a breathless groan. The sound tore my own free, deep, resonant, making me fist myself harder.

"I...want you," she whispered. "I want all of you."

"I want you, too...so much I can't fucking breathe." I drove my fist along my thickness. "I want to be where your fingers are. I could be so fucking gentle, Anna."

"What if I don't want that?" she asked as she drove her fingers deeper, *harder*.

Christ, I almost came.

"What if I want this?" She angled her wrist harder, thrusting and punishing.

I bit down on my lip so hard I tasted blood. "Let me come over," I groaned. "Let me...just..."

"Not tonight," she commanded.

She was the one calling the shots here. This was all on her terms.

"What the fuck are you doing here, Anna?" I moaned, and thrust my hips forward, my cock almost smashing into the camera.

Slickness glistened, shimmering in the camera's view as a teardrop bead welled on the head of my cock.

I wanted to smooth that all over her. I wanted to coat it on the inside of her thighs.

"Isn't it obvious?" she groaned, her fingers moving faster, slipping along her slit to rub her clit. She spread herself for me, sliding her touch low. Her fingers were slick and wet when they came free. "I'm fucking you," she moaned. "And you're fucking me, Finley."

I barked my release, unable to stop myself, as her hips rose from the bed and she cried out my name.

"Finley," she gasped. "Oh...*God.*"

Warmth closed around me as I gripped tight, catching every spasm, drawing free every grunt.

"You're going to ruin me, aren't you?" I muttered, the truth spilling free with my release.

"Not as much as you're going to ruin me," she answered, her fingers sliding from her body, glistening and trembling. "So tell me, Finley...what do we do now?"

20

Anna

"What do we do now?" My question hung in the air.

The tendons between my thighs ached from the stretch. I closed my legs and angled the camera higher. But it was my mind that was racing, outpacing even my heart.

Did I really just say that out loud?

Finley's face came into view, calm now...serious. But that haunted look still lingered as he met my gaze. "I don't know," he answered, and adjusted himself. "What do you want to happen, Anna?"

Thoughts and emotions collided. I waited to come down from the high of what we'd just done. I waited for the shame and humiliation to set in.

But they didn't.

There was only need when I looked into Finley's eyes, bone-deep and aching, strong enough to push everything else away. Baldeon was dead, and now we were different, especially me.

Loyalties collided. The need to get away from the Salvatores and put my own family first tore me apart.

What did I want?

The truth stood somewhere at the edge of his darkness, desperate to step into my light. "I don't know."

He closed his eyes for a second. I swallowed hard. *Wait!* I screamed in my head. *I want you...*

The words conjured the fantasy. The moment I said them, he'd come to me. The apartment was empty, guards standing at the entrance downstairs. Would they stand aside for Finley? *Yeah, they would.* There was no question about that. They'd let him walk through and take the elevator all the way up to my room.

Adrenaline burned in my veins.

And then?

Then there'd be no stopping this.

Maybe it was inevitable. Because to me, he wasn't a *cold fish* like everyone said. To me, he was...strong and familiar, buried deep under my skin. Kat was right, he *was* dangerous, only not like they all thought. He was fire, burning all the way deep into my soul

"Look at me," I demanded, desperate to claim that pain in his eyes. Dark eyes met mine through the camera. I wanted this, deep down. I'd wanted this forever. "This is going to change us now, isn't it?"

There was a flinch in the corner of his eye. His fingers combed his hair back. "Yeah, I guess it will."

This was the point of no return.

One simple phone call.

I hadn't meant for this to happen.

"You want me to forget this?" he questioned, his stare confronting. The camera angle shifted, coming closer. "Answer carefully, Anna. Once you do, there's no going back."

He was giving me an out here, and it was one more reason to feel even more for him. If I said yes...what then? Then he'd look at me like he looked at everyone else cold and distant, barely a second glance. He'd move on, burying that hunger hilt deep in one of the other Mafia daughters just waiting for their turn.

Could I handle that? Could I stand to see him with another? Something inside me quaked with fear. "No," I answered with barely a thought. "I don't want that at all."

One careful nod, and he eased the camera away. But the hard rush of an exhaled breath carried through the speaker of my phone. *Relief*...the clenched fist eased inside me. The image trembled as his phone let out a *beep*. Frustration sparkled in his gaze as he looked away and muttered, "I have to go."

"Okay." I readied myself for the blow.

"But Anna..."

"Yeah?"

"Don't go anywhere alone, okay? Not for a goddamn second, not for *anything* or *anyone*. You want something, you call me. Promise me." There was an urgency in his voice.

I gave a nod. "I promise."

"I..." he started, a small smile twitching at the corners of his mouth. "I enjoyed your call."

He may as well have said *I missed you, Anna. I missed your voice, your presence.* A tremble raced through my chest. "I enjoyed it, too."

"Sleep well," he murmured, his gaze meeting mine for a second before the video died.

And in the wake of that darkness, it all hit home.

Finley Salvatore. The first son of the Salvatore family.

The ache for him flared between my thighs.

I rolled over and slid under the sheets. I wished I was in his apartment, curled up in his bed. What would he smell like now? Deep, resonant, earth and blood. I closed my eyes as the thought bloomed and darkness descended, leaving the image burning in my mind.

Me in his bed...

⊏⊐

"HEY."

I cracked open my eyes to find Kat sitting beside me on the bed. Cool air danced across my thighs...my very exposed thighs.

"*Kat!*" I yelped, and pulled the covers over my ass.

She just scowled and her brows rose with a smile as she cocked her head. "It's a nice ass, Anna. But you don't have to hide it. I'm not into girls."

My cheeks burned as I turned over and clutched the sheets to my chest. "I fucking hate how there's no damn doors in this place."

She just shrugged. "You know me..."

"It wouldn't make a lick of difference, would it?" I grumbled.

Her damn smile said it all. No, it wouldn't.

"You okay?" I asked, searching her gaze.

"Yeah," she muttered with a wince. "I feel shitty for abandoning you, though."

The memory of last night rushed back in an instant, turning my voice husky. "It's fine."

"Looks like you had a party all your own," she probed, glancing at my phone. "What on earth did you get up to, anyway? On second thought," she lifted a hand, "I don't think I want to know. I like porn as much as the next person. You go, girl."

Heat rushed to my face. "It wasn't porn."

"It's okay," she said with a shrug, and rose. "Classes are back on, by the way."

"Classes?" The events of the party last night came back with a rush.

"Yeah, after everything that happened, can you believe that? They want our environment back to normal. But there's nothing *normal* about what they did to Baldeon." She took a step toward the doorway and lowered her head. "They said he died screaming, did they tell you that?"

*It was bad, Anna...*Finley's words sounded in my head. *It was so fucking bad.*

I slid from the bed, taking the sheet with me, and crossed the floor to grab her, pulling her against me. Tears shimmered, sliding down her cheeks.

"It's this fucking life," she said, and wrapped her arms around me. "He didn't deserve that."

"No," I answered, my mind filling the gaps of what they'd done to him. But when I thought of blood and death, all I saw was Finley.

Finley dead.

Finley screaming.

I gripped her tighter. "*No one* deserves that."

"All because of his goddamn name. I wish I wasn't a VanHalen. I wish that every fucking day. I fucking *hate it*, Anna. I fucking hate it with all I have."

She trembled as she spoke. I just stroked her hair and held her. "I know, let it all out."

Her body shuddered as she wept. Head down, unable to meet my gaze. We stayed like that for a while until, with a groan, she pulled away. "You must think I'm weak."

"God, no." I answered. "You're anything but weak, Kat. This is not a normal circumstance, and we are not normal people. We exist outside normal realms."

"You can stay that again," she agreed, and wiped her cheeks. The movement resurrected the image of her curled on the sofa. But she pulled away from me. "Better get ready, put on the game face."

She was gone before I could answer, striding from my room to disappear into her own. I followed her lead, turning into the bathroom to shower and dress. By the time I came out, Kat was in the kitchen eating a bowl of granola.

"Want some?" She held out her spoon.

I just shook my head. One minute, we were talking about a murder that happened right here on the island and the next, we were sharing breakfast. Nothing about this life should be normal. But here we were.

Kat's phone let out a *beep*, and mine did, a second later.

I grabbed it and glanced at the screen.

Security: Your escort is waiting in the foyer for your class.

"Escort, huh?" I muttered.

Kat emptied her bowl, rinsed it, and placed it in the sink before striding into her room once more. "Apparently we're to be guarded 24/7."

Twenty-four-seven...

Cold sank deep inside me as I listened to Kat brushing her teeth. It was all slipping through my fingers now, all falling away from me. I came to escape this life, not be drawn deeper inside. I closed my eyes and exhaled. But the truth was...that's exactly what was happening. Footsteps made me open my eyes once more and force a fake smile. First Kat, then Finley. Friends... desire. She ran her finger across freshly glossed lips. "Ready when you are."

I grabbed my phone and tucked a granola bar into my pocket before following her to the elevator. Our escorts were waiting downstairs, dressed in black suits and carrying weapons under their jackets. A careful nod and one of them fell in step.

"See you after class, okay?" Kat leaned in and kissed my cheek before she turned.

In an instant, she was back to her old self, head high, the mask firmly in place.

"Miss Eden." My escort motioned toward the door.

I glanced at him and moved forward, making my way through the automatic doors and outside.

A helicopter roared by overhead, so close I could make out the man behind the controls. The machine angled down, scanning the grounds before it moved to the other side of the island. I lowered my gaze and kept walking, catching movement in the distance. One of the male students strode out...he wasn't Mafia, not like Finley. But he held his head up and strode forward without hesitation.

As though this was all just so familiar.

My stomach felt filled with stones as I made my way toward building two, heading for class. I pushed through the double door, catching sight of more students...and their shadows. My neck tingled as I glanced behind, catching movement at my back.

He was so close...so damn close. Panic surged through me as I followed the others along the hallway, gravitating toward the sound of the class.

"I'll be waiting outside, Miss Eden."

I just gave a nod and slipped through the doorway. *Money Laundering and its Pitfalls* was scrawled across the whiteboard at the front of the class.

I flinched at the words and tried to breathe. They all looked my way...every single one of them. The lecturer watched me, his gaze scrutinizing. Heat burned in my face as I hurried to the first empty seat. But the murmurs were already starting as the roar of the helicopter sounded again overhead.

"They're coming."

I caught the snatch of conversation behind me and turned my head. Desperation fought the need to be invisible and I asked, "Who's coming?"

A familiar female gaze met mine. I recognized her from Damon's party. She scowled for a second, then her eyes widened as though she remembered me, too. "The Commission. *All of them,*" she said carefully.

My heart thundered. "Here?" The face of Dominic Salvatore filled my mind.

"The word is they're *pissed*," she continued. "They're saying Baldeon's killer is still here...and they're going to find them."

Find them...panic boomed inside my head.

Who else would they find? The answer sent a pang of desperation coursing through me as the lecturer stepped up to the podium, looked straight at me, and spoke. "Okay, let's find out who here knows anything about laundering."

21

Finley

I waited all fucking day. It was just like him not to show up... even as the rest of the Commission had descended in a flurry of howling winds and Sikorskys earlier in the day. But that wasn't good enough for Dominic Salvatore. It wasn't enough just to carry a name which made others look over their shoulders. No, he had to drive his status home by making the other heads of the families wait.

He was an outlier...in the worst possible way.

What a fucking legacy waiting for me.

I stood on the rise of the headland, in the exact same position I'd stood mere nights ago when Dillon Shaw had roared and demanded his daughter leave this place...and also on the night she'd come.

Anna Shaw.

The one person who was here to ruin me. The one person who made me question everything I knew. My chest tightened as I lifted my gaze to the darkening clouds, and the only person who made sense.

When I was with her, I sank into a bubble of calmness, swallowed by those perfect eyes and her quiet presence, the one quiet space in this screaming world of rage.

It was that screaming that grew louder as a black speck grew larger on the horizon. All fucking day I'd waited, pacing the floor in my apartment, the walls closing in until I'd gotten the text message not five minutes ago.

Father: Be waiting when I get there.

So here I was...waiting, just as he wanted.

Always as he wanted.

I didn't need to turn my head to feel them beside me, Pavlov on one side and Max on the other. Both men looked like shit, sunken eyes and twitchy fingers making them dangerous as hell. None of us had had any sleep, not knowing what was out there.

I drank after ending my call with Anna. Drank and thought about the shitstorm that was about to be unleashed on this island. A storm that was bearing down right now as the speck in the distance grew larger and larger.

Within minutes, the helicopter was making its descent, all shiny and black against the twilight sky. I never shifted my gaze, never lowered my head, even as the rotor blades whipped gusts of wind toward me. That clenched fist inside me trembled with the force as the machine landed and the doors opened.

The three of us waited as my father heaved himself down from the chopper and straightened his jacket before ducking his head and making his way toward us.

But he didn't stop to greet us, just kept walking straight past, making me turn and hurry after him. And all of a sudden, I was fucking five once more, running after the man with the massive strides, the one who never gave me a second glance—for my entire goddamn life.

"Where are we with the issue?" he enquired, glancing around on his way to Building One.

I lengthened my stride, and kept my voice low. "There's been nothing out of the ordinary."

"Apart from her father coming to the island to demand his daughter's return, you mean?"

I hid the flare of panic. "I had him followed."

"And lost him..." Disappointment was etched in his tone.

But then again, when wasn't it when it came to me?

Building One came into view and in a second, I was back there, carrying in a bottle of Macallan, ready to see Baldeon once more.

"Make sure you're waiting for me when I'm done...and Finley..." He turned his head then, those dark eyes seizing mine. "I'm disappointed I didn't hear it from you."

He pushed through the open door and into the foyer. I followed, knowing this was the way it always was with him. Only son or not...I was *never* more important than the man himself.

He stepped up to a closed door halfway along the darkened hallway, pushed the handle, and stepped through. I caught a glimpse of the others, their guarded gazes shifting to my father before they noticed me...until my father met my gaze, and closed the door in my face.

"Ouch." The low murmur came from the corner of the hallway.

I hadn't seen him, but I did now as Lazarus stepped out of the shadows. Anger burned through me, blazing like a comet across a darkened sky. My fists clenched and my breaths deepened. I wanted to introduce my knuckles to his face, wanted to unleash the hurricane inside. I *needed* it. So. Fucking. Much.

Instead, I just tore my gaze away.

I'm disappointed I didn't hear it from you...

Disappointed...

Disappointed. Disappointed. Fucking...disappointed.

Movement blurred into nothing. Because nothing was all I saw now. Not Anna...not my mother. Just darkness hovering at the rise of the steps. I shoved through the door and made my way to my building once more...flickers of last night pushing in. Blood pooling black against the filthy concrete floor.

Just a second son...right?

Not like they needed him, anyway. Not like they needed any of us. First son. Second son. *Dead son.* Nothing but pawns on the board. Pawns. But never the King...because to surrender the throne meant loss of control.

And that will never happen.

Not for a Salvatore.

Not for a Rossi.

Not for any of them.

I strode through the doors, not giving a fuck about Pavlov or Max in that moment, and smashed my fist against the button for the elevator. They stayed back...hovering just out of view.

I'm disappointed I didn't hear it from you...

My father's words played on repeat as the elevator doors opened and I made my way into the apartment above once more. Leale gave me a *chuff* and looked at me warily before advancing slowly. I clenched my jaw, hating that savage part of me.

In that moment I was too much like my father. Too violent...too *limitless*. All that hate. All that rage seething in my blood. I wasn't like the others, I didn't have another to share the poison of my father, not another brother or a sister. It was just me, just the son.

I strode to the counter. Two empty bottles sat there, glaring like a spotlight on my weakness. It should be empty clips, the bullets buried in the bodies of all those who'd had a hand in my mother's death. But it wasn't. My clips were still fresh, still full and waiting. I grabbed a bottle from the cupboard, bypassing the stack of food.

What was food when I could survive on rage?

I poured a glass and drank...*and waited*.

The clock moved painfully slowly, the numbers blurring as I paced, ate...then shoved my fingers down my throat and bent over the toilet. I drank once more, swiping my lips with the back of my hand. Desperate. That's what I was, *desperate*.

Until finally, the hum of the elevator sounded and the doors opened.

I turned at the heavy thud of footsteps as my father cut across the living room and stopped at the wall of glass overlooking the island. I waited for him to speak, waited for him to say *something*.

But he didn't. He just stared.

"The funeral," I started.

"Will be taken care of."

I knew better than to offer him a drink. Right now, the chopper would be refueled and on standby. I'd bet he couldn't wait to get away from me. He didn't look me in the eyes when he turned. He never did anymore...not since Mom...

"I sent you here to make sure the Shaw bitch was under control."

A fucking fist slammed against the inside of my chest. But I swallowed that word...*bitch.*

"So, when I hear that Dillon was demanding she leave, after begging me to send her here, it set off some red fucking flags."

"It was nothing."

"Nothing," he repeated, the word loaded like a weapon in his mouth.

He crossed the space between us faster than I could track. One minute, I was cold and steel, still swallowing that word, and the next, I was wrenched forward, hate an inferno in my father's eyes. *"Nothing?* Like your mother's death was *nothing?* Like this fucking attack on us...*is nothing?"*

I tried to pull away, but he had grabbed my shirtfront, daring me to raise my fists. I sank into that pit of fury, our gazes locked as he curled his top lip.

He was pale and pasty, smelling sweet and sickly. The smell plunged deep, rolling with the remnant of the Scotch and acid in my belly. If he was anyone else...*anyone else,* I'd smash this bottle and gouge him to death with the shards.

But he wasn't...he was my father.

By blood alone.

"I had it under control," I said carefully. "I'm watching her every second of the day."

"Are you? Are you tracking who she messages, who she talks to? Are you finding out where her damn father is?" He released my shirt, leaving creases behind. "Because the sonofabitch hasn't returned home, and I *don't have my fucking money."* He shoved me away, hard breaths expanding his massive chest. "I want to know exactly where she is." He stabbed his thick finger in the center of my chest hard enough to hurt. "And I need your head in the fucking game. There is not *nothing* here. They're either with us, or against us. There can be no middle...not for them...or for you."

No middle.

That's what it came down to.

Either I was all in...or I was all out.

"The next time I have to hear something like this from the Commander will be the last fucking time I hear anything about you at all. Do I make myself clear?" His dark eyes shone in the amber lights from the kitchen.

"Yeah," I answered slowly, hate and rage blistering my insides. "You have."

22

Anna

Lights flickered and danced in the distance, rising into the sky.

"Looks like they're leaving," Kat observed, and stabbed a sliver of smoked salmon on her plate.

The chef was gone and the kitchen had been cleaned, leaving a dinner for two behind. But I couldn't eat. I couldn't even *think* about eating...not after today. Instead, I felt sick.

I hadn't seen Finley at all, not in the classes that had passed by in a blur, or standing on the outskirts as the rest of the others gathered. I even found myself on the pathway to his building, staring up at the shimmering glass walls of his suite, too afraid to go to him.

There was a nagging feeling that something was wrong, something more than Baldeon's death...and more than the sudden arrival of *the Commission*. The Commission that Dominic Salvatore belonged to. Goosebumps raced across my skin...like someone had walked over my grave.

Still, I stared at those flickering lights climbing higher and higher into the darkness. The sparkle slowly faded away and I knew deep down that everything was about to change.

"That salmon was delicious," Kat sighed as she strode toward the kitchen, swapping her plate for a glass of white wine before heading back to where I stood.

She wasn't rocked, not like I was...or the other members of the families. The rich and the dangerous. I hadn't noticed there was a difference...but I did now. It was glaringly obvious that what touched one world didn't really affect the other. But where did I stand? I had money, more than I needed. But not the status...no, my feet were planted firmly on the wrong side of that line. In a second, all the dangerous shit I'd ever seen came rushing back.

The guy kneeling on the concrete floor in their house.

The hidden accounts.

All the money.

So much money.

The laws that'd been broken and the oaths we'd taken. Ones that hadn't meant much while Finley's mother had been alive. But in the wake of her death, everything had changed. I lifted my hand and glanced at my phone. Heaviness settled in my lungs. Each breath was like a belt cinched one notch too tight. I couldn't ease the strain.

Finley...

The ache in my chest had a name and it was his. My phone let out a *beep*. Was it Finley? I lifted my hand and swiped the screen, opening the messages.

Unknown: Button...we have a problem.

"Oh, Finley, huh?" Kat murmured over my shoulder.

My heart hammered as I spun, panic punching through. *Had she seen?* "What?"

Her gaze flicked to mine and stilled. She frowned and nodded her head toward my phone. "You're messaging Finley."

I licked my lips as my phone *beeped* once more. "Yes."

Kat just gave a slow, sly smile and murmured, "Good for you."

But it wasn't my messages to Finley I cared about now. "Excuse me for a second. It's my dad."

She just turned her gaze to the window once more as I hurried from the living room and raced for my room. My fingers flew across the keypad. *What's happened?*

Unknown: I need to call.

The phone rang in a second and the hard, panicked breaths of my father filled my ear. "I can't talk for long, but I'm being tracked."

My pulse sped. "Dad, are you okay?"

"I tried to shake them, but there're too many, they're everywhere. I heard about the attack on the island. Things are getting dangerous now, Button. I want you out of there...now."

Now...the word resounded. "Okay."

"I'm sending a message to the contact. It's now or never, Anna. If they can't get you out of there soon, I'll come and get you myself."

"I don't know," I murmured into the phone.

"I sent you there thinking you'd be protected," my dad growled. I'd never heard him growl before, never heard him so...*unhinged*. The hard gusts of his breath filled my ear. "I sent you there to get you out of all this. It's now or never, sweetheart. But don't worry, I'll keep Dominic busy. I'm releasing some of the funds. Hopefully, that will give us the time to get you away from those people."

He meant Finley...

The ache in my chest grew bolder, forcing me to choose a side. My heart...or my blood. "Whatever you need me to do, Dad."

"I'll send you a message with the time and place. I need you to be ready to go, Button. I'm getting you out of there. I'm going to keep you safe. I love you, Annalise."

I closed my eyes at the words. "I love you too, Dad."

"Be safe, Button. We'll be far away from this world soon, don't you worry."

I ended the call and just stood there at the far end of my bathroom, watching the screen of my phone go dark.

The faint clink of a glass drew my focus to Kat as she moved around in the apartment. The island felt different tonight. There were no more parties, no more lights. Only darkness waited now and it was both empty and hollow.

I made my way out into the kitchen, finding the plates cleared away.

"Everything okay?" Kat rose from the sofa, concern flaring in her eyes.

"Yeah, sure, everything's fine. Just checking in," I smiled.

Kat's phone illuminated with a *ping*. She glanced at the screen, her lips twitching into a smile before she tucked it away. Only one thing would cause a reaction like that...*or someone.* "Go," I forced a chuckle and motioned to her phone.

Hope shimmered in her eyes. "Are you sure?"

"Positive," I answered. "Go, have fun."

She squealed. "You're the best." And rushed toward me, grabbing me in a hug before planting a kiss on my cheek.

A memory rose with the motion. The scowl on Lazarus's face as he strode back in to the party last night. He'd seen something he didn't like...something that happened where Kat and Damon had disappeared to.

"You like him, right?" I asked as she pulled away. "Damon, I mean."

She just gave a shrug. "He's okay."

Just okay. I narrowed in on her excitement. "So, not mind blowing?"

A low chuckle escaped her as she took a step away. "No, not mind blowing, Anna. That kind of romance doesn't exist, except in books and movies. I'll have my cell on me and the guard will be downstairs. Call if you need me, okay?"

I could only nod. Romance like that didn't exist in her world... maybe it wouldn't in mine?

Finley's shadowed face filled my mind from last night. His desperation...his need. Maybe it was all just an illusion. I moved to the counter and grabbed a glass from the cabinet as she hurried for the elevator, pouring myself some wine. Maybe it *was* nothing more than a fairytale, one that didn't exist in this world.

Sweetness bloomed in my mouth as I drank and made my way to the window. Lights sparkled in the distance, but it wasn't the stars I looked at now, it was the emptiness in the direction of his building, the space where stars didn't glimmer. Instead, it was like a black hole, drawing me deeper and deeper...*and deeper*.

My phone gave a *beep*.

I lifted the cell higher, peering at the screen, secretly hoping it wasn't Dad.

Unknown: tomorrow night at 11. The small cove on the north side of the island.

An image followed, a map with an X.

Tomorrow night this would all be over.

The contact would be found.

And I'd leave Finley and this place behind.

The thought of that hurt more than it should.

23

Finley

My phone let out a *beep*.

Call tracking information: Caller Unknown. Duration: 1.30 minutes. Message received: 2 in total.

I stared at the information as a sinking feeling swept me away. She'd received a call...from an unknown number, and it didn't take a fucking genius to know who it was. But that had been four fucking hours ago and now it was close to midnight. I raked my fingers through my hair as my loyalties collided.

No matter how much I hated this...blood always won out.

There can be no middle...not for them...or for you.

I stared at the text, that weighted feeling pulling me down. Then I pushed up from the sofa, unable to stand the waiting any longer. Leale rose to pad alongside me as I strode toward the elevator, letting out a whine as I hit the button. But there was no ruffle of his ears this time and no careful command.

I just left him behind and rode the elevator down to the lower apartment, knowing Max would still be awake. The man survived on little to no sleep. He was always on always ready for war...always ready for my family. The pungent smell of coffee hit me as the doors opened. The drone of the TV was on, normal sounds of comfort, unlike my place where it was always quiet...and always cold.

"Fin?" Max called, and rose from the sofa, concern filling his gaze. "Everything okay?"

"I need Pav," I said.

The crease in his brow deepened before he gave a slow nod. "*Okay*, want to tell me what's going on?"

"No. I don't."

The bite was too hard, too brutal, especially for a man who'd been by my side for my entire life. A man who was more of a father than my own, a man I normally confided in like a friend. I ground my teeth and wrestled with my conscience. I was pushed to the wall here, my shirt still fisted in my father's hold. There could be no middle ground with this, no matter how much I wished for more. So this was me making sure my allegiance was firmly fixed on the family's side.

"I'll get him," Max said, his voice softening.

I couldn't meet his gaze, couldn't feel his tone. All I could do was give a nod and wait as my bodyguard made his way through the apartment. A soft knock sounded on the doorframe before he stepped into the room. Hushed voices, a quiet command, and the sound of someone rising from the bed.

Max returned a moment later, and we stood there as strangers. My skin was still raw, newly born in blood, pushed harder than ever before to change into the kind of man my father expected of me. Someone colder, someone dangerous, someone more like him.

"Fin," Pavlov called in greeting, shrugging a holster over his creased shirt. "Ready when you are."

"Max." I stared at the floor, then slowly lifted my gaze.

He just gave a careful nod, concern lingering in his dark eyes as I turned and headed for the elevator with the heavy thud of Pavlov's steps behind me. I said nothing even as my shadow stepped in beside me and rode the elevator all the way down to the foyer.

The doors opened and the cool night air rushed in, cooler than it had been before. "You have the swipe card?"

"I do," Pavlov answered, sleep still lingering in his voice.

I was betting he knew what this was now. I was betting he was waking all the way up to the fucking shit I was about to do. This wasn't just an invasion. It was a betrayal. *A fucking piece of shit obeying his father.*

I held out my hand and the card hit my palm. We walked in silence and I wanted it that way. I didn't want comfort. I wanted to be numb.

I lifted my gaze to her building as it came closer. Darkness filled the apartment. There were no faint lights, not even the shine of the TV. Cold wrapped around me as I walked the path and slowed at the reader outside the electric doors. One swipe and they opened, triggering movement from inside. The guard rose from a seat, a scowl on his face. It was easier before...before Baldeon died, when I could've done this without being noticed.

But I was noticed now...

"Can I help you?" the guard asked, looking from me to Pavlov.

"No," I answered. "He's going to keep you company."

The guard's eyes widened.

"Don't be a hero," Pavlov warned, stepping to the guard's side before he met my gaze.

One nod said it all. *Do what you came here to do.*

Loyalty was a concrete block wrapped around my feet as I swiped the card and stepped into her elevator. This wasn't the first time I'd been here, but it was the first time I'd ever had to do anything like this. I pressed the button and closed my eyes. *Piece of fucking shit.*

I reached for that numbness as the doors started to close. Movement came from the guard, but Pavlov moved swiftly, placing one hand on his arm. Then they were gone and I was rising... like a demon coming from Hell.

Darkness waited for me as the doors opened. I waited, my heart climbing into the back of my throat, and slowly took a step into the faintly familiar layout. Soft, throaty snores reached me as I moved quietly ahead. I scanned the darkness, glimpsing a single glass on the counter, and scowled. *Shouldn't there be two?*

A deep flare of annoyance burned as I made my way quietly to the first bedroom. It was dark, and quiet. I stepped into the doorway, my eyes adjusting to the gloom to find an empty bed. *Kat had left her alone...again.*

I clenched my jaw as that annoyance turned into something toxic and turned my head at the sound of her breaths. She hissed. I flinched at the sound, head cocked to the side, straining to listen before I moved. The sound came again, the sound long, riding an exhale before ending with the draw of her inward breath.

A flicker of longing rose inside me, but I shoved it down, moving quietly to her doorway. That tiny sound slipped from her lips once more. But I wasn't here to be drawn deeper into her.

I was already sinking into her depths, swallowed down by the current of obedience.

For a second, I couldn't move, frozen at the entrance to her bedroom. Her breath caught, and silence plunged through the room before she shifted under the sheets, turning her head from side to side. *Was she dreaming?*

The thought of that drew me closer. I took a step, breaching her privacy in a second.

A low moan tore from her lips, faint...*desperate.*

I glanced at the phone beside her and felt a flinch.

"Fin."

The sound of my name was a kick in the center of my chest. I jerked my gaze to her...and waited. But there was no lift of her head. No words of *what the fuck are you doing in my room?* But if there was? What would I do? Would I tell her my truth and demand the same from her?

What the fuck are you doing here, Anna?

Tell me. Now. Before it's too late...

But she didn't wake, just settled once more, one hand reaching across the bed as though she was *searching for me?*

"Fin...please."

My heart hammered with the sound of my name on her lips. That fucking ache sank fangs into my heart. I tore my gaze from the faint outline of her body, bent, and grabbed her phone before making my way out of her room without a sound.

I pressed the button, illuminating the screen, and punched in her old code, *Salvatoresucks.*

What do you know...she hadn't changed it.

Maybe Salvatore had sucked before, but now we were downright ruthless.

Her messages were illuminated. My gaze gravitated to my own name second from the top. I fought that need to consume her entire life. To unearth every fucking secret—*to expose her lies.*

But that sickening need wasn't for my father. No. In this moment, I wanted to know her for *myself.*

I lifted my gaze and turned my head in the doorway as the dangerous part of me took hold. Jealousy ripped through me like a damn drug. My hand shook, clutching her phone. She shouldn't be here. She should be at home, waiting there... secret...*safe.*

But she wasn't.

She was here.

That dangerous part of me danced with rage.

Forcing me to do this.

I jerked with the hunger. My hands trembled once more, but this time with rage. I pressed the top text open, the *unknown* number glaring like a neon fucking sign, and read the first message from that number.

I need to call.

Tomorrow night at 11. The small alcove on the north side of the island.

An image sat underneath. A map of the island, one I'd seen before, with an X on the isolated side of the island. I dragged my own phone from my pocket and took aim, the flash of the camera blinding in the dark. I didn't even care if she woke anymore. In fact, some part of me wished she would. That part of me would shove this into her face and demand the fucking truth.

It was just another betrayal.

Just one more person pushing me...*always pushing me*.

Mom.

Dad.

The fucking Commission.

And now Anna. The one person I'd thought was perfect. The one person I'd wanted to be perfect for me.

But she didn't wake, just continued with that low hiss of her breath. I strode back into her room, forcing myself not to look at her, and placed her phone beside her bed once more.

Just remember...you did this.

I threw the words into the emptiness and left, making my way past her lonely fucking glass on the counter, and strode into the elevator. I closed my eyes as I sank down to the foyer. There was no going back now...not after what I'd just done.

She'd never have anything to do with me, not after tonight.

It was the way it was supposed to be anyway, family before everything else, right?

I opened my eyes as the doors opened, the mask firmly in place as I swept a cold glare toward her guard. "Don't worry," I assured him, and headed for the door. "I didn't hurt her."

Not that it made a fucking difference.

Baldeon's frozen stare hovered in the back of my mind as I strode toward my building once more. Pavlov was silent beside me, saying nothing until we were in the elevator.

"Do you want to talk about it?" he asked, staring straight ahead.

I jerked my gaze to him, tortured by my emotions. "No."

He pressed the button for his floor, then mine. We stopped a moment later. "Night, Fin. Try and get some sleep," he urged, and left.

The doors closed and I was alone.

Again.

A tremor coursed through me as I rode to my apartment. The darkness blurred when the doors opened and Leale was sitting there waiting for me. Any other time, I would've taken comfort in his presence. Any other time, I would've looked at him and thought of my mom.

But not this time.

This time, the floor was cracked open under my feet and the world I once had was slowly slipping away.

I didn't even try to sleep. Instead, I strode toward the sofa facing the windows and sat. I couldn't shake the coldness, couldn't shake the pain. I couldn't do anything but sit, and stare...and wait for the sun to rise once more.

━━━

I WAS a ghost the next day, rising from the sofa as the sky started to brighten. I changed into sweats and made my way down to the gym. But the treadmill didn't punish me, not like it used to. I lifted and heaved, sweating until my body trembled with the strain. Still I couldn't shake the cold inside me, or the memory of what I'd done.

When I leaned against the elevator walls, my breaths heaving, then made my way into the apartment once more, I knew this would be my existence now. I was born anew. The brand new beast in me mewling and hungry, slowly coming awake.

The only thing still holding me back was my fucking conscience.

I showered, dressed, and drank an energy drink. The rooms were too fucking empty now, the sound of my own breath wearing me down. I needed noise. I needed warmth. I needed forgiveness for what I'd done. But I couldn't get any of that, not from the one person I needed it from the most.

Anna...

We were beyond that now, pushed down a path that led only one way. And that way was my father taking what he wanted and not giving a shit about anyone else. I glanced at the screen on my phone, at the screenshot taken from Anna's phone, the X on that map glaringly obvious. She was meeting someone else on the island...*or leaving.*

Leaving...

I closed my eyes, and deep down, I knew it was for good. Leaving me for good.

Just let her go.

The words slipped through the tiny cracks of my brand new armor, rising like a tendril of smoke. Let her go? I lifted my head to the dark clouds gathering on the horizon. The fight inside was torture.

I turned and went downstairs, stepping out of the elevator at the lower apartment.

"Hey, you good?" Max greeted me, draining the last of his coffee before rinsing his mug.

"Yeah." I met my bodyguard's gaze.

He froze, his dark eyes growing even darker. "Fin," he started. "Everything okay, you look—"

"I don't want to talk about it," I answered as Pavlov strode from his bedroom, dressed in a crisp black shirt and pressed black trousers. He slipped on his shoulder holster, adjusted the strap, and tugged on his jacket.

We made our way down to the foyer and out of the building. The weather had turned sometime during the night. Gone were the bright, glaring sun and clear blue sky. Now the wind was howling and vengeful.

A gust slammed into me the moment I stepped out. I lowered my head and made for her first class, some more bullshit on money laundering. Like she needed to learn more of that. My phone let out a *beep*.

Dad: Progress. 5m coming my way. Get the rest to me immediately.

Five million. We were getting five million. But it wasn't a drop in the bucket of what we had tucked away in cryptocurrency. I lifted my head, my eyes drying from the harsh salt spray. There was no *thank you*. No, *I'm proud of you*. No, *job well fucking done*.

Just, get me what I'm owed.

I don't care how you do it.

The only problem was, I'd had nothing to do with the sudden release of funds.

I'd neither asked nor spoken to Anna.

Instead, I wanted to be as far away from her as possible. But I couldn't...*could I*? No, that wouldn't go down with the mighty Dominic Salvatore and fuck if I needed that getting back to him. Not the way we were.

Others on the island ran from the wind, making their way to the buildings with their heads down, sheltering against the collars of their jackets. But I didn't hurry, just look my time, feeling every bit of the growing storm inside me, and pushed through the door.

Voices echoed louder than normal in the vast, empty space of the foyer, battling against the roar of the wind from outside. I turned and made my way to the far wall before stopping. Max and Pavlov melted into the background around me.

I saw nothing, not the others waiting to go to class, or the other shadows who watched me carefully. They all faded away, until the door opened and she walked in. My gut hardened and my jaw clenched. But I didn't turn my head, not even when I felt the weight of her stare.

Let her go...let her go...let her go...

The words were fucking torture.

But the demon inside me wrestled with teeth and claws.

Let her go...

I didn't think I could.

I just pushed off the wall when the classroom doors opened, and walked right past her.

"Fin," she called.

But I was already gone.

24

Anna

He didn't look at me when we gathered before the class. Instead, Fin just stood there, leaning against the wall, his gaze fixed across the room, darker than I'd ever seen before. He wasn't some perfect, brooding god now. He was vengeful, burning with wrath *and changing before my eyes.*

"Fin," I called as he strode past, heading to the classroom...but my voice was swallowed by the roar of the wind from outside.

It was as though I was invisible to him, like I didn't exist at all. The thought of that hurt deeper than it should.

Everything had changed in the wake of Baldeon's death. Gone was the perfect sunshine and endless parties, gone were the smiles and laughter, and the person I shared my apartment with. Now I sat listening to the howl of the oncoming storm as others hid their fear behind careful, stoic gazes. But the truth was, we were scared, scared to leave our apartments, and scared of being alone. But alone was where I found myself. I glanced toward Finley sitting across the room...now more than ever.

Still, I sat quietly through the class on laundering, which focused on false descriptions of trade goods, and under- and over-invoicing of goods and services. The lecture was good, even if it was outdated. That kind of hiding and layering was for chumps, for those with little reach and a small stream of income. It wasn't for the sharks like Dominic Salvatore.

He needed more...*always more*. Demanding and aggressive, pushing my dad to go without sleep for weeks, desperate to find a better, *faster* solution to clean the millions of illegal dollars that flowed through his pockets every goddamn month.

Dad was more than panicked. His back was against the wall, faced with disappointing someone who had a reputation of being extremely dangerous...a reputation we hadn't known about before. There was no way something as basic as illegal reporting was going to appease the kind of man we worked for.

Not worked for...worked with.

There was a difference. We could walk away any time we wanted, I reminded myself.

And this was us choosing to survive the bloodshed. This was us walking away.

Still, I stayed in the class, hoping somehow Finley might seek me out. But he didn't. Instead, he seemed to grow even colder, distancing himself from even his own shadows across the room.

Max and Pavlov just stood separate, hands clasped in front of them, their gazes scanning the room every so often. My pulse sped as they swept across me, but then they moved away. By the time the class was finished, I was desperate to end the torture.

"Okay, I think that's all for now," the lecturer announced.

But I was already rising from my seat and stepping around the others as I headed for the doors. The weight of their gazes settled on me as I hit the handle and let the door fly open and slam against the wall with a *bang!*

My hands fisted, my heart clenched and aching, I made my way out of the building and headed toward my apartment. Heavy steps from my shadow echoed behind me, driving the panic home. I stopped in the middle of the path to my building and turned, finding his dark gaze narrowing.

"Just, stop it." I lifted my hand. "Stop *all* of this. Leave me alone."

The island's security man just scanned the path around us, his hair lashing his face with the wind, and answered. "Can't do that, Miss Eden. I'm here for your pro—"

Panic was in the driver's seat now, desperation had its fist around the gears, driving me to step forward, cutting off his words as I growled, "You and I know that's *not* my real name. Now I'm asking you to *back the fuck off.*"

He shifted his weight and swallowed, but he said nothing, just stared at me with that careful gaze, the one that said he had bigger people to answer to than me. I clenched my fists, my gaze boring into his, until I tore away with a groan and stormed toward the building. I swiped my card and stabbed the button, tears burning my eyes.

But I couldn't shake the howl of the wind in my head, or the pang in my chest as I stepped inside and rode up to my apartment. When the doors opened, a sweet, delicious smell smacked into me. I strode out and past Kat, who was humming as she stirred a pot on the stove.

"Hey there, stranger," she called.

But I couldn't look at her. I couldn't barely hear her voice. Why the hell couldn't she have just stayed away until tomorrow? I kept walking, hoping to God she'd just leave me alone.

"Hey, Anna!" Kat called.

Shit.

"Not now, Kat."

"Whoa." She came around the counter as I strode into my bedroom.

But there were no goddamn doors in this place. *Why the fuck were there no doors?*

"What's going on?" Her eyes were riveted on me as I paced around my bed, unable to stop the movement. Tears welled inside me as the damn wall fractured, desperate to break.

"Nothing." I forced through clenched teeth.

"Something's wrong." She strode into my room and reached for me.

I didn't want to feel the warmth of her embrace, didn't want to feel the weight of her caring. I didn't want to find comfort as she pulled me close. But I did. I felt all those things and more as I buried my face against her neck.

"Hey there," Kat soothed, holding me tight. "Hey now."

I reached up, grasped her arms, and tried to push the pain away as a tremor ripped through me.

"What's going on?" She pulled back. "Talk to me."

I couldn't speak, couldn't even make a sound. My lies were wedged in the back of my throat. I swallowed again and again, but no matter how hard I tried, I couldn't ease the ache, or unburden my soul.

"It's the storm, isn't it?" she said finally.

Relief flickered inside me. Resigned to my fate, I gave a slow nod.

"I knew it. I hate them, too. Hate that caged, restless feeling. Hate how loud the wind sounds, and how the windows tremble. But I'm here now. I'm here and I'm going to stay. I told Damon if he wants to see me, he can come and stay here. I can't leave my best friend alone, not anymore."

Her face blurred under a sheen of tears as I lifted my gaze. Of all the fucking times for Kat to grow a damn conscience, she picked the one night I was going to leave! That was the real kicker, wasn't it? That's why I felt so caged, and heavy with the burden. It had nothing to do with the storm.

It was because I was leaving.

For good.

"That's why I made you my specialty," she said, and gave me a wink.

"Oh yeah?" I swiped my thumbs across my eyes. "I didn't take you for the cooking kind."

"See," she pulled away with a smile and stabbed me with a finger. "That's where you're wrong. I'm a phenomenal cook. I make the meanest hot chocolate you've ever tasted."

I couldn't help but smile. "Hot chocolate, huh?" I said as she strode from the room and headed to the kitchen, and I followed. "What else can you make?"

She grabbed the pan's handle with a towel and poured the chocolate milk into two cups, leaving just enough room for three perfect marshmallows. "That's basically it. Hot chocolate. So, you better like it, 'cause that's all you're gonna get, from me at least."

"Great, I'm gonna be as big as a whale," I complained with a smile.

"A very *awesome* whale," she corrected, handing me a cup.

But she didn't pick up her own. Instead, she just waited, watching me with stars in her eyes as I blew on the sticky mess and took a sip. But it was perfect, not too hot or too sweet. I scowled, stared at the melting marshmallows, and whispered, "This is actually damn good."

"See?" she smiled, and grabbed her own cup. "Come on, sit and tell me about your lecture."

I sank into her energy once more, finding myself doing just that, sitting beside her on the sofa, and started talking. She listened attentively as I ran through the lecture, touching on the high-lights of the antiquated version of laundering as she sipped her drink.

"You know," she murmured, sitting back against the soft black leather. "You've got the same look in your eye now that you did explaining it to Evan the other day. You really like this stuff, don't you, launderer?"

I froze at the words, my excitement growing cold. "What? No, I mean, I guess I have a passing interest."

"Bullshit," she disagreed. "You don't look like that with a passing interest. I've seen you look like that in two separate discussions...and only one of them was about laundering money."

My face burned. *Don't say it...don't say it...don't sa—*

"And the other was about Finley Salvatore."

The chocolate perfection turned chalky in my mouth. Her gaze narrowed for a second, then fixed on mine. "Okay, there's a whole lot going on in your eyes, Anna. Something's happened between you two, hasn't it?"

"You could say that." The words slipped free before I knew it.

And it was too late to take them back. It was too late to take this all back...every single minute of this damn island.

"You want to talk about it?"

Talk. The *one* thing I couldn't do. Not about the way I was feeling or the relationship between Finley Salvatore and me. "It's complicated."

Kat leaned forward. "Complicated how?"

I held her gaze, my voice small. "Complicated that it could get me in a lot of trouble."

She went quiet then, her gaze picking mine apart. "You're not just talking about feelings here, are you?"

Tell her. Confide in her. Goddamnit! You need to tell someone!

All I could do was slowly shake my head.

"Shit, Anna." Kat leaned backward, her brown eyes careful. "How fucking deep are we talking here?"

Easy, the voice warned. "Are you talking about my heart?" I answered with a smile. "Because I'm pretty sure I saw a sold sticker on there somewhere."

"I fucking knew it," she muttered. "It all makes sense now, all the weirdness around him and the night of the party. You're into him and he's totally into you, like head over heels into you."

"Bullshit" I denied.

But she wasn't done. "Like totally take a fucking bullet for you," she continued.

That time I couldn't meet her gaze.

Instead, I drank my chocolate, letting the conversation grow just as cold.

"I might not be the best person to talk to about the kind of things you're feeling here, but I'm a good listener," she said finally, then slowly rose and, with a wave of her hand, she offered, "My door is always open."

She drained the rest of her cup, rinsed it, and placed it in the dishwasher.

"That's because you have no door," I answered, and followed her.

"True," she admitted with a shrug, and stifled a yawn. "But the offer's there anyway."

"You sound tired," I said as I rinsed my own cup and placed it away.

She just turned and gave me a slow smile. "I should be."

"I don't want to know," I cried, lifting my hand.

"I just need a nap. Wake me in an hour if I'm not up, 'kay, and we'll do something fun."

"Sure," I answered, but even as I said the word, I knew it was a lie.

Instead, I just watched her walk into her room and flop onto her bed, and within minutes, her deep, even breaths bordered on snores. I went into my bedroom, grabbed my phone, and sat on the bed, flicking open my messages.

But it wasn't the map I pulled up and stared at. It was Finley's messages, the last ones we'd exchanged...and the ones I'd saved in a private folder on my phone before our lives had gone to hell.

FIN: *You know, you're pretty cute for a geek.*

Who are you calling a geek, thug?

Fin: thug, huh? I guess I am, aren't I?

Meh, as much as I'm a geek.

Fin: Night, Anna. See you next week.

Night, Fin.

FIN: *You didn't come with your father tonight, what gives?*

Why? Didn't think you'd notice my absence.

Fin: Looks like you were wrong. The numbers look shoddy. I think your dad is getting old.

You weren't even at the meeting, were you?

Fin: Busted. Maybe next time we'll see each other?

Fin: Are you asleep?

Fin: Anna...I need you...

I STARED at that last message Finley had sent me. The last one before my father had told me what Dominic Salvatore was planning. The last one before my father made plans to get us away from whatever war was brewing for the Salvatores.

You're into him and he's totally into you, like head over heels into you...like totally take a fucking bullet for you.

Kat's words surfaced as the wind picked up outside. A pang of pain drove through my chest. "I'm sorry, Fin. I'm so fucking sorry."

Lucky for him it'd never come to that.

I sat there, leaving Kat asleep while the afternoon slowly grew into dusk and the sky continued to darken. Then I rose, grabbed my bag and slowly started to pack. I took only what I needed, folding a warm jacket and stowing it in my backpack. Apart from a windbreaker, the rest of my stuff would stay. I thought of what would happen tomorrow when Kat realized I was gone. I thought of leaving her a note, but what would I say? *Sorry, Kat, I love you, but please don't come and try to find me.* Muscles along the back of my neck tensed, the deep throb on an oncoming migraine started. I was already a ghost, already hunkered under the tarpaulin and being speared away toward Dad.

The faint snarl of thunder drew my gaze. Through the tinted windows, the sky was black. It was still early, *too early.* I sat back down, my bag beside me on the bed, and brought up the photos of Finley.

There were three...

Three photos I'd taken when he wasn't looking.

They weren't of anything in particular. Him sitting behind the wheel of his sleek, black Camaro. He looked fierce and power-ful. He looked more like his father there, relentless...*commanding.* My pulse sped. I knew him now, knew him more than I'd ever known him before. I moved on to the next, the one taken as he hugged his mom.

Agony moved through my chest at the sight. His mom, who'd been taken from him.

We had too much in common now.

Far too close to home.

Maybe that's why I'd done what I had the other night...calling him, urging him to show me more of himself. Heat moved through me as the memory of his body came alive inside my mind. Jesus, I'd never seen anything so beautiful in my damn life. The way he worked his body with his hand, the way he'd stared into my eyes, his fueled with pain and desperation. *So fucking raw.* That's how he was. So beautiful and raw. If only things had been different.

Love like that only happens in fairytales.

Kat's words hit harder than ever before. She was right. There was no such thing as love. Not like that...and not in this world. There was only death...only destruction. The screen of my phone blurred with a *splat.* I lifted my hand and brushed my tears away. That ache inside me grew with the low rumble of thunder until I couldn't stand the waiting any more.

It was after nine now, who knew how long it'd take me to get to where I needed to be?

I rose from the bed, shrugged on my windbreaker, and zipped it high before grabbing my bag and making my way to the back of the apartment. There was a small balcony facing the coast of the island, one that led to a ladder fixed against the wall. I swallowed hard and turned my head at the sound of Kat's soft snores. Tears slipped down my cheeks as I stepped away, my heart heavier than it'd ever been in my life.

I moved faster, the lump in the back of my throat throbbing and aching. I slid open the door and closed it behind me, waiting for a moment to stare at the heavy steel ladder. *You can do this... come on...Dad's waiting.* My hands shook as I neared the railing, gripped the cold steel, and swung my leg over it.

I was terrified, my knees shaking, as I reached across, grabbed the ladder, and stepped.

A small, frightened sound tore free as the wind slapped my face. I pressed my body flat against the ladder, the cold steel burning against my cheek as I closed my eyes and waited for death. But my hands gripped like a vise, fingers clenched tightly around the rung, and when my knees finally relaxed enough to release, I slowly lowered myself.

One step at a time. I stopped, sucked in harsh breaths, and kept on moving, lower and lower until a blur in the darkness sharpened, turning into the thick palms that crowded the rear of the apartment building. One last step, and my boot hit the ground.

With a trembling hand, I reached into my pocket and grabbed my phone. The climb had taken longer than I'd expected. My cheeks burned, stung from the wind as I scanned the darkness, catching the faint light spilling from inside the foyer, and stepped away. The sound of my steps was swallowed by the faint boom of thunder as it growled all around me.

I lifted my head as the flicker of lightning danced behind thick black clouds. With my pulse booming in my ears, I hurried, making my way to the pavement, my backpack firmly fixed on my back. The map of the island on my phone was all I had to guide my way.

I pushed the image of Finley's face from my mind and hurried my strides until I was almost running. I focused on my dad, every pounding beat of my heart driving home the desperation to keep him safe.

He was all that mattered to me.

All that I focused on as a *boom* cracked directly above me. I looked at the map again, hurting and making my way along the island. I was taking too long...far too long. Minutes slipped away until it was well after ten. I jerked my gaze from the map, my jaw clenched tight as I ran along the path until my steps stumbled, my boots hitting soft earth instead of hard concrete.

The path had ended. I glanced over my shoulder at the faint sparkle of lights in the distance. Fire lashed my lungs as I sucked in the salty air. I was too far gone now, too far for me to turn back, even if I wanted to.

And I didn't want to.

With the memory of my father's blood-splattered shirt burning in my mind, I pushed on, inching closer and closer, the flashes of lightning chasing me. The island curved away in the distance. I pressed the button on my phone with trembling fingers, illuminating the map once more. It was up ahead, just a little further to go.

I pushed on, driving my boots into the ground as the soft dirt became sand.

I scanned the darkness as I made my way down to the small cove, searching for the faintest flicker of boat lights against the inky black waves. But there was none. My heart punched higher, clawing into the back of my throat, as I stumbled across the soft sand and made my way to the shoreline.

I glanced at my phone...it was just after eleven.

Was I too late?

Panic filled me as I searched the darkness. A sob tore free as movement came from the corner of my eye. Darkness closed around him as the figure strode toward me. "I'm sorry," I called. "I came as fast as I could."

But he never spoke, just strode toward me with long, commanding strides.

It was a man, that much I knew.

Darkness closed around him as the bestial snarl of thunder came again overhead.

As he came closer, more bright flickers of lightning followed the roar.

But it wasn't a stranger's face filled with chilling malice that was lit...*it was Finley's.*

"Expecting someone else, Anna?" he asked.

But his voice didn't fight the boom in the clouds above.

It bled into the sound.

In that moment...Finley Salvatore was *the goddamn storm.*

25

Finley

Her eyes widened until the whites were all I could see.

But it was all too late for her.

It was too late even for me.

I bent, grabbed her around the thighs, and hauled her over my shoulder. My boots sank into the sand, but rage and desperation supplied strength. I pushed harder, lengthening my stride. She was still for a whole fucking second before the shock wore off.

Then the kicking started.

"Put me down...*Finley!*"

I said nothing, just kept climbing, rage seething inside me.

"Finley, no...*put me down!*"

"Not doing to happen," I snarled in answer, and climbed to where the ground fell toward the sea.

She thought she could leave me. She'd thought wrong.

Her fists smashed against the back of my head, one blow driving against my ear hard enough to hurt like a bitch. I clenched my jaw and kept walking, even as she thrashed and bucked, her backpack sliding free to hit the ground behind us with a *thud*.

I left it behind. I left it all behind. Max and Pavlov. These punishing blows in my goddamn chest. All I felt was her.

"Stop! *Finley, just stop!*"

She slammed both hands down, hitting the nerve in my shoulder, triggering my hold to release...and she slipped off. Her feet hit the ground hard before she stumbled backwards and fell. I was already moving, lunging to grab her, when I slipped, as well. I hit her hard, driving my body against hers as lightning raced across the sky, illuminating her face, her perfect goddamn face. In a blinding instant, everything shattered.

I kissed her, slamming my lips against hers. There was nothing kind in me in that moment. There was nothing warm, nothing worth saving. I was all beast, all hunger...*all consumed.*

Her mouth was warm against mine, soft and yielding. I yanked the zipper of her windbreaker, tore the catch free, and shoved my hand under her shirt.

"*Finley,*" she cried my name again.

But it was swallowed by the thunder crashing inside my head.

My fingers slid against her warmth. "You think you can fucking *leave* me?" I jerked my gaze to hers, my lips curled with rage. "You think I'll *ever* allow that to happen?"

There was a tremor in her gaze. But it didn't matter...*none of it did.* I pinned her fucking stare and fumbled with the button of her jeans. There was no stopping now, no quenching this firestorm inside me. Her lips parted. Her eyes were impossibly wide, glassy and dark. I was past the point of no return...past the point of stopping this...*or was I?*

"*Tell me to fucking stop!*" I barked as I yanked her zipper down.

But she didn't. Instead, she just looked at me with that bone-gnawing ache, the icy touch I felt in my soul. With a sickening snarl, I shoved her panties aside and sank my fingers into her body.

Her hands fisted, and her eyes closed. Her breath was what I wanted.

So I took that, too.

I took everything.

Descending like a fucking monster, claiming her air with an unmerciful kiss, my touch sank deep inside her. I fucked her with my fingers, losing myself in her warmth. Jesus fucking *Christ.* Her thighs parted, her hips rising as I worked her body. My chest crushed hers but still, I couldn't let her go.

I *couldn't.*

Not now...*maybe not ever.*

Her moan filled my mouth. I stalled the tremble, sliding my thumb against her clit, making her shudder and shake. Until her nails dug into my skin. My lips curled as I pulled away. "I told you before, you belong to me, Anna. Maybe now you'll fucking understand your new reality."

Her hips rose as her core clamped around my fingers. Still, I worked her, sliding through that perfect slick until she cried out. Tiny tremors rocked her. I slowed my strokes, drew free until the elastic of her panties *snapped* against her skin...and slipped my fingers into my mouth.

Fuck me, she was delicious.

Salty and perfect.

I'd tasted her once before, then she'd distanced herself.

But no more.

A moan ripped from the back of her throat as I pulled away, rising above her, leaving her lying on the ground with her jeans open, just like those fucking lips. My cock pulsed hard and fucking brutal at the sight of her. Her gaze lowered to the bulge in the front of my jeans. I dropped my hand, feeling far too fucking savage to be kind, and gripped my length.

"He's gone...whoever you came here to see," I growled. "The next time you think of meeting him will be the last time he draws breath."

She trembled with fear.

Good.

She should.

My father's voice resounded in my head, the same one that spilled from my lips.

I took a step away, loathing myself in that moment.

"*Wait!*" she cried as I turned.

"There's no more waiting, Anna...not now...*not ever.*"

26

Anna

"Wait!" I screamed.

My body ached and burned as I shoved up from the ground. Lightning tore across the sky overhead, and neon white spilled across the island. *Except for him.* He was darkness. Violent and *wild.* Head down, striding away...leaving me alone with that hunger burning between my thighs. I scanned the ground, unable to see my backpack, and fumbled with my jeans.

My phone stuck out from my pocket. I shoved it down deeper and clutched my windbreaker closer against a battering gust of wind. The contact was gone...*had he meant dead?*

Terror filled me.

Had.

He.

Meant.

Dead?

"Finley! I roared until my throat burned, and stumbled forward in the darkness.

But no matter how fast I ran, he was gone...like he hadn't been there at all.

Confusion was a fog inside my mind. What the fuck was happening to me? I ran until the ground blurred, and the panic inside me blended with the pounding in my chest. I ran until the soft dirt turned harder and finally my boots smacked concrete.

Darkness moved at the edge of my vision. Still, he was like a mirage, elusive, and addictive, drawing me along the pathway until the lights of the buildings shimmered in the distance. I shouldn't be back here. I should be gone, hiding as the contact sped me away.

But there was no meeting...and no escaping—*not tonight.*

My phone gave a *beep.* But I didn't reach for it. Deep down, I knew who it was. Instead, I kept pushing until the hard *thud* of my steps pushed agony through my ankles. I raced past the first building and punched my fists into the air as my own building loomed.

I caught sight of the guard seated in the foyer, oblivious to my escape. But I wasn't escaping now, was I? No. I turned my focus to the pathway in front of me, driving my hurting feet along the path as I narrowed in on the lights that twinkled in the distance. I wasn't escaping at all.

"Salvatore!" His name burned along my throat.

I was too far gone now, heading toward building one, then past it, only slowing as agony moved through my side. I shoved my hand against the stitch as my breath caught.

I couldn't breathe, couldn't think, couldn't feel anything other than the wretched burn tearing through my veins. I wasn't myself now, wasn't in my right frame of mind. I was *just like he wanted me,* unhinged. reeling. Adrenaline numbed my thoughts as I stumbled toward his building, lifted my hand, and slammed my fist against the glass door.

The guard sitting in the foyer whipped his head up at the sound. "*Let. Me. In!*"

He rose from the sofa and lifted his hand, his lips moving as he spoke into a mic. Seconds passed like hours. That burn moved deeper, forcing me to slam my fist against the glass once more. But then he strode toward me and hit the button, letting me stumble inside.

Into the quiet.

And the dryness.

Hard breaths consumed me. For a second, I couldn't speak. A harsh rasp was all that came as I lifted my hand and pointed. "I want to see him."

"I don't kn—"

I curled my lips and whipped my glare toward the guard. "*NOW!*"

He moved fast, striding toward the elevator and swiping the card before pressing the button. The bright lights of the elevator were blinding as I staggered inside, grasped hold of the railing, and watched as the doors closed.

Sonofabitch...

Goddamn sonofabitch.

My body quaked as the elevator rose, inching slowly toward the top until it stopped with a jolt...and the doors opened.

The silence was eerie. Empty. *Vacant.* Not just as though the moment we'd shared was only my own private fantasy...but as though he'd never existed at all.

I stumbled into the apartment, finding faint outline of the leather sofa in the muted amber lights. Darkness pushed in, choking the life out of this world, leaving me to try to focus and scan the apartment.

"What are you doing here, Anna?"

I flinched at the desolation in his voice. Black moved on black, drawing my focus to the sofa. He sat, his arms splayed out on either side of him, until he pushed up and came toward me, his dark eyes shimmering with that same demented gaze.

"You." I sucked in hard breaths. *"What the fuck was that?"*

There was no answer, just a chilling curl of his lips.

Fear punched through me.

I'd never been scared of him...until now.

"What was that?" he repeated...sounding too much like his father. *"What. Was. That?"*

He stopped in front of me, forcing me to lift my gaze to meet his.

"I think you have it all wrong. I think it should be *me* asking *you* what the fuck was that? I mean, you're the one lying, aren't you? Where were you going, Anna?" He grabbed my arm and yanked me closer, his eyes blazing with rage. *"And who the fuck were you going with?"*

I yanked my arm from his hold and stepped around him. "Who said I was leaving with anyone?"

The low chuckle sent chills along my spine. "You take me for a goddamn fool?" He strode toward the sofa, bent, and held my backpack in the air. "Want to try again?"

I stared at the pack, then slowly turned, but I didn't leave him at my back. That low voice in my head was a warning now.

"It wasn't Kat...or your *new* best friends Evan or Xael. Were you planning on leaving with another man? Is that what this is...this goddamn *charade?*" He stalked closer and fear snaked down my spine. "Do you have a lover, Anna? Someone on the island...*someone I know?*"

I couldn't speak.

That malice in him had taken hold.

I stepped backwards as he advanced.

"It all makes sense now." A frightening bark of laughter ripped free. "All the running, all the fucking fighting. Is my little virgin no more? Did you finally give it up, Anna? Was I already too late?"

Through the dark windows, lightning speared across the sky.

"*Have. You. Fucked. Another. Man?*" he screamed at me.

I flinched at his roar. "*No!*" Desperation spilled free as I unleashed like the storm outside. "There's only ever been you, you selfish *bastard!* I waited...*I waited for you!*"

He was uncaring...*unkind.* Striding forward, with a sudden movement he lifted me into the air. But my body took over this time, wrapping my legs around his waist. I was just as hungry, just as depraved, meeting his lips with mine, my fingers spearing through his hair before I fisted tight.

A low, animalistic moan tore from his chest and spilled into my mouth. I kissed him until my lips burned, swallowing that sound before I broke away and stared into his eyes. "There's only ever been you, Finley, in my dreams, in my fantasies. I want you... more than I want to survive."

He didn't understand my words, not the real impact of them.

But I did.

243

I knew exactly what I'd just done.

I'd chosen Finley over my father.

Like the storm outside, electricity carved through my veins.

He strode forward, his hands tearing at my windbreaker before he threw me through the air. I hit his bed with a *thud* and watched as he slowly advanced. "You want me? Tell me, Anna, say the goddamn words I need to hear."

My body tensed as he came closer.

Tell him...

Tell him what you want.

I looked up at him and answered.

27

Finley

"I want you to do *anything you want*," she replied, looking up at me with those haunted doe eyes.

"Anything I want," I growled through clenched teeth, "will make you run and never look back."

"Try me," she whispered, her chin jutting high in defiance. "I might surprise you."

I moved to the wall and hit the switch for the bedroom lights. I needed to see her tonight, but it was more than that. *I needed her to see me*, every sick, twisted thought, every unholy need. A low amber glow spilled from the floor lights, illuminating just enough for us to see.

"Last chance, Anna," I warned, and dropped my shirt. She just lay there, fucking windbreaker still hanging from her arms, her legs bent, gaze heavy. "Before this is all over and there's no going back."

"I don't want to go back," she whispered, then sat up and leaned forward, tearing the windbreaker free.

I pounced, lunging onto the bed, driving her backwards. She lay flat on her back, staring up at me as I hovered over her. "You do things to me." I lifted my hand and grazed my fingers down her cheek. "Dark things, dangerous things...and I can't control who I am around you. There won't be any place you can run after this, or any*one* you can run to."

She just licked those lips.

Those perfect fucking lips.

My pulse was thumping. I was just a fucking liar, giving her an out. The truth was, there was no out...not for me. The thought of that was frightening.

Her boot hit the floor with a *thud,* the sound muffled by the roar of thunder overhead.

I fucking knew, maybe deep down I'd always known. All those women my father had pushed at me, all those perfect Mafia Princesses, they weren't her and she was one I wanted. Her other boot hit the floor. But she was already tearing at her shirt, that same hunger burning in her eyes.

I grabbed it as she yanked it over her head and tossed it to the floor. Her phone made a *beep,* the sound reminding me of her on the beach, her eyes wide, scanning the darkness...

"There won't be any leaving," I warned, watching her fumble with her jeans and shove them low. I lowered my gaze to her white cotton panties. "Not after this."

Her hands froze, the jeans stopped around her knees as she lifted her gaze to mine.

She saw me now.

Saw me raw.

My truth laid bare.

Her movements were slower now, her gaze fixed on mine as I yanked my shirt over my head and unbuttoned my jeans. One shove and I was naked. Her gaze slid low, taking in the hard length jutting toward her. It was all for her...*always for her*.

"Touch yourself," she requested, finding my gaze once more.

I did as she wanted, reaching down and cupping my balls before finding the base, dragging my fist all the way to the end. "This what you want to see?"

Her tongue snaked across her lips. It was all the answer I needed. I would fist myself for her and drive my cock between those pretty lips...*later*. Right now, my hunger was unmerciful and unkind, chasing another kind of high. I lifted my hand and strode toward the bed. I wasn't soft tonight, wasn't careful. I was all hard edges and burning need. I crawled onto the bed, slid my fingers under the sides of her panties, and yanked, wrenching them down her thighs with a jolt.

I caught her tremble as the barrier was gone, leaving her exposed. Fuck me, she was perfect. I reached across her body, yanked open the nightstand drawer, and grabbed a sleeve of condoms.

I was prepared to do the right thing, prepared to let a shimmer of decency shine through...*until she parted her legs*. All I saw was her innocence...all I saw was *mine*. I cast the condoms aside, scattering them on the bed beside me as that shameful part of my nature lifted its head and roared.

I couldn't stop myself, couldn't control the beast inside me.

I wanted her blood on my cock...

I wanted her filled with me.

I rose over her, stared into her eyes, and *thrust*.

She stiffened at the invasion, her hands fluttering to my back. I just pulled back, then drove in deep. Hungry, *poisoned with lust.* I lowered my head as a thunderous growl spilled from my lips, and bucked my hips forward, taking my fill.

But it wasn't enough...*it was never enough.*

Her breaths came hard and fast. The low, painful moan in my ears only increased my hunger, driving me deeper, harder...*faster.* She was all I knew, all I wanted, my forbidden little secret.

"More."

I froze with her whimper and lifted my head to stare into her soul. "What did you just say?"

"More, Finley...." She lifted her hips, urging me on. "Give me more."

That defiled part of me burned with her words. I'd just done the unthinkable...I'd taken her virginity raw but still her nails raked my back and her legs were splayed brutally wide under me. Her warmth waited for me. And I'd never felt so cold as I did in that moment. Never so...*beyond saving.*

I slowed my thrusts, feeling my orgasm unfurl from the base of my spine and reach my balls. With a savage growl, I tore myself free from her, my fucking cock *aching* for release.

"What are you..."

I moved down the bed and slid my hands under her ass. My lips met her heat, the most tender part of her brutalized by me. I licked her and moved one hand free, lifting my gaze to hers as I slid my fingers inside her.

She gave a moan, half tortured with pain...half ravenous with need.

Mine.

The word rose in the emptiness of my mind as she threw her head backwards and moaned. "Fin..."

My name echoed in the darkness. "Say it again."

"Finley."

I lowered my mouth, my tongue finding her throbbing little nub and dragged my teeth across her clit. She whimpered, clenching tight around my fingers. This was it now...past the point of no return. I drew my fingers free and moved up her body once more.

This time, I took it slowly, lowered my gaze, and guided the head of my cock inside her. The image did irreparable things to me. I was broken from her, shattered beyond anything I'd ever known before sinking deep inside her body.

She clawed for a hold, letting out a tormented sound. I thrust, hard, that heat inside building once more.

"Oh God." She arched her spine. "Oh...*my*...God."

She lowered her hands, gripping my ass as I hit home, her voice unleashing the storm inside me. The hard slaps of our bodies hitting together rang in my ear before she let out a cry, clamped tight around me, and stilled. I came a second later, hard and hot, spasming inside her.

Fuck me...

I hadn't meant for that to happen. I lowered my gaze to hers. I hadn't meant to come inside her like that. Hard, heavy breaths pressed her chest against mine. I was quiet, growing soft inside her before I pulled free. In the soft amber lights, she glistened between her thighs.

She reached down, her fingers fucking shaking as she probed between her legs. There wasn't any blood on her. I looked down, finding the small smear on me. *Jesus fucking Christ.* I closed my eyes for a second. But the truth was, it wasn't in disgust...*quite the opposite.*

"Are you okay?" I murmured.

She met my gaze, her eyes glistening with something that looked like pride. "Yes."

I tried to be smooth, tried to hide the movement of my hand as it slid down and fisted my soft cock. I fucking rubbed that smear of blood all over me, wearing it like a badge of goddamn honor. And in the wake of my predatory longing, the events of earlier tonight came rushing back.

"Why were you there, Anna?"

She flinched at the question, the dark pools in her eyes growing larger. She licked her lips, I could see the gathering lies inside her mind. She didn't know that by now I was attuned to her, every goddamn tremor, every twitch in her face. *Her perfect face...it haunted me.*

"I needed to get away for a while," she whispered. "Someplace where I could be alone."

Lies.

I didn't move, didn't give her any reason not to trust me. "You took your backpack, Anna. You were leaving. I want to know who with...and where were you going."

I could almost see her pulse jumping under her skin in that seductive hollow of her neck. I wanted to cover it with my hand, the webbing of my thumb pressed over the tremor. I wanted to capture every terrified thought inside her head and chain them to mine. My gaze moved to hers. *Let me in.*

But she didn't. Instead, she closed down...like a trap around my heart.

The soft padding of feet drew my focus. Leale gave a sigh and flopped down in his bed in the corner of the room. She sensed him, and I knew without looking that he sensed her. *Because he knew her.*

Just like I knew her.

I lowered my head and shifted my body.

"Fin."

"Shhh," I whispered, and pressed my face into her neck. "No more lies now. We can save that for later."

Somehow, I knew she wasn't going to be that easy.

She would test me still.

Push me to the boundaries of my existence.

And I was ready for the chase.

28

Anna

My body ached and throbbed as I shifted in his bed...*naked*.

He nuzzled my neck, his warm lips finding that spot behind my ear, the one that melted me from the inside, sending a flare of heat between my thighs. I was taken back to the kiss outside the classroom on that first day of classes. It felt like a lifetime ago now. So much had changed...in me.

Tell him, that small voice whispered. I closed my eyes, unable to distance myself from his touch. "Finley."

"Hmm?"

"I..." a tremor coursed through me as I fumbled for the words. "I need to use your bathroom."

He pulled back and met my gaze. Gone was the lightning in his eyes. He was unfathomable once more, the kind of depth I could never reach, not in a million years. Fear coursed through me as he stilled, his weight pinning me to the bed, until he finally rolled to the side.

Relief was instant, driving me to scurry from his bed and rush to the bathroom, to find that *his* bathroom had a damn door. I blinked at the sight and shoved it closed, hitting the light switch. The bright glare was instant, flooding the black and chrome bathroom.

I stumbled toward the toilet and sat, wrapping my arms tightly around my waist. *Jesus...Jesus.* Through the door, I could hear my phone *beep* again. There was only one person it could be. I emptied my bladder and winced at the swipe of toilet paper. But it didn't hurt as much as it should.

I liked the sting...I liked what it meant.

The bed creaked, drawing my focus. *Finley Salvatore.*

My body trembled at the name, coming alive even after what had just happened between us. *Holy shit, what the hell* had *just happened?* I lowered my gaze to the juncture of my thighs. I just had sex is what had happened. Hard, consuming sex. The kind of sex that would leave a mark.

"Anna." His voice came through the door. "Is everything okay?"

I stood and flushed the toilet before hurrying to the basin to wash my hands, and strode to the door. He was standing there in his boxers when I opened it, with a scowl on his face, one that smoothed as he scanned my naked body, lingering between my thighs.

"I'm fine," I answered. "But I want to go now."

There was a flare of panic as he jerked his gaze to mine. "You're really not going to tell me, are you?"

I tried to stop the tremble by crossing my arms across my chest. "There's nothing left to tell."

His lips curled, he gave a nod of his head, and he pushed away. He turned away from me, striding from the bedroom, leaving me behind. I hurried the moment he was gone, yanked on my clothes, and searched the bed for my phone.

My pulse sped as I found it on top of the nightstand. I shoved it into my backpack and snatched my windbreaker from the floor. Leale gave a chuff, but waited until I yanked on my boots before coming closer.

"Hey there, stranger," I murmured, glancing toward the kitchen, and ruffled his ears. "I missed you."

"He missed you, too," Finley spoke from the doorway.

I flinched, jerking my gaze to his, and straightened.

"And he wasn't the only one," Finley continued, and lifted a glass to his lips.

Pain filled his words. I made my way toward him. "Finley."

"Save it, Anna." He swung his gaze to mine. "Unless you plan on telling me the truth?"

I stopped in front of him. The heat of our passion had turned into something else now. Something *unsatisfied*. He wasn't going to leave this alone, not even after sex. "Just let me go, Finley," I pleaded.

He leaned closer, the heat of his body electric. "Not even if you begged me to. I warned you, Anna. You belong to me."

I swallowed hard, the throb of torment pulsing in my chest and between my thighs. I left him there, standing in the doorway to his bedroom, and made my way to the elevator. Everything was changed now. My father. The contact. *Me.*

The bright lights of the elevator were too much. I closed my eyes, opening them as it came to a stop. The guard said nothing as I made my way through the foyer and out into the windy, stormy night. The driving wind battered me as I made my way along the path. I glanced over my shoulder, finding Fin standing at the window, watching me.

I hurried back to my apartment, tears stinging my eyes as I swiped the card across the reader and the foyer doors opened. The guard jerked his gaze toward me and rose from the seat in the foyer.

"I don't want to hear it," I muttered, lifting my hand. "I just want to go to bed."

It was well after one AM when I made my way quietly through the apartment and into my bedroom once more. I dropped my backpack into my closet, dragged off my jeans, top, and bra, and crawled into bed. But sleep didn't find me. Not for a long time, not until I'd replayed what happened in Finley's bed over and over and over.

⊏────⊐

"ARE YOU AWAKE?"

I cracked open my eyes to the bright glare of sunlight and tried to focus.

"Jesus, are you sick or something?" Kat wondered, and came closer.

She blurred and swayed, even after I closed my eyes. "Go away, Kat."

"You look like hell."

I felt like it. I felt like I'd been chewed up and spat back out. A moan tore free as the corner of the bed dipped and in an instant, another moan slipped through my mind. Only this was a memory...*of what happened last night*. I jerked my eyes open and shoved up.

"Whoa, *okay*, settle down," Kat jolted from the movement, almost spilling her coffee. "It's like after nine and you haven't even moved. I thought you might be dead."

I swallowed hard, my heart thundering as I glanced at the backpack sitting in the closet doorway. I didn't need to reach between my thighs to know it was all real. *Every. Single. Moment.*

"I need a shower," I mumbled, and eyed her coffee. "And one of those, give." I held out my hand.

She just looked at me warily and handed it over. "What's gotten into you?"

Finley Salvatore, that's what.

I shoved the words aside and lifted the cup to my lips, taking a long swallow before handing it back. But it did little to quell the storm inside my head. I shoved the covers aside, moaned at the ache between my thighs, and stumbled into my bathroom.

I didn't even care that Kat was there. All I saw in my head was Finley's commanding gaze as I left his apartment.

"Something's changed," Kat called out as I stepped out of my panties and hit the faucets for the shower. "Are you pissed off with me or something?"

"No," I answered, and washed my hair, then my body, carefully sliding my hand between my thighs. "Of course not."

He came inside me.

The thought burned.

Shit.

It was lucky for me I'd only just finished my period. But that didn't mean it couldn't happen. *Pregnant...with Finley's baby.* The thought made me freeze, my soapy hand resting across my belly. That would be the kind of war I wasn't ready to handle. I dropped my head backwards and let the water run over my face.

Kat stepped onto the doorway as I wrapped a towel around my body. "So, what gives with the backpack?"

I winced, jerked my gaze to hers, and worked a comb through my wet hair. "Nothing, I went for a walk."

"A walk, huh?" She mulled over the words. "The walk didn't happen to end up in Finley Salvatore's bed, did it?"

My face burned as I lifted my gaze to the mirror. The reaction was so fucking obvious.

"I *knew it!*" Kat barked. "Holy shit, Anna."

"It's not a big deal, okay?" I protested, the burning spreading out from my neck.

But not making things a big deal wasn't how Kat rolled. She rushed into the bathroom and yanked me against her in a hug. "No, of course not. Not a big deal at all, *except that you punched your v-card.*"

I lowered my head, taking comfort in her hold.

It wasn't a big deal at all...*except it was.*

Kat pulled back to stare into my eyes, concern darkening hers. "It *was* consensual, right?"

I flinched. "Yes...*of course.*"

"Good," relief flooded her words on a slow exhale before she cocked her head to the side. "So, was it good?"

My face burned even hotter.

She just threw her head back and laughed. "I'm taking *that* as a yes."

I just tried to focus on my hair as she turned and walked from the bathroom, still laughing. "I guess that means stayovers and all the soppy shit that comes with infatuation?"

That burning on my face grew cold. *Just let me go, Finley.* My own words surfaced with a shudder.

Cozy and soppy? No, I had a feeling that wasn't how this was going to be. "Don't count on it."

"Oh, one and done, huh?" Kat called from the bedroom, striding into my closet. "I get that. They're like a drug. Do it once, get it all out of your system, then a hit of Narcan. You don't want to become addicted, especially to someone like Finley Salvatore. I heard his father is a real piece of fucking work."

A real piece of work...

I stared at my reflection as fear bloomed deep inside. "Yeah," I muttered. "You could say that."

"Did you say something?"

I jerked, tearing my gaze away from the mirror, and strode from the bathroom. "No, and what's all this?" My clothes were set out on the bed.

"You look like you need all the help you can get today and the island *so* isn't the place for comfy sweats and t-shirts."

My teal dress with spaghetti straps and my leather bomber jacket. Right. I glanced at the window and the brooding clouds that were starting to break up. "A dress, in this weather?"

"To accentuate your stunning legs. Besides, I heard that the sun is coming out." Kat turned to the doorway. "They want the island to return to normal...whatever normal means with a pack of misfits like us."

Normal. The word filled me as she left. I moved to the dresser, grabbed panties and a bra, and slipped them on before dressing in the clothes Kat had picked out for me. It was well after ten now. I'd already missed the first class on hand-to-hand combat techniques. But there was a shorter class on psychology in an hour I wanted to attend.

Just let me go, Finley.

The words haunted me as I tugged on my heeled boots and strode from the room. But it was Finley's response that chilled me to the bone. *Not even if you begged me to.*

"Thanks for the coffee." I grabbed the cup from the counter and drank. "And for taking care of me."

"That's what besties are for," she called from her bedroom. "Wait...are you leaving now?"

"Yeah, I'll meet you there, okay?"

"Sure." She appeared in her doorway, shrugging into her shirt.

There were bruises on her ribs, small...round, and another lower down, this one larger, yellowing. "Kat."

"Hmm?"

"You're okay, right? I mean, you asked about consent for me. But you and Damon, you're safe?"

She just swallowed hard and turned her gaze away. "We're fine, honey. I'll see you in class, okay? Save me a seat."

She seemed to close down in front of my eyes. I wanted to stay, to pull her into my arms like she did for me. I wanted to coax more from her. But how could I get her to talk to me when I barely knew how to talk myself. I gave a nod. I wasn't finished here. Somehow, I'd get Kat to tell me about the bruises I saw.

I left her then and made my way downstairs, to where a new guard waited. He stood as I approached. I just lifted my hand. "Save it. I'm going straight to class and Kat's upstairs. She needs you more than I do."

I grabbed my phone as I made my way out of the building, resigning myself to the phone call I'd been dreading. I found myself on the small beach where Kat and I had sat and talked. One glance around me as I sat and pressed the button, just to be safe. The unknown number rang three times before it was answered.

"Button," Dad's voice was strained and hoarse.

"I'm sorry," I started.

"What happened?"

I closed my eyes. *So much, Dad...so much and I can't tell you about any of it.* "There was a problem."

Dad's heavy breath was loud in my ear, making me wince.

"Are you still safe?" I questioned, hating how it'd come to this.

"For now. But I can't hide from them forever, Annalise."

I winced. He never called me by my whole name. I lifted my gaze to the dark clouds slowly moving away. "I'll try again."

"Button..." Dad said with a resigned sigh. "*It's done.*"

"No, Dad, *please.* Let me try again."

I heard movement through the phone as bedsprings groaned. "Do you want this, Anna? Say now if you've changed your mind. Say now if I need to run."

*On his own...*that's what he was really saying.

"I can make it so they never look at you." His words were filled with torment. "They'll have no cause to ever come after you."

"And what, sacrifice yourself?" I cried, hysteria a little too close.

"If it comes to that."

I closed my eyes as pain tore across my chest. "No, Dad. That's never going to happen. I'll make sure I'm there next time. I'll make sure I make it."

"Okay, sweetheart, we'll try again. And Button, I love you."

"I love you too, Dad." The words sounded hollow and strange. "I love you, too."

But the line was already dead. I glanced at the screen. Thirty seconds and not a second longer. All so they couldn't track him.

I shoved up from the ground and brushed the sand from my ass. Dad was in trouble and he was risking it all to keep me safe. If anything happened to him...I lowered my head and started walking. If anything happened to him, I'd be my fault.

I lifted my gaze to the buildings in the distance. It didn't matter what happened between me and Finley. Like Kat said, it was probably a one-and-done situation. I wrapped my arms around my middle as the wind picked up. I just needed to stay away from him and wait for the contact to try again.

Next time, I'd be more careful.

And make sure I was far away from Finley Salvatore.

29

Anna

I got to class just as the other students piled in through the open doors and made my way along the middle row of seats. There weren't as many bodyguards now. Not like there was before. Four or five hovered just inside the door as I slid into a seat. I was relieved Max or Pavlov wasn't one of them.

He wouldn't come to class.

"Anna," Evan called.

I smiled and waved. No, he wouldn't come, not with everyone else watching. "Hey, guys."

Xael sashayed in a few steps behind Evan, wearing her usual men's sweatpants and open baseball shirt. Not a sweats and t-shirt kind of island, my ass. But that woman took it to a whole other level. I swear she'd make a feed sack look sexy as fuck.

But they kept walking, making their way toward the other side of the room before sliding into their seats, Xael's thick Welsh accent drifting through the air.

"This seat for me?" I turned at Kat's voice as she slid into the seat beside me.

"Okay, ladies and gents," the lecturer called from the front of the room.

It was Mr. Former FBI, shuffling his papers before lifting his gaze and scanning us.

"You okay?" Kat murmured.

"Sure." I gave her a smile and turned back, waiting for a flicker of recognition as the lecturer's gaze settled on mine.

But there was none. He just swept past me without even a second glance.

"I so don't feel like doing this," Kat muttered.

Movement came from the doorway as Damon strode in. Kat stiffened as he headed our way and slowed at her seat to bend and kiss her cheek. I was absorbed by the movement, trapped by the way Kat seemed to shut down. Still, she lifted her head and kissed him back.

"Anna," Damon murmured, straightening to block my view.

"Damon, how are you?"

Movement came from the doorway again, but I was drawn by the way Kat became silent as Damon answered. "I'm good. Heard the storm played havoc on your nerves. I told Kat she should've brought you over. I'm sure I could've kept you both company through the howling winds."

The way he said it sent a chill along my spine.

"You have somewhere to be, Zakharov?"

I went cold with the tone and slowly turned my head as Finley sat down in the seat behind me. *Right behind me.* Damon's smile died in an instant. There was a sneer as he slid into the seat beside Kat in a perfect *fuck you.*

"Right. I want to talk today about something that might be a little close to home. Death and destruction, specifically aimed at the patriarchy and the unconventional archetypes that form within male-dominated structures that exist with the elite and dangerous."

A groan tore through the classroom, but I barely heard it.

My attention lay elsewhere.

Heat radiated along the nape of my neck as someone slipped into the seat beside Finley.

"Salvatore." The deep voice echoed behind me.

"Kilpatrick," Finley answered.

My pulse raced at the sound of Finley's voice. I tried to focus on the lecturer and Kat beside me, anything but the goddamn male behind me.

"I have some information about a certain someone," Kilpatrick murmured, leaning closer to Finley. "You know, for the initiation."

"He's all yours," Finley responded, keeping his voice low...still, not low enough that I didn't hear it. "I have a new target now."

"You want to share? You know the Commission thrives on getting dirt on the other families."

"No," Finley's tone was icy. "I don't want to share."

The conversation grew cold, leaving Kilpatrick to shift in his seat before finally saying, "So, you really don't want in on Rossi."

"Fuck off, Kilpatrick."

"Fine," the guy snapped, and rose as the lecturer droned on and on, talking about society's structures. It was enough to make the entire class yawn. But I was too busy being trapped by Finley's words as Kilpatrick slipped into another seat further along the row. Xael had told me the Commission was built on distrust, and that seemed to start here...in the Institute.

The initiation...

My mind raced with the word. I wanted to turn in my seat and confront him, to find out who the new target was. Goosebumps raced along my arms with the thought. Deep down, part of me already knew the answer. *Me...*

I felt it in the intensity of his stare, and shifted in my seat... praying for the class to be over.

But the minutes dragged on and the heat of his gaze only grew hotter.

Until it was all I could feel...

His breath on my neck.

His thoughts even pushing in on mine.

By the time Mr. Former FBI placed his notes on the desk beside him and said the words, "Well, I think I've bored you suffi-ciently for the—" I was already up, cutting Kat a careful stare.

"I'll see you later, okay?" I urged.

"Sure," she answered carefully with a frown.

My dress flared as I turned sideways and hurried for the door, triggering everyone else to get the hell out of there. I tore through the open door, giving Max a scowl, and strode into the hallway. They were already filing out after me, driving my panic deeper...*and harder.*

I scanned the hallway, finding darkness behind the glass panels of the doors. With my pulse booming, I lunged for the second door, shoved down the handle, and slipped inside the darkened classroom, quietly closing the door behind me.

My chest heaved with hard, consuming breaths. I pressed my spine against the wall, listening to the low murmur of voices as the others passed. Just wait...that's all I had to do, until he was gone and I could breathe.

But it was that ache in my chest that didn't ease, not even when the chatter died down outside. I waited until the hallway outside turned quiet...but then the handle of the door turned.

I shoved away from the wall as the door pushed open and Finley strode in...like he hadn't a care in the world.

"Did you think you could hide from me, Anna?" He lifted his gaze to mine and closed the door.

My cheeks burned as I stepped backwards.

He was toxic, a poison that burned in my veins. *One and done.* Kat's words filled me as I stuttered. "W-what are you doing here, Finley?"

His gaze raked along my body as he took a step closer. "Oh, I think you know exactly what I'm doing here, Anna."

Long strides closed the distance, no matter how fast I moved. I glanced at the closed door and his lips curled. *Try it,* the smile said. *Try it and see how far you get.*

He was carnal and all-consuming, hunting me through the gaps between the desks. "Tell me you don't want it too." I opened my mouth to say just that, but he lifted his thumb to his mouth. "I bet you're fucking wet right now."

Longing tingled between my legs.

"I bet you're sore, too." Those dark eyes bored into mine. "I bet every time you move it reminds you of what we did last night. How I fucked you."

"I—" I shook my head and smacked against the back wall.

There was nowhere else to go now. Nowhere I could run, nowhere I could escape him.

"Do you want me to take care of you, Anna?"

My nipples hardened at his words. His gaze shifted to my open jacket, his eyes narrowing. I didn't flinch as he lifted an arm and braced it on the wall above my head, trapping me. But my breath caught as he brushed the fingers of his other hand across my breasts. "I didn't take care of you last night." I shuddered at the touch. "Not like I should've. I'm ready to correct that now."

I jerked at the words, wrenching my gaze to his.

"Do you want that, Anna?" he murmured, and lowered his hand, cupping my sex through my dress.

I ached...*Jesus Christ, I ached.* But it wasn't in pain, not the raw kind of pain he delivered.

His hand moved between my thighs, pressing against my heat.

"I think you are wet." He clucked his tongue. "Do you think I should find out?"

His hand slipped under the hem of my dress before I could answer, his thick fingers pressing along my crease. I bit the inside of my mouth, stifling a whimper.

"How about if I finger this aching pussy? Would that help the pain?"

I closed my eyes at the words.

My knees trembled.

"I bet I could ease that for you." The elastic of my panties moved and he was inside, stroking, pushing. My legs widened on their own. I opened my eyes and reached for him, clinging to his shoulders. But he didn't kiss me, didn't make any attempt to hide my shame.

No, he just stood there in the dark, one hand flat against the wall boxing me in, the other curled knuckle deep inside me.

"Fuck me, you feel so goddamn good," he growled as a crack in his composure tore across his face.

Perfect lips parted as he worked his fingers inside me until, with a groan, he knelt at my feet.

"Let me take care of you, Anna." He looked up at me and met my gaze. "Will you do that?"

He touched me like I was forbidden. Like I was a secret. *His secret. One to keep...and destroy.*

One slow slide, and my panties were dragged to my ankles. My body betrayed me, lifting my feet, stepping out of the garment.

"What were you doing at the cove, Anna?" he whispered, and lifted my dress to my waist. He slid his hand along the back of my leg, lifting my foot until he placed it over his shoulder. "Tell me and we can put it behind us."

My hand went to his head, my fingers slid into his hair. I was already arching my back, my hips shifting forward to meet his mouth. A battleground existed inside me. Blood had been spilled, my battle cry filled the air, filled with torment as I opened my mouth to answer. My head and my body at war.

"Tell me," he urged as the door opened.

Giggles filled the room as a couple stumbled in, kissing, yanking at their clothes, oblivious to us. But Finley turned and lowered my dress. "Get the fuck out."

The guy jerked his gaze to Finley. His eyes widened, before they slowly moved to me. Heat burned in my cheeks before he shoved his companion back out the door, leaving us in the gloom once more.

A snarl echoed in the back of his throat as he lifted the hem of my dress again.

"He saw us," I whimpered, and lowered my hand. "Finley, he saw us."

"You think I give a fuck?" Anger burned in his eyes as he looked up at me, then narrowed his gaze. "Why, are you embarrassed to be seen with me, Anna?"

My stomach fluttered before he bent his head, his tongue finding my clit. He pushed my leg higher, parting my legs wider. "Are you embarrassed knowing how wet I make you?" He licked and sucked, moving deeper. "How I fucked you...*here.*"

I cried out as he slid his fingers deep.

"How hard I made you come."

A moan tore free as I fisted his hair. "Yes," I whimpered. "I'm embarrassed for you."

With a guttural snarl, he grabbed my hips and yanked me forward to meet his mouth. His head moved, sliding his tongue deeper. I couldn't stop myself, grinding against his face. My Mafia Prince. I had been his secret...but that secret was about to come out.

In that moment, I didn't care...not about his father, or mine. Only about how good he made me feel as my orgasm barreled in. I clamped my thighs around his face, burying him deep...*and came...hard.* He stayed there, his strong grip holding me still until he slowly eased my leg from his shoulder and rose.

His lips glistened, his gaze was intense as he leaned closer. "You think I'm the one embarrassed to be seen with you?"

I heaved harsh breaths. "Yes."

He just smiled, capturing my hand to press it against the front of his jeans. "I'm going to enjoy watching you change your mind about that."

30

Finley

She was embarrassed for me? I closed the door to the classroom and glanced along the hall, adjusting my jeans. Still I was hard as a fucking rock, desperate to be inside her. Jesus Christ, this woman was bringing me undone.

I dragged my fingers through my hair and caught the scent of her on them. My body froze, muscles trembling. That longing was a fucking animal inside me. It wasn't too late to go back inside, to make her eat those pretty fucking words along with the head of my cock.

The image of that consumed me, making me fucking shudder. Her on her knees, looking up at me as I pushed into her mouth. I wanted to own her, to have her in every way possible, to fill her pussy. *Not yet...*that voice in my head whispered. I wanted her scared, wanted her running from me. *I wanted her cornered with no place else to turn.*

Only then would she give into me, and if I knew Anna at all... she'd fight to the very fucking end. My lips curled into a smile, one I quickly smothered, and left her behind. I wanted her shaken and right now that's exactly what she was.

I strode along the hallway, catching the frantic thuds inside the classroom next to ours. *Constance.* That was the rich schmuck who'd burst into the damn room. It wouldn't take fucking long for it to get back to Zakharov and his band of fucking assholes.

Grunts echoed from the room.

"Jesus, I'm coming." The male snarl slipped through the door.

"What? *Already?*" his companion protested.

Yeah, the secret would be out in about two point five fucking seconds if that was anything to go by.

I smiled and kept on walking past the guards hovering at the end of the hall. Max and Pavlov stood at the entrance, cutting a stony glare at anyone who dared walk back this way.

"Let's go," I muttered, and kept on walking.

They fell in line as I strode across the foyer and out of the building once more. My phone let out a *beep*. I grabbed it and looked at the screen.

Dad: Make sure this call is secure.

I flinched, my satisfaction dying away in an instant, and lengthened my stride, heading to my apartment building once more. I typed back in a hurry.

Heading back to the apartment now. Will message when it's clear.

My gut clenched, and my excitement died. That message meant only one thing...*and it wasn't good.*

Max strode ahead and leaned into the scanner as I neared the foyer doors. His gaze was careful as it met mine. "Everything okay?"

"Fine." I just glanced from him to Pavlov, then stepped inside the elevator as it opened.

I lifted my gaze to my bodyguard as the doors closed. He'd never outright asked like that before, never *overstepped*. But here he was, treading the fine goddamn line. The feeling didn't sit well as I rode to my apartment and grabbed my phone.

I'm here.

The phone rang a second later and my father's biting growl cut through the speaker. "The fucking launderer. I want to know where the hell he is."

I swallowed hard, my mind racing. "I thought you had men tracking him down?"

"That's *not* what I fucking asked for, is it? The location...*now*."

But I didn't know the location. He'd slipped from Pavlov the moment he hit the mainland, sinking into the shadows, and hadn't surfaced yet. "I'll get some men on it."

A howl of agony in the background filled the handset. My grip clenched around the phone. "Is everything okay?" *Dad.* The word lodged in my throat.

"Five fucking million," my father growled, as behind him the screams of agony turned into words.

"I don't know where the fuck he is!" The howl of terror bled through the phone from behind him. *"I'm telling the truth! Please believe me...I'm telling the truth."*

Muffled sobs came after, low, sickening sounds. You'd think after all this time I'd have gotten used to them.

Thwack.

The sharp sound ended the cries.

There was only silence now. Chilling, foreboding silence that made my blood run cold.

"Five million," my father repeated coldly. "He has one hundred million of my money, and you think I'm okay with getting five?"

I didn't know what to say.

"I'm giving you five days, Finley...then I'll be taking matters into my own hands."

Harsh breaths did nothing to quell the pounding of my heart.

"What does that mean?" I asked.

But the line was already dead, my screen blank.

Still the chilling sound of a dead man's screams rang in my head. I lifted my gaze to the window. I needed her father...*that meant I needed her.*

Five days. That's all I had. Five days, then my father would descend on this island like a storm. One none of us would survive. I closed my eyes, still feeling the grind of her pussy against my mouth. The taste of her lingered, that ache a beast of its own.

I didn't have a minute to lose.

Not anymore.

I turned and stepped into the elevator once more, making my way downstairs. Max and Pavlov were still waiting in the foyer. Both men lifted their heads as I neared. "I'm heading to Building One. I don't need you for this."

"I don't think—" Max started, shaking his head.

"You don't think?" I repeated.

He became silent, searching my gaze, then gave a slow nod. "Whatever you need, Finley."

That was more like him.

What the fuck was this new attitude from him, anyway? I left them both behind and headed for Building One, hating how the memory of Baldeon surfaced again. First Mom, now Baldeon's second son. Someone was coming for us, picking us off one by one. The Commission were concerned and my father was calling for war.

But bloodshed wasn't just dirty business.

It was also fucking expensive.

"Anna." Her name slipped from my lips in a growl. "You'll belong to me, one way or another."

You mean my father's...right? Anna and her father will belong to mine.

I was nothing in his shadow. Not even a pathetic copy.

I pushed through the glass doors of Building One and made my way along the hallway, past the meeting room where the Commission had gathered yesterday, and headed for a wing hardly anyone ventured along. The air grew cooler the further I walked, until I stopped at a thick wooden door further along the back.

There was no card reader here, nothing that basic. I pressed my thumb to the scanner and waited for it to scan my fingerprint. Very few had access to this room on the island...and that was for a reason.

I pushed the handle and stepped inside. The dark hallway was short, leaving me to step into a large, specially built room. Monitors lined the walls, filled with images taken from every CCTV camera on the island. A guard turned his head as I stepped inside.

"Mr. Salvatore," he acknowledged me with a nod.

I didn't respond, just made my way into the small office at the rear of the control room and stepped inside before closing the door behind me. Everyone on the island knew they were being watched. If they didn't, then they didn't belong here.

Most were born with cameras shoved in their faces. After a while, they neither cared nor saw them at all. But there were still some of us that required privacy more than anything. But that was one of the joys of the island, wasn't it? *Nothing was off limits.*

I pulled the black-out blinds down and hit the lights, illuminating the computer and monitor in the middle of the desk. It was a computer hooked up to all feeds. One specifically available to a few. I was just one of those few. I sat, logged in, and brought up the feed of Anna's apartment building, narrowing in on the one illuminated apartment to watch.

"You don't want to tell me," I murmured. "That's fine. I'll find out on my own."

I knew she was getting phone calls from someone and I could only assume it was her father. That's who she was going to meet on the beach. *Then why come to the island at all?* The thought nagged me as I searched the images from the cameras in her apartment, watching on the live feed as she strode into her apartment and leaned on the counter, her head lowered...as though she was catching her breath.

Had she run all the way from the classroom where I'd left her? The thought of that made me smile. She pushed off and made her way into her bedroom. I switched feeds. Call it a fucking invasion of privacy...I didn't care, not in that moment. A thought rose inside me, one that sent heat through my veins. I rose from the seat and walked around the desk to open the door. "How can I get a direct feed sent to my phone?"

The guard swiveled in his seat. "How many feeds are we talking?"

I opened my mouth to answer, then changed my mind at the last moment. "Two."

"Two I can do. But I'm going to need your phone and I'll get it set up." He held out his hand.

I held the guard's gaze, then slowly unlocked the screen and handed it over.

"I'll get right on it, Mr. Salvatore."

"Thank you." I turned back into the office and closed the door.

There was more than a live feed of her bedroom I needed, no matter how fucking entertaining that was. She was sitting on the bed as I sat back down, her hand over her breast before it slowly slipped between her thighs. *Fuck me.*

I reluctantly tore my focus from her obvious torment and adjusted the commands, skipping to the recorded video. *Unfortunately,* there was no sound. The Commander felt that was one step too far, especially in the bedrooms...but that didn't mean there wasn't another device in the apartment. I rewound the footage to the night before, watching her moving backwards throughout the apartment as day slowly became night and she stumbled into her apartment in the early hours of the morning.

After us...

I hit the button and pressed play, watching her walk from the elevator to her room. Then I switched the feed as she dropped her backpack in the doorway of her closet and slowly peeled her clothes off. Memories pushed into my mind.

Her windbreaker hanging off her arms as she lay underneath me, then the slow slide of her panties as I dragged them free, revealing her body inch by perfect inch. I watched her now dropping the windbreaker to her floor, then her top and jeans as she stepped out of her boots.

Was she stunned...aching? A flare of panic tore through me. I licked my lips as the panic grew. Was this a good stunned reaction...*or a bad one?* I raked my fingers through my hair, transfixed as she shoved down the covers and slid into bed.

I wanted to be there with her, to take care of her like I should've done last night. I wanted to fucking hold her, to sleep beside her...*and love her.* That made my hand freeze, fingers fisted in my hair. *No...God, no.* That can't happen, not with someone like her.

This was nothing more than an infatuation, right? Nothing more than a job. My father's instructions had been clear. *Haunt her fucking steps, make sure she and her father deliver my money...and don't let her out of your goddamn sight.*

And she wasn't...even now.

I lowered my hand, catching the goddamn tremble as I rewound again, taking her past where she'd stumbled in, and kept going. The apartment was dark, the seconds the only thing moving as the time ran backwards. Then there was movement...from her bedroom.

"Shit." I hit the button and ran it forward.

She headed out of her room...but it wasn't to the elevator, it was somewhere deeper in the apartment. I leaned closer, intrigued. I ran it back, catching the movement once more. Her head was down, the backpack over her shoulder. *Where the hell are you going?*

She glanced toward Kat's bedroom, then moved deeper into the apartment, disappearing into the gloom. I scanned the other cameras, pressing each button, but none captured her again. So

I moved to the one outside her bedroom, and waited...and waited...*and waited*.

But she didn't return. I rescanned the others, clicking on the camera outside the building and ran it again from the time she disappeared. It felt like a damn hour until finally she stepped into view from outside the building. My mind raced, working out how the hell she'd managed to get from the top floor of the goddamn building to the ground without killing her damn self. There was only one logical conclusion, *she'd climbed*.

"Jesus, Anna," I muttered.

Goosebumps raced along my arms as she glanced toward the guard sitting in the foyer, then raced ahead, melting into the palms. I lost her as she ran, frantically switching from camera to camera, hoping like hell I caught sight of her.

But I didn't...she was lost to the night.

I paused the replay and leaned back against the seat. She'd avoided the damn guard and I swore there was sadness in her eyes as she'd slipped from her room and glanced toward Kat's. Whoever she was meeting with forced my little launderer to not only risk her damn life climbing down the outside of the building, but hurt her by making her leave her newfound friend behind.

I smothered the flare of annoyance at that.

I might not particularly like Kat VanHalen, but Anna did, and seeing her forced to hide and run from her pissed me the fuck off. I leaned forward as that seething knowledge burned, but before I switched off the camera feeds to her apartment, my hand stilled.

There was something she'd said to me the night I'd found Baldeon dead.

Something I hadn't been able to shake.

You said something to me. You told me you...touched yourself when you thought of me. That's what I want. It's only fair, right? After you saw me when you took my phone.

Saw her when I took her phone.

When she'd said it, I was too caught up in the moment, but since then, the words had nagged at me. I leaned forward, switching to the night her father had come to take her away, and moved the timing forward.

I'd instructed Pavlov to switch her phone with the new one, right before he followed her father and lost him when he hit the mainland. "Saw you when I took your phone, huh?" I murmured, and slowed the camera, leaving it playing.

She was in bed, tossing and turning. The whites of her eyes flared bright in the night vision camera until she closed them. I leaned closer as her hand moved, caressing her breast before slipping under the sheets. "Jesus, Anna."

I'd never wanted to invade her privacy so fucking bad and listen to her sweet little moans...

She shifted, worming that perfect body as her hand moved between her legs under the sheets. The control room office blurred into nothing as I watched her. She was the only one I wanted to see. Movement came from the corner of the screen. A towering dark shape headed for her room as Pavlov moved without a sound.

He was a former Navy SEAL. He was ruthless and dangerous. But most of all...he was loyal.

My pulse sped, my heart hammered, and even though I knew he was obeying *my* orders, my fists clenched as he slipped into her room and neared her bed. My eyes burned, unable to tear my gaze from the dark blur beside her bed.

She was oblivious, trapped by desire, left vulnerable by her own fucking heat.

The kind of heat that should be mine.

Pavlov didn't just switch the goddamn phone and leave. No, the dark blur stood there beside her bed, motionless...*mesmerized*. *My heart jerked as* the door to the control room office opened and the guard walked in.

"It's all done, Mr. Salvatore."

"Leave it and get out." I forced the words through clenched teeth.

Agony tore through my jaw as he left. Still, Pavlov just watched her as she arched her back, her other hand fisting the sheets as her orgasm engulfed her, claiming her senses.

She didn't know there was a man watching her.

A man I'd sent right to her bedside.

But the sonofabitch watching her did.

And he fucking knew better...

31

Anna

This can't be happening...

I closed my eyes with a shiver.

Not Finley...

Not now.

Of all the guys and of all the goddamn times...Maybe there was still a way out of this somehow? Maybe I could still save my dad...*but at what cost?* The tremor echoed with an answer. But it was the kind of answer I didn't want to hear. The kind of answer that lingered between my thighs and whispered only one name.

Save my dad, or be with Finley. I couldn't have both.

My phone gave a *beep* on the bed beside me. I opened my eyes and turned my head to stare at the unknown number before grabbing it and answering the call.

"Do you think this is a game, Anna?" the distorted voice on the other end asked.

The contact. It had to be. It couldn't be anyone else. An icy touch raced along my spine "No."

"Then why the fuck are you playing me?"

"I'm not...I'm not playing you."

"*I. Saw. You!*" he roared. I froze, unable to speak as a rush of hash breaths filled my ear. When he spoke again, he was more composed. "Saw you with *him.* You looked so cute together. But you seem to forget what's at stake here. Maybe that's my fault. I was too lenient, too soft. Maybe I needed to remind you what happens to those who get caught up with the Commission? No one is safe, not even their precious progeny."

A *beep* followed.

I pulled my phone down and tapped the screen, finding a message in my inbox. My damn hands shook as I opened it and stared at an image. Bright crimson invaded my world.

Blood. *So much blood.*

Baldeon's eyes were wide open, his mouth fixed in a silent scream. Dead...he was dead. I now knew what that looked like. In my head, Bladeon had been alive, screaming of retribution as they hauled him off the boat. But not anymore. The phone slipped from my hand, falling onto the bed before bouncing to the floor with a *thud.*

No...*no...no...no!* The scream was trapped in my throat, choking and hard, as that voice came through the speaker again. Instantly, I was lunging forward, dropping to my knees as I grabbed the phone and brought it to my ear.

"Now that you understand what's at stake here, I need you to be on board."

"I am." The hoarse words burned. "I am on board."

"That will be your father if you don't do what I say, do you understand that?"

I squeezed my eyes closed as the room swayed. "Yes."

"Finley Salvatore is nothing more than a puppet for his father. Why else do you think he's here on the island, if not to spy on you? Ask him, you'll see I'm telling the truth. Everything you do and say will be relayed back to Dominic Salvatore. If you don't believe me, check his phone, then you'll see I'm telling you truth. And, Anna..."

I waited.

"The next time I call and schedule a meet, you'd better be there."

"I will." The words left me in a rush as I opened my eyes.

"Stay away from Finley Salvatore. Before it's too late," the voice warned before he ended the call.

I sat there, staring at nothing, until my thumb skimmed the screen and I exited the image of Baldeon's face. Instead, I typed with trembling fingers, sending a message to the only person I could.

Dad, I need to talk to you.

I waited. Two seconds later, he responded.

Unknown: You okay, Button?"

Tears slipped from the corners of my eyes. It was just like him to only think of me. *Yeah, just shaken.* I closed my eyes and tried to breathe, before opening them once more. *I want this to be over.*

Unknown: Me, too. Wait a sec...

I waited, concern mounting as he didn't text back, until the phone vibrated in my hand. I answered in an instant. "Dad."

"Can't talk long, sweetheart," he gasped, sounding out of breath. "But I know you're scared."

"Dad," I whimpered. "I..." Sirens blared in the background, making me flinch. "Where are you?"

"Hiding in an abandoned house in Moris Dime. It's...dangerous, but safe from the Salvatores, I think."

Safe...it didn't sound safe to me.

"As soon as you make contact again, we'll get out of here, okay? Go somewhere nice, some-place we can lay low. Australia sounds nice."

I smiled. It was just like him to make me feel better. I swiped the tears from my face. "Yeah, Australia sounds really nice."

"Okay, I have to go, Button," he murmured. "We'll see each other soon, okay?"

"Okay, Dad."

The sound of the elevator thudded before slow footsteps drew my gaze. I lowered my phone with shaking hands as Kat headed to her room in silence. I swallowed hard and rose from my bed.

"Hey," I called, my words hollow and strange as I headed to Kat's room. "Everything okay?"

"Just tired," she smiled, and flopped down on her bed. "I've had this damn headache for two days now, can't seem to shake it."

I took a step closer as she lay her head on her pillow and covered her eyes with her forearm. "You want me to call the doctor?"

"No, I'm fine. I think I just need to sleep it off. Not the best roommate right now, am I?"

I sat on the edge of the bed beside her. "You think I care about that?"

"No," she answered. "Not someone like you." She shifted her arm and cracked one eye open, finding me. "What happened to you, anyway? You ran out of that class like the damn devil was chasing you."

The devil...yeah, you could say that.

I just gave a shake of my head. "Wasn't feeling well myself. I think I just needed air."

"You do look pale," she observed. "Maybe there's something going around."

"Maybe," I answered.

But deep down, I knew the truth. There was no sickness...not for me.

There was only Finley, and for him...there was no cure. My phone gave a *beep*.

I looked down.

Institute announcement: compulsory class. Building 1: Room 62.

"Now?" I moaned, and glanced at Kat's phone. But she hadn't received a message. She just lay there, her arm over her eyes, then she started to snore.

32

Finley

I left the control room and strode past Mateo's empty office, still consumed by the image of Pavlov standing over Anna's bed. I wouldn't go after him. That's not how things were done with the Salvatores.

No, that wasn't how we operated at all.

My phone *beeped.* I dragged it up and checked the notifications.

Call tracking information: Caller Unknown. Duration: 2.05 minutes. Message received: 1 in total.

I smiled. It didn't take her long to run to good old dad.

The burn of satisfaction flared. I wanted her running, wanted her confused.

I wanted her with nowhere to run to...but me.

I strode through the doors of my building and into the elevator, but instead of stopping at their rooms, I went higher. *Beep.* My phone sent another alert. With a snarl, I looked at the message.

Call tracking information: Caller Unknown. Duration: 1.02 minutes. Message received: 2 in total.

I stopped in the middle of stepping out of the elevator and scanned the previous message. Both caller IDs were unknown, but they were two separate logs. Two separate logs meant two separate cell towers. If that was the case...then there were two different callers. *If her dad was one...then who the fuck was the other?*

The elevator doors tried to close against me. I stepped out, forced myself to type out a message, and hit send. Almost instantly, there was a reply.

Max: On my way.

My phone *beeped* again. I fought the need to react and glanced down at an image. It was some kind of drug, the vial's label filling up the entire screen. The second I read the name, I froze...and my blood ran cold.

Sodium pentothal.

I exited the image and found the message.

Kilpatrick: You don't want to find out who killed your mother, then sit this one out like a fucking chump. But don't come begging when it's all done. You can run back to daddy instead...

My phone *beeped* once more. *Institute announcement: compulsory class. Building 1: Room 62.*

I clenched my jaw as I read the message. I knew it was him in a fucking instant.

What the fuck are you doing?

Kilpatrick: What you should be. Don't get in my way.

I jerked my gaze back to the vial. Fucking truth serum...that's what it was. Shit like that was fucking toxic. Goddamn initiation. It made us all fucking animals. But some more than others. Alexi had changed in the last twelve months. I guess his brother taking his own bullet to the head did that to someone. And just like that, the second son was forced to take his older brother's place.

That kinda thing could fuck you up for life. The only difference was...his brother had survived. Word was, six months in a mental institution had done nothing to help him. The fucker was still broken and dangerous. The first son was nothing more than a walking trigger.

Now his younger brother was taking every fucking attack as a personal battle, determined to find out who was behind it all. The elevator gave a *ding* and opened as I turned. Max strode out, hands fisted in his pockets, and lifted his head as I headed his way.

"Come with me," I ordered. I didn't have time to deal with Alexi's shit. But it looked like I needed to make time.

"Is there a problem?"

I winced, and forced a long, slow exhale. "Nothing I can't handle."

We stepped back into the elevator and waited for the doors to close. "Has Pavlov ever stepped over the line?"

I saw him flinch and slowly turn his gaze to mine. "Do you know something I don't?"

Didn't answer the question though, did it?

"Not that I know of," he continued.

"Well, he has...and he needs to be careful."

Max gave a slow nod. "Understood. Is there something specific you'd like me to discuss with him?"

We stopped at the foyer. "No, not yet. But I'll be watching."

It wasn't all I wanted to say, but right now it was all I had time for.

The doors opened as Max dragged his massive hands from his pockets. "You want an escort?"

I shook my head as Alexi's face filled my head. If anything, he was about to get his ass kicked. The fewer people who saw that, the better. "No. I'll be back soon."

"Okay, Fin," Max answered as I set my focus on the goddamn doors.

There was always fucking something. Always blood...always fucking danger. I dragged my teeth across my lip and headed for the door outside, chasing down the stupid motherfucker that was about to get his ass kicked. There was only one person I wanted to chase. Only one person I wanted to think about.

I lifted my phone as I headed for Building One and pressed the button, bringing up the CCTV feed to her bedroom. But Anna wasn't there, nor was she in the goddamn apartment. *Fuck.* I didn't have time to search the entire goddamn island for her.

What if she'd run again? Packed her backpack, and this time she's gone for good?

The text messages and calls. Two goddamn callers. *Two* callers. I didn't want to think about that. If Anna was gone, my father would see it as a personal betrayal. Then there wouldn't be a goddamn thing I could do to protect her.

The thought of that exploded inside my head. I raked my hair backwards, punched through the doors to Building One, and made for the lower levels. I knew the fucking classroom I was headed to, knew it all too goddamn well.

My jaw clenched...that fucking twitch was back with a vengeance. I needed to close this shit down with Kilpatrick and get out of there. I had bigger things to worry about.

Like keeping Anna alive.

But the sonofabitch had brought in my mother. The one fucking thing I wouldn't tolerate. Not from him...*not from anyone.* I strode down the ramp to the lower floor and along the hall, turned, and strode toward the end. Lights were on inside classroom 62. The door was ajar, even from here. I glanced at my phone and shoved the door open...finding the goddamn classroom empty.

I scanned the cleared benches, the weapons all put away. Figured. Plastic flapped and fluttered over the air vents. Fuck, it was hot in here. I yanked my collar as the heat moved in.

"I knew you'd come," Kilpatrick murmured behind me.

I spun, finding the stupid fucking asshole pushing off the wall.

"What the fuck have you done, Alexi?"

He just gave a shrug and stepped further inside the room. "If you're not interested in finding out if the Rossis ordered the hit on your mom, then I'll do it for you."

Rage howled inside me. I crossed the space in a blinding fucking blur to grab him by his shirt and yank him closer. "The *fuck did* you say to me?"

He was breathing hard, his dark eyes incensed with anger. He loomed over me, desperation mingling with rage in his eyes. He wanted to show me how much he *didn't* give a shit...but he did. He was fucking unraveling under that cold exterior. I saw it now, saw the fucking demon inside, the one who howled for vengeance. I knew what that felt like.

"What are you waiting for?" he growled, leaning into me.

For my goddamn father to give the word...that's what.

If he thought we hadn't entertained the idea that the fucking Rossis had ordered the hit, then he didn't know us at all. Thoughts of my father filled my head, incensed, consumed by wrath and calling for war. He was barely hanging on as it was. One fucking wrong word whispered in his ear and my world would be one huge fucking battlefield.

Alexi saw that...*he fucking saw that.*

And he wanted it.

I clenched my fist, desperate to punch the bastard in the face and leave...until I heard footsteps approaching along the hallway. I shoved him away as the door opened and in strode one of the rich assholes who hung out with Zakharov.

"This the right place?" the guy asked, glancing at us.

I jerked my gaze to Kilpatrick. "What the fuck is this?"

But his face was paling. He licked his lips. "Leon was supposed to send the message to you and Lazarus."

"Well, guess what?" I growled, and shoved the stupid goddamn idiot away. "Leon fucked up."

Still, the plastic flapped quietly as the thud of boots came from outside the door once more. I lifted my gaze to the plastic tape across the vents as the rage inside me turned to fear. What the fuck did he have planned? I jerked my gaze toward him, catching sight of something on the floor. Small canisters lay there. Two...*no, wait.* I scanned the room, finding two more, as the door swung open and Lazarus Rossi strode in.

"What bullshit class is this, Salvatore?" He cut me a chilling glare and peered at the rich asshole.

Until the poor bastard shifted nervously and took a step back.

"Don't fucking ask me," I answered, cutting Kilpatrick a glare. "I got the same text as you."

"Fucking compulsory classes, as if I come here to learn this bullshit."

Movement came from the doorway, a woman, small, petite, her long blonde hair shimmering over one shoulder. She lifted her gaze to me as she entered and, with a thick Russian accent, murmured, "Am I late?"

"Fuck no, you're not late," Lazarus snapped, folded his arms across his chest, and turned to Alexi. "What the fuck is wrong with you, Kilpatrick? You look nervous..."

Alexi just flinched. "No, I'm not nervous," he answered as the door started to close.

I glimpsed the guard through the glass panel just as a familiar voice called along the hallway. *"Wait!"*

My heart lunged, and panic bloomed inside my head as she barreled through the doorway.

"Anna?" I growled.

Her eyes widened with surprise as she slowly glanced from me, to Lazarus, then to Kilpatrick. "What's going on?"

"That's what I was asking," Lazarus snapped.

Then the door closed with a *thud* and the click of the lock sounded.

The slow hiss of the canisters was barely audible, but the sharp, bitter tang in the air burned my fucking eyes. Kilpatrick turned, grabbed one of the masks from the bench, and yanked it over his head before tossing me the other one. All of a sudden, the chilling grip of fear plunged deep.

I grasped the mask as the room started to sway. *"Anna."* I jerked my gaze toward her.

Movement came from the corner of my eye as my stomach rolled violently and clenched.

"Cover your fucking face, Salvatore," Kilpatrick barked, snatching the mask from my hand before shoving it over my head and securing it over my face. "Breathe, Fin."

I sucked hard, deep breaths as low, brutal groans filled my ears. Lazarus stumbled forward and shoved out a hand. *"What the fuck are you doing?"* he roared, wrenching his gaze to me, then to Kilpatrick.

I almost gave a shit, but I was too busy shoving him aside and scanning the room for Anna.

I found her on the floor, on her knees, gagging and retching, one hand over her nose. Through the blur of my tears, she lifted her gaze to mine. "Fin..."

"It's truth serum. I rigged it," Kilpatrick barked.

The petite blonde hit the floor with a thud and she didn't move. *Shit.*

"Anna, come on, honey." I pulled her toward me, yanking the mask over my head to press it against her face.

"It's too late. The drug's already in her system," Kilpatrick growled as he made his way toward Lazarus.

Still, the asshole didn't go down. He just gripped the corner of the bench, his unfocused gaze trying to narrow in on Kilpatrick as he slurred, "I'm going to fucking kill you."

Alexi neared Lazarus and through his mask, he asked the question. "Did the Rossis order the hit on the Salvatores?"

My eyes watered as I pressed the mask over Anna's face. "Anna...come on, *breathe*."

She did, but it did nothing to help. Instead, she just retched again, before blindly shoving the mask away. With a snarl, I yanked it down over my face once more and shoved up from the floor. The rich asshole was on the floor now, spine curled, his knees drawn to his chest, moaning loudly. At least I knew he was still alive. I pushed past him, slammed down on the door handle, and screamed at the guard on the other side. *"Open this fucking door! NOW!"*

"The truth, Rossi," Kilpatrick commanded through his fucking mask.

"Open this door!" I roared at the guard again.

He just shook his head, his muffled words coming through the door. "I can't."

"Fuck!" I swiveled to Alexi. "You're fucking killing them, you get that, right?"

He just jerked his head up and shook it. "No. It'll be out of their systems in five hours."

Five *fucking* hours. As I met his gaze, I knew...he'd done this before. *Jesus fucking Christ.* Anna released a low, tortured moan as her arms buckled, sending her body crashing to the floor.

I wrenched my gaze above my head to the fucking flapping plastic. I couldn't feel my damn feet as I moved, couldn't feel much at all as I dragged a stool out from under a bench and tried to focus.

"Tell me the truth," Kilpatrick cried, yanking Lazarus up by his shirt.

"Get the fuck off me," Lazarus slurred, and tried to shove him away.

But Alexi wasn't backing down. He grabbed Lazarus as he started to slide, and took him to the floor. "Tell me the truth, Rossi."

"No," Lazarus mumbled. "No, we didn't order the goddamn hit. You think we'd do that?"

Alexi froze, his hands still fisted in Lazarus's shirt. He let one hand go and reached for his pocket, dragging his phone free. One press of a button and he aimed the camera at Lazarus once more. "Who ordered the hit, then?"

"I don't fucking know," he insisted, then shoved Alexi away and rolled, his spine bowing as he heaved. "You think we'd do something like that? We're not fucking animals."

"Can't trust..." Anna murmured, drawing my gaze.

Alexi straightened and lowered his phone.

"Can't trust the Salvatores. They'll kill us."

My blood ran cold as she murmured.

"Launder their money and run. They'll kill us...that's what he said. Can't trust...can't trust any of them."

That icy touch moved deeper as I took a step toward her.

"Going to war," she whispered. "They're going to start a war."

I snapped my head to Alexi. But it was too late, the phone was aimed at her face, capturing every word.

"He's going to find where Dad is hiding. He's going to kill us all..."

"Anna," I croaked, and moved closer.

"The Ghost," she murmured. "They'll all find out I'm The Ghost."

"No..." panic roared in my ears. "Anna, *no!*"

"Jesus fucking Christ," Alexi muttered, and slowly lifted his gaze to mine.

The goddamn initiation.

He'd come thinking he was trapping Rossi...

And he'd trapped me instead.

There was only one thing to do now.

Only one way to keep this from getting out. Only one way to keep my secrets.

"Alexi..." I murmured, and stepped toward him. "*I told you not to do this.*"

33

Finley

I lunged and snatched the phone from Alexi, smashing it against the side of the bench with a *crunch*. Plastic shattered in my hand, shards slicing the meat of my palm before they clattered to the ground.

But he never said a word...he just stood there, stunned.

That savage fucking hunger gone from his goddamn eyes for now.

I wanted to smash him...no matter the cost to my body. He just cast a careful look toward Anna, moaning and gasping on the floor, and mumbled, "She's the Ghost?"

I sucked in hard breaths and stabbed him in the chest with a bloodied finger. "One fucking word, Alexi, not one mother-fucking word."

He just lifted his hands in surrender.

Goddamnit!

Anna just heaved and whimpered, struggling to push up from the floor. Of all the fucking people and all the fucking times.

"Open that door, or I swear to God, I'll shove your head through it."

"Leon," Alexi called behind me and the door gave a click before it opened.

I yanked off my mask and cast it aside. The petite blonde was barely moving. She was probably fucking dead. "Take care of her. It's the least you can fucking do."

"Salvatore," he started behind me, but I was already kneeling beside Anna and sliding my arms under her body.

"Can't trust," Anna mumbled. "Can't trust a Salvatore."

"Yeah," I forced through clenched teeth, and shoved up to stand. "I heard you the first fucking time."

She closed her eyes and let out a moan as I took a step.

"Hold on to me, Anna...just hold on."

I strode through the open door, casting the guard a savage glare. "If I were you, I wouldn't sleep...not for a very long fucking time. Because when Lazarus rises, you can bet your ass I'm sending him your way."

The asshole swallowed hard and jerked his gaze toward the male moaning and pushing up from the floor. If there was anything I respected about Lazarus Rossi, it was his murderous fucking rage, and these assholes were about to get a firsthand taste.

Thud.

I slowed, stumbled. and glanced over my shoulder, watching Lazarus wobble on his feet, then crash to the floor in silence. I switched my gaze to Alexi, who had a heavy wrench in his hand. Fuck me, there was going to be bloodshed, and my goddamn fingerprints were all over.

"Can't trust you," Anna slurred in my arms.

As much as I hated to hear the words...right now, I didn't fucking blame her.

I hefted her higher, still lightheaded from the gas, and stumbled forward. I moved so damn slow, only one slow goddamn step at a time. My stomach rolled, and my chest felt crushed, like a fucking ton of concrete weighed me down. Maybe it was... maybe it was my fucking tomb calling.

He knew...he fucking knew who she was.

Of all the goddamn people, now I had to deal with the fucking Welsh?

I thought about calling my father, thought about coming clean. Jesus Christ, I could hear his fucking screaming already. I was a failure in his eyes anyway, how much further could I fucking fall?

"You won't find him," Anna murmured as I forced myself to stride faster and faster, desperate to get out of the goddamn building and into fresh air. "Hiding...hiding in Moris Dime."

I lowered my gaze as she whispered. She didn't know what she was saying.

And didn't know who she was saying it to.

Ninety-five million dollars.

That's how much that little piece of information was worth.

One expensive fucking secret.

"Won't find him," she whispered, her eyes jerking under the lids.

"Quiet now," I soothed, and pulled her higher as I stepped out of the hallway and into the foyer.

My breaths were lighter, but my feet weighed down. Not as heavy as my fucking heart though. I lowered my head as movement came from outside the door. Mateo headed toward me, his commanding strides saying he meant business. He lifted his gaze, catching my movement through the glass doors, and yanked them open as I neared.

He took one look at Anna in my arms and his expression darkened.

"She's fine," I growled. "But you might want to get a doctor down to room 62. There's others down there."

"Jesus fucking Christ," he muttered.

I just barged forward, almost pushing the bastard out of the way. It was all his fault anyway. Him and every other motherfucker that sat on the Commission. Fucking rats. That's all they were, scurrying on a sinking fucking ship, desperate to bite and infect anyone they could on their way out.

The Commission was failing.

They knew it.

I knew it.

But until it shattered and fell, there wasn't a damn thing I could do about it. So I played my part of the first son and tried to stay away from their fucking games...*this time I'd almost made it.*

Sunlight hit her face, making her whimper and reach for me. Her nails dug deep into my arm. The goddamn slice along my palm was opening even more, pulsing and stinging. I could almost smell my blood. But I kept going, lifted my head to the building in the distance, and focused.

Step by step.

Whimper by whimper.

The doors to my apartment building opened.

The elevator was next. Max strode out, his gaze moving over me before finding her in my arms. "What happened?"

"Sodium thiopental happened."

"Jesus." He winced and jerked his gaze to mine.

"You okay?"

"Yeah." I pushed through the door and into the elevator. "But you might want to head off Rossi's shadows. They'll be gunning for someone."

"Is that someone you?"

I winced as the doors started to close. "I sure fucking hope not."

We were done, rising above the stench of it all. But we could never really rise, could we? We couldn't crawl out of that mold, couldn't not be what we were born to be. A beast was still a beast. It still had that same sickening need. Infected from birth. I closed my eyes and held her against me.

But Mom had tried. Her blinding light tried to cast the darkness away.

But it was back now...*and it was hungry*.

Anna gave a whimper. I opened my eyes as the doors thumped open.

"I think I'm going to be sick." She lifted her head as I carried her through my apartment, into the bedroom. She was already heaving as I strode into the bathroom, already turning her head. Warmth hit my arm as I eased her down to her knees.

"Careful now." I held the hair back from her face as she clung to the toilet.

The smell was sharp and bitter, lifting from my arm as her vomit splashed into the bowl. She moaned and heaved, her spine bowing with the effort. I pressed my hand against her back. Soft, comforting words were all I could offer.

Until after a while. the heaving eased...and the shakes started.

"F-fin," she cried out, her teeth gnashing as her body shook.

I rose quickly, grabbed a cup next to the sink then a clean wash-cloth from the cupboard and ran it under the faucet. A stranger met my gaze in the mirror, haunted, detached. Anna's words running a loop inside my head.

You won't find him...hiding...hiding in Moris Dime.

You won't find him...hiding...hiding in Moris Dime...

You won't find him...

Won't find him.

"I-I...I ca-can't s-stop sh-sha-shaking."

I shut off the water and turned away from the mongrel in the mirror. I knew what he wanted...and it made me fucking sick to my stomach. "Shh..." I murmured, and knelt beside her, holding her hair back as I ran the cool cloth over her face and across her lips.

She turned her head. The frown was instant, as confusion clouded those perfect eyes. "Fin?"

"I'm right here, Anna," I reassured her. "Right here. Here, rinse your mouth, let me take care of you."

She sank against me, her hands running up my arms to grab tight, the shaking lessened as she took a mouthful, swished and then swallowed.

"Hold onto me." Acid rolled in my stomach with every word. "Hold onto me, Anna, I've got you."

I held her as we sat on the floor of the bathroom, and pulled her hair back again as her stomach clenched with dry heaves. I rubbed her back when she turned to me for comfort, and when she was done and her clothes were soaked with sweat, I gently eased them from her body.

She looked at me with a detached, haunted gaze.

"It's okay," I murmured. "Let me take care of you."

She seemed confused...and scared. But then she gave me a small nod and lifted her arms so I could slide her jacket free.

"My head feels strange," she grumbled.

"You came into contact with something toxic," I explained as I knelt at her feet. "But you're going to be okay now."

It felt so strange now, not sexy...but still seductive in a way. In a way that was only for me. She was still my secret, only now she was the secret that led straight to my heart. She looked at me shyly, waiting for me to react. But I kept my focus, rose to my feet, and lifted her gently under her arms until she was steady enough on her feet.

"Finley," she cried, clutching hold of the of the towel rack with one hand as I sank to my knees.

I looked up at her and gently grasped the back of her leg, as memories collided. Jesus, it was only hours ago when I'd done this exact same thing. She looked at me with so much fucking trust as I lifted her leg and removed her boots, stuffing her socks inside before rising.

She gave a tremble as I reached for the zipper of her dress, lowering it carefully all the way down to the small of her back.

The thin straps slipped from her shoulders and I couldn't stop myself from laying my hands on her, spreading the thin fabric wide, revealing every inch of her. I stared at the bones of her shoulders, so fucking delicate, so goddamn small. I unhooked her bra, watching as she reached up with one hand to cup her clothing to her chest.

"I'm not going to have sex with you," I said as I gently coaxed her hand down. "If that's what you're worried about."

"Why?"

Why?

The whisper may as well have been a howl of rage. I flinched and fought the need to snap at her. "Because I'm not a fucking animal, that's why."

She just held my gaze, even when her knees started to tremble once more.

"Easy," I growled, catching her as her knees buckled.

She clung to me, her skin icy. "Fuck me, you're freezing!" I reached out, and turned the faucets on, then adjusted the temperature, waiting for the heat to rush through.

But I was too fucking awkward...to *unused* to caring for someone other than my own damn self, and when the heat hit her skin, she cried out, falling forward, her arms winding around me again.

"*Fuck!*" I barked, and tested the water.

It was warm...but not scalding.

Except, for her it was.

I swallowed hard, hating myself more than ever before. I curled my fists, aching to lash out and drive my own knuckles into the side of my face. But I shifted the temperature, holding her hard against me.

I licked my lips. "Easy."

She lowered her head to my chest and stepped backwards. A moan tore free. My fucking heart slammed against my chest. "Is that too hot, babe?"

She lifted her head and stared into my eyes as she shook her head. "No...it's good."

Her body shuddered and shook. I stood there, half holding her, as the needle-like spray hit both of us. It didn't take long until my shirt was soaked through. I eased one hand from her and tugged at the buttons, peeling the sodden material from my body, until it hit the floor with a *splat*.

She just watched me, those unfocused eyes suddenly sharp and clear, staring at my chest. I trembled as the cool, air-conditioned air teased my nipples, making them tighten. Then I stepped forward once more, reaching behind her to grab my soap, and squeezed some onto the washcloth.

She closed her eyes, her breath coming slow and deep as I ran it across her shoulders. She melted against me, and for the first time in my damn life, I knew what it was to care for another...*to really care for them.* While my hands ran down her spine and to the small of her back, I pressed her a little harder against me.

Suddenly, I didn't care that my two-thousand-dollar Givenchys squelched when I moved. I wanted more, craving her, desperate for her. My fucking hands were shaking as I pressed the wash-cloth against the small of her back, hating that I was using the pretense of caring for her to ease my own basal need.

The sound of footsteps pressed in, throwing me off balance as Max's voice called out, "Fin?"

Panic filled her gaze as she wrenched her eyes to mine.

I jerked my gaze over my shoulder, glimpsing movement in the doorway. "Stay the fuck out!"

He froze, lifting his hand to shield his eyes. "Got the doc here to check her."

I swung back, shielding her as best as I could, and turned the faucets, ending the spray. My thick bathrobe hung close. I moved fast, grabbing it and holding it out, and waited as she slipped her arms into the sleeves.

"I can't, Fin," she moaned as she closed her eyes and swayed on her feet. "I feel like I'm going to..."

Before her knees could give way, I bent and lifted her, carrying her with squelching shoes into the bedroom.

Max didn't meet my gaze as I passed. But the doc took one look at her and frowned.

"Be careful when you touch her," I warned and eased her down until her head hit the pillow.

She clutched her stomach and rolled as I straightened and stepped away, leaving the doc to do his thing. I was too tuned to her, too on fucking edge listening to the doc as he asked her questions and touched her skin.

"Fin." Max held my stare as I turned. "What the fuck happened?"

I kicked off my boots and peeled my wet socks free. "Alexi, that's what happened."

The elevator doors opened and out strode the Commander. He looked fucking pissed.

"Finley," he muttered, casting a glance toward the bedroom where the doc's voice murmured. "Is she going to be okay?"

"Mateo." I acknowledged him, and swallowed a shudder of rage. "Yeah."

"It went too far."

"No fucking shit," I muttered, taking a step toward the Albanian. They all whispered behind his back, said he'd suffered...said he was fucking scared. "You know what happens here. But you still fucking encourage the games."

"It's different this time...the attacks."

"The fucking attacks?" I couldn't believe the fucking asshole.

With a sigh, he gave a slow nod. "You're right." He stilled, closing down before my eyes, becoming the cold-hearted sonofabitch the Commission required once more as footsteps came from behind me.

"She's going to be fine," the doc reported. "I gave her a shot to counter the nasty side effects. She's going to be sleeping for a while, but she'll be okay."

"Will she need to be monitored?" Mateo asked.

The doc just shook his head. "No need. She's going to be out of it for the next eight to twelve hours, and probably have a nasty headache when she wakes up. But other than that, she'll be fine."

The Commander gave a deep exhale. "And the others?"

"The young woman isn't so lucky, unfortunately. I'll be keeping her in for monitoring."

Mateo gave a low groan before he turned away. "Thanks, Hugh."

One curt nod and the doctor left, with Max as an escort.

But I could feel the rage building and brewing.

I turned away and headed for the bedroom.

"Finley…" there was a warning in the Commander's tone.

But I was past giving a fucking shit. "Stay out of this, Mateo. He has it fucking coming."

34

Finley

She slept, and I watched her, pacing the damn floor like an idiot as the afternoon wore on and slowly the shadows took hold once more. I changed from the wet clothes into a t-shirt and cut-off sweats. Every damn moan had me striding to her side, checking her forehead with trembling fingers. But still, it wasn't enough. When her eyelids fluttered, I sat beside her.

"Anna?" I whispered. "I'm here."

She seemed to ease at the sound of my voice, and slowly, steady breaths took her deeper into the darkness and farther away from me. I brushed her forehead with the cool washcloth, watching as she turned toward me in her sleep. Even slumber wasn't strong enough to keep us apart.

You won't find him...

You won't find him...

You won't find him...

I curled my fingers at the words as they rose. Her face half bathed in shadows. "You should've kept that secret to yourself." I caressed her cheek with my curled knuckle.

But she didn't, did she? She has to unburden herself in my arms.

And now I didn't know what to do with that information.

I closed my eyes as the battle raged inside me. *Tell him...tell my father. Get our money...find those responsible for Mom's death, and go to war.* It's what any good son would do, right? It's what a *Salvatore* would do.

Her lips parted, her breaths coming harder now. She thrashed her head and threw her hand out from her side.

"Easy," I murmured, and brushed a lock of hair from her face.

But she moved from my touch, twisting in the bed until my bathrobe she was wearing parted. I swallowed hard as the opening revealed part of her breast, her soft, perfect, pink skin. I licked my lips and glanced at her face, only to find her eyes still closed.

Her breaths were deeper now, slow and controlled. But it was the sight of her body that drew my gaze back. The dusty pink of her nipple was fucking intoxicating. My damn fingers trembled as I touched the thick fabric of the robe and eased it aside.

Fuck me.

That tender flesh was tight and puckered, the tiny point perfect and hard. Christ, I ached at the sight. My mouth watered...my cock came alive. That fucking thunder in my head was insistent, forcing me to touch her. Warmth danced across my callused thumb as I skimmed the edges, then moved across the peak.

A moan tore from her lips, low, bestial...*hungry.*

I was already moving before I knew it, leaning down until I kissed the peak. But I didn't just stop there...I didn't do what any man with morals might do...*because that wasn't who I was.*

Instead, I closed my eyes and shifted closer, taking her deeper into my mouth. My tongue dancing over that nub in my mouth. I was a bastard. A sick, foul piece of shit that didn't deserve to touch her like this. I didn't deserve to touch her at all. Not look at her. Not even know she existed.

I'd dirtied her with my touch.

I'd tainted her with my goddamn need.

I'd fucking *ruined her*.

I closed my eyes as that echoed in my head. The taste of my soap still clung to her skin. I breathed in the scent and pressed harder, driving my body against her. She let out another moan, drawing my gaze, and damn me if her lips weren't parted with desire.

I rested my hand on her hip before pulling away, but the robe parted further as my hand slipped. Her thighs moved and her knees slid against each other before they parted. The hunger raged inside me. The beast that howled for blood. If I was anywhere else...*with anyone else,* I'd be terrifying. But here... with her, I stood in the eye of my own fucking storm.

I stared at the juncture of her thighs and thought about bloodshed.

"Fin?" she whispered, drawing my gaze.

Heat burned in my cheeks as I met her stare. But there was no confusion in her eyes, no disjointed and dreamy glaze as she fought the effects of the sedative. Her eyes were as clear as ever.

I swallowed hard. "Anna?"

"What happened?" she asked.

I brushed my thumb across her cheek. "What do you remember?"

Her brow furrowed in concentration. It was a look I'd seen many damn times. Her hunched over the keyboard as the rolling screens cast splashes of black and green and red across her face.

Her cheeks blushed as she murmured, "I remember us."

Us? It took me a second to register. Then the memory of the classroom came flooding back. Before my world was turned upside down and Alexi found out the Ghost was right under his goddamn nose.

I came back to the present and to her stare. "Anything after that?"

Her gaze changed, became more distant. "I remember sitting on my bed..."

But do you remember what you told me? That was the real question.

The only question that mattered.

"...then everything is a blur."

I released a breath as she narrowed her gaze and looked down at her bare body. I knew the instant she realized what had happened. I waited for the shock and the horror...but there was none of that. Heat flared in her gaze as she lifted her eyes to mine.

My length throbbed under my sweats. I reached for her hip, but instead of moving the robe back in place, I grabbed the tie and slowly dragged it from around her. There were no words in that moment, just pure lust. She lifted her hand as I reached for her. Our fingers entwined in a heartbeat, as though unconsciously we craved to be one...*always.*

You won't find him...

Her words surfaced again as I wrapped the tie around our hands. I unclasped her fingers and turned my wrist, placing my hand over hers. "I couldn't help myself," I murmured. "Seeing you lying there like that, like a damn fantasy come to life in my bed. I touched you, kissed you...I wanted you."

Her breaths grew deeper as I moved, rising to kneel on the end of the bed. "So, it's only fair, right?"

She was mesmerized as I pressed her hand against my stomach. She caught on, her eyes widening as I moved her touch lower, until our fingers slipped under the waistband of my shorts, finding me hard and bare underneath the soft cotton.

"Oh, fuck me," she groaned.

Christ, yes, that was the plan.

Her breath stuttered, her throat worked. Her hard swallow was intoxicating as I cupped her hand around my length. One tug with my other hand, and I pushed my shorts lower, letting her see.

"You wanted to watch me, remember?" My cock twitched as she fisted it tight. I wanted to come right there in her hand. "So...*watch*."

Her gaze was fixed on me as I pressed those perfect, slender fingers around the base. The vein bulged as she worked me, sliding the slick skin all the way to the head of my cock. The slick bead was waiting as I spread her fingers over it, smoothing the precum against my skin...just like her blood the night I'd taken her virginity.

Her breaths were harder now, deep, *plunging*.

She moved fast, leaning forward, her hair cascading as she bent. Warmth closed around me as she took my cock into her mouth. I'd never felt anything so goddamn wonderful. I looked down at her, brushing her hair to the side so I could watch her.

She took me deeper...*deeper*.

Consuming me inch by inch...and heartbeat by heartbeat.

But it wasn't just my body she claimed.

I closed my eyes.

No, it wasn't just my body.

I opened my eyes.

This thing between us had been brewing, brooding, and thundering, crashing with bolts of lightning with the kind of current that razed buildings to the ground. I'd known it was happening, the slow slide of my loyalty. It might've started that day we'd first met, while I'd commanded the brutal beating of a man who'd betrayed us.

But it was happening still.

It was happening as I'd washed her in the shower, as I held her while she trembled and vomited. It was happening now as she shifted her body closer, her hand trapped within mine, fisting, moving *up and down...up and down,* her tongue dancing across the tip of me.

"Anna." Her name was a hoarse whimper.

But I was too far gone, winding her hair through my fingers as I gently pushed down on the back of her head. With a brutal cry, I came in her mouth, bucking and jerking, spilling against her warmth. *Aching for more.*

I wanted more.

I would have more.

I'd fucking kill.

I'd murder.

I'd betray.

That slow slide had started years ago. But I'd been lost then, blind and helpless...wandering around with no tether to my name. But that was changed now.

Now I had someone to protect.

To save.

Alexi's face pushed into my mind as she gave me a soft lick and lifted her head. I'd smashed the bastard's phone, the recording was gone. But *he* knew now...he knew who she was. He knew *where* she was. And if he knew, then she was vulnerable.

And that could not stand.

I smiled down at her. But it was a cruel smile, robbing myself of that moment of perfection.

Because inside my head, she was already tucked safely inside her apartment, guarded and free from danger.

And Kilpatrick was mine...

35

Anna

"Let's get you home," he said, looking down at me.

I wiped the corners of my mouth. *Now?* Confusion flared. Had I done something wrong? "Okay," I answered, and moved away.

But he captured me, his hand gripping my jaw gently, stopping me cold. "You are more perfect than I deserve. I want you to know that."

My pulse raced at the words. More perfect than he deserved? But didn't he realize he *was* perfection?

Finley Salvatore, the god.

Finley Salvatore, the lover.

My lover.

Still, I couldn't stop the sting as I pulled away.

"Anna."

I met his gaze. "Yeah?"

He licked his lips and combed stiff fingers through his hair. "What would you say if I asked you to stay here...with me?"

Wow...

"I mean, it's closer to your classes."

My stomach sank.

"And you'd be safer. I mean, I could keep you safe. Here...with me."

He looked away awkwardly, combing his fingers through his hair again, as though he was...*nervous.* "You want me to live here because it's closer to my classes and I'd be safer? I mean, I don't mind the walking and as for safer...I don't think I could be any safer than living with a billionaire heiress."

He jerked his head up, fire blazing in his eyes. "You know and I know that means fucking nothing in this world." He winced, adjusted his shorts, and rose from the bed, only to turn and lean over me. "I want you here...period, and not because it's fucking closer to your goddamn classes. I want you here because...because I want you in my fucking bed."

"If you haven't noticed, I'm already in your bed, Fin." I pushed him, forcing him to face me...*I forced him to face himself.*

That desperation rose once more, like a beast behind his eyes at war. His top lip trembled. Dangerous. That's what he was in the moment...*he was dangerous.* "I want you in my goddamn bed every day. I'd fucking chain you here if I could. I want you to turn and I'm there. I want you to fucking hiccup and *I'm fucking there.*"

My heart boomed, filling my head with a thunderous roar. I wanted to give into him. I *ached* to give into him. I opened my mouth, and Kat's face filled my mind.

But it wasn't her smiling and happy. It was her the day I'd come back to the apartment early, only to find her curled up on the sofa, the shiny trail of freshly shed tears on her face.

"I can't just up and leave, Fin," I murmured. "I want to, but I can't."

"Can't or *won't?*"

Was there a difference?

"I've made friends here. Ones I can't just abandon." Even as I said the words, I felt the trap spring shut around me.

Finley just smiled that sadistic, seductive smile and rose. "But you were prepared to only days ago"

I tried to keep the panic from my eyes, tried to quell the booming in my chest.

"You waited for your father on that beach, ready to climb aboard his damn boat, even after we..." He inhaled hard as betrayal flared across his face.

Even after we'd...had sex?

Heat moved through my cheeks as I murmured, "That was before."

"Before what?" he snapped, pushing me.

"Before it all changed. Before *we* changed." The words seemed to pour out of me. "Before I felt this way about you."

He stilled, hard breaths punching through his chest. I waited for him to say something, to acknowledge what we had. But he didn't. He just shut down, closed his eyes, and swayed.

"Sure." I shoved the bedsheets aside and crawled out the other side. "I get it...I'm nobody, right."

"Anna," he croaked.

But it was all too late. Pain moved through me and turned quickly to anger. "Fuck you, Finley."

I had nowhere to turn, so instead, I marched into the bathroom and found my clothes in a pile on the floor. The skirt of my dress was damp, but I yanked it on and found my panties in the corner. I tracked his footsteps as he moved through the apartment, but he didn't come for me...*instead, Leale did.* Heavy pants filled my ears. I turned, zipping up my dress, and knelt, reaching for him. "Hey, boy."

He moved closer, pressing his big body against me. God, I'd forgotten how much I loved that...how much I craved it. I wound my arms around his neck and buried my face against his body, breathing in the scent of his doggy fur. "God, I missed you."

I pulled away and stared into his beautiful eyes. Love echoed in there. The kind of love that had no barriers and knew no bounds. The kind of love I wanted. Figured. Maybe if this wasn't going to work out with Finley, I could take his dog, instead?

I gave a small bark of laughter. But it quickly died as Fin stepped into the doorway. He glanced from me to Leale, and there was that tortured look once more. The one that said he was holding back.

That was fine.

But I wasn't...not anymore.

I rose from the floor, striding past him before grabbing my jacket, and proceeded through the apartment. Finley met me at the elevator and stepped in beside me without a sound. The ride to the foyer was painful, but the moment the doors opened, I was out.

I wobbled a little when the fresh island air hit me. I threw out a hand, reaching for the doorjamb. But Finley caught me instead, grabbing my hand. "Easy, hold on to me."

I met his gaze, that ache flaring inside me. Didn't he see I was trying hard not to do exactly that? But he didn't give me an option as he wound his arm around my waist and pulled me close. We walked like that, close...together. By the time we reached my building, my cheeks were burning.

Others had seen us...like this.

But the closer we came to my apartment, the more detached he became. Anger brewed under the surface. Even if he didn't show it, I still felt it. That coldness...*that rage*. I dropped my hold around him and stepped away as the doors opened to my apartment.

I took a step, then another, before realizing I was alone. Fin hadn't stepped out. He met my gaze as I turned.

"Stay in the apartment, Anna," he ordered as the doors started to close. "I'll keep you—"

But then he was gone.

"I'll keep you *what?*" I called, and rushed to the closed elevator doors. *"I'll keep you what, Finley?"*

36

Finley

"Safe," I said to the closed elevator doors. "I'll keep you safe."

I clenched my fists as my phone let out a *beep*. Guilt and desperation pushed to the surface as I dragged my phone free and glanced at the message.

Dad: Time is almost up, Finley...for you and the launderer.

I didn't need to be a fucking genius to figure it out. First son or not, I'd be disowned.

But he wouldn't do it outright. Oh, no. That wasn't the *Salvatore fucking way*. I'd be shut out, frozen from any kind of family matters. I'd be my father's son in name only, and that'd be all.

Instead of handing over the reins to me when it was time, he looked to my cousins, instead. My pathetic, spineless, weak fucking cousins who hadn't done a damn thing to earn the fucking seat but be goddamn born.

The elevators doors opened. Be born. That's what I needed to do.

But I wanted to be reborn anew, bathed in some motherfucker's blood...and take the seat for myself.

The thought of that filled me as I strode out of her building and pressed the button on my phone.

"Fin," Max answered on the first ring.

"Alexi?"

"He's in the infirmary," my bodyguard answered.

"Playing the fucking victim? The man has reached an all-time fucking low."

"No...he's—"

"It doesn't matter," I cut him off. "I'm heading over there now."

"Fin," he started. "Have you spoken to your father about this?"

Have I spoken to my father? "No," I answered.

"I just thought, seeing as how the launderer..."

My gut clenched. Panic shifted under my skin. "Not until I have something to go to him with, Max."

"Of course," he responded. "I'm here if you need me, Fin."

He ended the call. Still, there was a bad taste in my mouth as I strode toward building one, a real bad fucking taste. I couldn't ease that tension inside me, couldn't stop the thoughts from racing through my mind as I headed toward the infirmary, to settle this once and for all.

The doors opened to building one as I came close. Deja vu hit me like a train as I strode along the hall, heading tino the island's medical facility.

Baldeon's death was a little too fucking real right now. A little too raw, as the echoes of my boots rang through the empty hallway. I hadn't let myself think about him, not about the hole in the family he'd left behind, or as a...*friend*. If you could call us friends. More like comrades in the same bloody war. Sometimes those comrades were an ally...and other times, my damn enemy.

I lifted my head and pushed through the door to the infirmary. A faint murmur drew my gaze in the distance. The bastard was already whining like a fucking bitch. I clenched my fist until my knuckles strained. I guess it was lucky he was here. *He's was going to need a doctor by the time I was done.*

Movement came at the end of the hallway. The same doc that had treated Baldeon lifted his head from a file in his hand, took one look at me, and froze. I didn't slow, just slipped through the doorway and into the room.

"Things will change after this..." Alexi's low voice reached me as I lifted my fists.

"Damn right they will," I growled, yanking the plastic curtain aside, and lunged.

The scrape of a chair squealed against the floor...but everything else was *wrong*.

Alexi shot to his feet as the chair toppled. He lifted his hands for protection, but it wasn't for himself. It took me a second to see the petrified stare of the blonde in the bed. But my anger was unrelenting, punching through my veins like a merciless shot of heroin. I grabbed him by the shirtfront as his eyes widened.

"Fin," he warned, casting a glance toward the petite blonde.

"I fucking warned you, Alexi," I snarled as I drove him backwards. "I fucking warned you."

He lashed out in desperation, grabbing my shirt as he struggled us away from the bed and lowered his voice. "I haven't said a damn thing."

"And you fucking won't..." the words were more than a warning.

They were a goddamn promise.

The Kilpatricks were the closest we had to my mother's kin. But I swear to God, that savagery in me was calling for blood. Alexi just licked his lips, not caring about himself. His hands fisted tighter in my shirt and he leaned close. "Not in front of her, okay?"

I froze.

Since when did Alexi give a shit about anyone but himself? I glanced over my shoulder to the blonde in the bed as she gripped the steel railing and forced herself to sit up.

"No," she protested, her eyes fixed on me. "Do not hurt him."

I could almost hear church bells ringing inside my head, drawing me back to the past we shared.

"I didn't say a damn thing," he repeated, drawing my eyes back to his gaze. "It's not any of my business what the Salvatores do." He licked his lips as desperation roared in his gaze. "Fuck me, Fin. We're practically kin."

"That wouldn't stop you exposing me," I forced the words through clenched teeth. "Or her."

He flinched, and released his hold. "You really think I'd do something like that?"

"It's all part of the initiation, right?" I only drew him closer, clenching until the fabric tore in my grip.

He just held my gaze, sinking into the depths of my rage.

"You think I'd *ever* go after you that way? I've been your fucking ally from the goddamn beginning. All of that...*all of fucking that was to find out the truth!*"

He dropped his hands, leaving me the only one burning with rage.

"I stood beside you at your mother's funeral." He stared into my eyes. "If that means nothing to you, then by all means, have at it. But I'm not going to fight you, Finley. Not now...not ever."

The words were a blow all of their own.

And in my head, those church bells continued to toll.

One for every year my mother had been alive.

I could almost smell the cold, dank earth as I had the day we'd put her in the ground.

Almost feel that detached torment.

Almost feel that icy rage.

I licked my lips and forced the words. "You never heard what she said."

He didn't look away. "I never heard what she said."

"Your phone..."

"Is smashed and already disposed of."

I clicked my lips. "And the backup?"

"What backup? You know better than to have anything leading to any kind of external account."

I sucked in a harsh breath, and slowly unfurled my fists. Even if he was taller, I would've made him hurt. I just kept his stare. "Just as well, I'd hate to hurt that pretty jawline of yours."

He gave a cocky smirk and rubbed his chin. "It is one of a kind."

I couldn't help but chuckle. "Yeah, well. It was a bullshit stunt."

"I know." Jesus, he even looked remorseful as he cast the petite blonde a careful glance.

I followed his gaze, finding her gaze riveted on me. "I didn't catch your name."

"Leila," she answered in a thick Russian accent. "Leila Ivanov."

"The Ivanovs." I crossed the floor to take her hand in mine.

Jesus, she was small, all skin and bones, cold skin. It made me wince as I let her hand go. I glanced along her bed, then met her blue eyes. "So, you're okay?"

"Yes," she answered automatically. "I will be fine."

"She fainted, so the doctor just wants to keep an eye on her for tonight."

I cast him a careful glance. I hadn't missed the fact we had a murderer on the island, and the last place anyone saw Baldeon was when he was discharged from here. But as I met Alexi's stare, I saw the same haunting realization in his eyes.

"You'll have security here?" I asked.

"I'll be here," he answered.

I lowered my gaze to his chest, then further, to the waistband of his pants, searching for the bulge of a weapon. It didn't take me long to find it as he made his way back to her bedside. His shirt stretched taut over the outline of the gun tucked into the small of his back under his pulled-out shirt.

So, the sonofabitch was going to play bodyguard.

For some reason, that didn't sit right with me.

No, for some reason, I didn't like that at all.

"Your shadows?" I murmured.

He met my gaze. Something dangerous shifted in his eyes. "Will be right outside the door."

I just gave him a nod. "I'm sending over Pavlov."

He scowled and opened his mouth to protest. But I was already turning and giving Leila a careful nod. "It's already done, Kilpatrick. No need to get all gushy."

"Asshole," He muttered under his breath as he grinned.

"Exactly, brother," I agreed as I headed for the door. "Exactly."

I grabbed my phone and sent a text to Max, giving the instruction for Pavlov to provide extra security to Kilpatrick and the blonde billionaire heiress, and headed along the corridor once more. There was one more thing I wanted while I was here. One more thing that needed a special set of skills. As I turned right and headed for the control room, Anna's words from yesterday surfaced.

I pressed the code and unlocked the door before stepping inside. My boots resounded in the gloom as I made my way back to the operator. It was the same male as I'd encountered yesterday.

He lifted his head as I came around the end of the hallway. "Mr. Salvatore."

My pulse was booming as I met his gaze. "You're military trained, correct?"

"Yes, sir," he answered, his gaze narrowing. "Special Forces, specialist in recon."

"Recon," I repeated. "And if I ask you to pull up a satellite image, I can trust it stays between us?"

He licked his lips and inhaled, before answering carefully. "Well, it depends. Is this a personal matter, sir? Or does it concern the Commission?"

"Smart," I murmured, mulling over the question and its implications. "Let's call it personal."

One careful nod. "Then I see no reason to report it to the Commander. Especially if we're, say...checking out some hotties on the coast of..."

"Mauritius," I answered.

He gave a smile and swiveled his chair over to a computer. "Mauritius it is."

I moved closer, watching as his fingers flew across the keyboard, punching in passwords and login information. Before I knew it, he was pulling up a satellite image and narrowing in.

"Moris Dime," I urged, watching the image sweep across the city and zoom in.

"The Dime." The operator winced. "Not the place I'd look for a stunner, but..."

I licked my lips as abandoned ruin after abandoned ruin filled the screen. "Can you filter down to isolated buildings?"

"Sure can. Any specific one?"

"Just give me them all."

One nod and it was done. He punched in details in a separate window, panning out to track specific roads. The printer beside him whirred and started spitting out six by eight images of houses.

"I'll send a copy of this to a special backup file on your phone I set up for the cameras," he explained, punching in the details.

Barely a second later, and my phone gave a *beep*. I pulled it up, finding the file information displayed on the screen. He grabbed the printed images, tapped them on the desk beside him, and handed them over. "Moris Dime is a dangerous place, Mr. Salvatore."

"It is," I agreed, taking them from his hand. "Lucky thing danger is my line of work."

I turned and made my way out of the control room, folding the images carefully before tucking them under the tail of my shirt as I made my way back to the apartment. Anna's father was hiding out in some filthy, rat-infested building far away from the safety of his own house.

He had no plans to go back there.

And she had all intentions of leaving.

I needed to know why...before my father did.

For both their sakes.

37

Anna

I turned from the closed elevator doors and stepped inside the quiet apartment. "Kat?" But there was no answer, not a soft snore from her bedroom or the rush of the shower telling me she was here at all. "Okay," I muttered, and walked toward my bedroom.

Kat's bed was empty, the sheets clean and straightened. The maid had obviously been in, it was either that or she hadn't stayed here last night. I winced at the stabbing pain in my head. But even through the agony, worry pushed in.

Kat had been different in the last few days with Damon. I'd thought that with Damon, she'd be happy and glowing. But the truth was, she was the opposite, withdrawn and tired. Gone was the spark of excitement in her eyes. They were haunted now, surrounded by dark circles. She'd withdrawn from me. But maybe that was Kat? What did I know?

I made my way into my bedroom, tugging the zipper of my dress before stepping out of it and tossing it into the laundry basket. The throb in my head grew bolder. I winced, shielded my eyes, and stumbled to the window, pressing the button to close the black-out shutters.

Sweet relief came as the shutters closed, throwing my bedroom into gloom. I wasted no time crawling between my sheets and putting my phone on charge before I lay my head on the pillow and closed my eyes.

Darkness came to stake its claim. I couldn't fight it, giving myself over to the growing ache behind my eyes.

Finley's face haunted me as I sank deeper.

I could still feel his fingers on my skin.

Still feel the hunger in his eyes.

Still feel his hold on the back of my head and his cock pushing into my throat.

I swallowed and gave a sigh before sleep claimed me.

THUD.

The sound woke me. I cracked open my eyes and moaned. *What the hell had happened to me?* Memories were slow to filter in, until a low moan dragged me fully awake. I blinked, opened my eyes, and pushed up from the pillow. The moan came again, only this time it was softer.

Darkness shrouded my room. The blinds were closed, but it was darker than I remembered. "Kat?" I called out. "Is that you?"

"Hey," she replied, and stepped into the edge of the doorway, giving me a small smile. "Sorry if I woke you."

I yawned and stretched. "No, I was awake."

Her smile only grew wider. "No, you weren't."

She clung to the doorframe, almost like she was hiding from me. "What's going on?"

"Damon wanted to come over later," she murmured, the smile slipping.

"Oh, okay. You want me to disappear?" I shoved the covers over and pushed myself up from the bed, dressed in panties and bra.

"No," she answered quickly. "I was just about to take a shower and head out with him, anyway. Apparently tonight is cards night, some kind of boardroom set-up in building three where they play and drink...*and barter...women, as well as favors.*"

"Oh." I stilled, my mind instantly going to Finley. Pain stabbed through my chest, maybe that's where he'd been headed in a hurry. "Okay."

She just gave me a smile. "Missed you last night."

Heat moved to my cheek as the memory of what had happened pushed in. Something about a classroom...and a...*gas leak in one of the buildings?* I couldn't quite remember, Finley's words were nothing more than a jumble. But I hadn't forgotten the look he'd given me, like I'd just murdered his best friend. That was the kind of torture I didn't want to relive.

"I think I'll take a shower, too," I decided, and gave her a smile. "And I promise to stay out of your way tonight. I'll be quiet as a damn churchmouse. You won't even know I'm here. Earbuds and Netflix for the win."

She just chuckled and stepped inside, coming toward me before I knew it. She wrapped her arms around me, hugging tight. "I missed you."

I hugged her back, my gaze drawn down to her bare arm...and three distinct bruises across her arm, almost like a grip mark. "I missed you, too."

It wasn't the first bruise I'd seen on her. But when I pulled back, she looked down.

"Kat," I pushed. "Is everything okay with you?"

She gave me that laugh again, the one I didn't quite believe. "Yes, Anna," she answered, and met my gaze.

"Do you promise?"

"I...*promise*." She made a cross over her breast. "Cross my heart."

But that nagging feeling drew stronger. "Why don't I believe you?"

"Because," she said, leaning closer and kissing me on the cheek. "Under this mask made of meek and mild that you think is fooling everyone, you're a little brawler, aren't you?"

"A brawler?" I chuckled. "That's one word I've never been called."

But she did it again, deflected and turned, sauntering away, making me feel like I was prying into things I shouldn't be.

"My little brawler," she repeated, and disappeared around the doorway and into her own room.

I stood there until the hiss of the shower drifted to my ears, then slowly turned, making my way into my own bathroom. *Bartering women and favors.* Yeah, that sounded like Cosa Nostra to me. No wonder Finley was distant. As hard as I tried, I couldn't push the thought out of my head.

"You're a fucking idiot," I whispered to myself, reaching around to unhook my bra. "A stupid fucking idiot."

I was going to get my damn heart trampled by a stampede of pain.

I just knew it.

I washed and soaked, taking time to shampoo my hair.

Wait! The memory of my own voice drifted from the darkness as I dropped my head backwards into the srpay.

Anna? Finley's voice followed.

Fragments of images filled me. The bright overhead glare of the classroom lights slipped in, bringing with it a sharp, cloying stench, one that plunged down my throat.

Anna! Finley's roar was desperate now.

I lifted my hand with the memory of something pressing over my face. My pulse sped, making me slam the faucets and turn off the spray. I stumbled out of the shower, still dripping, and grabbed hold of the vanity.

"A gas leak?" I whispered, and met my own haunted gaze in the mirror.

But the memories I had weren't of a gas leak...

Anna, come on, honey. Finley's voice resounded.

It's too late. The drug's already in her system, someone else said.

Someone who wasn't Finley...and who knew what had happened to me. I clung to the vanity until the water cooled on my bare skin. "I was drugged," I whispered, and grabbed a towel from the rack. "*I was goddamn drugged.*"

I tried to piece it all together. But the moment I started, the ache in my head came back with a vengeance. Knots of agony throbbed along the base of my neck. I reached behind me, pressing and kneading the muscles as they clenched.

"I'm going!" Kat called out. "We'll be back later!"

"Okay!" I forced through clenched teeth as my brain exploded in agony.

I wrapped the towel around my body and stumbled to the bed. There was two of my phones when I sat down...actually there were two beds, as well...and two closets. I closed my eyes and lay back down. It was too much...automatically, I reached for the phone to call Finley. But the moment I pressed the button and stared at the blurry screen, I remembered what Kat had said.

Poker night and women...coming to my damn rescue once more sounded like a mood killer for sure. So I slid my phone along the bed and closed my eyes. I dozed, waking sometime later when it was still night.

The pain wasn't as bad, moving to behind my eyes like a damn migraine. I rose slowly, pulled the towel from my body, and slipped on a pair of sweat pants and a t-shirt. Finley's t-shirt. One I'd worn before that'd been washed, folded, and placed back into my closet.

I made my way into the kitchen and found a container of fresh pasta and carbonara sauce. I heated some up and made my way back to my room. A few mouthfuls, and I was feeling much better. My phone gave a *beep,* and when I looked over, there was only one now...which was a massive improvement.

I grabbed my cell as I stabbed the handmade pasta and twirled.

Fin: Are you okay?

I could imagine him now, dressed to perfection in black pants, and the open neckline of his black shirt as he texted me with one hand and cast a thousand-dollar chip across the table with the other. Heat burned through me as I thought about Kat being there. She'd look stunning...

I shoved the ache of jealousy aside and pressed the button, taking me out of messages to my Netflix app...*enter account information.*

Oh, that's right, a brand new phone.

I logged in my details as the sound of the elevator came. Footsteps echoed. Was she back already? I lifted my gaze, waiting for the...*I'm back,* from Kat. But there wasn't any of that...just the sound of a drunken slur, followed by a *slap!*

"Fucking dirty bitch."

I froze at the sinister snarl and slipped my phone into my pocket.

"You want to look at someone else?"

"No..." Kat's voice was barely audible. But I knew trouble when I heard it.

A low tortured groan came from her lips, before a hard *thump.* One that sounded like it came from the living room. I rose from the bed and made my way to the doorway. My heart was thundering and fear punched into the back of my throat as I watched Damon tower over her on the sofa. He braced one hand on the cushion beside her head and reached between her legs with the other.

A low, sickening sound came from her before the words, "Stop...*Damon, stop.* You're hurting me."

"Hurting you?" he growled, and thrust his fingers between her legs even harder.

"Get the fuck away from her!" I yelled as I stepped out of the doorway.

Kat just moaned, her head lolling to the side. But that wasn't drunk...*I knew drunk.*

"What the fuck did you do?" I cried as I stepped closer.

She tried to push his hand away, but the sick piece of shit just laughed.

That sound did something to me, shattering some barrier, and primal instinct roared to the surface. *You fucking bastard!* I took two steps and rushed him, unleashing a savage cry. I hit him with all I had, driving my shoulder into his side.

He stumbled, tripped, and fell to the floor. But I couldn't stop, punching and screaming until my throat burned. All I could hear was Kat's moan...and those goddamn bruises on her arms. Bruises I should've done something about. "I'll fucking kill you for hurting her! *I'll. Fucking. Kill. You!*" Hard breaths savaged my chest. I tried to breathe, tried to control the rage as I put myself between him and Kat. "Kat...go to the elevator," I urged her. *"Go right now."*

She just whimpered and sobbed as Damon slowly pushed himself up from the floor. But his attention wasn't on her anymore...it was on me. *Good.*

"You want to take her place, little Anna?" He licked his lips and took a step closer. "I'm down for that. But you know what I like now...drugged and compliant."

"You fucking drugged her?" I whimpered, fighting the desperate need to glance at her. His smile made my stomach roll. "You... piece of fucking shit," I shouted, then lunged, landing on him.

I clawed, and swung. But he was bigger, laughing and deflecting blow after pathetic blow. I punched and kicked, catching him on the shins with my bare feet. Agony roared with the *crack* in my toes as his smile faltered. I saw his true face then, as the mask slipped. I saw a soul made of tar. He wasn't just sick...*he was cruel.*

And I saw how truly terrifying it was to be in his way...and right now, I was in his way.

He lashed out with a fist, glancing my cheek. My head snapped to the side, spinning me with the impact, and that agony howled through my head once more.

"Anna...*No!*" Kat screamed.

But Damon was on top of me, grabbing a fistful of my hair. His menacing sneer blurred, so close now. "You want to fucking play?"

His fist came again, driving into my face as he held my hair. Stars burst behind my eyes with the savage blow. Screams filled my ears. But they weren't my screams.

"*NO!*" Kat shrieked as she kicked and clawed like a wildcat.

But his hold slipped. Fractured images hit me, but Kat's howls were dull now, hollow and warped. Everything moved slowly as I tried to fight the darkness hovering behind the bright sparks in my eyes. The room blurred as I kicked out, driving myself slowly backwards. My hand hit something hard, something that slid against the floor. I blinked, tried to think, and lifted it to my face. It was my phone...*my phone.*

Those stars in my eyes blurred my movements. I didn't think... *couldn't think* as the agony consumed my head and plunged down my spine. Movement came at the corner of my eye and a terrifying *thump* followed. My fingers were already moving, pressing something I didn't know as Kat wobbled on her feet...*then hit the floor.*

"Anna?"

"Please..." I gasped. "Please help me."

"*Anna?*" Finley's voice roared from my phone.

"He's going to kill her...Damon's going to kill Kat."

"What the fuck! *Anna, are you at home?*"

"Yes."

"Did he...did he hurt you?" I didn't recognize the voice on the other end of the phone. *Dark. Terrifying*. The thud of boots resounded like a heartbeat.

Was that my heartbeat? "I think he broke something in my face."

"He's a *fucking dead man!* Hold on...I'm almost there. Anna... *I'm almost there!*"

But I couldn't...not anymore. The phone slipped from my hold to smack against the tiled floor. All I could see was Kat, motionless, as Damon slowly pushed himself up from the sofa. The sound of his harsh breaths filled the room as he turned his attention to me.

"You shouldn't have done that, Anna..." He swayed and took a step toward me. "Now I'm going to have to hurt you too."

38

Finley

"*Anna!*" I screamed. But the phone was dead now...*dead.*

"Fin?"

I swiveled toward the voice, panic punching through me. Pavlov just stood there, hands fisted at his sides as he glared at the phone in my hand, worry hardening his tone. "What's wrong?"

I took a step toward him, stabbed him in the chest with my finger as desperation roared. "Do the fucking job I gave you, Pavlov...and this time, *make sure no one but me and you knows. Understand?*"

The former Special Forces operative gave a hard nod.

"No one else, Pavlov." I turned and lunged toward the elevator, frantically stabbing the button. "*And make sure he stays alive.*"

Help me...

Help *me.*

He's going to kill her...Damon's going to kill Kat.

With a snarl, I spun, my heart booming in my head.

Help me...

I tore through my apartment and shoved the stairwell door open, leaving it to slam behind me with a *bang!* The sound was too much like a gunshot, *far too much*. Stairs were a blur under my feet as I lunged, taking three and four at a time, and shoved through into the foyer.

Hard breaths claimed me.

But it was empty...*it was fucking empty*.

Max.

I clenched my jaw and tore through the open glass door and out into the light. *Get to her...GET TO HER!* The night was a blur as I drove my body harder...slamming my boots against the pathway as I raced toward building one and rounded the corner.

Movement came out of nowhere at me, stepping out of the garden filled with thick green palms. I slammed into something hard. Someone who seethed with anger. Lazarus Rossi's blue eyes were wild as he cocked his fist and swung.

"Fucking running from me, *Salvatore?*" Lazarus barked.

Hate burned in his gaze. Forbidding and infernal, like the blue flames of Hell. I jerked my gaze to the building in the distance and tried to catch my breath. "Get the fuck out of my way, Rossi!"

"Get the fuck out of *your way?*" His cold, controlled words belied his rage. "Get the fuck. Out. Of. Your. Way? You fucking *drugged* me Salvatore!"

"Drugged?' I jerked my gaze to him, shaking my head. "No...it wasn't me."

"Wasn't you?"

Every second I stood here...every goddamn second.

Please...help me.

I lunged, trying to flanking Lazarus, but the fucker was quick. He was so fucking quick, lunging in my way to slam his fist against my chest, driving me backwards. My breath left in a rush, hard and brutal, tearing from my lungs...and for a second, none rushed back in.

I stumbled, and doubled over, sucking in a harsh breath. But there was nothing, just a void of pressure, one I couldn't break. The world dulled around me. Movement came from the side, but still I pushed upwards, driving toward him as my chest blazed and spasmed along my throat.

"Anna..." Her name was a wheeze.

But Lazarus wasn't listening. He was consumed, flanking my goddamn side, his body taut and tensed, fists tight. "You fucking drugged me...*because of a goddamn initiation?*"

"Anna...is..." A thin trickle of air rushed in. *Kat*...the word didn't reach my lips. "He's going to kill her."

Rossi's head snapped toward me. "What the fuck did you say?"

"Kat...Damon's hurting Kat and Anna...*he's going to fucking kill them.*"

The color bled from his face and those piercing blue eyes darkened to inky black. "The *fuck* he is..."

Air rushed down my throat now. My head swam with blinding white stars as I gasped. "Damon...he's hurting them."

"Sonofa—" He didn't finish., just turned his head toward their building and took off at a dead sprint.

I shoved forward, senses firing as heavy breaths sawed deep. But Lazarus was like a fucking bull, head down, charging forward.

I dug deep, Anna's desperate plea driving me harder than I'd ever moved before. Building after building flew past until Lazarus lifted his hand and plunged through the thick gardens outside her building door.

"Open the fucking door!" he roared as I caught up.

The sensor flashed red as he slammed his card against the reader. I shoved my hand into my pocket, dragging mine free as a faint scream came from above. Lazarus jerked his gaze upwards as I slammed my card against the screen. The sensor light turned green and the electric doors opened in an instant.

Lazarus was gone, driving his body through the door and toward the stairwell. I was close behind, matching him stride for stride. That urgency howled as I shoved the door wide and plunged into darkness once more. The sound of our boots was thunder in the stairwell. Higher and higher, Lazarus took the stairs two and three at a time. Fire moved through my lungs as I grabbed the railing, forcing myself to keep up.

By the time we hit the penthouse floor, my legs were numb.

A scream came once more, piercing...*shattering*.

"Kat," Lazarus gasped, sucking in hard breaths as he raced forward.

I shoved forward, slamming my card against the lock of their door and in an instant, we were through. Damon was towering over both of them on the floor, one hand fisted in Anna's hair, the other wrapped around Kat's throat. Anna kicked and screamed, yanking against his hold, her eyes wide with terror.

Her shirt was ripped...the collar torn, exposing her breast.

"I'm going to fucking kill you, you goddamn bitch!" Damon roared.

Hate plunged deep as Lazarus took one step inside the apartment and growled, "The *fuck* you are!"

He moved like a soldier, head down, charging like a man possessed. Damon never heard him...and never stood a chance. With a roar, Lazarus hit him, tearing his hand from Kat, sending him flying. But the bastard's fingers were knotted in Anna's hair.

I lunged as she was dragged away. "Anna!"

Her wide, terrified eyes found mine. The look unearthed something deep inside me, something forbidden...*something foul*. I grabbed his hand clutching her hair as the bastard fell, and squeezed with all I had.

Something snapped under my grip, and a howl of agony followed. I pulled her hair free, leaving her to drop to the floor and crawl away.

"Kat," she whimpered. "Kat...*Kat!*"

Lazarus swung his gaze toward them, that bestial glare narrowed in on the redhead.

"You..." I growled and took a step closer. Hard breaths punctured every word. "You're a fucking dead man."

The bastard just gripped his wrist and screamed. Bent fingers, bloodied and broken. It was nothing compared to what I wanted to do to him.

"What the fuck did you give her?" Anna yelled at Damon.

Lazarus stiffened and whipped his gaze toward her. "What?"

"Gave her something," Anna whimpered, and lifted a trembling hand to Kat's cheek. "Drugged her...raped—"

Lazarus lunged, grabbing Damon by his shirt. "What the fuck did you give her?"

"Just a little E..." he shouted. *"That's ALL!"*

"You gave her fucking E?" Lazarus loomed over him, dragging the male closer by his shirt. "You gave her fucking E and raped her?"

"He's been doing it for days," Anna insisted, her eyes wild with rage. "Leaving bruises...I saw them..."

Kat just clenched her legs tighter and curled into a ball. "It doesn't matter...it's what they all do."

"They fuck...they...do," Lazarus howled.

The blow was brutal...and fast. Lazarus unleashed, driving his fist into Damon's face over and over *and over*. The sickening *crunches* filled my ears. I couldn't have stopped Lazarus, even if I'd wanted to...*and I didn't want to.*

In that moment, we were savages...in that moment, we were wrath.

Drops of blood splattered the marble floor. Damon didn't fight back...he couldn't. He could only take blow after punishing blow until Lazarus let out a primal howl of fury and stopped, his bloodied fist hovering in the air, trembling with need.

"Lazarus," Kat's voice was hoarse...faint.

But that one fucking word drew the monster from his kill and Lazarus Rossi turned his head toward her.

Kat sat there on the floor, one hand gripping Anna's, her eyes shell-shocked and glazed.

Lazarus sucked in hard breaths and let the mangled mess that was Damon Zakharov drop to the floor. His face was fucking ruined, lips split in several places, a busted eye socket that was already beginning to swell, and it looked like his cheek was fractured...in three places. But that wasn't the worst of it. Oh fuck no. The bastard was going to need multiple surgeries to correct what was left of his nose.

A sickening high-pitched wheeze was coming from him, one that made my stomach clench.

The elevator doors opened at that moment...and the Commander strode out. He took one look at us and the goddamn mess of Damon's face, and let out a groan. "Jesus fucking *Christ*."

Lazarus's bodyguards stepped out behind the Commander, and Max was half a step behind. I straightened as the Commander gave me a once-over, and moved his gaze to Lazarus...then to Zakharov.

"A second son is murdered and now this?" Mateo muttered, and shook his head. The stairwell door opened and two of the island's security guards strode out.

"He fucking drugged her and raped her. What the fuck did you think was going to happen?" Lazarus snarled, angling his body toward the Commander.

The Albanian just stilled, his brows narrowing as he cast Kat a glance. "Is that true?"

Anna didn't answer, just turned to Kat, holding onto her hand. "It's okay, honey. You can tell him the truth."

But there was something in Kat's eyes. It was more than detachment. It was total shut-down.

"I saw him rape her," Anna finally answered, turning to the Commander. "I heard her tell him to stop, but he didn't."

Lazarus sucked in several hard breaths and stabbed a finger at the broken piece of shit. "He's fucking lucky I didn't put a bullet in his brain."

"Fuck me," the Commander muttered, and turned his head to his security guards. "Take him to the goddamn infirmary. I want the bastard watched, no fucking phone calls, no *anything* until I say."

The bigger of the guards gave a nod, then turned his attention to Lazarus.

But Lazarus's men were at his sides, and no one was passing... not until Rossi gave the order.

"I want to end you," Lazarus snarled, clenching a fist. "I want to fucking beat you until I'm the last fucking thing you ever see, then I want to dump you in the water, still alive...and watch the goddamn sharks feed."

A shiver raced along my spine at the words. "And I'll be right there," I added. "Watching every goddamn second."

"No," Kat whispered, and slowly shook her head. "Let him live. Lazarus..."

Rossi's first son turned toward her. "Yeah?"

She licked her lips and slid her hand from Anna's, commanding with a stony look, "Get me out of here."

I'd never seen anyone command Lazarus like she did. In an instant, his focus wasn't on the mutilated almost-dead man at his feet, *but on her.* He cast a last glance at Damon and turned toward her, taking two strides until he crouched at her side where she still huddled against the sofa.

One of his men moved to help. "Don't fucking touch her," Lazarus snapped, stopping the bodyguard cold.

With deliberate, gentle movements, he slid one hand under her knees and circled her torso with the other. "Hold on...hold on to me," he urged, and grimaced.

The male looked awkward and way out of his fucking depth as he lifted Kat and angled her against his chest. But there wasn't a damn word spoken as he strode across the apartment and headed for the elevator. His men were right there with him, half a step away. One stabbed the button for the elevator, then tugged off his jacket and draped it over her as the doors opened.

I turned my focus to Anna, but she was already moving, shoving up from the floor and gripping her torn shirt closed. *No, not her shirt, my shirt, the one I'd wanted her to have.* Her damn legs shook as she stepped forward, coming face to face with the Commander, and stared him in the eyes. "She gets seen by the doctor before that piece of shit."

"His injuries—" the Albanian started.

Then she curled her lip, baring her teeth. "Think very hard about your next words, Commander."

Fuck. Me.

A shiver raced along my skin. This was no quiet nobody, no regular millionaire heiress, either. I *knew* who she really was— the most skilled money launderer we ever knew of, brilliant, not just in her ability to navigate the US Treasury but to outsmart, and outplay every other two-bit hacker who had tried to take us down—and so did the Commander.

He stilled, those careful eyes boring into hers before he gave a small nod. "Taking into account the severity—"

Anna didn't even wait for him to finish his sentence. Instead, she glanced toward where the island's security guards stood over the whimpering piece of shit.

"I'm going to fucking *end you!*" Damon howled as the guards lifted him to his feet. "I'll bury you, I'll bury you so goddamn deep. I'll use every penny I have to do it if I have to." He wobbled with rage, clawing hold of the guards as Anna stepped closer. "You...*you* fucking *bitch*."

She just stood in front of him, all five-foot-five of her, and lifted her gaze to his. "Imagine you woke up one day and all your money was gone...*poof,* just like that."

He paled, but it did nothing to ease the pure hatred in his gaze. "That's *never* going to happen."

She just gave a smile, one that was savagely malicious...and filled with dogged determination. "Never say never, asshole."

They carried him toward the elevator, each step filled with whimpering, threats, and howls of pain. I just stood there, not really knowing what to say. "I came to rescue you."

She waited for the Commander to leave and glanced at Max before answering. "You did."

I took a look around at the shoved aside sofa and blood splatter on the floor. "Wanna get out of here?"

She gave me a smile then, one that was fragile and sad...and the Anna I knew. "I thought you'd never ask."

39

Anna

Finley looked at me like I was a stranger, glancing from me to Max and back again.

"I'll be in the foyer when you need me," his bodyguard murmured, and cast me a glance before nodding. "Anna."

As he followed the Commander when the elevator doors opened, my shaking hands clutched the torn t-shirt across my chest.

I waited for them to leave, unable to move a muscle. But the moment the doors closed, leaving us in silence, I shuddered so hard my knees buckled.

Finley rushed forward to catch me. "I got you," he murmured, holding me against him.

Tears started, blurring my vision as I wrapped my arms around him and buried my face into his chest.

"Let it all out, baby," he soothed as a sob tore free.

My head was screaming. The muscles along the back of my head, knotted and angry, were throwing fists of fury against the inside of my skull. I clung to him, giving into the panic and the terror that'd held me hostage. "I thought...I thought he was going to kill us."

Hard muscles bulged under my hands. He slid his finger under my chin and forced my gaze to his.

"That's *never* going to happen."

There was truth in his eyes, the kind I'd never seen before. Steely. *Lethal.* Then he lowered his head and kissed me. I closed my eyes to the feel of his lips and the warmth of his body. Gone was that fleeting flare of jealousy I'd felt only minutes ago. I didn't care about any damn poker night...I didn't care about anything other than the fact he was here...*with me.*

Curled knuckles grazed along my jaw as he took my mouth. That tremble inside turned into a wildfire, one that burned through what little control I had left. I threw my arms around his neck and pulled him into me. His hands were everywhere, sliding up my back to my shoulders. I stiffened and groaned as he touched the back of my neck, pulling away.

Concern darkened his gaze. "What is it?"

I winced, my fingers probing the base of my skull. "My head, the pain..."

"Jesus, Anna," he snapped, and gently pressed against my neck. "Did you fall? Did you hit your head?"

I could already feel the throb in my face, my eye was already tight...and starting to swell. "He punched me."

Merciless rage made him freeze. "Where?"

I pressed gently against my cheekbone and whimpered.

"Motherfucker."

He gently turned my head and scanned every inch of me. "Here?" He touched my eyebrow.

I gave a careful nod.

"He busted your fucking eye." He left me then, striding into the kitchen and yanking open the freezer, then grabbed a clean dishtowel, wrapping up a handful of ice cubes before coming back. "Here." He pressed the icepack against my eye. "Tell me what you want to bring."

He strode into my bedroom like a man possessed, throwing my bag onto the bed with a *thud*. Clothes flew from my closet, sailing through the air to land on my bed. I watched the frenzy in horror. "What are you doing?"

"What does it look like?" He forced through clenched teeth. "Packing your shit."

"Why?"

He stilled, then spun. *"Why? Why?* Because...because you... *belong...with...me."*

I'd never seen him so frantic, never seen him so consumed by fear.

"Because you're not leaving, not now...*not ever."* He said the last words under his breath before he turned back to the task of filling my suitcase. But I heard them.

I'd tried...tried to get us away from them...*the Salvatores*. I'd tried to protect us. Dad was waiting, depending on me to do the right thing...and here I was, doing the complete opposite. When Finley was finished decimating my wardrobe, he disappeared into the bathroom, reappearing seconds later with his arms full of my toiletries, and tossed them into the suitcase right on top of my clothes.

"Finley."

He didn't stop, just disappeared into the bathroom once more and cast more of my stuff into the bag before yanking the zipper closed. But my clothes were sticking out the side, catching in the zipper.

"*FUCK!*" he roared, and punched it.

Honestly, if he'd had a weapon, I was sure he'd have emptied the clip into my brand new Valentino.

He just stopped, breathing hard, his hands braced against the suitcase, and turned his head to me. "I can't do this."

My heart dropped.

"I can't live like this, not knowing you're vulnerable." He straightened, then strode toward me. "I can't lose you too."

Cracks formed in my heart, shattering my resolve like fine china. All I saw was his pain, his loneliness...the void his mother had left behind. I lowered the ice from my face, wrapping my arms around him as we came together. "You're not going to lose me," I murmured, meeting his lips. "Never going to lose me."

The deal was already done.

My heart, my body...my soul.

Were his.

I kissed him, touching him, and realized something that shook me to the core. My heart had only two settings, all or nothing. There was no in-between. When it came to Finley, he held it in his hands. "I love you."

He froze, lips loving mine, stealing breath from my lungs, and slowly pulled back. "What did you just say?"

There was no stopping now, no saving my heart anymore. It was destined to be ruined by this Mafia Prince.

This First Son of a powerful Mafia family.

I tried not to think about that. Not about the implications of what that might mean.

Whatever happened between us after this moment would be up to fate.

"I love you, too, Anna."

I sucked in a hard breath and searched his gaze. "You do?"

"Yeah. I do."

He kissed me, reached down to grab the towel filled with ice, and pressed it to my cheek. "Now hold the damn ice to your face so I can get you the hell out of here."

I felt giddy as he turned and grabbed my suitcase, then my laptop and phone. "Everything else can wait."

He strode from my room, carrying my overstuffed, half-zipped suitcase with him.

We made our way through the apartment, my gaze shifting to the mess in the living room.

"Hey," Fin called, drawing my attention. "Before we really do this...let's just get one thing straight."

Panic flared as I followed him to the elevator, watching as he punched the button and turned toward me. "Keep your possessive mitts off my damn dog. No funny ideas about claiming him. The pain in the ass is mine."

He gave me a small smirk as the elevator opened.

"How did you know?" I muttered as I followed him inside.

"Because, Anna...I know a lot more about you than you might think."

But there was no smirk now, just a steely determination. One that made me break his gaze and look away.

40

Finley

"Wait," I barked as the elevator doors opened to my apartment.

Anna just turned, already halfway out of the elevator, and her brows rose as she stepped to the side. "Okay."

I gave her a smile and strode forward. "Leale!" I called.

The big lug heaved himself up from his lambswool-cushioned bed against the window and gave a shake, stretching and yawning.

"Look who's come to stay with us," I urged, hating myself just a little fucking more.

"Leale," Anna called. "Come here, boy!"

He strode forward, walking painfully slow, and lifted his gaze to mine as if to say *make up your mind, will you?* I gave a jerk of my head toward her and muttered, "Just do your fucking duty."

The padding of paws slipped behind me, a groan of affection came from Anna a moment later. "Hey, there," she murmured. I didn't need to look to know she had her arms wrapped around his neck and was hugging him fiercely. *I was counting on it.*

I strode to the bedroom, dropped her suitcase on the bed, and watched a shirt slip free of the partially open zipper. Moving fast, I strode toward the island in the kitchen. My gaze moved to the spread of photographs, ones I had printed only hours before...ones I'd showed Pavlov as I gave him instructions. My gut clenched as I swiped my hand across the slick surface, gathering them all in one sweep, and strode toward the office.

"Everything okay?" Anna called.

"Fine, just putting away dirty underwear," I lied.

Because it came so fucking natural.

I strode through the doorway of the office and turned to the small safe embedded in the wall. One press of my thumb, and the lock released, leaving me to yank the door open and shove the black and white surveillance images inside.

"Must be pretty bad," she murmured from the doorway as I pushed the door closed and twisted the lock. "If you have to lock them in the safe."

I forced a chuckle and shook my head. "Busted."

Her gaze moved to the safe behind me as I stepped toward her, grabbing her hand to lead her away. "How about we get you cleaned up and into some fresh clothes, and I can take a look at what that bastard did to you?"

She didn't move at first, her focus firmly fixed on the safe filled with my secrets. Secrets that would ruin her...*secrets that would ruin* us. Then she finally gave in, allowing me to lead her from the office, past the open shutters, and into the expansive bedroom.

The island glittered tonight. Stars sparkled through the panoramic windows as I led her into our room...*our room.* Something trembled in my chest at the words. "A warm shower, then fresh clothes."

She just looked down at her shirt, pain slashing across her face. "He ruined your shirt."

"I have a hundred more for you to wear," I answered, pulling her into my arms. "If need be, I'll buy the entire fucking brand."

But it was more than the shirt, and more than the cost to replace it. I saw the flare of pain as she clenched her jaw. Fire blazed inside her, one that wouldn't be quenched in a hurry. "It's okay," she whispered, stepping away from my hold, and headed for the bathroom. "You won't need to buy anymore."

The words were ominous. Still, I started to follow, taking a step.

"I'm okay, Fin," she said, stopping me in my tracks.

But I couldn't help but linger in the damn doorway as she turned her back, easing the shirt along one arm, then the other, before tugging it over her head. The faint beginnings of a bruise along her side made me let out a savage sound.

She stilled, then slowly turned, revealing the darkening mark inch by inch. I couldn't look at it, couldn't look at her, not the perfect span of her belly, or the gorgeous tilt of her breasts. I couldn't look at her without wanting to put a bullet through Zakharov's head once and for fucking all.

So I turned, leaving her to shower in peace without me hovering like a fucking idiot. Instead, I did what I did best. I fucked things up a little more and grabbed my phone, sending a message to Pavlov. *Status update.*

Pavlov: Target acquired. Waiting to make contact.

Waiting to make contact. Any moment now...any goddamn moment. The hiss of the shower drew my attention. I rounded the island and opened the refrigerator. Was she hungry?

Thirsty? Did she need...chocolate and a damn movie? Did she want me to talk to her...or pretend none of this happened?

I raked my fingers through my hair as my thoughts collided. What the fuck was I doing? I didn't know how to help someone like Anna. I didn't know a fucking thing about taking care of her needs. I thought of Mom, and all the times I'd found her alone, quiet, with fresh tears in her eyes. I knew about the other women he had, knew about the whores, too. I knew all about his fetish to inflict pain.

Sometimes, being the first son was staring into the eyes of the monster you'd eventually become and hating yourself even more. A quiet stillness came over me at the thought, like the heavy weight I'd been fighting all this time finally settled. *Click, click, click.* Locks engaged as a knowing was born inside me, one that made something deep inside me squirm with unease. But that chilling stillness hunted it down, strangling the worry with a savage grip.

Beep.

I glanced down and grabbed my phone.

Dad: We need to talk.

Didn't we always? A twitch came at the corner of my mouth as the phone rang a second later.

"You don't fucking reply to my messages anymore?" my father snapped.

"I answered the call, didn't I?"

There was a low snarl on the other end of the line. "You've made no fucking progress. You don't answer my *fucking* calls. What the fuck is going on over there? You think this is a goddamn *holiday?*"

I said nothing. That quiet resolve hardening anything that'd once been soft and vulnerable.

Hard breaths replaced the snarl as the bull on the other end of the phone growled. "Where the fuck is the launderer, Finley? I'm starting to get a real bad fucking feeling about this...*a real bad feeling*, and you know what happens next."

I knew what happened next. I knew he'd react like he always did, and it wouldn't be good for any of us...especially that aching thing that pulsed in my chest. I just lifted my gaze to the bedroom doorway, listening to Anna in the shower. "I know what happens."

Blood happened.

And death...

And loss.

"You'll get your money," I finished.

"You have two fucking days, Finley. Then I'm sending in a team. I'll take the girl. I'll find the father...then we'll be looking for a new way to clean."

A new way to clean.

Because Anna and her dad would be dead.

"I understand," I answered carefully. "All too well."

"You'd better," he snapped, and ended the call.

The rush of the shower was all I heard as I lowered the phone. I stared into the refrigerator and pulled out what I knew, hoping like hell she didn't see me for the fucking idiot I was.

I busied myself pulling out a chopping board, a knife, and ingredients from the pantry and set to work. Precision was the key here...it was all skill as I placed the main element on the board, slicing, spreading, forcing every damn inch of it as I slaved away.

And when I was done, I stopped and lifted my head as Anna stepped out of the doorway of my bedroom, her hair damp and piled into a messy bun on top of her head. She wore one of my shirts. Clean, navy. the soft cotton hugging the peaks of her breasts. Her face was still flushed from the shower, her lips pink and full as she took a step closer and stared at my masterpiece. Suddenly, under her gaze I wasn't so sure anymore.

"You made that for me?" she murmured as she met my gaze.

"Yeah...I did. Took all my skill, too," I bragged.

One perfect brow rose as she took a step forward and stared at the meal I'd prepared. Christ, she was stunning. I held my breath and waited as she reached out, picked up a morsel, put it into her mouth, and chewed. "Hmmm..."

"Good?" I hated how fucking needy that sounded.

She just chewed again and nodded before swallowing. "It's the best I've ever had."

I exhaled slowly.

"Yeah, it is. I particularly like how you spread the butter to the edges of the bread. Very impressed."

I smiled.

"And the peanut butter doesn't fight the jelly. They're the perfect consistency, not too thick or too thin," she continued. "And your skill with a blade is astounding, how you cut those crusts right off."

I nodded. "One of my many talents."

Her eyes sparkled as she ate the half of the sandwich. "I'm looking forward to finding out the rest of those talents."

It was the first time she'd spoken of a future, the first time she looked almost *resigned*. My damn pulse sped at the thought. She wasn't running, or looking for the door. She wasn't halfway gone. She was all the way here...now, of all times, when my father's threat still rang in my ears. I stared at her, knowing exactly what he'd plan, and the haunting image of Baldeon's face filled my head once more.

"Can I eat the rest of this at the table?" she asked, reaching for the plate and the remaining half a sandwich.

"It's your apartment." I gave a shrug, "do whatever you like."

Still, curiosity coursed through me like a charge.

"Thanks." She smiled, grabbed the plate, and made her way to the table, giving Leale a scratch on the head as she passed. "I don't think peanut butter and jelly is good for dogs."

But she didn't sit. Instead, she placed the plate down and went back to the bedroom, returning moments later. She plugged a cord into an outlet, and sat, opened the screen on her computer, and started typing. "Fin."

"Yeah?"

"What's the Commander's cell number?"

I frowned and dragged out my phone, brought up the contacts, and read out the number.

"Thanks."

Her fingers flew across the keyboard, and colors lit up, reflecting against her face. She was lost to me, in a world I couldn't comprehend. Still, I watched her as she stopped after a while to take another bite of her sandwich.

Beep!

I glanced down at my phone.

Pavlov: On our way back.

On our way...*our way*...he'd done it. Fuck me...he'd done it! That dangerous feeling inside me swelled.

My phone flashed red as an alert came. *Warning! Possible security breach. WARNING...WARNING...WARNING...*

"Anna..."

"Hmmm?" She never looked up.

I stared at the alert flashing and buzzing, then at the slow smile that spread across her face. "Never mind."

She didn't...barely giving it a second thought. I figured I was better off not knowing. The woman was in her own world, one where guns and fists didn't rule.

I left her, strode to the bathroom, and placed my phone on the vanity before I stripped and stepped into the shower. It buzzed and rang, vibrating across the surface. It didn't take a genius to work out who it was. The Commander had his problems...and they were about to get a whole lot worse. I took my time under the searing spray, letting the water cascade across my shoulders and down my chest. Images flashed across my mind, Lazarus in a fit of rage, driving his fist against Zakharov's face.

I'd wanted to be the one who split the bastard open. I'd wanted to be the one to quell the rage, but that hollowed-out look from Kat surfaced, and fuck me if I didn't understand how Rossi needed it more. If the bastard had touched Anna like that...*if he'd touched what was mine,* there wouldn't be a code in existence that'd save him.

My phone buzzed and danced as I ended the spray and stepped out. I wrapped a towel around my waist, grabbed my cell, and stepped out of the bathroom. *Tap...tap...tap.* The sound was so damn familiar, reminding me of the good times, of the nights she'd spent working at our house while our fathers made plans.

Everyone wanted to name Dillon Shaw as the Ghost, but I knew better. I knew he was just the man who'd started this, a man who'd gotten in way too deep. A man who turned to his daughter when it all became too much...and she'd come up with a way to take over the damn world.

Buzz...buzz...

I looked down. Fifteen missed calls and...a screen filled with notifications. I smiled and strode toward her. "How's my little hacker?"

She just lifted her head, the savage determination in her gaze filled with glee. "Almost done."

"I bet he is..."

She gave a dangerous smile. The island's information was mostly safe. My launderer worked with singleminded ferocity. I pitied Zakharov in that moment, just a little at least. A fist to his face and he'd heal. I stepped around her, watching her fingers flying as screen after screen zipped by. But all his damn accounts frozen? *Jesus, she was good.* She hacked into account after account, including all the offshore ones under aliases, the list of them on a spreadsheet a mile long.

"The Treasury is going to have a field day," I muttered gleefully.

"Oh, they're not the only ones. Look what else I found..." she chuckled, pulling up a file. "It was locked down, but nothing I couldn't break."

I stepped closer. It was a video. The moment she pressed play, I knew that it was...men dressed in expensive tuxedos wearing white masks.

"Turn it off," I snapped, my gut clenching.

Anna just looked at me. "Why?"

I stepped forward on instinct, stabbed the button, and froze the view. If I looked harder, I'd find it was a bedroom. One of many. "Anna...I said turn it off."

She just shook her head. Of course she didn't. She existed in my world, but she wasn't part of it. She didn't wade in the filth and the blood. She didn't know what the White Mask Society was all about. But I did.

"What is it?" she questioned.

"Nothing." I closed the screen. "Get away from it, corrupt it, delete it, and forget you ever saw it."

"Fin," she protested, those beautiful, innocent eyes of hers flashing with anger.

"Do you trust me?" I asked, brushing my fingers along her jaw.

It took her a second longer than what I would've liked to answer. But that answer lingered there...yeah, that answer I was counting on. "Yes."

"Then delete it and forget it," I urged. "*Please.*"

Her forehead creased with annoyance, but she did as I asked, punching in the details and tracing back to the server. I watched her work, knowing what the Zakharovs were involved in. It made me sick. I shoved it to the back of my mind and strode toward the bedroom. They wouldn't touch Anna, not men who liked to hurt and control.

Not men like Damon...

Not men like my father.

Not again...*never again.*

41

Anna

"Who are they, Fin?" I pushed the point even as I punched in the command to not only remove the video from the internet, but to unleash a greedy goddamn virus along with it.

He looked at me with that careful, stony stare, and answered. "The kind of men you'll never have to worry about, Anna...not if I can help it."

I saw him close down then. His gaze hardened and his jaw clenched. That slow, calculated blink told me that was all I was going to get. But that didn't mean I was satisfied. I turned my attention back to the screen and finished searching the directories, punching in code after code. Laundering was less about money and more about hiding...and if there was anything I was good at, it was finding those dark, dirty corners of the internet. After all...it was where I unleashed the market for our cryptocurrency.

Those with bloodstained hands ate it up, jumping on board the moment it filtered through the dark web. They saw the advantages all hidden under anonymous trades; Altcoin became the new US Dollar. Whatever you wanted, you could buy, drugs, women, even take out a hit if you knew where to look and how to play. But this was no *Silk Road*. This was no exchange of physical products like drugs and paraphernalia, this was all numbers.

We provided a way for money to exchange hands for services... without knowing who they were at all. The beauty of it was, we held all the power. Each transaction was held in our escrow service, the one I'd built and designed from scratch. One the US government would *never find*. Because it didn't exist, not in the way they expected. It was mirrored and bounced, changing every time I updated the passwords.

Beep.

Fin's phone dragged his attention elsewhere, long enough for me to punch in a few commands. *White mask, expensive suits, dangerous men, who are they?* And logged back out as Fin lifted his gaze to the screen.

"Almost done?"

I smiled, punched in the last command, and watched as account after account on the Zakharovs' list of aliases all flashed red with the words *ACCOUNT FROZEN PLEASE CONTACT UNITED STATES TREASURY*.

I smiled. "He is now." I leaned back, my breaths deep and hard. Wrath took a lot of energy, especially in the cat and mouse game I played.

I switched screens, logged into Binance, and checked the market. "Congratulations, Altcoin and Bitcoin are at an all-time high, you just made another fifty million overnight."

He stilled at the words, those dark eyes unfathomable. His touch was careful as his fingers brushed my cheek. "You know my father will never let you go, don't you?"

My stomach clenched tight. His father...*or him?*

I swallowed hard and forced a smile. Inside, I was reeling, my pulse tripping and thundering as he leaned down and brushed his lips over mine. "You know what we have to do now, don't you?"

My skin pebbled under his touch, but still I closed my eyes and whispered against his mouth. "What is that?"

His answer was to take my hand and gently pull me from the seat. I left the open laptop behind, letting him lead me toward the bedroom. Memories pushed in, violent memories, and Kat's screams rang in my head for a second before he turned.

"You're here now, this is me," he reassured me, and pressed my palm flat against his chest. "Feel that?"

I breathed deep, feeling the faint tremor against my hand. "Yes."

"While that muscle is pumping, that's how you know you're safe. I'll always be there, Anna."

I lifted my gaze to his. "Where?"

"Where all the goddamn rules and codes stop protecting you. That's where I'll be...ready to kill anyone who looks your way."

I couldn't breathe, couldn't think, only stare into the darkened depths of his soul to find my own reflection. He lifted the bottom of my shirt and pulled it over my head. Cool air danced across my skin, making me shiver.

"Don't worry," he whispered, lowering his head to gently lick my nipple. "You won't be cold for long."

I closed my eyes as he took me deeper. A low groan rumbled in the back of my throat as I drove my fingers through his hair.

He picked me up in an instant, carrying me to the bed. My head hit the pillow as he slid his hand down my thighs. Stars sparkled in his eyes. I took it all in. The night sky and the island through the window…and Finley as the low amber lights of his bedroom cast faint shadows against his skin.

He reached over his shoulder and dragged his shirt free. His sweatpants were next, leaving him gorgeous and bare. Thick and heavy, his cock swung as he moved. I was transfixed by the sight of his body. But my attention didn't linger as he braced his hands on either side of my hips and bent down, kissing my thighs. One gentle caress and he parted my thighs. He lifted his gaze to mine, the connection burning like fire. Desire engulfed me as he moved in close, kissing his way toward my crease.

"Jesus, you're beautiful," he groaned as he slid his finger down my crease. "Just like this."

I moaned, arching my spine as he slid inside me.

"Just…like this," he repeated with a sigh.

I couldn't help but widen my thighs. My body wasn't mine to control when he was around. Warm breath tickled the tenderest part of me. He kissed and licked, taking his time. We'd been here before…a number of times now. We'd done this dance and fed this hunger. Still, it blazed hotter than ever.

His tongue moved lower, spearing inside with the slow thrust of his finger. He fucked me, branded me. I was barren without him, empty and hollow. My heart ached for him. My hips rose to meet his mouth as he sucked and thrust, replacing one finger with two. Fire leaped inside me, licking with greedy tongues, until he pulled away.

"Turn over, Anna."

I was helpless to fight, doing exactly as he instructed.

"On your hands and knees."

My breath caught as I drew my body onto all fours.

The low, guttural growl this time was all male, primal and urgent as he slid his finger along the crease of my ass, then down. I shivered when he brushed the ring of muscle. Panic flared, scattering my desire for a second, until he slid his fingers down and inside me once more and shifted his weight, coming closer.

"We're going to have to fix this..." he murmured as his slick fingers left a trail on my hips as he pulled my weight backwards. "I need to protect you, but goddamn, you just feel so damn good."

Pressure pushed against my opening. Just a little, just enough to slip inside before he pulled out once more.

Teasing.

Torturing.

I closed my eyes with a whimper as my body trembled, reaching for more.

"Or fucking not," he growled, pulling my body against his. Still, he never gave in fully, slipping in and out, making me clench around him. "Fuck me..."

I spread my legs wider and drove back harder, grinding my hips, desperate for more. "Fin," I cried as that urgency came back with a roar. *"Fuck me."*

He obeyed, driving up with those powerful thighs, slamming into me. I cried out with the impact, throwing my head back and moaning.

"Jesus Christ...do that again," he growled.

So I did, letting the hunger for more of him ripple through my chest and spill through my lips. Hard breaths were punctuated with brutal thrusts. We were always headed for this, always destined to collide.

"Mine," he growled, and dropped his weight against me, slamming my hips against the bed. He loomed over me, caging me under him. His arms enclosed mine, his thick thighs slamming against me. *"Do you hear me? Mine...mine."*

I was lost as he hammered his words home. I closed my eyes and fisted the sheets as that fire burned through me...leaving stars behind. I cried out as my body shuddered, that ache inside clenching and throbbing.

Fin came with a grunt and stilled inside me.

He dropped his head, brushing his lips across my back as he sucked in hard breaths. "No. One. Else. Touches. You."

I lay flat on the bed, but turned my head toward him, sucking in deep breaths. I knew what he was saying, knew that once we left the island, there was no going back for us. Whatever this was...it was permanent.

The only problem was...Finley answered to his father.

And once his father found out we planned to run...we'd be dead.

42

Finley

"You hear me, Anna?" I wanted to be sure she understood.

My body pinned her to the bed, but I couldn't move. Not just yet. Her head turned to the side on the pillow. Her lips were flushed and parted as she panted, then I leaned down, taking her mouth, claiming her air. That beast rose inside me, the one that wanted to control every aspect of her, the way she lived, the way she breathed, the way she affected me.

That *was* where it came from, right? I wanted to control her the way she somehow controlled me.

She moaned under my mouth, straining to lift her head higher, wanting more. I pulled away just enough to stare into her eyes. "You are mine."

She didn't answer. That both annoyed the fuck out of me and excited me even more. My phone gave a beep beside the bed, shattering the moment. She dropped her head to the pillow and stretched her arms out underneath me.

I rolled and reached for my phone to stare at the text.

Max: Have you heard from P?

I shifted, my senses coming back from that euphoric high, and typed. *He's on a job.*

My gut tightened as a second later, *Max: Anything I should know about?*

I stared at the words. *Was* it something he should know about? Instinct pushed to the surface as I hit the button, shutting down the screen, and slid my phone to the nightstand.

You can trust me, Fin. Pavlov's words rang inside my head. They weren't the only things he'd said to me when I'd pulled him aside to discuss the footage I'd seen, the one where he'd watched Anna touching herself. I'd wanted to stab the bastard in the eyes for watching her like that. But the moment I opened my mouth to nail the bastard to the wall, something else rose inside me, something that'd been nagging me for a while now...*especially since I'd come to the island.* I listened to that voice inside me and showed him the images instead, the ones taken over Moris Dime, and gave him his orders.

I was playing with danger, I knew that. More than that, I was playing with *her life.* I glanced at Anna, lying beside me on the bed. But loyalty was always being tested, none more than it was being tested now. I wrapped my arms around her as she closed her eyes and sighed.

"Sleepy?" I pulled her back against me, curling my legs behind hers.

Fuck, we fit perfectly, nestled, warm. The faint blossom scent of her shampoo filled my nose.

"Yeah," she answered, and reached for my hand, drawing me harder against her.

Any harder and I'd be inside. The mere thought made me fucking hard again. She let out a moan and shifted her ass, pressing against my stiffening cock.

"Fin."

"Yeah?" I pressed my face into her hair. Having her here... knowing she wasn't going anywhere. It was fucking torture.

She didn't speak, just moved once more, only her movements were purposeful, pushing...*grinding*.

"Fuck me, Anna," I grumbled.

"That's what I'm trying to do," she responded, turning her head to find my gaze. "Now, if you'd only move a little more to the right..."

With a growl, I grabbed her thigh, parted her legs, and thrust inside her.

Jesus Christ, it was like coming home. Only it was a home I'd never been to, a home I'd only dreamed about. That feeling of falling, *always falling*. She reached over her shoulder to grasp my neck.

I kissed her and slammed into her, making her breasts bounce with every...jutting...thrust. I gave into the burgeoning frenzy and slid right into the beast. With a savage growl, I moved my hand from her thigh to the tiny nub of her clit, circling, dancing, sliding the length of my finger over that trembling peak. "Better get used to this, launderer. I'm going to fuck you until you can't stand."

She curled her back, driving her ass against me. The friction grew where we connected, drawing my balls tight.

"Is that a promise?" she taunted breathlessly.

I let out a sharp bark of laugher and slid out, forcing her onto her back before I moved between her thighs. Here I could command her, here I could control her. "Look down. Look at us."

She obeyed, lifting her head from the pillow to watch as I pulled out. I was fucking slick and shiny, the head of my cock throbbing to release. She gave a low moan as I probed her opening, barely sliding in and out.

"Fin," she gasped, opening her legs wide, driving that sweet ass low to meet the collision. "Fin, *please.*"

I braced my weight on my elbow and reached up, grabbing her jaw. "Please what, launderer?"

I knew I drove her wild, saw the need unhinged and glinting in her eyes as she curled her lip and glared at me. "Please give me what I need."

I smiled with savage glee, angled my hips, and plunged.

Her eyes fluttered as she dropped her head back. *"Oh, yesss."*

I drove my focus to that tipping point, feeling the rake of her nails along my back as she squeezed her eyes closed and clenched tight around my cock buried deep inside her. I leaned further in as my balls drew tight, and let go. A part of me wanted to fill her belly. I wanted her ripe and round. I wanted her to forever be tied to me, unable to go.

Deep down I knew it was the only way we'd ever be accepted.

By my father and the rest of the Commission.

My perfect, tenacious little launderer was going to be my ticket to take the Salvatore seat, whether she knew it or not. I pulled out and flopped over against the mattress, spent...exhausted. I closed my eyes, sensing her just as keenly as I had watching her.

"I...can't...move," she gasped.

I just smiled. "Good, then don't."

Leale padded into the bedroom and, with one massive grunt, hauled himself onto the bed. I cracked open my eyes and lifted my head. "Leale..."

"Don't," Anna commanded, rubbing her hand against my thigh. "Let him stay."

"I've already lost him, haven't I?" I complained, and dropped my head on the pillow. I knew when I was fighting a losing battle.

The asshole had the gall to grunt and sigh, before settling on her side of the damn bed. *Her side.* My own words in my head stole my annoyance. I cracked open my eyes again. Only that time, it was to watch her as she reached out with her eyes still closed to ruffle his damn ear. The asshole turned his head and gave me a look that said, *see, bro, she likes me better than you.*

"Asshole," I growled under my breath, and dropped my head.

"Did you say something?" she asked as she pushed up from the bed.

"Nope. Not a damn thing."

I listened to her steps as she went into the bathroom. I could track everything she did and everything she touched as the toilet flushed and the faucet ran as she washed her hands. She stepped out, stopping on my side of the bed before the whisper of fabric came. Leale lifted his head as she rounded the foot and climbed back under the covers. But then she was mine, working her way across the bed to curl up against me.

I smiled at her careful movements as she adjusted her body to press against mine and settled. It didn't take long before her breaths slowed and deepened. I let myself relax, let myself give into the moment for just a little while at least.

But as the darkness rose up and wrapped its claws around me, taking me deep into slumber, I felt the bed shift beside me...then I knew no more.

43

Anna

I shifted my weight and pressed against Fin. The touch was comforting, warm and relaxing. His hand slowly dropped from his abdomen to fall against my hip, and that's where it stayed. My body was humming, flooded with adrenaline. Kat's screams still resounded in my head, and the images of what that piece of shit had done to her...but it wasn't only that.

It was Fin...

And Lazarus.

It was the way they'd set upon Damon with fists and fury. There was no stopping them, no changing the utter annihilation they were desperate to inflict. I'd seen violence, seen it from the very first day I'd stepped inside the Salvatore home. But I'd never seen it from *him*...not like that.

I closed my eyes as Damon's screams filled my head again, piercing screams, *howling screams*. Something trembled inside me and what bloomed from the darkest depths wasn't what I expected. I wasn't horrified, I wasn't scared, I was *resigned*, and that scared me most of all.

That was the way they were. That was how they protected their own...*and I was now one of those people.* If Fin knew how bad Damon had hurt me, there would've been no stopping him. I wouldn't be worried about a few broken bones. I'd be trying to figure out how to hide a goddamn body.

I turned my head and glanced over my shoulder. Fin lay with one arm curled under the pillow, his powerful muscles shimmering under the soft amber lights. His full lips parted with deep, easy breaths. His face lit up for a second and it took me far too long to realize why.

I rolled, making sure I didn't disturb him, and grabbed my phone. One press of the button, and my pulse started to race.

Unknown number: What the fuck have you done, Anna?

I scowled, lifting my head from the pillow. *What the fuck have I done?* My mind raced. I'd missed the meet. I'd fucked up the schedule. I'd done a lot of things. Leale lifted his head, giving me a low *chuff* as I slid my feet from under the covers and sat on the side of the bed.

My fingers flew across the keypad as I replied: *What are you talking about?*

I waited for an answer. Waited and waited and waited. Lightning flickered and danced in the distance. I pressed the screen over and over...waiting. But there was nothing. I typed: *Answer me, what are you talking about?*

The sky came alive, arcing and blazing, severing the darkness with a brilliant white glow. Still there was no reply. I tried to lie back down...tried to push the text from my mind. But sleep wouldn't come. Instead, I lay there as both Fin and Leale started to snore...then I got back up, and tiptoed from the bedroom.

I made my way to the table, hit the button on my laptop, and the screen came alive. *What have I done? What have I done? What have I done?* I stared at the screen and the list of Zakharov accounts. An icy chill swept over me. *He couldn't mean...*

I just stared at that list. "No...no, that can't be the contact..."

The sheets shifted in the bedroom, drawing my gaze just as my phone lit up with a text.

Unknown: Your father is now a dead man.

A video symbol appeared. I gripped my phone tightly and pressed play, my heart in my damn throat as the stupid thing buffered and finally started. But there was nothing but darkness, nothing but shadows...until my father's voice came through loud and clear.

"I'll go back...*do you hear me? I'll go back to Dominic. We didn't tell them anything about the Salvatores. I swear!*"

"Dad," I gasped, shoving up from the chair.

"Get in the fucking boat, Dillon." My heart hammered. I knew that voice...*I knew that voice...I knew that voice!*

The video narrowed in, taken from somewhere in the distance. The shadows sharpened, showing the glint of lights against dark, choppy waters. It was a marina. One on Mauritius. It had to be. I caught the panicked face of my father, his hands cuffed behind him. But the camera narrowed in on the man next to him. The one dressed in black as he shoved my dad into a boat to take him god knows where.

As the man turned, giving me full view of his face, my blood ran cold, hard features, a stony stare. I knew his voice...of course I did. I lifted my gaze to Finley, still asleep in the bed. I knew his face because I'd seen it only today as Pavlov had stood at Finley's side.

No...

No, he couldn't do this. Not to me...not to me. I closed my eyes and squeezed them shut, praying this was all just a bad dream. My phone vibrated in my hand, forcing me to not only open my eyes, but accept reality. Everything had been a lie. All of this. There was no love, no desire. Finley Salvatore had used me. He'd used me...and I fell for it. I fell for it all.

Agony stabbed through my chest, sawing and severing, until I was sure my heart detached.

Unknown: If you want to see your father alive, meet me now. You have twenty minutes to get to building o, before your boyfriend delivers your father to Dominic Salvatore as a traitor.

For a second, my feet wouldn't move. I willed them...*MOVE NOW!* Leale lifted his head to look at me as I stumbled away from the table.

Tears blurred my path as I quietly made my way into the bedroom and tore off Fin's shirt. I wanted it far from me, desperate for my own clothes once more. I watched him, riveted by the rhythmic rise and fall of his chest as I quietly tugged the zipper on my bag and speared my hands inside. I grabbed what I could. A bra, panties, a button-up shirt, and jeans. My jacket was shoved at the bottom. I lifted my gaze, there was no way I could get it free without waking him.

Beep.

I wrenched my gaze to his phone. I was moving before I knew it, desperate to quiet the sound, and snatched his phone from the nightstand. *Call tracking information: Caller Unknown. Message received: 4 in total.*

Call tracking information?

Heat burned all the way up my cheeks. He was tracking my phone? *He was tracking my damn phone...*I took a step backwards as fire burned all the way through my chest and into my face. He'd not only played me...he'd betrayed my father as well.

He shifted in the bed, reaching out his hand. Was he searching for me? Even as his betrayal played out in front of me? What kind of callous bastard *was* he? He was a Salvatore alright. *Like father...like son.*

I stepped back, unable to take my eyes off the man I'd given myself to. I wanted to scrub away the feel of his body. I wanted to burn away my own sick desires. But as I stepped quietly away, I knew I'd never be free...not from craving him...or from what I'd done.

I looked down at his phone and swiped down, disabling the WiFi and mobile data before pressing airplane mode and calculator. My fingers worked fast, punching in numbers to exit and turn the phone to the side. One more swipe and I was in, no passcode and no fucking remorse. Not anymore. I'd never do this, never betray his trust like this. I'd never put to use all the things I'd learned from hundreds of hours spent hacking, coding, laundering, if it hadn't come to this.

He shifted in the bed, mumbling something, then clearly, "*Anna...*"

He called for me...even in his sleep.

I was rocked by the ache in his voice. But it was all just a play, right? All just a deceitful fucking lie. My stomach clenched as a wave of nausea swept through me. And all of a sudden, it made sense.

I have some information about a certain someone. You know, for the initiation. Kilpatrick's words returned to me and Finley's answer followed. *He's all yours. I have a new target now.*

He had a new target alright...and that target was me.

I forced myself to look away from him as something hit the screen of his phone with a *splat*. Tears slipped down my cheeks before I brushed them away with the swipe of my thumb and stared at the screen. I swiped left, to the lesser apps he used, finding one marked *Cameras*. I clicked on the icon, finding the black and white real-time footage of the camera outside my building... *then the camera inside*.

Not only did he monitor my calls and texts...he watched me.

My insides turned to water as I found another folder marked *Saved*. I opened it, finding one video. It was more than curiosity now. It was a *need* to know. I opened the saved video and watched it play out. At first, it was hard to see...until I saw myself shift in the bed.

"*Fin...*" My own throaty voice drifted from his phone.

My cheeks burned as I saw the darkness shift beside me. Movement came, a figure stepped close and lingered near the bed.

"Fin, *please*," I whispered, my hand moving under the sheets.

But as the shadow moved, it hit me. It was the same build as the one from tonight...the same male who'd shoved my dad toward a boat. *It was Pavlov.*

Pavlov had seen me...*touching myself*.

And Fin knew it.

"Anna?" I jerked my gaze to the bed as Fin moved, shoving his hand out. He lifted his head and I stumbled backwards. "Anna?"

He was more awake now, lifting his head from the pillow and searching the dark. I dropped his phone and it hit the carpeted floor with a *thud*.

"What are you doing?" he mumbled.

"I...*ah*. I need to go and see Kat." Panic flared in my head as I moved backwards.

"Now?" he groaned, and pushed up on his elbows.

"Yes, Fin, now." I tried to stop the anger from spilling into my tone. But as hard as I tried, I couldn't stop it. I wanted to hurt him...I wanted to hurt him like he'd hurt me.

I turned, strode barefoot to the table, and took my phone. The sheets rustled behind me as he sat up. I didn't have time to stop and find my shoes, didn't have time to do anything but haul ass toward the elevator.

A *thud* sounded as I hurried and stabbed the button for the elevator.

"Anna?" Fin growled, sounding pissed off now. "Anna, wait a second. You're going to Kat's now? Why, is something wrong?"

Yeah, you fucking asshole. Something is very...very wrong. "No." I forced the words through clenched teeth. "Nothing's wrong."

I could hear him yanking on pants as the rumble of the elevator came close.

"Where's the fuck is my..." he muttered, then stopped. "Anna," he called as the doors opened.

I hurried inside and pressed the door closed button, then the one for the ground floor.

"Anna, *wait!*"

But there was no waiting, not anymore. Tears burned as they spilled free. I stared at the closing doors as Fin raced toward me.

"Anna!" *Boom!* The sound of his fist against the door made me flinch. I stepped backwards until I hit the rear wall.

But then I was gone, sinking lower and lower. I lifted my phone and started typing.

On my way. Need directions to building o.

I waited, not really expecting an answer, but a second later, he replied.

Unknown: Follow the map.

An image followed, one similar to the one of the island. I blinked my tears away, focusing on the blur, and searched for building zero as the elevator came to a shuddering halt. The doors opened and I strode through, quickening my steps toward the foyer doors.

Thunder came from the stairwell...thunder and the roar of my name.

Finley was coming for me.

But this time it was far too late.

"You did this." I fought the agony and raced through the doors out into the night.

44

Finley

"Anna!" I lunged and lashed out, slamming the handle of the stairwell door before charging through. But she wasn't there...

You fucking idiot! I turned, stared at the closed elevator doors, and strode toward it, pressing the button. It opened immediately. That meant she was gone.

She was gone.

I clenched my fist around my phone and jerked my gaze to the outside door. She was out there...running, scared, pissed off... what the fuck had she seen? I pressed the button on my phone and punched in the code. The saved video was still open, playing...with Pavlov standing over her bed, watching her as she cried out my goddamn name and pleasured herself. *"Shit!"*

I ran a hand through my hair and tugged my boots on properly, yanking the laces before tying them tight. This was all falling apart and it was all my damn fault. *Fucking idiot!* I glanced at my phone once more, shutting down the damn video feed, and saw the text.

The phone tracking notification. The one that showed texts sent to her phone.

Texts I knew for a fact hadn't come from her dad.

I pressed the buttons to call Pavlov, and strode through the doors out into the night. The wind was brutal, slamming into me the moment I stepped out. I lowered my head, fighting the force, and kept on walking.

"Yeah?" he answered on the third ring.

"Is he secure?"

"Yeah, he's secure. Everything okay?" Concern etched his words.

I tried to keep the bite of frustration and anger from my words, but it was fucking useless. "Where the fuck are you right now?"

A grunt came in the background, then the choppy slap of the waves as he battled the wind as my bodyguard answered. "We're just getting off the boat and heading for the building now."

Kat...she said she was going to Kat...

Was it all just a lie?

I sucked in hard breaths and tried to think like her. Maybe the texts were from Kat? Maybe Kat somehow had an unknown fucking number and maybe that warning in my gut was right.

"Everything okay?" Pavlov barked. "Something I should know about?"

Something I should know about. It was the same words Max had used. The same fucking words my father used. The same words that said only one thing. *I wasn't fucking trusted to handle things on my own.*

"No," I answered. "Text me when he's secure, and Pavlov."

"Yeah?"

"You haven't spoken to anyone about this, have you?"

"Not a fucking word. Just like you instructed."

"Good..." I exhaled hard, losing that flare of anger, and kept on walking. "Good."

"I'll text when he's secure," Pavlov repeated, then hung up.

I lifted my gaze to the lights of the buildings as a bolt of lightning speared the sky in the distance. A damn storm was coming. I tucked my phone into my pocket, my steps slowing on their own, and stopped. Something was nagging me, some flare of instinct in my gut.

That same instinct made me turn my head and lift my gaze to the windows of my apartment. Through the expansive glass, I caught movement. My gut clenched...*Anna.* I almost turned around, almost took off at a sprint back to the fucking building... almost stepped out of the damn shadows of building one.

But it wasn't Anna at all...

I watched as Max stepped into our bedroom and moved around the bed. I knew exactly what he was seeing. Anna's open suitcase filled full of her belongings, and the rumpled sheets, the air still heady with the scent of sex. But that wasn't what he was after...he left the bedroom and moved into the office, turned the light on, and closed the door.

My gut clenched and panic raged, mingling with the low growl in the clouds overhead. He was in the fucking office, and I was betting that right now he was trying the combinations of the safe. The combination I'd changed at the very last minute. My phone lit up as I stood there.

Max: Fin, everything okay?

I clenched my jaw tight and turned away.

Max: Do you need an escort?

I tore my gaze from the text and focused on the building in the distance. I knew exactly what he was doing. The sonofabitch was watching me at all damn times, sneaking into my apartment when he thought I wasn't watching. There was only one reason to betray me like that...and that was for my father.

Don't you think your father should know about this?

How many damn times had he said those words? Too many to count. That cold-seated anger burned inside me as I stepped up to the scanner, swiped my card, and the doors opened. But that's where I stopped, as two massive bodyguards rose from their seats.

"I need to see him," I growled.

One just shook his head. "Sorry, Mr. Salvatore. Mr. Rossi has asked not to be disturbed."

I clenched my fist, looked the asshole in the eyes, and let that savage part of me rise to the surface. "I don't give a *fuck* what he said. Call him right now and tell him *I* need to fucking *see him*."

The bastard flinched and glanced nervously at his partner. One nod from his partner, and the bodyguard turned away, grabbing his phone. I paced the fucking foyer, running my hands through my hair as the asshole's low murmur drifted through the space.

"Yes, Mr. Rossi...I understand. I'll let Mr. Salvatore know."

Mr. fucking Salvatore. I hated that fucking name, hated it with a goddamn vengeance. I hated the weight and the looks that came with it. The same look that found me now as the bodyguard glanced my way. "He's on his way, Mr. Salvatore."

"Finley," I muttered.

Confusion flared in his gaze. "Sorry?"

"I said, my damn name is Finley," I snarled through clenched teeth, and tore my gaze away.

But the darkened view outside was no better. Palms swayed and lashed as the winds rose. A high-pitched whistle forced between the doors as the elevator opened. Lazarus stepped out, still tugging a shirt over rippling fucking abs.

He gave a nod toward his bodyguards and strode bare-foot toward me. "Finley."

"Where the fuck is she?" I snarled, turning on him.

His blue eyes darkened. There was a furrow of annoyance as he lifted his hand and combed back his hair. His knuckles were bloodied and raw, still fresh from the fucking beating he'd given Zakharov. The fucking beating *I* should've given him...if I wasn't such a goddamn fucking failure.

"What do you want with her?"

That's all the bastard said...*what do I want with her?* I took a step forward, watching the two big fucking assholes shift nervously, until Lazarus lifted his hand, stilling their movement.

"What do I want with her?" I stopped in front of him, glaring into his eyes. *"What do I want with her?"*

There was a tic of his jaw, but he didn't move an inch. "You want to tell me what's going on here, Fin?"

Through the windows, lightning slashed in the distance as I answered. "Anna's fucking gone and the last thing she said was she was coming to see Kat."

Relief swept through those blue eyes. Gone were the furrow and the snarl as he smiled and shook his head. "She's not here."

"Bullshit."

"*Bullshit?*" he repeated, one eyebrow rising. "I said, she's not here."

I stepped forward until I bumped the asshole's chest. There was fucking bad blood between us...*real bad blood.* And it wasn't the first time a Rossi had tried to claim what was ours. "Forgive me if I don't fucking believe you."

That smirk grew wider and a little more savage. "You know what, Fin? I don't give a fuck what you believe, how's that?"

He started to turn away, leaving. "Wait." I grabbed his arm, wrenching him back.

He just took one look at my hand, then at me. But danger moved deeper, cutting through his blue eyes like a fucking shark. "You wanna take your fucking hand off me?"

No, I didn't want to. I didn't want to at all. Part of me was ready to go to war. He could see that, see the desperation...the same desperation he'd had racing toward Anna's building to save Kat.

With a sigh, he muttered. "Fine. You want to come up and see for your fucking self, then be my goddamn guest."

I followed as he headed for the elevator. Maybe he as bluffing, maybe he was outright lying. For all I knew, she could've snuck back down through the stairwell and was ready to slip out into the night the moment I stepped onto the elevator. But something inside me didn't think that was the case. It was that menacing drive that forced me into the elevator and all the way to the penthouse floor.

I clenched my jaw and stared straight ahead.

"Fin," Lazarus called as the doors opened.

But I didn't stop, just strode into the damn apartment.

"Fin," he called again, *louder.*

I stopped, sucking in a hard breath as movement came from the bedroom.

"Just give me a fucking second, okay?" he warned.

Heat rushed to my cheeks as Kat called out, "Lazarus?"

He just glared at me. "Yeah, it's me," he answered her.

I waited as he passed me heading toward Kat, hating how that feeling of desperation led to coercion.

"What's going on?" Concern filled Kat's voice.

"It's Fin," Lazarus explained, keeping his voice low. "He's worried about Anna."

There was a sudden shift in the bed. "What about Anna?"

With a sigh that carried through the apartment, Lazarus growled. "It seems she's gone missing."

There was silence, then the soft padding of bare feet as Kat stepped around Lazarus in the doorway and stalked my way, her eyes sparkling with anger. "What happened?" she demanded.

For a moment, I'd forgotten who she was...all I saw was the bruised eye...and the dark circles under her eyes. But that all faded away as she came closer and grabbed my shirt. "Fin...*what the fuck happened?*"

I couldn't answer her, because...*I didn't know.* "She left."

Kat stilled. "Just like that?"

I swallowed hard. "Yeah."

"Did you...hurt her?"

Did I hurt *her?* The question was a punch to my gut. Did I hurt her...

Her words filled me. *I...ah. I need to go and see Kat.*

Now? I'd asked.

Yes, Fin, now.

She'd seen the video of Pavlov, that I knew for sure. But the tracking information was what filled me with fear. "I think she's in trouble...and she's about to do something fucking stupid. Something I won't be able to fix."

"What the fuck," Lazarus growled, and jerked his gaze from Kat to me. "You think she's going to talk? How much does she even fucking know about you, anyway?"

I just met the eyes of the heir of the Rossi line and answered "She knows it all."

His dark eyes widened.

I just clenched my jaw. I couldn't say any more, not without risking her damn life even more. Because the problem was...she couldn't know all about the Salvatores' dealings without knowing the Rossis', the Baldeons', Valachis' and the Kilpatricks'. All five fucking seats on the damn Commission were at stake and in that moment, Lazarus knew it.

"Then you'd better hope you find her, Fin...before it's too late."

I left with those words resounding in my head and prayed this wasn't over.

For the both of us.

45

Anna

I glanced at the map on my phone and lifted my gaze to the darkness. Building zero wasn't just a building. It was a towering warehouse set back from the rest of the island. I hurried, leaving the path behind, and ran across the grass toward the faint light that shone through the rear door in the middle of the imposing structure.

But the closer I came, the more I realized this was no ordinary warehouse. The wide asphalt that stretched far into the distance toward the end of the island could only be for one thing...the island's own private jet. My pulse raced as I hurried. I hadn't seen this before. I glanced over my shoulder at the faint sparkle of lights in the distance. Why would I have? It was far from everything I'd known. Not even the small cove I'd run to had been on this side. Not only was it far away from everything else, it was hidden in shadows.

I slowed my steps as fear took root inside me. All I could hear was Dad's voice as he'd pleaded. *I'll go back...do you hear me? I'll go back to Dominic. We didn't tell them anything about the Salvatores. I swear!*

Desperation forced me toward the dull light shining through the doorway. The closer I came, the more terror took hold. What if I was too late? What if the contact couldn't save Dad? A sob lodged in my throat as I quickened my steps, running toward that doorway. They had to be here...they had to know of a way.

The moment my hand closed around the handle, something hard clamped around my mouth. I was yanked backwards, my feet dragging for a second before panic kicked in. *No!* I screamed, thrashing and fighting.

"Stop it, Ms. Shaw. Unless you don't want to see your dad again."

Ms. Shaw. *Ms. Shaw.* The only person who called me that was...*the contact.*

Instead of fighting, I stepped backwards, following him as he almost dragged me toward the far side of the building. I grabbed the thick, muscled arm for balance and risked a glance upwards. My stomach clenched as he looked over his shoulder, then down at me.

"You?" I whispered.

He stopped, pulling me closer. "Me," Mr. Former FBI acknowledged. He scowled and glanced toward the apartment buildings. "Were you followed?"

Was I followed? "No," I answered, my mind instantly shifting to Finley. "No, I wasn't followed."

Pain drove through my chest as I brushed off my jeans and took a step backwards, desperate for a little distance. He just glared down at my bare feet. "Where the hell are your shoes?"

"Where are my shoes?" I forced through clenched teeth. "Where are my goddamn shoes? How about, where the *fuck* is my father?"

He just lifted his gaze to mine, and the memory of that first class came roaring back to me. The day he'd called Finley and the others down to the front of the class...for the so called *initiation,* and the way he'd so carefully brushed me aside. "You knew about it all, didn't you? The initiation, the Commission. You knew who we were...and who we worked for."

"I knew enough to know you needed help," he responded. "And if you don't get inside the building, you're going to need more than I can deliver."

It all made sense now. The *contact* who'd reached out to Dad... was FBI. He had to be. I opened my mouth to ask as he took a step, grabbed my arm, and shoved me forward. "Inside, now."

"What's the plan?' The words came out instead. "How are we going to get my father now?"

But he didn't answer, just shoved me step after step around the corner of the hangar and toward the front. The moment I left the rear of the building behind, fear found me. I was out of sight from the others now ...*from Fin.* Lightning tore across the sky again as I put my head down and stepped onto the asphalt.

Over there!" he barked in my ear, fighting the roar of the wind. I lifted my gaze to a doorway, one that was all the way open, yet darkness waited for me inside. My feet stopped. I forced myself to turn. "Where is my dad?"

He just looked at me with confusion before jerking his gaze ahead. "Inside and I'll tell you the fucking plan, now *move!*"

I'll go back...do you hear me? I'll go back to Dominic.

Those words rang in my head. This was my only chance now. The only way to save Dad and get us away from these people and their goddamn lies and deceit. As fear gripped me, I took a step, fighting the gale, and headed for the doorway. Still that howl resounded in my head the moment I stepped inside.

Mr. FBI yanked the door closed behind him with a *boom*, leaving me standing in the dark. "Just keep walking," he barked.

I was too far in now, way too far over my head to try to back out. I just glanced around, waiting for my eyes to adjust, and started walking toward the faint outline of a doorway.

"My dad."

"Has been taken by one of your boyfriend's bodyguards. I thought that was plain to see."

"He's not my boyfriend," I bit back.

"Sure looked that way to me."

"But you can get him back, right?" I asked hopefully.

He was silent for a second, the thud of his boots matching the throbbing of my pulse. I stepped through the doorway and into a room. The thud of a door came and a second later, a light was switched on. We were in an office of some kind. The light from a desk lamp showed a desk and chairs inside the small room. One nod toward it, and Mr. FBI commanded, "Sit, and don't move."

I did as he said, curling my bruised toes against the industrial carpet.

"I warned you not to get involved with him." I winced from the tone as the contact paced the floor. "But did you listen? No...so now it's too late."

"My dad..."

He jerked that cold glare toward me as his phone *beeped*. A glance at the screen and he muttered apprehensively, "They're here."

They're here?

They're here?

I pushed up from the seat. "*Who's* here?"

But he didn't answer, just looked at me with a calculating glare and motioned toward the doorway.

"*I said...who's here,*" I forced the words through clenched teeth, refusing to move.

But Mr. FBI just turned, apparently sick of my questions, grabbed my arm, and shoved me forward. I stumbled, throwing out my hands to keep from hitting the door.

This wasn't right...

None of it. I twisted the handle and yanked. As I stepped through the doorway, I caught movement from behind me. I turned my head just enough to catch him drawing his gun. "You're not FBI, are you?"

He didn't answer, just gave me a shove, and all I could think about was the pain when Fin had spoken about Baldeon that night. *It was bad, Anna. It was so fucking bad.*

We'd stayed inside after that. We'd had bodyguards...*and each other.* But I didn't have any of that now, did I? And as I walked, a sudden surge of regret found me. A gnawing terror filled me, weighing down my feet as I moved slowly ahead.

Tears slipped from my eyes as I walked in the dark, heading down a long hallway toward the far end of the hangar. "Tell me one thing. Were you even going to try to get us out of this alive?"

"Alive?" the contact muttered. "See, I only needed one of you... and lucky for you, your father was never the target. You were."

I closed my eyes for a second, then opened them, striding toward the red exit light over the hangar door.

"Wait!" the contact barked behind me. I slowed my steps as he rushed forward, driving my shoulder hard against the wall as he pushed through. "Don't even think about running."

The wind howled through the gaps in the door as he grabbed the handle, turned, and opened it.

"Surprise," Pavlov snarled, and lashed out, driving his fist into the contact's face.

"Anna?" Dad's voice came from behind him. I lifted my head as Pavlov lunged, driving Mr. FBI backwards and slamming him into the wall.

"Anna!" Dad roared.

Everything happened in a blur. One minute I was standing there, looking at my dad in handcuffs...and the next, I was on the floor.

Fists flew in an onslaught as Pavlov and the contact traded blow after sickening blow, slamming each other into the wall.

"Dad!" I screamed as my father stumbled through the door and lunged toward me. His eyes were wide, tearing from the fight...to me.

Until a deafening *boom* tore through the air.

I jerked my gaze from Dad as Pavlov stumbled backwards, a dark stain spreading across his stomach. He turned his head toward me and whispered, *"Run."*

"You do," the contact sucked in hard gasps and leveled his gun at my father's head, "and your father is dead."

46

Finley

I did this...I did this...I...

I stepped out of the elevator as Lazarus's guard lifted his gaze from his phone. One fucking look, and I knew he'd done *something*. "Who the fuck are you texting?" I growled, and jerked my gaze to his phone.

"Mr. Salvatore," he gulped, and shook his head.

"I said...*who the fuck are you texting?*" I repeated, reaching behind me.

His eyes widened at the movement as he shook his head again.

"*Whoa!*" His partner lifted a hand in surrender and took a step forward. "I told him to. Told him to let your bodyguard know you needed him."

"*What?*" Panic roared through me. *Max?* "No..."

I jerked my gaze to the doors as my phone gave a *beep*.

Pavlov: Can't talk. Head to hangar now! She's there.

She's there. *She's there...*what the fuck was she doing at the hangar? I lunged toward the door, hitting the glass with a *thud* and slipping through. *The hangar...the hangar...the hangar. She's leaving me.* The words were a like a dagger to my chest. I lowered my head and charged into the howling wind. Lightning slashed the sky, forking and brightening for a second.

"*Fin!*" The roar rivalled the deafening boom of thunder.

I jerked my head toward the movement as Max charged from between the palms and headed for me.

"What the *fuck* is going on?" he barked, grabbing my arm and jerking me to a stop.

But I couldn't stop...not when she was leaving.

"*Fin!*" Max growled, stepping in my way.

I tried to move around him, but the bastard blocked every goddamn lunge. "*Get the fuck out of my way, Max!*"

"What the fuck has gotten into you?" he yelled, his hold like a steel clamp around my arm.

Panic surged as I jerked my gaze to his. *Tell him! Tell him you saw him. Tell him you don't fucking trust him where Anna is concerned.* But as I settled on his gaze, I said none of that. I just wrenched my arm from his hold and forced through clenched teeth, "She's at the hangar...and she's in trouble."

But inside, I was panicking. What about Pavlov...what about her dad?

"She's at the damn hangar? What the hell is she doing there?"

"I don't have time to fucking discuss this with you!" I took a step, gathering all that Salvatore rage. "Now, either help me or get out of my goddamn way."

I'd never spoken to him like that, never spoken to *anyone* like that. Not before Anna. Not before...*before I had something worth fighting for.* Max searched my eyes, then lifted his gaze to the brightening sky. "Fine," he grunted. "Whatever you want, Fin, but I'm coming with you."

I had no time to argue as he turned and took off at a run. I drove myself forward, my boots slamming against the pavement as I raced past the apartment buildings and into the darkness.

Anna...she consumed me, drove me. The pain and anger in her words driving me ever harder and faster. I caught up with Max, then passed him, lifting my gaze to the towering warehouse in the distance. I'd sent Pavlov to get her father. To keep him safe... safe for her.

It was supposed to be an easy fucking mission, in and out, keep her father hostage in one of the unused buildings until I could figure out a way to get out of this, until I could figure out a way to get them free. There was no way I could stop the inevitable now, no way I could stop my father from finding out about her plan to leave us once and for all.

But could I let her go?

That was the demon I battled, the one that wore the face of my father and sounded like my mother. The one who screamed *NO!* but at the same time ached for *yes*...For Anna to have the kind of life someone kind and sweet like her deserved. Not one that was called by the hands of a tyrant...like...*me?*

The thought slammed into me as I raced toward the hangar. *Bang!* The sound of a gunshot tore a scream of terror from me. But Max was already shoving his arm out wide, driving against my shoulder...pushing me out of the way as he charged through the open side door, disappearing into the dimness inside.

Anna's screams resounded in the space, coming from somewhere deeper within.

But then lightning lit up the sky. The brilliance lingered, splashing against the walls of the hangar hallway for a second... and the smear of fresh blood. Blood that was...blood that could be...*hers*. "Anna!" I screamed, racing after Max.

Boots thundered. The blinding white light flickered and dimmed behind me before it was gone. I was in the darkness once more, hurtling forward as Anna's screams were followed by a deafening *boom!* I left the endless hallway behind and stumbled into the open warehouse area. The faint white glow of a jet sat in the middle, but behind it, the grunts and thuds of men fighting echoed. I threw myself forward, then kicked something hard and heavy. I stumbled, windmilling my arms before I hit the concrete floor hard.

"What the fuck." I threw my gaze behind me and stared into the wide open eyes of my bodyguard...*Pavlov*.

The sight, froze me for a second before I shoved close and felt for a pulse at his neck. There was none, and the memory of that blood along the hallway spurred me on more than ever before. Grunts and roars came from the shadows. But they weren't the low, guttural sounds of Max when he fought. They were from a man fighting for his life, from a man who wasn't used to violence...*they came from Anna's dad*.

"Leave him the fuck alone!" Anna screamed.

I shoved forward at the sound and ran past the luxury jet, right into the back of the man who'd grabbed her, wrestling her to the floor as she tried to save her father.

"Get your fucking hands off her!" I screamed, and drove my fist into the asshole's face.

The bastard whirled and fought me.

But there were two more.

Two that were circling Max. I caught the glint of steel, a knife... a gun, I wasn't sure.

"Max, watch out!" I barked a warning.

He didn't look back, didn't take his eyes off the two who flanked him. *"Take her and get the fuck out of here, Fin!"*

"You fucker!" the bastard in front of me lashed out. Catching the blur from the corner of my eye, I ducked at the last second, then tucked my chin and charged him. There was no way they were taking her. No way they were hurting her. No way they'd kill my fucking bodyguard without me taking at least one of them.

No way they were surviving.

Not now...*not ever*.

I didn't care who I had to hurt.

Not if it meant saving her.

47

Finley

"Finley?" Anna screamed. *"Finley, NO!"*

But I took the bastard down and hit him with all I had, driving my fist into his cheek until his head snapped to the side. *"YOU ARE NOT LEAVING WITH HER!"*

Steel glinted in the corner of my eye as he thrust upward, and I felt the sharp sting in my side. But Anna was there, lunging at his hand and tearing at his fingers as she tried to knee him in the balls, and it became all too clear that the glint had been a knife.

I gave a grunt before a bellow. "Anna!"

Then she was beside me, her perfect face so fucking clear to me in the darkness as she let out a piercing cry and punched the bastard in the face. "He tried to kill us..." Punch. *"Tried to kill us all. Just like they killed Baldeon."*

I froze at the words, caught by the sight of the anguish on her face as she lifted her gaze to mine. "I'm so sorry...I thought you took my dad to kill him!" Her tears shimmered in the dark. "I thought...I thought..."

I lowered my gaze to the bastard underneath me as my focus adjusted to the dark. It was the instructor...the same one from that first class. The same one I'd seen outside the classroom after making love to Anna, the same one who'd lurked and hovered and *seen*.

He'd seen too much.

He *knew* too much. "Is that true? You killed Baldeon?"

"Fin!" Max grunted as the sickening wet thuds of fists on flesh sounded. "Your mother."

"He told us he's keep us safe," Anna cried. "Told us your father was going to war and that we'd be nothing more than collateral damage."

I fisted the bastard's shirt as that sting in my side grew talons and claws, spearing all the way inside my chest. But that pain was nothing, that pain *didn't fucking exist*. Not in the wake of her words. "And yet you believed him?"

"What the *fuck*!" Max roared, and charged, slamming into one guy and lifting him into the air. "She fucking betrayed us? *Fin... she fucking betrayed us!*"

Everything moved in slow motion as Anna's dad tried to reach for her from the floor. "Anna, no..."

His hands were still cuffed, and his face was a bloody, swollen mess. He was badly hurt from fighting two men, trying to save his daughter. I saw it all now, every cruel connection as they slipped into place. She came here, not to be one of us. She came here to leave with the FBI.

But as I looked down, I saw that piece of shit was no fucking fed. The bastard smiled as Max let out a grunt behind me, then one assailant hit the floor and didn't move. One down...one to go. After that, it'd all be over.

"Fin..." Anna whimpered. "I love you."

Those words drove deeper and colder than anything I'd ever felt before.

That was no warm, comforting love.

That was cruel and inviting and controlling, all at the same time.

I love you. Those words rang inside my head as I grabbed the asshole's wrist and squeezed, putting everything into that aching desperation until the *snap* of bone filled my ears. The bastard screamed, he bucked and thrashed under my grip as I twisted, lifted my legs, and clamped my thighs around his hips.

He'd killed Baldeon.

Killed my mother.

If he didn't, then he knew who had.

Boom! The gunshot echoed in the space. Max was a blur, lunging toward me as I reached down and grabbed the knife. Steel met flesh as I hefted the knife and drove the blade into his throat, then shoved, cutting all the way until there was nothing but the hiss of air.

"Fin! HE KNEW WHO KILLED YOUR MOTHER!" Max roared as I kicked, shoving the bastard from me, and rose. "

Agony ripped through my side. Agony and desperation, a noxious cocktail with only one way to explode...*and that was her.* My hand shook as I reached around to the back of my jeans.

Max dropped next to the bastard, grabbing him by the shirt. "Tell me who fucking sent you! *Tell me who killed Cian Salvatore!"*

That's all he cared about...delivering the wrath of my father.

I could see it now, see it as plain as the spilled blood before me.

Loyalty raged in my bodyguard's veins.

But it wasn't loyalty to me.

It was to my father, and always would be.

It all came back to that bastard in the basement. The one we killed after they tried to take out Baldeon the first time. His screams still rang in my head.

You think they'd send someone who had any family left? You have no idea who these people are. They're about to unleash a fucking shitstorm on your precious little island and you with it

"It doesn't matter," I murmured, my words sounding hollow and strange. "Nothing else matters."

I lifted my gaze and my hand at the same time. Max punched the assassin. "Tell me who sent you!"

But there was no more speaking, no more breath, no more life. No more of anything. I lifted my head. The whites of Anna's eyes glowed in the dimness. I guessed it was always going to come down to this...

My father or me.

Choose.

Max stiffened as I slid my finger against the trigger. My heart was in the driver's seat now, pushing me harder than my will ever could.

"Fin?" Max murmured and stilled.

Bang!

Anna screamed as Max slumped forward across the assassin. She lifted her gaze as I stood and stumbled toward her father. Pain ripped through my side. I didn't have much time...someone would be here soon enough and there was still too much to do. I fought the need to find her as Anna knelt in front of the bodies.

The small red light blinked from a camera high up on the wall.

But I couldn't worry about that now.

"Get up." I bent and yanked Dillon's arm, forcing him up onto his feet.

His face was busted, one eye already swollen shut, and he swayed as he fought for balance.

"What are you..." he muttered. "What are you doing?"

Like Anna, he glanced toward Max's body with shock and terror on his face.

"Move, Mr. Shaw," I growled, shoving him forward. "Don't make me ask twice."

Agony tore through my side, making me stumble and clutch my arm against my ribs. The gun wavered in my hand, but I gripped it tight, my finger far away from the trigger. Dillon Shaw glanced over his shoulder as I clenched my jaw and drove him forward, through an office door and into the room.

The place was small and cluttered. A desk lamp was on, the glow barely brightening the room. But it was enough. I glanced around, and pulled out a chair. "Sit."

He did as I instructed, looking shocked, hurt. *Scared.*

"Fin," Anna cried behind me. "Fin, what are you doing?"

"The only thing I can." I yanked the phone from the desk and tore the cords free, then knelt in front of Dillon to bind his ankles together. "What did you think was going to happen when my father found out?"

Anna's father let out sob and shook his head.

"When you disappeared with *a hundred and ninety-five million dollars?*" I barked.

He just froze, his visible eye glassy. The other one was swollen shut, and his lips were bloody and raw. "I was going to send it...I was going to send it all," he whimpered. "I swear."

"You swear?" I stood at the words.

That savage part of me took hold, like poison in my veins.

But it wasn't the blood of my father that corrupted me.

It wasn't the hate and the rage of my mother's death that pushed me to the brink and beyond.

It was her...Anna Shaw.

I took a step, grabbed her arm, and yanked.

"Fin!" She fought, trying her best to yank herself from my hold.

But there was no going back now. Not for me...*or for her.*

I lifted my gaze to a doorway on the other side of the office. "Move, Anna," I growled.

My body was alive.

But my soul was scorched.

There was only us now.

Only her and me...and fuck me, I had to own her...*or die trying.*

48

Anna

"Fin...Fin, what are you doing?" I jerked my gaze over my shoulder as he pushed me through the doorway and into what looked like some kind of storeroom.

One flick and a light brightened above us, then he closed the door, leaving us alone.

"Anna!" Dad roared in the other room.

But it was a bit muffled now, locked away. I turned and took a step backwards, glancing at the blood on Fin's shirt and the madness in his eyes. "Fin...talk to me."

"Talk to you?" he murmured, and combed his fingers through his hair. *"Talk to you?* What the fuck do you want me to say, Anna? That I just...killed for you? That I *fucking* murdered for you? That if my father knew what you'd planned all along, it'd be *your* fucking body getting cold out there?"

I flinched with the hatred in his tone.

But it wasn't hate...was it?

Not the kind I'd expected.

"Max would've told him." His voice deepened as he lowered his gaze. "He would've told my father, then there'd be nothing I could do..." he met my gaze, "to protect you."

Protect me...

I swallowed hard, staring at the blood shining black on his fingers. Fear gripped me, making my knees and my words tremble as I took a step forward. "But you did protect me, Fin." He flinched at the words, watching me with those careful eyes as I came closer. "You did what you had to do."

It was our lives on the line here...and my heart. A pang of agony tore through my chest. "You found me, you found me and you did what you had to do."

Carefully, I reached for him, waiting for him to move. But he didn't, just stood there with those unfathomable eyes. "You showed me how you truly felt."

One flare of his jaw and he lashed out, grasping the back of my neck. "Showed you how I felt? *Showed you how I felt?* I fucking made love to you. I protected you...I *took care of you.*" Rage sparked in his gaze. He drove me backwards with long strides, pushing me off balance...driving me toward the far end of the room.

Boxes lined the walls. There were heavy coverings over what looked like stored furniture. I reached out, grasping the corner of something to steady myself before hitting the far wall. Fabric slipped under my grip, sliding from the top of an ornate mirror. The light bounced in the reflection as Finley stepped closer. "I took care of you, even when I knew you were lying."

My stomach clenched with the pain in his voice. But I couldn't make myself move...couldn't fight that cold caress of fear. He was changing, morphing into someone else right in front of my eyes.

"But all that is behind us now. *I* put it behind us. Max is dead, Pavlov is dead, no one but me knows what you were planning to do." He took another step closer, pushing me against the wall. The scent of blood filled my nose as he brushed his thumb across my cheek. "My father will never know...that's why you won't work for him anymore."

My stomach roiled.

"You will work for me instead." He lifted his gaze to mine. "You will launder for me, you will clean money for me. You will find new ways of hiding money *for me*...and when the time comes, you will take my side."

Take his side? "What does that mean, Fin?"

He stepped closer, lowering his hand to my shirt. Bloodied fingers worked the buttons, opening them one by one as he dipped his head. "We can take our time, plan out the rest of our lives. But make no mistake, there is no life for me without you in it."

Thunder clashed overhead. "What are you saying?"

"I will own you. I *will* have you," he whispered in my ear. The brush of his lips at my neck made my heart race. But that sickening, heavy feeling gripped my stomach as his words finally took hold.

This was not agreement...*this was coercion.*

"Mine," he growled. "You will be mine."

I slid out from against him and stumbled away. "You want me to, what? Obey you? To lie for you? To...*love you?*" I sucked in hard breaths. "What do you want, Fin? Tell me, because I don't understand this at all!"

"Lie, love, fuck, marry," he growled through clenched teeth as he turned toward me. "I want it all when it comes to you. There are no boundaries I won't cross, no lies I won't tell...*no blood I will not spill."*

His gaze shifted when he said those words, as though in that moment, he understood the lengths he'd go to. Cold wrapped itself around me. I was frozen to the core, numb, and yet filled with burning hunger all at the same time. He didn't look toward the doorway, didn't draw my attention to my father's life hanging in the balance...*he didn't have to.*

That's how they worked, right? They drew you in, then took you under. They made you want, made you love, made you trust more than you thought possible.

"I will protect you," he said carefully. "I will make sure no one ever finds out."

"For money," I said as the cold moved through me.

"For love," he answered. "Your father's and mine."

"Do you really think I can love you after this?"

He flinched at the words and came toward me, flanking my side to stand at my back. I lifted my gaze to us in the uncovered mirror. "I hope so," he murmured, and caressed my body, spreading his hand wide to cup my breast. "Jesus, Anna." He rocked backwards, and the haunted look in his eyes grew darker. "There's no other way. No other way that doesn't end with you, or your dad dying at the hands of my father."

The panicked thud ached. It was like someone was squeezing my heart, clenching until all the blood drained free. Is this what it meant to love someone like Finley? Is this what I meant to fall for a Mafia Prince?

"If not love, then I'll take whatever you can give me." He murmured.

"What if that is hate?" I growled, and yet even as I said the words, I knew they were a lie.

"I'll take it." He kneaded my breast and dropped his head to my neck, kissing and biting, hard enough for me to know how savage he was feeling in that moment. "I'll take it all, however you come to me...*just as long as you come to me.*"

He slid his hands to the front of my jeans, his fingers working the button before plunging inside my panties. I lifted my arms, reaching over his shoulders as he slid his finger along my slit. "Now, are you going to launder for me, Anna?" He bent lower, slipping a finger inside me. "Or will you force me to do something I'll fucking regret?"

I grasped the back of his neck, pulling him hard against me, craving his touch, his brutal fucking touch.

"Take it off, Anna," Finley murmured in my ear. "Take it off and tell me you're mine...*forever.*"

Forever.

"Anna...no!" my father screamed in the room next door. *"Let her go, you fucking bastard!"*

I held Finley's gaze in the mirror as he reached into the pocket of his jeans and drew out a wad of money. "Make your decision, launderer. Will you be mine?"

He had blood on his knuckles, blood he'd spilled for me.

He'd said he'd fight for me, said he'd inflict the kind of violence that'd make me scared of him. I already knew what he did...and knew he was capable of more. I knew this because he had everything now.

My loyalty and my lies.

I lifted my hands to the buttons of my filthy shirt and opened them one by one.

They were all his now, every dark and dirty secret I'd ever owned.

They were his demons to carry around now.

If I had a chance to do it over, would I have come here to this place...to *Cosa Nostra Institute?* I wanted to say no. The sight of Max's dead body pushed into my mind. I wanted to say the price was too great. You see, when you lie down with lions, you aren't really protected at all. You're just like them.

A hunter.

I'd done things on the island...terrible things.

"Make your decision, Anna," Fin urged in my ear, holding the wad of cash in one hand, and reached to clamp my throat with theother. "Tell me what I want to know?"

A million dollars laundered?

A billion?

It didn't matter, money was useless...money was *never* what I'd wanted.

It had always been him.

"Yes," I answered, and dropped my shirt to the floor. "I will be yours."

I reached around and unhooked my bra. The bright splash of blood smeared across my breasts with his touch.

"Damn right." He lowered his hand.

Money fluttered to the floor as he gripped my jeans and pushed them down.

"I will fucking have you, Anna." His hand slid along my back, pushing me forward.

I bent at the waist and closed my eyes. The sound of his zipper came before he pushed inside me. I moaned with relief. Hard thrusts jolted me, forcing my eyes open. I held onto the mirror as Finley rose behind me, his gaze locked on mine.

I love him...

I love him.

I...love...him...

I pushed backwards as he thrust, meeting his brutal blows until he pulled me against him. His hands were all over me, sliding along my belly, cupping my breasts. His cock was buried deep inside...and I'd never felt more alive.

I wanted this...I wanted him. "Fin..." I cried, my body clenching as stars burst behind my eyelids. "I..."

He came with a growl, hard breaths scattering my hair, and turned his head. "I love you," he whispered against my neck. "Anna...I love you."

I knew in his own way he did. His love was brutal and controlling. *And I wanted it all.*

Deep shudders wracked his body. I lifted my gaze to the reflection of him in the mirror, tears shimmered in his gaze. The sight of them made the ache in my chest clench tighter. I pulled forward, leaving him to slip free and then turned.

"It's going to be okay, you hear me?" I grabbed his face, his perfect goddamn face. The one that haunted my dreams. "It'll be okay because I *choose you*."

God help me I did. I chose Finley, somehow I always knew I would. I chose him...and he chose me.

One nod of his head and I leaned close, kissing the salty trail from his cheeks.

"We have to hurry." He lifted his gaze, kissed me and then bent, grabbing my panties and jeans, sliding them up my thighs. "They'll be here soon and we need to get our story straight."

I sucked in deep breaths and tugged my clothes into place, buttoning my jeans and sliding on my bra and shirt. A minute was all it took, but to me it felt like a lifetime.

"You ready?"

I tucked in my shirt and curled my hair behind my ear. "I guess so."

This would be the hard part, meeting my dad's gaze...knowing what to say.

Fin slid his hand in mine and pulled me toward the door.

Dad's head snapped up as the door opened and Fin and I walked out. He'd been crying, slick tears still shone on his cheeks. But Fin moved fast, letting my hand go to stride out into the hangar space.

"What did he do to you?" Dad cried, searching my gaze.

"Do to her?" Fin growled as he returned.

Dad flinched as Fin used the contact's knife to cut the ties around his ankles, then shoved the key into the handcuffs, tearing them free. "I saved your lives, how's that?"

"Dad," I started, and took a step forward. "I need you to listen to me. I need you to understand what I'm about to say."

Dad just looked at Fin, who rose to stand next to me, then shifted his gaze to me.

Revulsion sparkled in his eyes. "Anna...no."

I swallowed hard as a roar cut through the hangar. *"FIN!"*

"Dad." I stepped closer, the words spilling from my mouth. The more I spoke the more he looked at me like I was a stranger.

I was trying to save his life.

Trying to save mine, too.

"This is the only way." I finished as the thunder of boots grew louder. "The way it has to be."

Dad said nothing as flashlights cut through the darkness and into our eyes, and the Commission's guards followed.

"Fin!" the Commander roared, his eyes wild as they scanned the room, then moved to Finley.

"I'm okay," Fin answered. "We're all okay."

The Commander looked at me, then my dad, and jerked his gaze back to Fin. *"What the fuck happened?"*

49

Anna

Lies.

They consume us.

So does love.

I stood at the dock in the slanting rain and watched my dad leave for the second time since coming to the island. Only this time, he wasn't roaring and raging, desperate to save me. This time, he didn't look at me at all. Instead, he just sat there, defeated, while the yacht sailed away.

"Come on," Fin murmured as he pulled me away. "It's been a helluva night."

The steel gray sky was brightening. But I couldn't leave, not yet. Rain battered me as I stared, hoping he'd turn to look at me. But he didn't, he just grew smaller...and smaller and smaller.

Until eventually I let Fin pull me away.

We made our way back to Fin's apartment building and stepped, dripping, into the foyer.

"Mr. Salvatore." I jerked my gaze up at the voice and stared at two bodyguards I'd never seen before. "Ms. Shaw." One nodded my way in greeting.

I could only nod back.

Fin pulled me toward the elevator and we stepped inside, rising silently to the apartment.

I felt numb inside, aching with pain for my dad. I knew he didn't understand, knew he didn't like what'd happened. But there was no other way.

"I don't know about you, but I need a hot shower and some sleep." Fin left my side, striding toward the bedroom.

Leale hauled himself to his feet and padded slowly toward me. I dropped to my knees and hugged him tight. *There was no other way,* I told myself again. No other way that didn't result in collateral damage.

I refused to be collateral damage.

Or anyone I loved.

Fin dragged his sodden shirt over his head, the wound in his side now bandaged and taped. It'd been chaos from the moment the Commander found us, bright lights, people everywhere, and questions asked over and over again. Fin finally took over, rubbing my arm when the words choked in the back of my throat.

He explained how my dad had been kidnapped, and the men who took him had tried to take me as well. He told them how he'd found out and raced to save me, with Max and Pavlov at his side.

He told them how his bodyguards had died saving his life.

How devastated he was with the loss.

How they'd both been loyal right to the end.

The doctor came and checked us over, taking Fin back to the infirmary to stitch and bandage his wounds before he called his father. Dominic Salvatore took the news in stoic silence before asking to speak to the Commander.

Mateo Ristani, the Commander of Cosa Nostra Institute, confirmed everything Fin said, glancing my way as he repeated what had happened not once, but twice. By the time we were done...it was almost daylight again.

Now Dad was gone.

And I was here with Fin.

"Anna?" he called from the bedroom. "Are you coming?"

I turned to the bedroom, because to do anything else was hopeless.

I belonged to Finley Salvatore now...*maybe I always had...*

50

Anna

Months later...

THE CAMERA BLINKED ABOVE ME, moving to scan my office for the hundredth time, distracting me. Watched, controlled. That was my life now. It was what it'd been like since coming back from the island six months ago. I tried to not look up. Tried to pretend not to notice how guarded I was. Instead, I grabbed my water and unscrewed the cap.

My eyes blurred. I squinted, the screen a haze of scrolling numbers as the program scanned the accounts. I'd worked harder than ever before after the Island, days, most nights. I tilted back the bottle, spying the camera with the movement, and swallowed.

I hated them...

Dominic Salvatore and the other members of the Commission.

Hated him more than ever. I hated his control, his power. I hated how he infected everyone and everything. But more than anything, I hated how he ruled his son...the man I'd fallen in love with.

Finley Salvatore.

I screwed the top back on my bottle and turned back to the scrolling accounts on the screen, wrestling with my damn heart. Footsteps thudded outside the locked door, drawing my focus.

The shadow neared, stopped, peering through the slits of glass in the door. I felt his gaze raking me, searching the room, making sure I was still here working away like a good fucking dog.

A nerve twitched in the corner of my eye as I set my gaze on the monitors, adjusting run times and expanding out to new parameters. I'd searched for Bitcoin accounts, finding ways to hide the billions of unwashed Salvatore money only to have it return squeaky clean.

The moment my father had come home bloody and desperate, telling me he'd found himself in trouble with the dangerous Mafia family, I knew I had to help. This was the only way I could. I knew the network, knew how to infiltrate the many servers. I'd spent my entire life watching my father create network after network, spending my nights hunkered behind my laptop, creating my own future...

Only for it to be traded for my father's life.

Now I worked for *them*.

The Salvatores.

I typed, my fingers flying across the keyboard before I hit the command and expanded into new networks, cleaning even more money and driving it all back into Salvatore accounts. With a few strokes, I turned two hundred million dollars of blood money into something untouchable by any kind of federal enforcement agency, foreign and domestic.

They were rich beyond anyone else on the planet. "Take that, Musk," I whispered, fighting that knife-edge of power play between pride and disgust.

I looked up, searching for the guard peering through the door and into the room, but he was gone. I scowled, looked at the clock...*gone from like an hour ago.*

Footsteps resounded, two of them...my pulse stuttered, narrowing in on that heavy, purposeful gait. I knew that gait... heard it in my dreams...felt it in my body.

My breaths deepened as a surge of adrenaline tore through me. Shadows spilled across the door, too many for one person. The tiny beep of the electronic lock sounded before two men invaded my world. One hung back. I didn't look at him. Instead, I leaned forward, activated the keystrokes of the triple-encrypted locking system I'd set up for my own foolproof program.

They couldn't access it, not even if they tried. They might control every aspect of my life...but I'd be damned if they got their hands on my father's. The guard's focus dropped to my fingers flying across the keyboard, activating the encryption before I turned, meeting his gaze.

He was smart, this one. Cold, calculating blue eyes that reminded me a little of Lazarus Rossi. But he wasn't a Rossi. Lazarus wouldn't spy on me. Not for all the money or power in the world. Instead, he'd tell Dominic Salvatore to go fuck himself. But not this guy parading as security. He was a computer science major from Berkeley, graduated top of his field. As if they could send someone my way and not expect I'd pick apart every aspect of his life.

If they did, then they were dumber than I expected.

"Ms. Shaw." He moved closer, scanning my desk before waiting for me to stand.

I didn't smile or acknowledge. We were far beyond niceties.

I knew he was sent to gain information about my program. After all, that was what we traded, wasn't it? Lies and lives as currency. I laundered their filthy money, and they let my father live. I rose from my seat and turned my attention to the other male in the room. The one who made my pulse race and my body a traitor.

Finely stood at the doorway, dressed immaculately as always. There wasn't a crease in his white-collared shirt, not a hair out of place, either. He'd became bigger, more muscled, spending countless hours in the gym we had at home in the months we escaped the Island off Mauritius. The one controlled by the Commission which had come under attack.

We'd barely made it out alive...*some of us didn't.*

I lifted my arms as the 'guard' passed behind me, waving a wand over my body. His hands were next, sliding along my arms. I held Finley's gaze as those hands rounded my stomach, searching a little too hard.

There was a twitch in Finley's stare as the man behind me knelt, holding on to my hips, his hands running along the backs of my thighs.

"Sorry, Ms. Shaw." He moved down the inside of my thighs and my pants, his fingers dangerously close to my crease.

Finley's jaw clenched. Muscles flaring. He hated it. Hated them putting their hands on me, and yet every fucking day they did, knowing there was no reason to. This was just another game his father played, another flex of his power over me...

Over us.

"You're all clear." The guard rose to his feet.

My body shuddered with the violation which made me sick. Hard breaths moved though me. Finley said nothing, but he didn't have to. Rage sparked in his gaze as he turned to the asshole who he knew was untouchable...*for now.*

"Mr. Salvatore." The guard nodded as he rounded my desk and strode out of the room, closing the door behind him.

But there wasn't the click of the lock this time. Seemed like they were letting me out...for now. I grabbed my purse and my jacket from the back of the chair and strode around the desk.

"Anna..." Fin called.

But I couldn't look at him. Couldn't want him...couldn't listen to his goddamn excuses. Instead, I twisted the handle and shoved open the door, striding out into the stark white hallway.

My heels resounded until they were smothered by the heavy thud of boots. Fin said nothing as he followed behind me. The chill from his silence at my back said it all as I clutched my card, pressed it to the scanner, ignoring the five cameras swiveling my way as I waited for the doors to open.

They always waited a second longer than necessary before letting me leave. As though they wanted to get the point across one last goddamn time.

We own you.

It couldn't be any more obvious. The door opened with a rush, and fresh air hit me. I stepped out into darkness. It felt a lot like my life. Darkness surrounded me. Darkness claimed me...*darkness became me.*

Headlights flashed from the Maserati parked at the entrance. Finley strode ahead to the passenger's door and opened, waiting for me to climb in. For a second, I didn't want to. I lifted my gaze to the empty parking lot. Freedom waited out there beyond the towering, razor-wire-tipped fence line and the reach of Dominic Salvatore. Far beyond the murky gloom and the trees, and the road that led to the Facility.

The Facility.

That was what I called it. But it may as well be called *The Prison*, because that was what it was for me in the days since I escaped the carnage with Finley. His father bought me back from the island and delivered me here, to the secure room where I was watched every damn second of the day.

I could leave...one chance, that was all I needed. I'd run and never look back. Change my name. Change my hair and my clothes. I'd become someone else...someone who wasn't controlled. Someone who wasn't *me*. A pang tore across my chest at the thought. But there were two things making me stay. My father, and my damn heart.

"Anna," Fin called, drawing me back to the waiting car. "*Please*."

I pulled away from thoughts of running away and resigned myself to my fate. Lights from the dashboard spilled into the footwell of the car. I focused on that, on the asphalt under my boots, on the smell of rich leather, on *anything* apart from *him*, and climbed in.

Because I just couldn't stand the pain.

Fin shut the door behind me carefully. The headlights spilled over his muscular body as he rounded the sports car. Then he was here, so damn close. The seductive scent of his body so fucking delicious, making my body react in ways that unnerved me.

As though he knew what I was feeling, he turned his head, those perfect brown eyes finding me in the dark. Desperation collided in his eyes. His chest rose a little harder with a breath before he lowered his gaze to the curve of my breasts.

HIs hand moved in the dark. I didn't leave his gaze as he worked the button of my white collared blouse. Just one button...the one that was in his way. The back of his finger caressed my lace bra, grazing my nipple, finding me puckered and tight.

"I missed you today," he murmured, his voice deep and hunky as his finger slipped under the cup.

I flinched with the contact, the warmth of his finger drawing shudders through my body.

"I'm going to take you home now," he continued. "And straight to bed."

"I'm not tired," I lied.

"Who said anything about being tired, Anna?"

My insides clenched. That need bloomed deep inside me. He was the only man I knew and the only man I wanted to. I just wished I didn't want to.

I broke his gaze, forcing my focus to the front of the car and the grounds of the place I hated more than anything. Finley stabbed the button for the engine, and started the car.

We were driving through the secure gate and past the armed personnel in an instant, pulling out onto the quiet darkened road that was closed to the rest of the world.

"Are you ever going to talk to me?"

I winced at the words. We didn't talk. Not like how he wanted to. Minimal words...all heat, our hunger did our talking us. Even that I wished I could kill. Finley slowed the car, pulling out past the signs marking Private Property and Trespassers Will Be Prosecuted signs and out to the main road that would lead us toward the city to the house we shared.

A house owned by Salvatore money.

Money I'd laundered.

Fin's fists tightened around the steering wheel, strangling it as he punched the accelerator. Headlights cut through the darkness. The sleek sports car hugged the corners, never missing a beat as it took us home.

Home was a battleground of emotions. I could hate the facility. I could slam doors and throw pens. I could curl my lips and bare my teeth at the cameras. But here...here I couldn't do any of that. The sensor on the dashboard blinked, and the towering black steel gate slid open, leaving us to drive to the house.

I was already yanking the handle before he killed the engine. He swore hard as I stepped out, slamming the door closed behind me.

"Anna...*wait, for fucks sake!*"

But I wasn't waiting. I strode toward the front door and pressed my thumb against the scanner before unlocking the door.

"*Anna!*" Fin growled behind me.

I headed inside, making my way to the rear of the house.

"*God damnit!*"

The heavy thud of his steps boomed behind me. He grabbed my arm as I stepped through our bedroom door, turning me to face him.

Anger and desperation burned in his eyes as he roared, "When the fuck are you going to talk to me?"

I stared at him, hating him. Needing him. God, I needed him. I wrenched my arm from his hold and turned away, moving through the expansive bedroom to my wardrobe.

This place felt empty...stark...cold...and expensive. It was all a pretense. Everything about my life was like that. Since I'd stepped off the plane coming from the island, there'd not been a second for the real me.

Because she no longer existed.

I kicked off my shoes and reached around, unzipping my slacks, letting them fall to the floor.

"Are you going to say anything?" He glared at me as I walked past, heading to the bathroom.

The stark lights were blinding, flicking on the moment I stepped inside. I worked the buttons of my blouse as Finley moved deeper into the house.

"I'm tired," I muttered, not bothering to meet his gaze.

I didn't need to. The bathroom almost trembled with the thunder on his face. "Thought you said you weren't?" He stepped up behind me, pressing against my back. "So which is it, Anna? Either you're tired or you're not?"

I lifted my head, meeting his glare over my shoulder. "Both."

He scowled, driving his body harder against me. He was already erect, the bulge forced against my ass. I sighed. So we were doing this...after all this time, we were really doing this. "Look, Fin, I—"

He reached up, wrapped his hand around my throat, squeezing hard enough to shock me. Savage breaths drove his chest against my back as he pressed into me, growling in my ear, "You fucking push me, Anna...you fucking push me to my goddamn limit."

Hard. Savage. I melted in his strength and unleashed a moan as he pushed my head down, bending me over the basin and, with his other hand, tore off my panties. He fumbled with the front of his pants, yanking the button, and shoved down his zipper.

I splayed my hands against the basin, lifting my head enough to find the animal in his eyes. His finger slipped between my legs, seeking, spreading, slipping into my core only to slip out and find my clit.

"I'm going mad." He growled, circling before he fucked me with his finger. "You hear me? *You're driving me mad.*"

"Good." I moaned. *"Good."*

"Good?" His tone was dangerous.

Anyone else would be terrified of that tone. Anyone else would be terrified of him...

I drove my ass against his hand until I pressed against his hard cock. "Yes." I hissed. *"Good."*

51

Finley

"Good?" I pushed my finger inside, watching as she dropped her head forward and moaned. "You stop fucking talking to me, stop wanting me." I thrust inside her, fucking her, claiming her. "You barely fucking look at me, and this..."

I slipped my finger free, grabbed her ass, and spread her pussy wide before I knelt between her legs. The scent of her hit me, driving all the way to my cock. "This is the only time I can have you. It's all you give me."

I moved closer, licking her core. She shuddered, trembling, hating...*me*.

She hated me.

I slid my tongue inside, driving my face deeper, reaching as far as I could until I pulled away. I couldn't wait...couldn't stop myself. I rose, sliding my hand along her back to grab the back of her neck and slammed my hips forward.

My cock rammed in hard, all the way to the hilt. She bucked from the invasion, fighting against my hold. But I gripped her, sliding out only to drive back in once more.

This was what she made me...*a beast.*

She unleashed a moan. And fuck me if I didn't need that sound. I needed the guttural rawness. I needed her, even if it was only like this...*I needed her.*

I gripped her back and thrust back in, watching her shove her hands against the mirror, driving back against me to meet my thrusts, and instantly I plunged back into that night. To the night I'd fucked her in that warehouse on the island, covered in another man's blood, while her father screamed in the room next to us.

Make your decision, launderer. Be mine forever. My own words rang in my ears.

Anna...no! Her father screamed in the room next door. *Let her go, you fucking bastard!*

But I'd never let her go. I rammed my hips forward, thudding her body against the basin as that look of savage ecstasy tore across her face.

"If this is all you give me, Anna..." I grunted as my balls clenched, and that sweeping dangerous need drove through me. "Then...this...is...what...*I'll...take.*"

She cried out, throwing her head backward, her pussy clenching and throbbing around me as I came hard, my warmth melting deep into her body. My breaths were harsh, tearing from my chest, just like she tore out my damn heart.

"When are you going to forgive me?" I asked, the words fighting my gasps.

She shoved backward, tearing from my hold, and headed for the shower. "Never."

I just stood there, watching her shed the rest of her clothes and hit the taps. That cold, hard truth hit me like a slap. She hated me...*she fucking hated me*. Christ. The thunder in my head was deafening, making me panicked and unmerciful. I clenched my fists, hating that seething rage inside.

But she never looked my way as she stepped into the spray, leaving the water to cascade down her body. A pang tore through my chest as I followed the rivulets down her breasts, then her stomach. My gaze moving to the thin patch of hair between her legs.

God, I still wanted her...

I turned away from the sight, grabbed my pants, and walked out of the bathroom. The hiss of the shower was like nails down a damn chalkboard. I wanted to go back in there, wanted to fuck her again...and keep fucking her until she came back to me.

But she wouldn't come back, and it wouldn't matter how many times I made her come. Knowing that was eating me alive. I crossed the room, unbuttoned my shirt, dropping it inside the walk-in robe and tugged on a t-shirt before grabbing a pair of sweats and leaving.

The hiss of the shower carried, haunting me as I made my way back along the mammoth fucking house to turn down the east wing and the gym I'd had purpose-built.

The faint scent of chlorine hit me as I pushed through the doors. This place was a fucking mansion, too big for the two of us. *And what...you expected more?*

My thoughts turned to Lazarus and Kat, who now had a perfect baby girl. The guy was still an asshole. But now, with two women to protect, he was a dangerous asshole. But that kid... Christ, she was perfect.

Lights flickered on with the movement. I bent, hit the button, and started the stereo, listening to Ghostemane fill the room. If only it was that fucking easy to fill my heart. I stepped up to the treadmill, starting with a walk, then pushed into a jog, then I upped the speed all the way as hard as I dared.

I wanted to punish myself.

A thousand times over.

I wanted to hurt myself for not being the man she needed.

For not standing up to my father when she needed me. For being the spineless fucking asshole and...*keeping them safe, the only way I knew how.*

Family.

Always fucking family.

I pushed harder, striding out until the burn moved through my thighs. I focused on the darkness outside through the double-glazed windows, and my mind turned to the money.

It was always the money.

So much fucking money.

She made it all...a thousand times over. There was no way he was going to let her go...*or hurt her.* But that didn't mean he wouldn't hurt her dad. There I found myself. I was her warden, her protector, her lover. But what I wanted to be was her fucking husband.

I wanted what Lazarus had.

A wife. A family. More than anything, I wanted her, the real her. The one she kept locked up in that fucking cage around her heart. My breaths ripped from my chest as I punched the button and slowed the pace, stepping off with shaking legs. I grabbed a towel from the rack and wiped the sweat from my body.

I was caught in a trap of my own making. Fuck, this would be easier if I wasn't obsessed with her...if I wasn't so...*riled*. I cast the towel to the floor and then turned, heading for the weights.

I'd burn her out of my system. Either that or I'd run myself to the damn ground. I rounded the weights and grabbed the bar. The first rep hurt, then the second one burned. By the time I was an hour in, I was fueled by fire...and the image of her anger burning in my mind.

By the time I was done, I couldn't walk.

I thought about sleeping on the hard mats in the gym...but the moment I did, my body ached with the kind of fever I couldn't take. Her alone...in our bed...I gave a sigh and made for the door, killing the music as I made my way through the empty house.

It was empty...cold, hollow. Devoid of her life.

She was nothing more than a shape in the bed when I stepped in. I headed to the bathroom, closing the door before the light came on. I showered, scrubbed the sweat from my body, and stepped out, wrapping a towel around my waist before lifting my gaze to the mirror.

I was hard, ripped. I spread my hand over my pecs, feeling the muscles tighten before I tugged the towel and looked down, remembering her bent over here two hours ago. Legs spread, her pussy against my lips. My cock hardened with the memory. But I didn't reach down, I didn't relive the fantasy. I walked into the bedroom as the light shone and climbed into the bed next to her.

The sounds of rhythmic breaths beside me were confusingly comforting. She was asleep. I knew that. I knew her sounds, knew her whimpers, knew her tortured moans.

"Fin... *no*," she murmured beside me. *"Please."*

I scowled in the dark, sliding my hand up and under my head. I lay like that, listening to her nightmares...ones which were always about me. I closed my eyes, willing sleep to come, but as always it stayed away, until that hollow ache inside me became the emptiness I so desperately needed.

Maybe this was rest for me.

A cruel, sadistic slumber.

It's what I deserve...

Thud.

The sound woke me. I cracked open my eyes, coming back to reality with a heavy thud of my heart. I jerked my gaze beside me, finding the bed empty. "Anna?"

I shoved up, climbed out of bed, the scent of her perfume heavy in the air. "*Anna?*"

The faint sound of her car came from outside. I lunged, ignoring the fact I was naked, and charged for the front door. By the time I yanked open the door and raced outside, she was already turning onto the road with the security gate closing behind her. "*Shit!*" I roared, turning back inside.

Panic moved through me. She knew...*she fucking knew*. I moved back to the bedroom, snatching my phone from the charger beside the bed, and dialed her number.

"*Hi, you've reached Anna—*"

I stabbed the button, ending the call, and redialed.

"*Hi, you've reach—*"

"Answer the goddamn phone!" I stabbed the button once more, desperation driving through me.

She answered. "What, Fin?"

"What the fuck are you doing?" Panic punched through me as reality hit home.

She never left...not since her father went into hiding and my own exerted his control. She was to be guarded twenty-four-seven. Watched by either the guards at the facility, or by me.

"Driving," she answered, coldly. "That's what I'm doing."

I raked my fingers through my hair. "You know what I mean. *You* know what he'll do—"

"I don't care."

I stiffened, my stomach dropping. "What do you mean, you don't care?"

"I'm tired, Fin. Tired of this, tired of..."

You. She didn't have to say it. But she was tired of me, tired of my name, tired of the fucking terror I bought into her life.

"Come back home," I demanded. "Come back home and we'll figure it out."

"We *did* that, remember?"

I winced at the words and shook my head. "We'll do it again. We'll do it again and we'll keep doing it. Just give me a goddamn chance..."

"Why?"

The word hung in the air. I closed my eyes. "Because...because I can't live without you."

Silence, just the faint sound of tires through the speaker as the car slowed, then braked to a stop. She was listening...that was all I needed.

"Tell me what I can do." I opened my eyes. "Whatever it is, I'll do it."

She knew what I had to do to stop this. The only thing that'd put an end to this control...*kill my father.*

"Say the words, Anna," I whispered, knowing I was past the point of blood loyalty at this moment.

If she told me to put a bullet in his head, I'd do it. I'd do it and I'd live with consequences.

"I can't." She whimpered. "I just can't."

The phone went dead in an instant. My heart punched through my chest as I forced myself to move, striding into the bedroom and made for my wardrobe. I pulled on anything I could, t-shirt, jeans before shoving my feet into boots and raced for the car. But as I shoved open the front door and tore halfway down the stairs, I heard the rumble of the automatic gate once more.

The front grille of her midnight-blue Audi appeared, nosing up to the gate before driving through. I watched her pull past my Maserati and head for the garage at the rear of the house. Then I followed, because it was all I could do not to burn the entire world to the ground.

My boots crunched on the gravel as I rounded the side of the house. She climbed out, closing the door and locking the car behind her. Tears slick and shining on her cheeks. I closed the distance between us in an instant, wrapping my arms around her, and pulled her hard against my chest.

Her body trembled, shuddering in my arms.

"Jesus...*Jesus, Anna.*" I clung to her, driving her against me in a desperate attempt to pull her inside.

Her hands trembled, sliding around me as I lowered my head to the crook of her neck, breathing her scent deep into my lungs. "Don't do that again...*okay? Just don't ever leave me.*"

Her nails dug into my side as she fisted my shirt. I winced, welcoming the sting. Cool air licked my back as she tugged my shirt.

I met her gaze. Her movements were frenzied, tearing off her shirt.

"Fuck me." She growled. "Fin, *just fuck me.*"

I tore off my shirt and grabbed her, lifting her feet from the floor and drove her backward against the side of her car. Her black skirt rode high, bunching around her waist as I fumbled with my zipper. I was already hard, already desperate to be inside her.

"My panties." She clawed my back, pulling me against her.

I didn't have time to waste, the need for her howling like a beast inside me. I reached down, yanked her panties aside, and drove inside her. She hissed, lips curled, teeth bared. There was nothing soft or careful about this moment.

This was raw...

This was savage...and more alive than she'd felt after stepping off that damn island. I gripped the back of her neck, holding her head still, her gaze fixed on mine as I drove my cock inside her.

"You're *mine.*" I grunted, driving deep. "You understand that?"

Rage sparked in her eyes. But there was a hunger in there...one that gave me a spark of hope. I took it, clenching my ass, thrusting inside her. I took it all.

"You leave me again, Anna, and I swear to you, I'll burn that place to the ground...and everyone in it."

She arched her back, her nails digging into my shoulders. The sting was cruel and unmerciful. I welcomed it. *I needed it*. She cried out, her face twisted in perfect agony.

Hard breaths punched through my words as that need to claim overtook me. "You...are mine...Anna. Always will be..."

With a savage snarl, my body tensed. Heat rushed through me as I came inside her. She clung to me, her sharp touch turning soft and needing as she pulled me against her. I wound my arm around her, cradling her body as she shook and shuddered.

"I can't...I can't keep doing this." Her words were warm against my neck.

I held her, sliding my hand along her spine. "You have to." I closed my eyes, giving in to this tormented moment. "We have no choice. We do what he says." I lifted my head, pulling away from her. "Because if he ever found out the truth, then it wouldn't just be your father's life on the table."

She stared into my eyes, her own fresh with tears.

Panic moved through them...as she finally understood.

52

Anna

"It's not just your father's life…"

The words hit me. My father's life was used against me. But it wasn't just Dad's life…*it was Fin's.*

"No." I shook my head. "He wouldn't…"

"Wouldn't he?" He stared into my eyes. "He doesn't need me… not when he has the money."

I stilled, then shook my head, my body clenching around him as he softened inside me.

"You know what he's like," Fin whispered. Sparks collided in his eyes.

I knew…only too well.

I swallowed hard, my breaths deepening as those shudders ripped through me. Would Dominic Salvatore kill his only son? His heir to his Mafia fortune? Would he be that callous and cold?

Yes…yes, he would.

Warmth slipped down my cheeks as Fin pulled me close. "Fin, what the fuck have we done?"

"Survived." He pressed me against him. "That's all we've done. Nothing more."

I closed my eyes, taking in his warmth as a *beep* on his cell sounded. He pulled away and grabbed it from his pocket, scowling as he read the message.

"Come on." He stepped away, glancing toward the road. "Let's go inside."

"What is it?" I followed his gaze, finding a dark-gray sedan slowly creep past the closed gate as he tugged me toward the house. "Are they spying on us?"

"Looking after their investment, they called it," Fin muttered, tugging on my hand to lead me back inside.

I followed him through the door and into the bedroom. The bed was a mess, covers cast aside in his panic to get to me. I stared at that, and for some reason, it hit me. Those fucking covers...his fear of losing me.

He was losing me. I could feel myself slipping away, and the truth was, I didn't know how to stop the slide.

"Anna?" he called from the doorway of the bathroom.

There was so much hope in his eyes...so much love, so much loyalty. Even if he was the catalyst, he wasn't the beginning. No, I had my father to blame for that. I followed him, kicking off my shoes, and tugged off my t-shirt before yanking the zipper of my skirt. Fin undressed in an instant, leaving me to watch him as he moved. His body was thicker now, solid muscle and raw power.

He fucked like he looked...*hard.*

I unhooked my bra and slid my panties to the floor as he started the shower and stepped in, dropping his head to the water. He waited for me, grabbing the loofah, washing my body.

"We'll figure this out, okay?" he whispered. "*I'll* figure it out."

I turned around, staring into his eyes. "If you can't?"

He scowled, licked his lips, the water beading on the flesh. "Then I'll do whatever I need to do to keep you safe."

I stood there, knowing he would, without a doubt. I was his family. Just me, no one else. Not since his mom died. I let him wash me, let him take comfort in this small act. Then I took care of him. By the time we were done, it was almost ready to leave.

I slipped on gray slacks and a white collar shirt. Fin glanced my way, his gaze grazing down my pants. He knew why I wore them. Because the feel of that asshole's hands on my body made me want to vomit.

That was why Fin tried to be there as much as he could. Especially after the first time he'd slid his hands along my bare thigh and brushed my panties. No doubt it was under Dominic's instruction. The man was a pig.

"Ready?" Fin adjusted the black belt against midnight blue trousers. His black collared shirt gaped at his hard chest as he moved.

Christ, he was gorgeous. Strong. Dangerous...*and hungry*. He lifted his gaze to mine, and I was hit by just how strong and determined he was...and how, for some crazy reason, he was in love with me.

Thank God for that, because without his desire...without his love, my life would be over. I licked my lips, watching his body as he strode toward me, holding out his hand.

"Anna, everything okay?"

I smiled, heat rushing to my cheeks as my pulse raced. "Yeah." I looked away, heady with the rush of him all over again, and took his hand.

It didn't matter how many times I had him. I wanted him more. More of his body, more of his soul. I was thoroughly addicted to Finley, maybe even more now than I had been on that island.

The thought of that terrified me.

I let him lead me back through the house, grabbing my purse and jacket as I went. The same sedan slowly drove past as we headed out of the gate in Fin's car. I glanced at the driver as we passed. But he never even glanced my way. *Protecting their investment, my ass.* They were watching us.

Day and night.

There was no escape.

53

Finley

I pulled up outside the facility and killed the engine, that tension building inside me like a damn hurricane. I hated her being here. Hated the way my father exerted his control over her. But that was the game, wasn't it? See how far he could push me...*before I snapped.*

I shoved open the door and rounded the front of the car, opening Anna's door for her. She rose, touching my hand as she went. My pulse ignited with the contact, instantly racing to my fucking cock.

She smiled, the tiny smirk growing as I sucked in a hard breath and shoved the door closed behind her. My phone gave a *beep.* I grabbed it from my pocket, looking at the message.

Dad: Meeting in my office...when you're finished.

I winced, then turned, following her up the wide brick stairs to the double-glazed door. She pressed her card against the scanner, and the door unlocked. A wand search by the security guard and we were making our way down to the secure bank of offices and to her damn prison.

The asshole was standing there, waiting for her. He smiled when he saw her coming, then glanced at me. That smirk trembled, fading in an instant.

"Ms. Shaw," he muttered as she stepped close, eyeing the open door to her office.

She said nothing, just let my hand go and made her way inside. I lingered near the doorway and clenched my jaw, fighting back the black, murderous rage as he put his hands on her.

"Arms, Ms. Shaw," he demanded, his hands running down her waist.

Mine...

The word rose. I clenched my jaw as he focused on sliding down my wife's body. *But she wasn't my wife, was she?* I winced. That savage need to tear this guy's face off screamed inside me.

"All done. You're clear," he murmured, looking my way as he rose.

He stepped around the desk like he always did. "Finley." He nodded at me as he passed.

I lunged, grabbing the asshole, and shoved him against the doorframe. "Mr. Salvatore to you."

He paled, eyes widened for a second, like he didn't think I'd react. One nod, and he answered. "Yes, sir."

I sucked in a hard breath and shoved him out of the door and away from her. "Make sure you remember that."

Anna just stared at me as he left. "Thanks." She muttered, moving around her desk and starting her monitor. "That alpha-asshole display is going to help me so much the next time he puts his damn hands on me."

In an instant, she was pissed at me again. I closed the space, braced against the edge of her desk, and leaned over. "He puts his hands on you inappropriately again and he knows who he's dealing with."

She just stared at me. That coldness I'd fought so hard to warm came roaring back in her gaze. "Goodbye, Fin. I'll see you this afternoon."

Dismissed...just like that. No one else would dare.

But she wasn't anyone else, was she?

Marry me...marry me, and he'll stop fucking pushing us. I stared at her, desperate to say the words. But she sat in her chair, grabbed her wrist guard, and slipped it on before she started punching in commands for her damn program.

I shoved myself away. That twitch in the corner of my eye as I turned and strode toward the door. "He gives you problems, Anna, then I want to know about it."

"Sure," she muttered. "Whatever you say, *Mr. Salvatore.*"

The muscles in my jaw bulged as I strode through the door and back along the hall.

Beep.

I shoved through the door as my phone sounded. I didn't need to look down to know who it was. I climbed back onto the Maserati and started the engine, kicking up stones under the car as I tore out of there.

I headed for the city, leaving the towering trees of the forest behind. My thoughts returned to those moments on the island. The night where everything changed between us. Where I became not the man she knew and fell for...but the beast she feared.

It was simple, her life for her father's.

The only problem was...her heart wasn't something I could bargain with. I gripped the wheel and punched the accelerator, sweeping around the cars like they were standing still and made my way to my father's compound on the Upper East Side.

Familiar cars sat parked in the parking lot. Only one was a permanent reminder of how far I'd fallen. Max's Chevy sat in the corner, still there from the moment he'd left with me to go to the island. The only problem was...he'd never returned.

Fin?

His deep growl rang in my head as I pulled into the car space and killed the engine. The morning sun was blinding as I climbed out, hit the locks, and headed inside. Darkness swept around me, the faint stench of cigar and stale sex. Mom had been dead for over six months now. Dead at the hands of someone hunting the members of the Commission.

I wanted to spill blood all over again.

Only I wasn't the one who had revenge.

No, it was the Commander.

A ruthless Albanian who controlled Cosa Nostra Island.

My father told everyone he killed in the Salvatore name, but the truth was, he killed for himself and left the Commission and its dark, brutal secrets behind for a life with the woman he loved, Xael Davies.

"Fin."

I flinched with the quiet murmur of my name as I made my way through the meeting room. I cut my gaze toward the darkness and slowed. He melted into the shadows, sleek, soundless...the perfect hitman. Christ, you'd never see him coming.

"Edon." I called the Devil by his name, and the Commander's brother stepped out into the light.

He narrowed that cold, stony gaze on me. "You've been summoned again."

I winced, knowing what was coming. "Yeah, well..."

"He hasn't found it." The hitman turned and started to walk away. "Whatever he says otherwise."

I stared, watching him. His steps were soundless. This guy didn't really fucking exist...until he saw you. A shiver tore along my spine. I *never* wanted a man like Edon Ristani to see me.

But his loyalty to my father was strained. He stayed to keep my father from forcing the Commander to come back. But I knew it was only a matter of time before it blew up.

He hasn't found it...

The words sent a surge of panic through me as I kept walking, heading to the large, darkened office at the back of the building. Other men moved around, men loyal to my father. I nodded as they passed, heading out to do whatever deed they were assigned this time.

I strode along the hallway, stepped through the open door, and closed it softly behind me. He never looked up, not at first. My father had a way of making everyone react in his own time. I turned away, refusing to play his games, and walked over to the bookcase that ran the entire length of the darkened room, stilling when a soft knock on the door came.

"Dom, honey." A female's voice came from the door.

I turned, watching a blonde with fake tits stride into the room. She cast me a glare, turning her thousand-watt smile on for my father.

"Baby, when you're done with the help..." She dragged her fingers along my father's meaty arm.

"Help?" I muttered, glaring at her.

My father smirked, narrowing his gaze in on me. "Honey, this is my son, Finley."

She stilled, narrowed her gaze, no doubt sizing up the competition. I was sure when she looked at my father all she saw was dollar signs. Only she didn't know what it took to get all that money.

"Your son?" She fluttered her lashes.

I wanted to fucking groan. Instead, I cut a glare toward my father, and turned. "Let me know when you're done with your whore, then we can talk."

"Whore? Who the fuck—"

"It's okay, honey. I haven't had a chance to tell Fin yet."

I froze, a chill sweeping along my spine as I turned back.

"We're going to be married." The fake bitch beamed, lifting her hand to show me the massive rock on her finger.

A rock my mom wouldn't have worn in a million years. It was ugly and gaudy and cost more than my damn car.

"You going to say something?" she asked, waving her fingers in front of me.

I glared to my father. "I saw Edon out in the hallway...I wonder if he has room on his schedule."

My father's smirk grew wider. "Now, now, Fin." He glanced at her. "Honey, I'll message you when I'm ready, okay, sweetheart?"

Sweetheart? I wanted to be sick. Instead, I looked at the photo of my mother on his desk. It was black and white, taken about five years so. My mom, beautiful, fierce, her thick braided hair draped over one shoulder, and her smile...her smile that shone even from the murky gray.

"Okay, baby." She leaned closer, kissing my father in front of me.

If I wasn't thoroughly pissed off before, then this sure did the fucking trick. I never looked away from him as she tottered around the desk like a fucking idiot and left the room.

The smirk stayed, the glint shining like diamonds in his eyes.

Diamonds I wanted to crush under my fucking boot.

"So what's the game? Is this a threat?"

"Threat?" he repeated carefully. "I don't know what you mean, Fin."

It was a game. It was always one fucking game with him.

He thought by dragging some bitch in here and flaunting her in my face that I'd panic? Having a son at his age. He'd be an old man by the time the kid even came close to being a rival. If I let it come to that.

That savage side in me rose to the surface. All I saw was me, standing over the bitch with a gun to her belly. Then it hit me. *This is what he wanted.*

He leaned back in his chair. "I heard there was a problem this morning."

I waited, knowing damn well that wasn't a question.

"Anything I need to be made aware of?"

"No."

"No?" My father shifted forward. "The reports say otherwise."

"The reports can go to fucking hell...and if the reports drive past my house one more time without my direct approval, I'll put a bullet in them."

One brow rose from my father. "You look...strained."

"I wonder why?" I stepped closer. "You have what you wanted."

He shook his head. "No, not all." He crossed his arms over his big belly, and I braced myself for what was to come with Edon's warning ringing in my ears. "Tell me...tell me about that night."

"We've already gone over this...a number of times."

"See, it just doesn't make sense." He muttered. "Max was highly trained. I've seen him take down three guys at one time, so when you tell me one man got the drop on him, it just...ugh, I don't know." He rubbed his chest like he was in pain. But it wasn't a heart attack.

I couldn't be that fucking lucky.

"It just doesn't sit right. Maybe the recordings will help me see things a little more clearly."

My pulse sped, and my stomach tightened. But I didn't react. Not like he was expecting. "I hope so," I answered. "As hard as it was to relive that night, I would, just to ease your conscience, since you clearly can't take my word."

His brow rose. "It's not that I don't believe you."

"Of course not," I added, standing across his desk. "I'd only be happy to watch the recording with you. Is it here?"

He held my gaze, knowing too fucking well he didn't have it.

Because if he did, I wouldn't be standing here.

I'd be in a dark room, most likely on my knees...with Anna hurt and screaming beside me. There was one thing my father didn't tolerate...and that was betrayal—no matter who it was.

If he'd watched that footage from that night in the warehouse, he'd see it wasn't the assassins who'd stormed the island, who'd killed his most loyal protector...*it was me.*

And I'd do it again...if protecting Anna was on the line.

I'd do it a hundred times over.

And I wouldn't fucking care.

54

Finley

"No," my father answered. "But I'm sure it's only a matter of time before it's located."

"Call me when it is," I answered, turning toward the door. "Good luck with Bobby."

"Honey," Dad snarled as I grabbed the door and yanked it open.

"Whatever," I answered, leaving him and his child bride behind.

I looked for the hitman when I left, but of course, he was long gone...or not interested in finding me.

He hasn't found it...

The words haunted me when I climbed in and started the car. I waited until I pulled out and made for the heart of the city. I didn't trust my car, didn't even trust my house. I glanced into the rearview mirror. I trusted nothing when it came to my father. So I took the streets slowly, watching for a tail that I knew was there, until I spotted the navy sedan about four cars behind me.

I drove toward the freeway, knowing damn well I could lose him. The Maserati ate the asphalt as I climbed onto the on-ramp and accelerated hard. I took the long way, doubling back to find my way along the long stretch of water.

There was no doubt a tracker in the car, but I'd at least have a few minutes to myself. I parked near the water and climbed out, grabbing my cell free and hit the number. I knew he'd be waiting, and he was.

"Fin."

"Mateo," I muttered.

"Edon found you?"

"Yeah." I combed my fingers through my hair and breathed in the salty bracken scent of the river. "The recording."

"Hasn't surfaced...as yet."

"Is that Fin?" I caught Xael's voice in the background. "Tell him I'm ready."

I let out a chuckle. "She ready to go to war with my father, is she?"

"You know the woman as well as I do. What do you think?" The tone was one of exhaustion but etched with pride.

"I think we'd better find this damn recording and figure out how the fuck it got off the island."

"It was uploaded. The sonovabitch had it on a secure server."

"Not so damn secure," I glanced to the road behind me. I was running out of time. "If you need Anna involved, she can trace it."

"It's too damn risky." Mateo growled. "We'll handle it on our end."

"Commander..."

"We'll find it, Fin. If we don't...let's just say my brother's happy to hang around."

I let out a hard exhale. "Sure," I answered. "Give my love to the wildcat."

I hung up the call, glanced at my watch. Eleven. He'd be waiting. I strode across the road, heading to a bar, and stepped inside. I made for the darkened back, ignoring the stare of the waitress who was setting up the tables for the lunch room rush.

"Help you?" the barman called from the other side.

"Can I use your phone?" I grabbed my billfold from my pocket, peeled off a twenty, and tossed it to the bar.

He gave a jerk of his head. "In the back."

I walked in, located the ancient thing miraculously still attached to the wall, and dialed the number I knew off by heart. The one number that kept us connected with Anna's father.

He answered on the second ring. "Fin."

"Everything okay?"

"Fine, Anna?"

"She's safe," I started. "But we're going to need some more time."

"How much more time?"

"I wish I knew. We're working on it, that's all I can say."

"And when you locate it, that's only part of the issue, Fin. When can I come home? When can I see my daughter?"

I felt the guy's agony. "I don't know, D. I wish I had something to tell you."

"*Then figure it the fuck out*," he snapped, his hard breaths a roar in my ear. "I'm sorry."

"Don't be. We'll find it, we'll negotiate a way you can get back home. I just need you..."

"To say hidden," he answered for me.

"Right."

"Until tomorrow," he muttered, defeated, and ended the call.

I hung up and walked back out, past the bartender still wiping glasses and the waitress, who smiled and walked toward me.

"Hi," She started.

But I kept going, striding across the street, ready to stab some motherfucker in the eye. The dark sedan pulled up a second before I climbed back into the Maserati. I never looked at my father's spy, just climbed into the car and started the engine, driving off and heading for the city.

I needed to find a way out of this. Needed to keep all the balls in the goddamn air. Dillon, my father...and Anna. There was only one person who knew my pain. Lazarus Rossi.

I punched the accelerator, aiming for the freeway, my gaze moving to the rearview mirror. But there was no sign of the tail. It didn't matter. They'd know exactly where I was going. The tracker in the car would show them the way.

Only that was all they'd know. My father wouldn't dare put a bug in the Rossi compound. Not unless he wanted to start a war. The freeway blurred in front of me as I put miles on the odometer, speeding across the other side of the city and to the Rossi compound.

By the time I slowed and pulled into their street, it was almost midday. I slowed, then drove the sports car into the darkened alley next to the nightclub. The place was always on, always alive. Dark, seedy music invaded the alley, reaching my ears as I climbed out of the car, locked it, and made for the closed door.

"Fin."

I glanced toward the voice, slowing as the Rossi protector stepped out of the shadows. "Logan, he in?"

The bodyguard just smiled. "Brother, he's always in, except when he's out."

I laughed hard at this. Lazarus was the most hot-headed asshole God ever put breath in. The guy was on, all the damn time. Only I thought now with the baby he'd be a little more *mellow*. But he wasn't.

If anything, he was even more savage, protecting a child who was his by name only. Kat had come to the island with a secret. One she'd kept hidden...One we never expected would turn into something like this.

"Later," I muttered to the bodyguard, waiting for him to nod before I headed to the door and stepped inside.

Heads snapped toward me as I entered, and it took me a moment to adjust my stride, meeting each gaze. Then to realize they still didn't trust me. That they didn't know the camaraderie we'd formed in those hallow nights fighting to find the woman Lazarus loved.

When they'd taken Kat captive, he was a wounded animal caught in a trap. I was there, searching alongside him. I was there in those dark moments when he thought all hope had been lost. Which was the only reason I was here now.

The Stidda Prince was no longer my rival. He was my friend, my ally.

"Asshole." The growl came from behind me.

I winced at the crassness and glanced his way. I wasn't the only one who'd hardened since coming back. Lazarus was more toned than ever and intimidating as fuck.

"Prick," I answered back.

He gave a jerk of his head, and I followed him to the back, glancing around the darkened room. There was once a time this was a place for the dancers to hang out. Where Laz didn't flinch at the sight of tits and pussy on display. But as I stepped through, he closed the door, shutting the sound of the music and the club out. He breathed a sigh of relief.

"Goddamn that shit, gets on my nerves," he muttered, grabbing a bottle of water from the refrigerator. "Water?" he offered.

I shook my head. "No, thanks. Sounds like you need a new place, Rossi."

He cut me a glare. "You're telling me, but it seems I've been outvoted. So, the titty bar it is...for now." He cracked open the water and drank, leaning against the sofa. "What is it?"

The way he said the words made me turn and pace the floor. He knew...*some things*. But not all.

"Salvatore." He gave a sigh. "You want to spill what's eating you?"

I met those crystal-blue eyes. "You remember that night...the night they attacked?"

That haunted look returned. "Like it was yesterday."

"They didn't get the drop on Max in that hangar."

He stilled, his gaze frozen on me as those clear blue eyes darkened. "Go on."

"It was me."

The furrow of his brow rose. "You killed your own bodyguard?"

"No, I killed the man loyal to my father and not me."

"Interesting." He was starting to get it now. "You making a play, brother?"

I swallowed hard and looked away, pacing the floor. "Yes, *no.* I don't know."

"Because if you are, then you should be hauling ass away from this damn city and taking Anna with you."

"If I could, then I would."

"Because your old man has the recording and is holding it over your head?"

I licked my lips. "Close enough."

"You want my loyalty, Fin, then it's yours, brother." He shoved off the desk and stepped toward me. "But before we all go to our fucking deaths over this, be damned sure before unleashing the hounds."

I saw it all. It'd be utter carnage. I knew that. My father's men would defend him to the death. But Christ...he was my damn blood.

"I need the recording of that night in the hangar and I need it yesterday."

"The Commander?"

"Is looking for it."

He nodded. "Good, if there's anyone who can hunt them down, it'll be him."

"Then you have my back if it comes to that. I can count on the Rossi?"

He came closer, grasped my forearm, and stared me dead in the eyes. "After what you did for me...you have my loyalty for life."

55

Anna

The thud of books invaded. Something scraped against the door. I winced and tried to block out the sound. But it'd been the second time in the last hour he'd made his presence known.

I stiffened at the squeal of the handle, tearing my gaze from the command prompt in front of me and quickly hit the sleep button, killing the screen as he strode in. They called him Archer. But his real name was Arnold Smutter. An asshole with a heavily padded pocket.

"Are you going on break?" he asked, lifting the wand.

I scowled at the asshole. Ever since this morning with Fin, he'd been haunting me. "No."

He licked his lips and kept walking, rounding my desk. I glanced at the closed door, my senses on fire. I'd been here before with assholes like him, locked classrooms, me all alone. Only this time, Fin wasn't here to save me. I dropped my hand to the side of my keyboard and grabbed the steel letter opener and fisted the hilt.

The movement was lost on Arnold. He stilled at the edge of the desk and then took a slow step toward me. "You going to use that, Anna?"

"I just might."

He took another step, forcing me to rise from my seat.

"Back the fuck off."

"Or?" He took another step, coming to the close edge of the desk, within stabbing distance. But he didn't come closer. Instead, he glanced at the notepad beside my keyboard. "Writing down algorithms?"

"That's none of your business."

"It is while you work for Mr. Salvatore," he answered. "And codes, any commands." He met my gaze. "And ideas you might have belong to him."

I stiffened with the words. "You have your head so far up *Mr. Salvatore's* ass you almost share the same set of lungs, don't you?"

He flinched with words, and a twitch came from the corner of his eye. "You know I'm close to cracking your algo, don't you?"

This time, I was the one who stepped closer. "Oh yeah? Good luck with that, buddy. You've just inspired me to make a whole new level of protection."

That flinch came again before he stepped forward, closing the distance in the blink of an eye. I stepped backward until I hit the wall. My fist clamped around the hilt of the letter opener as he pushed against me, driving me against the wall. "You think because you're fucking him, you're indispensable? You're not. We're looking for that hard drive. *I'm* looking for that hard drive. When I find it, then we'll know the truth."

This fucking guy...

"Who the fuck are you?" I whispered with my spine forced to the wall.

He just stared into my eyes, and for a second, hate raged. The kind of hate I didn't understand until he spoke. "Didn't anyone tell you? I'm Max's brother."

I froze. *No, that can't be right, I would've found it.* "Brother?"

He smiled. "That's right. Adopted, still, we were closer than blood." He growled against me. "I don't believe the events you gave about that night...and neither does Mr. Salvatore."

I couldn't think. Couldn't breathe. In my head, I was panicking, trying to put all the pieces together. Did Fin know? Was that the reason he was always here, always watching? Did he think I was in immediate danger from this guy?

My office door opened, drawing my gaze. In walked Dominic Salvatore, filling up the room and stealing the surrounding air. Just like he stole everything. He glanced at the asshole in front of me, then met my gaze. "Is there a problem?"

"Only that your *dog* is getting a little too excited," I spat.

There was no love lost between us. Not when he'd backed my father into a corner, one that drove him to contact the FBI and sent me to the damn island to meet him. Because of that, my world changed. It didn't help that my father stole the Salvatore fortune to bargain with in exchange for my safety.

Look how that turned out.

"Archer," Dominic murmured, never once leaving my gaze. "Thank you for your dedication. I can take it from here."

From the corner of my eye, I caught the asshole shift his gaze to his master.

"Woof," I whispered as the asshole scowled, then took a step backward.

I was done playing games, done with trying to pretend that I didn't have anything other than an utter distaste for Dominic Salvatore and any other spineless fucking pig who did his bidding.

Like Fin?

The words rose in my head. No, not like Fin. His loyalty was by blood alone...and even that was waning. The asshole turned and left, closing the door with a loud *thud*.

"There were some problems this morning?" Dominic said carefully.

I stiffened, trying to comb my memory...this morning...this morning. My brain was a blur of code.

"At the house," he prompted, and a chill raced along my spine. That smugness rose in his eyes. He was a viper, a cold-blooded viper, with no shame.

I crossed my arms. "What happens between me and Fin is none of your business."

"I disagree." He took a step closer, and I couldn't help but flinch. "Everything about you is very much *my* business, including what happens at home."

My breath caught. Eyes widened.

"So let me ask you again." Dominic said, "What happened this morning?"

Panic surged through me. To tell him the truth would mean to let the Devil in, and there was no way that was happening. "We ran out of milk."

"You ran out of milk," he repeated.

"And you know how pissy your son is without his coffee."

A twitch came from the corner of his eye. He didn't believe me, but I was giving nothing away. Nothing he could use against me anyway.

"Then that's good to hear. Maybe you need to speak to the service for failing in their duties. I can take care of that for you."

I swallowed hard. Letting this man anywhere near the staff to grill and probe and threaten was terrifying. Maybe he already had...maybe I was fighting a losing battle. Still, it wasn't in me not to fight. "Thank you," I murmured. "But no, I'm sure Fin and I can handle our own affairs."

One nod. That was all he gave me before he turned and made for the door. His hand was on the handle before he stopped. "Oh, and Anna...give my best to your father."

56

Finley

I drove back to the facility, to her office. By the time I got there, it was afternoon. The sun already losing its bite. I pulled into the parking lot and climbed out, making my way to the front doors.

They watched me carefully when I strode through the building, all the way to Anna's office, but when I opened the door and stepped in, I didn't find her inside. I glanced around, then left, making my way along the corridor to the small tearoom.

I found her standing at the window, staring out to the side of the parking lot and the trees in the distance. "Anna?"

She stiffened at my voice and turned. Her eyes were red-rimmed, glassy and wide.

I closed the distance in a heartbeat, keeping my voice low. "What happened?"

She shook her head. But I knew...I knew she needed to get out of here.

"Get your things. We're leaving."

She shook her head, looking so damn vulnerable. "I can't, I—"

"Can and are. Get your things, Anna. I'm getting you the hell out of here."

"Your father..." she started.

I clenched my jaw. "Fuck my father."

Her eyes widened with a expression of shock, and the old Anna roared to the surface.

"Get your things, geek. We're going away for a few days."

A look of terror washed over her. "Fin."

"I'll text my damn father from the car," I answered. It was a blur of a moment's decision, but the more I thought about it, the more solid it became. "We're getting out of here *now*."

She stumbled backward and then turned and left. Hurrying along the hallway to her office once more. I needed to get her away from here. Away from my father...*while I made up my mind.*

You making a play, brother?

Rossi's words rang in my head. Was I making a play?

It sure felt like it.

I followed her, striding toward the office. She had her things and was shutting down her computer by the time I moved to the door, then stepped backwards, peeking along the hallway, almost hearing the heavy thud of steps. "Hurry, Anna."

She snatched her jacket from the back of the chair and rounded the desk as that loud *thud...thud...thud* of boots became clear. But we were already out of there, closing the door behind us as Archer skirted the corner and lifted his gaze to us.

"Hey," he called.

But I just yanked her office door closed and placed my hand on the small of her back, ushering her forward.

"Fin!" the guard called out.

But I never slowed, just kept striding, pushing her toward the front of the building. But there were guards waiting when we reached the front door, closing around us. I gripped her hand. "Stay with me, Princess." And pulled her with me as I turned to the guard in front of me. "Get the fuck out of my way."

His eyes widened as I reached behind my back and grabbed my Sig. "Put your hands on us and I'll take that as a direct threat on my and my wife's life."

Anna jerked her gaze toward me. But I was done playing...on all goddamn fronts.

The guard never moved as I strode toward the door, pushing Anna out in front as it opened. I didn't need to tell her to hurry. Her steps lengthened as she headed for the car. I released her hold, grabbed the keys, and hit the button, unlocking the door.

We were inside in a heartbeat. As I started the car and backed out, I caught Archer striding out of the door behind us, lifting his phone to his ear.

"Fin."

I shoved the car into gear, never taking my eyes off the mother-fucker behind us. I knew he was onto us, knew he wasn't just watching Anna, but behind the scenes, he was the one hunting down the hard drive from the island.

One call was all it'd take, and I'd have Laz take the bastard out. He'd do it, too. I punched the accelerator, driving us through the gate and out onto the quiet stretch of road. But I wouldn't make the call...

I'd do it my damn self.

I drove us along the isolated stretch of road back home and pulled into the gates. "Grab your things, jackets, jeans, hiking boots. We're going camping."

"Really?" She looked surprised.

"Really." I pulled the Maserati around the rear of the house and pulled into the garage, parking it next to the Explorer.

I killed the engine and climbed out, waiting for Anna to head to the rear of the house before closing that side of the garage. A firm the Commander trusted had fit the house with security, and if he trusted them, then so did I. Still, I knew we were vulnerable, more now than ever.

Right on time, my phone started ringing as I followed Anna to the rear door and then inside. I didn't need to glance at the display to know who it was. I grabbed the cell and answered. "Yeah?"

"You want to tell me what the fuck is going on?" my father snapped.

"I have this damn pulse in the back of my head." I started nodding to Anna when she glanced my way.

The movement couldn't be more obvious...*hurry.*

"You what?"

"A pulse. It's more like a throbbing, really." I made for my wardrobe, grabbed my back pack, and walked out, throwing it on the bed as Anna rushed around like a madwoman, kicking off her shoes and yanking her blouse from her body.

She was alive, more alive than I'd seen her in months.

"What the fuck does that have to do with you walking out and taking my property?"

That savage side of me rose in an instant, making me stop at the side of the bed. "See, that's the problem. That's why I can't get rid of this damn throbbing in my head." My voice was low and dangerous. "It's fucking eating me up, the constant throb, throb, throb. It's because it's you...you and this fucking bullshit. You want *your* property, Father. Then you're going to have to come through me to get it."

I hung up the call and tossed the cell to the bed like it was on fire.

But there was no movement in the room.

Anna stood there, her eyes wide, mouth open before she closed it carefully and spoke. "Finally...my Fin is back."

That chokehold of terror released its grip around me as she took a step, closing the distance in a heartbeat to lunge. I grabbed her, pulling her against me as she wound her arms around my neck and kissed me.

The burn between us ignited like wildfire, unleashing her desire. She speared her fingers through my hair and kissed me, hard. I held her, smashing her cheek against mine. Fuck if she didn't feel so damn good. But then she broke the kiss, her lips red and full.

"Are you staying?"

"Here?" I asked, confused.

"No." She held my gaze. "Is this Fin going to stay?" She unwound her legs from around my waist and dropped her feet to the floor. "Because I'd say yes to this Fin if he asked me."

Yes to this Fin...

The words hit me. I knew exactly what she was saying. I swallowed hard, searching her eyes. "Yes. I'm here to stay."

She gave a nod, her eyes glinting with happiness. "Good. Now let's get the fuck out of here."

She left me, stepping away to find her clothes and shoes and everything else we'd bought to go hiking. I dressed in jeans, boots, and a t-shirt and warm jacket, leaving her to pack the rest of the bags as I went to the secure room in the house.

I punched in the code and waited for the locks to disengage before opening the door and walking in. Lights flickered and blinked on, revealing walls loaded with weapons. Enough to go to war, if I had to...*and right now I was feeling like I had to.*

I grabbed the guns, loaded them into a pack along with a heap of ammo, and left. But by the time I strode out of the house and headed to the open doors of the Explorer, Anna had already stowed our bags into the back and was hunting the shelves in the garage for our tent.

I made my way to her, finding cooking equipment and a cooler and tossed it all into the back. "Wait here, I'll lock the house. Everything else we'll get on the way."

She gave a nod, moving to close the doors and climbing into the passenger seat of the car. I'd forgotten how strong she was, forgotten a lot of things it seemed—including myself.

I made my way through the house and was heading back out when my phone gave a *beep*.

Mateo: Call me.

I flinched with the command, sucked in a hard breath, and locked the door as I headed to the Explorer.

Anna looked my way, yanking her seatbelt across her, and stilled. "What is it?"

"Not sure," I answered, starting the engine before hitting the Commander's number.

"Here," he answered a second later. He sounded rushed, heavy steps thudding in the background. "There's been a development. Is Anna with you?"

"Here," she said beside me as I shoved the four-wheel drive into gear and backed out of the garage, hitting the button.

"I don't want you to freakin' out."

I cut her a glance as the garage closed. My heart was already thundering as I shoved the car into gear and made for the front gate.

"Okay," she said.

"They've found him."

I jerked my gaze to Anna. She paled in an instant, turning deathly gray.

"So he's on the run. I have guys head his way to meet him. But he's going to have to get himself to somewhere that's safe enough for the pickup."

She shook her head as the front gate closed. "He can't do that. That's not him. He'll..."

"He will if he wants out of there," Mateo murmured. "It's amazing what the need to survive pushes us to do. He did the impossible once before, sending you to the island to protect you, so he'll do it again. Have faith. I'll call you as soon as I know more...and Fin..."

"Yeah?" I answered, turning the wheel and accelerating.

"You might want to make plans."

I swallowed hard, knowing exactly what he was saying and thought of the duffle bag loaded with guns in the back. "Already on it."

"Lie low. I'll call you when we've picked him up," he finished.

I hung up the call, speeding the four-wheel drive along the quiet, lonely road and scanned the rearview mirror for my father's watchers who would surely come.

57

Anna

I closed my eyes as Fin hung up the phone. They were going to find him...they were going to find my dad. I wrapped my arms around my body and rocked forward.

"Hey, no." Fin placed his hand on my back, the warmth melting through my thick buttoned shirt. "Don't fall apart on me here."

I shook my head, fighting back tears. I'd handled a lot of shit. The Facility. The fucking guard who put his hands on me as he threatened me. I even handled Fin with his cold, Salvatore demeanor. I did it all to keep my father safe.

But that was all over...*they'd find him and they'd kill him.*

I just knew it.

Warmth slipped free and slipped from the corner of my eye. "I did this...*Oh God. I did this.*"

"No, you didn't...I did."

I winced.

"I was the one who killed Max in that warehouse."

I opened my eyes, my cheeks wet and slick. "To protect me."

He turned his gaze back to the road. "The why doesn't matter. Now we need to find a way out of this damn mess and wait for Mateo to find your father. Because he *will* find him."

"He's the Commander," I murmured.

Fin glanced my way. But he didn't need to answer. I knew about the men in his dangerous world where he lived. I knew about them all too well. I once wanted to run from them...wanted to get as far away from them as possible.

But that was before.

I looked across the seat as he worked the gears and watched the rearview mirror, driving us where, I didn't know. He leaned forward, hit the button on his cell. Laz's number flashed across the screen before he answered.

"That was fast, Salvatore," he muttered. "You in or what?"

"I have your backing?"

My pulse sped with the words.

"One hundred percent." He growled. I could almost see the savagery in his eyes. "It's about time for fresh blood."

"I'm heading to the outpost." Fin glanced at the rearview mirror, then reached under the dashboard and hit a switch. "Tracking off."

"See you then, brother." Laz sounded almost excited.

I just stared at where his hand had been as he pressed the button and hung up the call. A chill coursed through my body as it hit me. "You knew...you knew this was coming, didn't you?"

He gave me a look and kept on driving.

His silence said more than words ever could.

I didn't know if I should be terrified or turned on. "How long?"

"Ever since we came back," he answered.

"You were planning to make a play." I pushed back against the seat, stunned. "All this time."

He cut me a glare. "You think I'd allow you to work in that prison forever?"

"Honestly? I don't know. Yes, maybe yes." The truth stung.

He winced. "Then that's one hundred percent on me." His voice was quiet, hurt. "I obviously failed to show you the kind of man I am."

A man who'd kill to protect me.

A man who'd lie to his own father...and now go to war.

"Lazarus is in this?"

Fin turned off onto a crossroad. "His father's been wanting to step aside for a while now. But he couldn't."

"Why?"

Fin glared. "Because of Dominic."

The slow nod was the trigger for it to all fall into place. Benjamin Rossi wouldn't step aside and hand over his seat on the Commission, not while a savage bastard like Dominic still occupied the seat. But Fin...

Fin was a whole other matter entirely. My mind raced, trying to put it all together, retracing the events that happened on the island as I tried to find the moment when this was all decided. "The other seats?"

"Will be handed down, by force if it comes to that."

"Wow," I muttered.

Fin drove, watching the rearview mirror as we made our way to some place he had ready for this exact purpose. Thirty minutes later, we slowed and turned onto a dirt track. I gripped the seat as the four-wheel drive bounced and jostled, taking us toward a bank of trees in the distance.

"It was always going to happen, Anna. This is just the catalyst." He grunted as we hit a pothole and bounced.

"Will you kill him, your father, I mean?"

He didn't answer. *Jesus...he didn't answer.* I wrapped my arms around my stomach. I was going to be sick. I was going to be sick all over Fin's nice new four-wheel drive.

The four-wheel drive he'd bought a month before and had specifically 'adjusted' was the word he used. I glanced at the dashboard where he flipped the switch. A switch that killed any kind of communication, whether it be a transmitter or recording equipment. So we were invisible.

"I'm never going back there," I whispered, unable to believe it until I spoke the words.

"No. You're not. Not if I have anything to do with it."

I let those words ripple through me as we drove through the trees and out the other side. There was a small cabin in the distance. One surrounded by a towering fence and a locked gate. But the place was neat and hidden. So well, you'd never see it if you weren't specifically on this track. "Is this yours?"

"Ours." He never took his gaze from the road as he neared. "Everything is ours, Anna."

He shifted the gears as we dipped down, the tires skidding before they caught on the graveled road, then we climbed all the way to the gate. He pulled up, shoved the car into gear, and stepped out, rounding the front to the locks on the gate.

I stared at the place, finding an outpost on the edge and what looked like a barrier of some kind at the rear. This wasn't just a cabin...it was a compound. One designed to keep us safe. Fin shoved the gate open, drawing my focus. He did this...all while I was pulling away from him.

I thought he'd given up on us.

Thought he'd given up on me.

When he'd bought me back from the island and set my dad free, I thought he was just as bad as his own father. His loyalties were murky at best. But now I saw that was a lie. He was loyal, biding his time, getting things prepared.

He climbed back into the four-wheel drive. His gaze moved to mine. "You okay?"

A flare of desire coursed through me. "Yeah," I answered, my breaths deepening.

The movement wasn't lost on him. There was a flicker of a scowl as he searched my eyes, then dropped lower.

My body reacted to him, like it always did. I thought the way I reacted to him had been the thing that held me prisoner. But it wasn't...it was my head. I took in the rolled sleeves against his forearms. Corded muscles flexed as he yanked the door closed, shoved the Explorer into gear, and drove through the gate.

"The others, they're coming?" I asked.

"Soon."

"How long do we have?"

One brow rose before the corner of his lips tugged into a smile. "Long enough."

He pulled the four-wheel drive up to the cabin, then killed the engine and climbed out, hurrying back to the gate to secure it. I moved to the back, grabbed our bags, and looked around. The place was beautiful and rustic. The sounds of the birds in the trees sounded so peaceful.

"Wait here." Fin unlocked the door, reached around his back, and drew out his gun before stepping inside.

He came back, barely a minute later, hitting the lights on his way. "It's clear. You can go in now."

I hauled our bags inside while he went to the four-wheel drive, carrying in the rest of the bags while I walked around the cabin, taking in the small kitchen, living room with a fireplace and rustic sofa with thick throws and a massive brown rug in the middle of the room.

Then I moved to the room, finding two bedrooms. One equipped with a stunning queen-sized bed that looked like it'd been carved straight out of a tree trunk.

"Where in the hell did you find time to organize all of this?" I couldn't stop from staring.

He dropped our bags onto the bed and followed my gaze. "The guy who sold me the place did most of it. The rest I handled on my own."

I glanced at the bed, the comforter in a rose-colored hue...my favorite color. My pulse sped at the sight, then I stepped into the expansive bathroom with slate brown floor tiles and the biggest claw-foot bathtub I'd ever seen.

"That's new." He came up behind me. "Took forever to get that through customs from Italy."

I spun, my mouth gaping open. "You had that sent from Italy?"

He just gave a shrug, his cheeks reddening. "I saw it, knew you'd love it. So I bought it, no big deal."

But it was a big deal...*a very big deal*—to me.

I stepped closer, pressing my chest against his. But I didn't reach for him, just stared into those beautiful brown eyes. This was the man I felt for, the broody, quiet, dangerous guy who stole my heart.

His breaths deepened. He inched his mouth closer to mine. "If I knew a tub would turn you on so much, Anna, I'd buy you the entire goddamn factory."

He could, too...that I knew, without a doubt.

But it wasn't about money. It was the fact that he'd thought of me.

I reached up, sliding my hands around his neck. "Such a shame to rumple that perfect comforter."

"Then I'll take you on the floor," he answered. "Bent over that tub. How does that sound to you, *wife?*"

A surge of excitement coursed through me with the word. I swallowed, then slowly reached for the buttons of my shirt. "I think I like the sound of that, *husband.*"

I tugged off my top, then moved for the button of my jeans, kicking off my boots as I went. Fin undressed in a second, tugging his shirt over his head, before he dropped his hand to the button of his jeans, then surged forward, grabbing me around the waist.

He lifted me like I weighed nothing, leaving me to wrap my legs around his waist, my fingers buried in those thick, soft curls. Christ, I wanted him more than I'd ever wanted him before. I kissed him hard, biting down on his lower lip until he unleashed a groan from the back of his throat.

The scent of the forest. The feeling of freedom.

Knowing he had always been thinking of me.

He shoved his jeans down, his hand sliding between us. His fingers skirted my crease, finding my clit as he rubbed. Heat radiated from me. God, this man knew how to get me wet.

"Christ, you feel amazing." He groaned.

He wasn't a talker, wasn't overly affectionate. He was a thunderstorm at the edge of my horizon, always brewing, always thundering...*always there*. He slipped his fingers inside, his thumb taking control of that sensitive nub.

I arched my back, holding on to his shoulders. He held on to me as we sank to the floor. I released my hold around his neck, sliding my hands along his arms until I lay on the floor. The cold floor tiles made me flinch, but the heat of his hands made it all melt away.

He lowered his head, kissing the inside of my thighs before sliding to my center. He didn't do this, not kiss me this way. Not my stony Mafia prince. But the moment his tongue licked me, I let out a guttural moan. "Oh God, yes."

"Yes?" He slid his finger inside, working my body like he'd never done before.

I shuddered, that tremor coursing through my belly until I lifted my head, finding his gaze. "Yes, Fin...*yes.*"

He held my gaze, sliding his fingers inside and leaned forward to lick that sensitive flesh. I bit my lip, watching the most dangerous man I knew take me into his mouth. This man killed for me...and was about to kill again.

I closed my eyes and moaned at the thought of that. Christ, if that wasn't the hottest thing I'd ever had. These bloodied hands now fucked me. I opened my eyes. "I want you," I demanded. "Now, Fin...I want you now."

He lifted his head. Hunger darkened those amber eyes to midnight brown. He rose, shoved his jeans lower, and grabbed my hips, lifting my lower body over thick thighs. The head of his cock butted against my core. Tendons stretched as I spread wider. I watched him looking down between us as he fisted his length and guided himself slowly in.

"Oh fuck," I moaned, arching my back. Christ, slow...so fucking slow. My pussy stretched as he slid inside, then pulled back out. I let out a desperate moan. "Please, Fin."

"You going to marry me now, Anna?" He pushed against me, the head thick.

I clamped my legs around his waist and drove against him, aching for one more inch...one more thrust. I was desperate for him. "Yes."

"And kids..." He gripped my hips, setting the pace as he thrust all the way inside. "Do I get kids?"

My body trembled. It was what I'd always wanted. I'd just kept it from him. "Yes, Fin...*yes.*"

He released my hips, rising to lean over me. "Good." He stared into my eyes and bucked his hips, slamming all the way inside me to the hilt.

I unleashed a whimper, holding on to his muscled arms as he drove his body inside me. "I want you big and pregnant." He dragged his teeth across his lips and slammed his hips against mine.

My body jolted with the impact. "I want that...Fin. God, I want that."

He braced his body on his arms on either side of me, caging me in. I slid my hands along his back, pulling him against me as he drove deeper. The brutal strength of his passion driving me closer to that edge. "Fuck me," I whispered. "Make me yours."

He let out a savage sound and picked up pace. "You...are always mine, Anna...*never forget it.*"

I let out a cry, holding on to him as my body quivered and quaked.

And in the blinding release, my walls came crashing down.

I gave myself to him. Body, heart, and soul.

Tears slipped from the corner of my eye as he let out a grunt and stilled, emptying himself deep inside me.

58

Finley

Fuck, she was perfect. I closed my eyes, my cock buried deep inside and felt that hunger ripple through me. I had to protect her, no matter what. Anna wasn't just anyone to me...

She was family.

She was mine.

She let out a moan, her breaths racing, forcing me to open my eyes. I looked down at her, and it hit me like a sledgehammer... just how lucky I was. I was so fucking lucky...so fucking blessed to have found her.

A woman who knew the ugly truth about who I was...and still stayed.

I eased out of her body, leaned down, and kissed her. "Better get prepared."

She just nodded, staring up at me. I hated leaving her, hated letting that heat I finally captured once more, cool between us. But Lazarus and the Commander would be here soon. Then plans would be made. Plans to go to war against my father, and pray we came out alive.

I pushed up from the floor, holding out my hand for her. Together, we walked out into the bedroom and got dressed. I spent the next few hours checking out the compound, getting the cabin ready and thinking of the plan in my head. When the sound of an engine drew my gaze, I knew instantly who it was.

I lifted my cell, pulling up the hidden cameras along the track and caught the black blur of Lazarus' gunmetal-gray Silverado as it cut through the fence line and headed toward the compound. I slipped my phone into my pocket, watching as he climbed out. Then Kat followed, her red hair vibrant in the sun.

She glanced my way, then looked behind me to the cabin as Anna stepped close. Kat left the door to the four-wheel drive open and raced toward us, tearing past me to throw her arms around Anna.

They hadn't seen each other in months, not since... the Facility. Ann let out a sob, hugging her back just as fiercely as Lazarus rounded the front of the truck and moved to the backseat, pulling out the most beautiful raven-haired baby girl I'd ever seen.

But I knew...

I knew as soon as I looked at her...

Knew who her father was, and it wasn't Lazarus. Still, he handled the child with the kind of love only given to those he loved. He strode forward, meeting my gaze before he glanced to Anna as Kat released her and turned, taking the baby from his arms.

"Anna," he murmured. "It's good to see you."

"Laz," she answered. "You look...well."

"Come on." Kat grabbed her hand, holding the baby against her. "Show me this gorgeous little hideaway."

No one would think she was one of the richest women in the country. Not unless she shared her former last name. The VanHalens were not just filthy rich and powerful, they were dangerous, too. But they paled in the face of Kat's father's most trusted friend, Haelstrom Hale. The most sadistic and foul piece of shit who ever walked the face of the earth.

And the father of her baby.

"Brother," I greeted Laz as he watched Kat and Anna disappear.

The fire in his eyes burned until he shifted that searing focus my way. I knew he wanted to kill Hale. Knew he'd tried to as well. But power came with protection, and there was no one more protected than Hale.

"We doing this?" he asked.

I nodded. "Yeah, we're doing this." I walked with him back to the truck and hauled his things out, most of them for the baby, and carried them to the cabin.

We settled them in the second bedroom, which was big enough to fit the portable crib as well. Then we went outside, checking the perimeter.

"You know you might have to kill him, right?" Lazarus turned to me as I checked the camera. "I need you to be okay with that. Because it has to be you, brother. No one else."

I nodded, lifting my focus. "Let's just hope it doesn't come down to that."

Beep.

My cell gave a buzz. I glanced down at the message.

Mateo: We have him. We'll see you in three hours.

"They have him. They have Anna's father."

"Thank fuck," Lazarus muttered. "Now all we need is for this damn hard drive to surface and we can close this damn chapter once and for all."

I couldn't agree more.

We spent the next few hours drinking a few beers, listening to our women chatter, sinking into the feeling of what life could be like, and slowly the clock ticked and time passed.

Beep.

I grabbed my cell.

Mateo: We're here.

"Anna," I called out, lifting my focus. "They're here."

She stilled, her eyes widening before she glanced to the windows, then slowly rose from the sofa.

We headed out, and I lifted my gaze to the darkening sky. Headlights cut through the bank of trees as Anna reached out and grabbed my hand.

Her smile was small, hesitant. Nervous. She was nervous about seeing her dad...or was it the Commander?

The black Hummer pulled up just outside of range. Jesus, the man never stopped being careful, did he? But then the passenger door shoved open, and a hurricane followed. A hurricane who was Xael Davies.

"Anna! Kat! *Bitches, come over here!*" she roared as the driver's door opened.

Mateo Ristani stepped out, his attention consumed by the woman who charged toward Anna and Kat. But the rear door opened, and a man followed. A man who was gaunt and quiet. A man who was the sole reason we were in this damn mess in the first place.

Anna hugged Xael before the tornado moved to Kat, leaving to *ooh* and *ahh* over the baby. But it was Anna's father we focused on as he stepped into the glare of the headlights, and I saw how the guy really looked.

"Jesus." The word slipped out before I knew.

He winced at the sound, but he didn't look my way, only held his daughter's gaze.

"Daddy." She stepped forward, until she broke away with a rush, lunging at him and wrapping her arms around his neck.

He grabbed her as best he could, but the man was thin...too thin. He stumbled under the weight, gripped her arm, and buried her head against her neck. "Anna."

I glanced away when they hugged. Hating how she clung to him and sobbed. It was all because of me. Me and my fucked-up father. A flare of jealousy tore through me. I wished I had that kind of love. I wished I had any kind of love.

Something more than the cold, controlling fist of hate my father gave me. I watched as the man's shoulders jerked and trembled, looking away when the thick sobs came.

"I thought I'd never see you again," Anna cried.

Christ, that fist in my chest gripped tighter, driving my hate a little deeper. If only my father had been reasonable and not been the savage bastard who'd made her father's existence impossible.

But he didn't need her father, not when he now had Anna.

He'd never let her go, not now he was seeing the vast amounts of money coming in. Anna pulled away, glanced at me, her eyes shining with tears. "Let's get you inside so you can eat."

"You and I need to talk." Mateo stared at me. "You, too, Rossi."

I felt the weight of that stare and turned to Lazarus as Anna, Kat, and her dad left us, heading inside.

"It surfaced," Mateo started as soon as they were gone. "But before you could get your hopes up, it was gone before my men could even reach out."

"Gone?" I winced, my pulse stuttering. "What the fuck do you mean, gone?"

Mateo pinned me with that unflinching stare. "It was an under-the-table transaction. The word surfaced and was snuffed out like a damn flame."

"*Fuck!*" I roared, turning away. I took a step, then stopped, my mind racing as I raked my fingers through my hair. "So, did we find out who the buyer is?"

"Arnold Smutter," Mateo answered. "My guys tracked his IP through about twelve different countries. He made it hard, that's for sure."

"But not impossible." I sucked in a hard breath. "He wanted us to know."

"Yes," Mateo answered.

"Fuck." I groaned.

If my father had the hard drive, then there was no way out of this. He'd watch the footage. He'd know exactly what had happened to Max that night in the hangar...and he'd know what I did to protect Anna. I looked to the cabin, listening to her laugh with Xael at the baby. "Then we go to war."

59

Anna

I lifted my gaze from the perfect bundle of joy when they walked back in. Fin's eyes were dark, darker than I'd ever seen them...that meant something was wrong. Lazarus moved to Kat, leaning down to kiss her first before touching his daughter's cheek. Even Mateo went to Xael's side, pulling her hard against him with a jerk. Her arms slid around his waist as she looked into his eyes.

This wasn't good...

This wasn't good at all.

I slowly rose as Fin moved toward me. He didn't hug me, not like the others. No, he refused my gaze, searching the rooms of the cabin behind me instead. His avoidance sent a chill along my spine. "What is it?"

Mateo was silent. Lazarus looked to Fin, licked his lips, then muttered, "She deserves to know."

"Know what?" I stepped closer, forcing Fin's focus to me. "Know *what?*"

"They found it," he answered. "They found the hard drive."

I rocked back on my heels. My mind frozen with denial. "That can't..." I shook my head.

"They can," Fin murmured, reaching for me.

I now understood the tortured look in his eyes. "Oh shit, it's him, isn't it?" I searched for the truth. "That sonovabitch."

I knew...knew in an instant. Smutter's sadistic smirk came back to me. He'd found the one thing he'd said he would. He'd beaten us...but... "How?" I glanced at Mateo. "I thought you said you had this handled?"

"I did," he answered and winced.

"Obviously not well enough." It was all I said.

This was not a time for *'you should've let me handle it like I said'* moment. But he knew without me saying the words. I wanted to put trackers out there, wanted to flood the damn dark web for traces of anything associated with the island or that piece-of-shit delusional psychopath who came to the island to destroy us.

"So we're going to get it back...or try to at least," Lazarus said behind me.

I turned, glanced over my shoulder as Fin moved away, heading to the bedroom.

"Don't worry." Laz brushed his thumb down Kat's cheek. "The Commander is staying here."

I glanced at Mateo, but I said nothing as Finley strode back toward me, the bag of weapons strung over his shoulder.

"It's okay," he said, meeting my stare. "You'll be safe."

"Of course I will," I answered. "Because I'm coming with you."

494

He froze, then scowled. "That's not happening."

I crossed my arms over my chest. Now he was just pissing me off. "I'm not asking."

"Anna, it's dangerous—" Laz started and froze with Kat's glare.

"You think she doesn't know that?" Kat snapped, looking up at him.

"She's right." Xael strode forward. "She has just as much at stake in this as you do, Fin. So stop being a schmuck."

Fin was growing colder. "A *schmuck* who wants to keep the woman I love alive."

"Give her a little damn credit. It's not the damn 1960s." She reached under her black leather jacket and drew out a gleaming silver handgun, grabbed the grip, and handed it to me. "She knows how to shoot a damn gun."

I clenched tight around it. Sig Sauer. The feel was nice, smaller...perfect actually. "I do, thank you, Xael."

Since the island, I'd spent time at an indoor gun range. I wasn't about to put my life in someone else's hands ever again, nor was I ready to trust someone else to protect Fin, not even Lazarus.

He'd help him, sure...

But would he die to protect him? The answer was simple: no.

"I'm coming," I said, sliding the gun into the waistband of my jeans. "Whether you want me to or not. So either you accept that and put me to work, or we stand here and argue. Choice is yours."

He looked at me like I was a stranger, then strode closer, wrapped his arm around my waist, and yanked me close. "Fuck, you're gorgeous when you're determined."

But he pulled the gun from around my back instantly, then turned it in his grasp, checking the safety and then reached around, sliding it back into place as he stared into my eyes. The primal glare couldn't be more erotic.

Excitement tore through me like a charge. If we didn't have a damn war to go to, or a cabin full of our friends, we'd fuck...in a damn instant.

"So I take it that's a yes?" Xael muttered slowly. "Or should we all give you a two a minute?"

"That's a yes." Fin stepped back, never once looking away. "Mateo."

"I'll make the call," the Commander answered.

"Then let's do this." Lazarus bent low, kissing Kat. "Kitten."

We were leaving in a blur of the booming of my heart.

"Stay safe," Xael called out as I followed Fin out of the cabin.

My mind was racing when I climbed into the backseat of the four-wheel drive. Fin heaved the bag of weapons, placing it between the front seats within easy reach. He started the engine, headlights lighting the way when Laz strode out, then climbed into the passenger's seat and closed the door.

We were rolling before I knew. Laz reached across and hit the stereo, letting the music fill the cabin. Fin tilted the rearview mirror, and our gaze collided in the reflection. He was scared. Hell, I was scared. But there was no way I was letting him do this without me.

I settled back, leaving silence to fill the void as we made our way along the dirt track, leaving the cabin behind. Headlights splashed along the asphalt when we climbed back onto the road.

"We go in hard," Laz murmured, eyeing the bag of guns.

I knew what *'going in hard'* meant. It meant if it moved, we killed it.

They weren't playing. But could Fin do that when it came to his father?

God, I hoped so.

The thought of that consumed me as we headed to get our damn life back.

"Do we know if they accessed the hard drive? Are there a safety triggers set in place when it's accessed?" I asked, my mind instantly trying to find hope in this madness. "Surely there would be...I mean, there'd *have to be.*"

"Even if there was," Laz muttered in front of me, "There's no one to send the trigger to."

He was right. I knew he was right.

The asshole from the island was dead.

Even if he sent the footage across the servers and off grid, there was no one who knew what kind of security mechanisms were in place. I mean, Smutter might not have had time to break the code yet...he might not've seen what there was to see.

But if he had...

If he saw the footage of Fin. If he saw it, then he'd know. The memory slammed into me. In an instant, that howling wind of the cyclone, the gunfire when those mercenaries attacked. Gunfire cracked in my head, the sound a little dull now as I sat here in the backseat of the four-wheel drive, but it was there. The...*crack...crack...crack...*filled me, white flashes filled my mind.

And bathed in the light, I saw it. Fin standing behind Max when he knelt on the ground, pointing a gun to the back of his head.

Bang!

I flinched. Fin caught the movement in the reflection and looked my way. But he said nothing, almost like he knew what consumed me...almost like it was the same memory that consumed him as well.

60

Finley

"Anna, stay with me," I murmured, catching the tiny flicker of a light from the darkness at my right.

I pulled up hard. The headlights were already dead, leaving me to drive by moonlight alone. I reached up, flicking off the interior lights before anyone opened the door and climbed out. She climbed out, closing the door with barely a sound. I didn't want her here. Not at Smutter's house or anywhere near this goddamn war.

But I had to trust her.

Trust she was strong.

Trust that she was lethal.

She reached behind her back and pulled out the gun Xael gave her as I reached into the bag and pulled out two filled clips and handed them to her.

The whites of her eyes were neon in the dark. Wide. Panicked. Her breaths were loud in my ears. I turned my head at the movement. Black on black shifted without making a sound. Any other time I would've been panicked, swinging my gun up at the movement. But I knew who it was.

I glanced up as Edon came closer, glancing at Anna without making a sound.

Still, I saw annoyance flash in his eyes.

This wasn't because she was female...wasn't because she wasn't strong...it was because she was a liability...*to me.*

"You ready for this?" he asked.

"As ready as I'll ever be." I winced, as ready as you could be, knowing you were about to kill your own father.

Lazarus rounded the car, tucking his phone back into his pocket. A pang tore across my chest. No doubt the Rossi Prince said his goodbyes...

I glanced at the hitman...the one they called the Albanian. He was ruthless, cold...and Mateo's younger brother. One I was damn grateful for.

"I'll go ahead." Edon took a step away. "Watch your damn backs."

He left us behind, melting into the night like he was part of it. I looked at Lazarus, who had a gun in his hand like he'd been born with it and a set of bolt cutters in the other. He gave a nod, leaving me to look to Anna. She looked scared, so fucking scared.

Still, she gripped her gun and murmured, "Let's get this done."

My heart swelled. I'd never seen her so damn beautiful before.

I gripped my Sig in one hand and the bag of guns with the other, then turned toward the compound and the house that sat toward the back. Steel shone from Lazarus' hand as he strode forward.

We moved fast, watching the compound for guards and monitors. Lazarus rushed forward, bent low. The *clip...clip...clip...*barely reaching my ears before he yanked the fence up and waited. I glanced at Anna, but she was already rushing forward and hitting the ground, scurrying through and was out the other side.

She rushed forward, racing toward the corner of the steel building in front of us. My pulse raced with the movement, triggered by the sight of her disappearing from view. Lazarus was next, racing ahead. I ducked, scraping the snapped edges of the steel links along my back.

Pain slashed, making me bite down on a snarl and shove through. Then I was running, tearing across the dark, a little louder than I wanted. But fuck me, I couldn't see her.

Then I caught sight of her, dressed in dark blue, her pale skin reflecting the moonlight. The plan was simple: get in. Find Smutter and the hard drive, get the information we came for, then kill him and get out.

All I needed to know was if he'd accessed it...and who else had seen the footage if he had.

Crack!

The gunshot tore through the air...followed by *crack...crack...crack!*

"Shit!" I jerked my gaze to the blur as Lazarus raced forward, his gun held high. Then I saw them, the rush of dark blurs heading toward us...right in Anna's path.

I saw her freeze. Saw one of the gunmen lift his gun and take aim...saw my entire future fade into darkness. But then the gunman dropped to the ground with barely a *pop!* And he never rose.

A.K. ROSE

I looked to where the shot came from, but the hitman was no longer there.

Crack...crack...CRACK!

The night erupted with gunfire.

Crack! Anna squeezed off a shot, missed, then took aim once more as Lazarus glanced her way, panicked. *Crack!* She pulled the trigger again, and this time hit her target.

The guy went down hard as I raced to her side. "Come on." I tacked the movement. As four more came out of nowhere, charging forward, gunfire erupting.

PING!

The corner of the steel garage took the shot near my head. Anna jerked her gaze to the bullet hole, then to me. Her lips curled, and a look of pure savagery tore across her face as she turned back, stepped forward, and unleashed a scream.

CRACK...CRACK...CRACK! She pulled the trigger time and time again.

Lazarus rushed toward the house at the rear of the compound and spun, slamming his back against the outside as the door opened and two more armed security came rushing out.

Crack...crack!

They went down before they took three steps from the doorway.

He was inside in a blur, making me pushing harder as I ran. Anna was behind me, fucking fierce and ruthless. I lifted my gun, plunging through the doorway after Lazarus and was inside in a heartbeat.

The place was old and big, with no lights on inside to light the way.

A grunt came from in front...one that sounded like Lazarus.

A *slam* followed. I caught the sight of Lazarus being lifted and hurtled through the air. *Like fuck!* I dropped the bag full of guns and charged, lunging for the asshole, tackling him around the middle.

But the dude was a beast. Big and muscled. He barely moved as I hit. Instead, he dropped Lazarus, right on top of me.

"Fin!" Anna cried.

From the corner of my eye, I caught her trying to take aim. But Laz was driving upward, letting out a brutal roar and unleashed his fists on the towering bull of a man. Seconds blurred, and with it, everything else.

I followed, shoved upward. Rage consumed me, mingled with the desperation to survive, I gripped the gun, shoved it into the asshole's side, and pulled the trigger.

The mountain flinched.

Boom...

Boom!

I squeezed twice more until the guard dropped to his knees. Hard breaths consumed me. I stepped backward and then turned. But the hallway behind me was empty. "Anna?"

I moved forwards, moving to the spot where she'd been a second ago, scanning the darkness.

 But she wasn't here...

She was gone.

61

Anna

The hand over my mouth was cruel, smashing my lips against my teeth until piercing pain bloomed. I fought, trying my best to throw him off. But he was too strong, picking me up until my feet left the ground, then drove me face-first into the wall.

Stars collided in my eyes as agony tore through my head. I let out a whimper as the dark hallway faded. Hard breaths were all I focused on as he pulled me toward him. I dropped my hand then reached around to the small of my back, before he beat me to it, but his cruel grip closed over mine and clenched my fingers together.

"Don't bother." The growl came near my ear. "You'd be dead before your finger found the trigger."

I thrashed and kicked. Memories of the island came roaring back. I refused to be back there, refused to be that woman again. I yanked my head to the side, opened my mouth, and bit.

"*Fuck!*" my attacker barked and wrenched his hand away.

Giving me enough time to spin, shove, and then stumble away. *Fin...*

I lunged, driving myself toward him until the fucker grabbed me by the hair and wrenched me backward.

"Fucking *bitch!*" he roared.

The blur came too fast for me to move. My head snapped backward with the blow, and the metallic taste of blood bloomed in my mouth.

"Do that again, I dare you," he warned.

I just stood there, trying to keep calm while inside I was screaming.

"Move!" He shoved me forward so hard my head snapped backward. I stumbled forward, heading to where the light at the end of the hallway spilled out from under the door.

Boom!

Boom!

Lazarus let out a roar. One that sounded savage and painful. Fin was all I thought about. I shoved away, bouncing off the wall and lunged, but not for the door behind us, to where Fin was.

My attacker let out a. *"Fuck!"* and grabbed me around the waist, hauling me backward and shoved me through the door.

"FIN!" I screamed.

"ANNA!"

Boom! BOOM! Boomboomboom!

He unleashed a clip into whatever stood in the way between us. Light blinded me as I was shoved inside. I stumbled backward as the sound of thunder came, matching the roar in my chest.

He shoved through the door, his eyes wild, searching for me... until he found me.

My attacker wound his arm around my throat and yanked me backward. Panic reared with the pressure, cutting off my air. I tried to suck in a breath and fight, but Fin lifted his gun and took aim at the asshole behind me.

"Let her go or you're fucking dead."

"Fin." The commanding voice came from further back in the room.

I hadn't even looked at the rest of the room. But Fin jerked his gaze toward the sound as Lazarus stumbled inside behind him, taking in the piece of shit behind me.

But Fin wasn't playing...not anymore. He lifted his gun, taking aim as Dominic Salvatore stilled. I felt the asshole behind me turn his head. His focus shifted elsewhere. I lifted my foot, wrenched it forward, then rammed it back, driving it into his shin.

The hold around my throat slipped as he let out a scream. I was lunging sideways before I knew.

Boom!

The shot tore through the room, slamming into my attacker, driving him backward, until he fell. I didn't have time to care about the blood that bloomed in the center of his chest. Instead, I drove myself forward, my pulse racing as I slammed into Fin's side.

His arms wrapped around me, pulling me against his side.

"You okay?" He searched my eyes, his gun never once wavering from his father as he found my busted lips. "Did he do that to you?"

I didn't answer. I didn't need to. He swiveled his gun toward the bleeding mercenary and unleashed another shot. This time in the center of his forehead, making him slump against the floor.

Dominic Salvatore stood toward the end of the study. Three men were at his side, and Arnold Stutter was behind the desk, his hands raised in the air as Lazarus and Finley moved deeper into the room.

I glanced at Fin who just stepped forward, his gun moving from Stutter to his father.

"Finley," Dominic murmured, never once flinching as we entered the room, even with the guns trained on him.

"Get away from the keyboard." Fin jerked his gun, urging Smutter away.

My pulse was racing. Still, I forced myself forward, drawn by panic and that need to know. I rounded the other side of the desk, out of the firing line. Smutter lifted his gaze, and that cold, savage stare found me.

I stared at the screen, finding the prompt screen open and the rows and rows of commands, with *incorrect command...incorrect command,* triggered over and over again.

He didn't get in...

He didn't get in.

I looked to Fin who was waiting for me and shook my head.

That panicked glint turned stony as Dominic murmured, "I was wondering how long it'd take for you to get here. Wondering who you had in your corner, too." He glanced to Lazarus, then to me, before his gaze moved to the doorway.

From the corner of my eye, Edon stepped inside, dressed in black, a sniper's rifle in his hand. "I see you have quite the arsenal."

I knelt over the keyboard, glancing at the file still locked, and then the list of commands and IP addresses on the screen, until I stopped. One of the IP addresses looked familiar. *Too familiar*.

I moved forward, backtracking his commands.

"What the fuck are you doing?" Smutter snapped, watching me as I narrowed in on that address, and instead of trying to hack my way into the file for the hard drive, I focused on that.

I tracked the details, pulling the address apart, using the skills I'd honed to track the address through different servers and locations until I came up with only one...

I lifted my gaze...my heart stuttering as I turned.

"You?" I whispered to Finley's dad. "You were the one who put the drive up?"

Those careful eyes glinted.

"What are you talking about?" Smutter growled. "I'm just about to crack it. Just about to expose the fucking truth...*that you killed my brother*."

BOOM!

Smutter jerked in the chair, then fell silent, a thick bead of blood slipping from the bullet wound in his head. I flinched with the sound and looked to Finley whose gun was still trained on the spot where he stood.

"You had the drive." He turned back to his father and took aim. "You played us."

"Not played...*tested*."

My mind was racing, unable to keep up as I straightened.

"It was always going to come to this. You needed a trigger, or you'd never see yourself as worthy of the seat. Don't you see?"

"*See?*" Fin snapped. "You forced my goddamn hand when you went after Anna. *You fucking brought this on yourself!*"

"I needed *you* to see you were ready." He stared at me, then Lazarus and Edon. "I always knew you were."

"Ready?" Fin repeated.

"To take the seat. It's what you came for, isn't it?"

Fin just scowled, his gun wavering, aimed at his father, before he paled. He looked at me, licked his lips, then turned back. "You'll move aside?"

"Will you give me a choice?"

"No." The answer was simple. He wouldn't, not when there was too much on the line.

My life.

My father's life.

There was no way Fin would play with that.

"Then you have your answer," Dominic murmured, a hint of a smile cresting his lips. He fucking *wanted this all along*. "Mr. Salvatore."

Mr. Salvatore.

The way he said it, he played into Fin's ego. Was this a setup from the beginning? I glanced at the screen and the IP address, the same address Fin had triggered when sending documents from his father's house to me at the Facility.

"The Facility?" I murmured.

Dominic looked at me like I was nothing more than a speck on his shoe. "That's up to the head of the Salvatore line. I'm out... I'm retiring."

"You're retiring?" I didn't believe it.

His gaze was cold and unflinching. "I'll expect my money to continue. But if Finley wants to take over the seat on the Commission, and it looks to me like he has, then I'll concede."

He'll concede...

I looked to Fin. Could it really be this easy? I glanced at Arnold Smutter's still body. Now it all made sense. He'd brought Max's brother here with the sole purpose of triggering this entire catalyst.

He wanted Fin to step up...and he used me to do it.

"You fucking bastard." I met his ruthless gaze, finding the corner of his lips curling at the edges.

"Welcome to the family, Anna," he took a step, reaching up to pat Finley on the shoulder like he was proud. "It's nice to see you're a good influence on my son."

Then he left, just strolled past Lazarus and Edon like he'd finished what he'd come here to do, leaving us all to stare at each other with the resounding thud of Dominic Salvatore's steps.

Book two in the The Institute series is next!
Read on for a sneak peak of the first chapter!

Ruthless Protector - Chapter One
KAT

12 years old...

I squeezed my eyes closed. One hand rested on the door handle of my room and waited.

No...please, no. Not this again. I could run away...just like Mom did. Run away and never come back. Not for anything. But where would I go? I closed my eyes at the thought. For a second, freedom burned bright and shining in my mind. Happiness, laughter, kicking sand at the beach as I ate cotton candy and played. Freedom. That's what it looked like...until the warmth dulled and reality sank in. I had nowhere to go...and no one to come for me. *Not anymore.*

"Ms. VanHalen," the servant murmured through the door. "He's expecting you."

Still, I said nothing, just waited for that fight to die inside me... and for emptiness to take hold. Slowly, the image of freedom slipped away, taking the echoes of laugher with it. I lifted my head to the ornately carved door and twisted the handle before stepping out.

The servant's eyes widened before she took a step backwards. "There she is." She forced a smile and met my gaze. "Your father—"

But I turned and left her behind, not bothering to listen as I headed for the stairs. My heels clicked on the marble. Shimmering, polished surfaces gleamed as I reached out, placing my hand on the handrail. With each step, I left that calling behind, the call with the sound of laughter. Because that wasn't real. It was a fantasy and I was old enough to know the difference. Old enough to want for more...more than money could ever buy.

I had everything a girl could ever want. A stable of horses for me to ride. Holidays to Aspen and Italy. Pink diamonds to match my pretty white dress and knee length socks. I caught sight of myself in the looming hall mirror as I hit the last stair and made my way across the foyer. I looked perfect. Not a strand of hair out of place. Not a wrinkle in my brand new dress...a dress my father had bought for me...*for his perfect Princess.*

But as I caught my reflection, I avoided my eyes.

There was something in them I didn't like.

Something that made that ache inside me twist and moan.

Something that made the dull thud in my ears race.

As I stepped forward, that image of freedom sank further down than ever before.

I tore my gaze from the sight and kept walking, through the open doors of the foyer and into the living room. White and gray closed in around me, blindingly perfect and intricate. There wasn't a thing out of place here, not a chair too far to the right, even the flames of the fire flickered and danced in unison.

The crackle and hiss were the only sounds here. This was a place of hardness. A place where hope came to die. I swallowed hard and lifted my head. My steps slowed now, each movement like wading through water as I lifted my gaze to the closed black doors in the distance, to the wing of the house where only certain servants ventured, but not on nights like this when the double doors were closed.

Where monsters hid behind masks.

And the sickening scent of their cigars made me tremble.

I reached out, grasped the door handles, and pushed them wide before stepping in and closing them behind me. Laughter spilled from behind a closed door at the end of the dark hall. I turned, leaving the bright white furnishings behind to find myself in a different living room. One that was consumed by black.

Black leather shimmered, reflecting the amber flames from the obsidian hearth. Black walls...black carpet. This was my father's domain. The place where deep, resounding laugher spilled from through the door and where power stained the air. Where power stained everything, tainting my perfect world black.

He's expecting you. The servant's words came back to me as I forced myself to move. But it was so hard now, my muscles trembling, fighting my will. *He's expecting you...he's expecting you... he's...expecting...*

I tried to swallow, and reached for the door. But my heart was lodged in the back of my throat, thumping and aching. My hand trembled as I gripped the handle, twisted, and pushed, before stopping in the doorway.

Heads turned toward me. But there was only one person I looked for, the man sitting at the head of the table, the one with cards in one hand and a cigar in the other. The sounds of laughter dulled. Sparkling dark eyes glinted as the man sitting closest to my father fixed his gaze on me.

But Dad never looked at me, never even lifted his gaze from the cards in his hand. That smile was etched onto his face. Cold and cruel, nothing more than a faded slash on his pale skin. Thick gold rings sparkled as he moved his hand.

"Good, you're here," he muttered, his jaw barely moving with the words. "Took your time."

But I said nothing, just waited, like a good daughter. I waited for him to look at me. For him to see the deep red hair like my mother's and the emptiness in my eyes, the hate and the hurt he'd created. Instead, he just murmured, "You remember Mr. Hale?"

Only then did I face the monster.

The one with sparkling eyes.

The one who smiled at me and rose carefully from his seat.

My heart thundered, beating out of control now as it crawled higher in my throat.

Yes, I wanted to scream. *I remember Mr. Hale. I remember him all too well.*

The devil moved around my father, giving him a pat on the shoulder as he passed.

"Katerina," the devil whispered, eyes shining with hunger as he came toward me. "It's so good to see you again...*so very...very good.*"

Link for RUTHLESS PROTECTOR HERE:

Grab this free sexy, short additional scene with Justice and Ruth!